SORT OF RICH

SORT OF RICH

A

NOVEL

BY

JAMES WILCOX

1817

HARPER & ROW, PUBLISHERS, New York
Grand Rapids, Philadelphia, St. Louis, San Francisco
London, Singapore, Sydney, Tokyo

FIRST EDITION

Designed by Karen Savary

Library of Congress Cataloging-in-Publication Data

Wilcox, James.
  Sort of rich.

  I. Title.
PS3573.I396S67   1989   813'.54   88-45919
ISBN 0-06-016099-3

89 90 91 92 93 CC/HC 10 9 8 7 6 5 4 3 2 1

F Wil

For Mariapaz Ramos-Englis

PART I

CHAPTER ONE

Do you think Henry would like to feed the catfish?"

"No, Frank. Let him rest."

"Is he sleeping?"

"Mm."

"I thought he was out back."

Mr. and Mrs. Dambar had many such discussions during the course of Henry's visit. They were concerned that he might not be having enough fun. Gretchen Dambar adored her cousin Henry and was anxious for him to like both Louisiana and Frank, her new husband. A consensus among Gretchen's friends in New York had given the marriage a year or two at most, and she was determined to prove them wrong. Fifty-four years old, a former widower with the most darling grin, Frank could not be sweeter, and she still got goose bumps whenever he walked into the room.

"Are you sure he's sleeping?" Mr. Dambar asked, hovering over her desk. She was writing a letter to the editor of the *New York Times*, a scathing indictment of Imelda Marcos. Gretchen had once had tea with Mrs. Marcos at a friend's Sutton Place apartment, and she was using this experience as a backdrop for her letter. It would be signed with her new name, Dambar, pronounced "Denner." She had asked her husband about the curious discrepancy between spelling and pronunciation, but he had no explanation. In any case, if the *Times* printed the letter, then the new name and new address (Tula

Springs, LA) would perhaps seem a little more real to her. Again, Mr. Dambar had no explanation when she had asked him what the town's name meant. And he seemed somewhat offended when she said she thought Tula was a Russian name. There were no Russians in Tula Springs, he insisted. Never had been. As a matter of fact, there weren't even any springs.

"What, dear?"

"Are you sure he's not out back?"

"Who?"

Mr. Dambar patted his wife's soft frizzy hair, a patchwork of gray and faded red. When he had first met her three months ago in a souvenir shop in the French Quarter, he had thought she was letting dyed or rinsed hair grow out. But he had since learned that the effect was completely natural. This, along with her frumpy outfit and a somewhat uninhibited way of speaking—her voice projecting to the farthest corner of the store—had led him to believe that she must be a maid or waitress on holiday. And quite a handsome, strapping maid at that. Yet it turned out she was from a distinguished New England family that had supplied statesmen, senators, and judges for a good two centuries. To tell the truth, he was vaguely disappointed when she set him straight about her background. It had been much more romantic to think he had been smitten by a woman who served up grilled cheese at Woolworth's, an overworked spinster whom he would raise up from servitude to a life of comparative luxury and ease.

Just when Mrs. Dambar was about to complain, fondly, that he was making it hard for her to think, Henry wandered into the study, as Mrs. Dambar called it, or den, as Mr. Dambar would have it.

"I was just wondering if you might like to go feed the catfish," Mr. Dambar said to the lithe, deeply tanned cousin.

Henry was Gretchen's age, around forty, but looked much younger, an impression he reinforced by acting so, especially at the table, where he dined with the happy abandon of a ten-year-old. He had just arrived unannounced from South America—Quito, where he had been doing an emergency rewrite of a low-budget movie about a giant ant. Henry had only taken this job as a favor for a friend who was coproducing the movie. His real in-

4

terest was something he called performance art. Mr. Dambar had some idea that this involved video cameras and possibly occasional nudity and let it go at that. He was not really terribly curious about the matter.

Henry yawned and stretched with unorthodox abandon. "I thought I'd take your scull out," he said to his cousin.

The smile on Mrs. Dambar's lightly freckled face stiffened. She had rowed for Radcliffe and up until the time of her marriage, had made a practice of getting out to the Columbia boathouse at the northern tip of Manhattan once or twice a week. Henry had rowed for Yale, but he was rough, unskilled, and she hated the idea of any interference with the karma of her sixty-five-hundred-dollar scull. "Really, Henry, there's nowhere to row around here."

"What about that thing?"

"What thing?"

"You know . . ."

"Tula Creek? Impossible. There's all sorts of logs and alligators and stuff. Why don't you and Frank go feed the fish? That would be nice."

The pond was about a half mile from the house on an irregular strip of property belonging somewhat ambiguously to both the state and one of Mr. Dambar's companies. Leo, the handyman, had convinced Mr. Dambar that it would be a good idea to stock the pond with catfish. On Tuesdays and Fridays Leo sat on the shoulder of the Old Jeff Davis Highway selling these catfish. Mrs. Dambar didn't think this was quite right since he was being paid full salary on those days. She had mentioned this to her husband once or twice, but had not pressed the issue. The marriage was too new, and she was concerned that she might appear overly assertive. Her husband, after all, was so smooth and gracious; the least bit of discord seemed to jar on his nerves.

"Go on," she prompted cheerfully. She was hoping that Frank and Henry would spend some time alone getting to know each other. But it was obvious they were reluctant to leave without her. Mr. Dambar was preoccupied with a squeak in the globe next to the window, and Henry was picking the scab of a macaw bite on his elbow.

With a sigh she switched off the electric typewriter. "All right," she said, and they followed her out the door.

The road they lived on, a dead end, was in the country, three miles from the city limits and two from the nearest 7-Eleven, yet none of the neighbors were actual farmers. The houses were substantial, and even though there might be a chicken coop, a tractor, or a sizable vegetable garden in the front yard, the back would be devoted to a pool or maybe tennis courts. Mr. Dambar's neighbors were lawyers, doctors, and such, who kept a horse or two for their daughters, and in one case—a bank president's—Nubian goats for the wife. Farming here was a hobby, and many of the vegetables had to be thrown away. After all, one family could eat just so many zucchinis and tomatoes.

Mr. Dambar's sprawling brick house was next to last before the dead end. "Did you spray yourself?" he inquired as they walked into the feathery grass where the asphalt petered out into a footpath. This was the shortcut to the pond, where, out walking with Henry the day before, Mrs. Dambar had suffered chigger bites on her calves and ankles. This evening she had on jeans and socks, but her cousin's powerful, corded legs were bare practically to the crotch. He was wearing extremely short khakis, somewhat reminiscent of lederhosen. Mr. Dambar repeated his question.

"Me?" Henry said. "No." And he strode ahead.

Mr. and Mrs. Dambar were holding hands. Gretchen had found that whenever she had doubts about the step she had taken, her faith was restored by mere physical contact. Then, the sense that she was nowhere that mattered, cut off from everything that was important, would dissolve—and even the Louisiana winter would seem less strange. There were some cold days, admittedly, and the green of the pines and water oaks was hardly lush or tropical. Yet at the same time she couldn't get over the feeling that she was in the midst of one long Indian summer, that the many warm afternoons were deceptive and the wildflowers still flourishing among the brittle undergrowth, premature. She never realized how much she would miss a definitive winter. Even on the morning the pipes froze, fat, officious robins were inspecting the emerald lawn, and by midafternoon the banker's wife was out feeding her goats in skirt and blouse.

Walking beside him Mrs. Dambar would occasionally steal a glance at her husband. She always took fresh pleasure seeing him in profile, when he was intent on something in the distance, unconscious of her. She read there a calmness, perhaps even a nobility of sorts, but certainly a wholeness so at odds with her own sense of being fragmented, incomplete. So what if he wasn't the most brilliant man she had ever met, if his sense of humor left something to be desired. None of this mattered compared to the almost spiritual sense she had of him. He was *right,* a word that could not be applied to any of her friends back East, male or female. And she so wanted Henry to see this, too.

Gretchen had met Frank quite by accident on a business trip to New Orleans. She and Molly Gribbel, an old friend from Radcliffe, had been thinking of starting a line of artistic jewelry using seashells and were calling upon a collector in New Orleans who was reputed to be an expert on Louis Quinze shell designs. Although Gretchen and Molly were fascinated to learn from him that the term "rococo" derives from *rocaille,* which in turn is a corruption of *travail de coquille,* they were dismayed by the smell of his French Quarter apartment and by the specious quality of his prized possessions. It was at this low point, when Gretchen realized that it had been a mistake to have let Molly talk her into coming all the way down to New Orleans, that she had almost literally stumbled upon Frank in a tourist-trap souvenir shop on Bourbon Street. Gretchen enjoyed sending tacky postcards to stuffy friends. Drawn by a rack of especially lurid photos, she swerved just in time to avoid colliding with a man on his hands and knees. This was Frank, searching for a buffalo nickel he had dropped, but Gretchen at the time thought something was very wrong, that he had collapsed, fainted. Before she really knew what she was doing, she had placed a hand on his shoulder, meaning to help him up, perhaps.

"And that's when I felt it," she had told Henry yesterday when they had walked this way alone. "I'd never felt anything like it before, really. The only way I can describe it—well, it was like a current going through me from head to foot. I hadn't even seen his face, what he looked like, nothing. I mean, I thought he was just some sort of horrible tourist or something. Henry, I know you'll laugh, but it was almost like a religious experience, like one of those faith healers putting their hands on your head and suddenly you're cured. You know what I mean?"

Henry had regarded her with his cold, gray, somewhat slanted eyes and smiled. It was as if he had not believed a word she said. Gretchen tried again, discarding the religious metaphor and substituting something more artistic. But Henry had interrupted her and started talking about the gallery in Tribeca he had designed. Apparently, the gallery owners turned out to be crooks and wanted Henry to work for half the agreed-upon fee. In revenge Henry had splashed orange paint all over their floor—and they had loved it, given him almost the full fee.

"Look at this," Mr. Dambar said as he peered into the shed beside the pond. A twenty-five-pound bag of Purina Floating Catfish Chow was lying on its side, open, on the dirt floor. "I asked Leo to be careful, always seal it up."

"Perhaps it was a raccoon," Mrs. Dambar ventured as he set it upright.

"Maybe, could be . . ." He tied it up neatly.

"Then again, Leo is sometimes negligent and—"

"Well, I—What's that?"

A splash made them both turn and look intently at the pond; the ripples in the café-au-lait water swayed a clump of cattails near the shore, but aside from this the surface was undisturbed. With fear and intense excitement Mrs. Dambar wondered if an alligator were feasting upon Leo's fish. Although she had casually mentioned the beasts to Henry, she had never seen one herself. She couldn't decide whether she was frightened of them or not, even though, since moving to Louisiana, she had dreamed of them frequently, mostly in the context of rowing past their partially submerged backs. Her fingers dug into the yellow zigzag on her husband's burnt-sienna sweater.

A sleek head emerged in the center of the pond. It belonged to Henry.

"Well," Mr. Dambar began, but did not go on. He had always had his suspicions about his wife's cousin, and this seemed to confirm them. To dive fully clothed into a fish pond in the middle of winter—obviously, the kid had a screw loose. "Did you ever?"

"Henry," Mrs. Dambar called out as he glided back to shore with an effortless breaststroke, "what are you doing?" For her husband's sake she tried to look worried and upset. But in truth, she was deeply thrilled. To think that anyone would have the courage to leap into such forbidding, murky water. Just about anything could be in there. And it was a bit chilly today, too.

"Not very deep," Henry commented as he waded through sawgrass, his long legs black with mud. Mrs. Dambar plucked a glob of algae from the back of his baggy, hand-painted shirt.

"You might have upset the fish," she commented, anxious to demonstrate her disapproval. But her wide-set green eyes, dark with admiration, gave her away. Henry had no fear. He did exactly what he wanted every moment of his life. And he got away with it. Everyone adored him. He had more friends than any one person could know what to do with. Gorgeous women threw themselves at his feet. And as for his work, he refused to be compromised, turning down lucrative projects if they violated his integrity. Gretchen had been dazzled by his bravery ever since that day he had visited her at Foxcroft and ridden bareback on Jolly Beans, who had gone mad and was scheduled to be shot. In fact, it was Henry's example, his ability to plunge into the midst of any situation without needless bourgeois scruples, that had inspired Gretchen. For it had taken a lot of courage to marry Frank, knowing so little about him and having to rely completely upon instinct, something she had never done before.

"I believe you've lost a sandal," Mr. Dambar said.

Mrs. Dambar looked down at her cousin's slimy feet; her husband was right. "Never mind," she said, going to the shed and clamping the padlock on the door. "We better get back before Henry catches cold."

"That's OK. You guys go on," Henry said. "I'm going to take a look around."

He trudged off unevenly toward the woods, picking up a

9

gnarled stick along the way and whacking the grass beside the pond.

Mr. Dambar remained planted where he stood, his tasseled loafers caked with mud. Finally, with a shrug that seemed to end some internal debate, he called out to his wife, who had been eyeing him furtively, "Gretch, why did you lock the shed?"

She said something about the danger of overfeeding the fish. Actually, neither she nor Mr. Dambar knew much about catfish and had to rely upon vague, often contradictory fragments of advice from Leo. It seemed to her, though, that since goldfish often died from overeating, it was probably best to adopt a minimalist attitude toward the chow.

"But why did you come out here to feed them, then?" her husband wondered as they made their way back to the house.

"It was you who wanted to feed them, dear."

"Well, Leo said—"

"Please, let's not talk about him. Anyone who listens to that man must be . . ." Mrs. Dambar checked herself. She knew this wouldn't be the appropriate time to air her feelings about the handyman. Frank was sure to counter with some observations about Henry, and she didn't want to find herself at a disadvantage. When she decided the right moment had arrived to discuss Leo's dismissal—for this was what she decided would be best, for all concerned—she wanted to broach the topic from a position of strength. "By the way, Frank, have you seen my jeans?"

"What jeans?"

"I had some in the wash."

He shrugged. Though he was trying his best to get used to jeans on a woman her age, they still had a jarring effect. "Well, they must be there."

"Where?"

"In the wash."

They parted at the front door with a distracted kiss. Mr. Dambar informed her that he would be out back on the patio cleaning his shoes. "All right," she said, going inside. "I want to finish my letter before dinner."

As Gretchen entered the study, Shaerl looked up from the

royal blue wall-to-wall carpeting that Mr. Dambar's late wife had installed there. For the time being Gretchen had to endure the taste of the deceased, who had wall-to-walled not only the study, but the entire house, in the same intense shade of royal blue. Louis Quinze reproductions, a trifle too exuberant, filled every room, mirrors, sconces, and footstools complementing the heavier pieces with plodding fidelity. The overall effect the former Mrs. Dambar had achieved with this decorating scheme was to make the house seem somewhat impersonal, rather like a hotel lobby. It was embarrassing to have Henry see the house this way, before she had time to redo it. He really should have given her more time to get settled.

"Are you going to be here?" Shaerl asked from the floor.

"Be here? Yes, I'm going to finish my letter."

Because she was a recent college graduate, Mr. and Mrs. Dambar balked at the idea of referring to Shaerl as the maid, especially since she was here on a temporary basis, planning to go on to graduate school. Until that time she was installed out back on the edge of a small pasture in her stepuncle Leo's trailer. Neither Mr. nor Mrs. Dambar was entirely happy with these living arrangements, even though Shaerl had her own bedroom and Leo slept on the trailer's living room sofa. But they put up with it because Shaerl was hard up for money and didn't seem to be the type of young woman who would stand for any nonsense.

Picking up the application for graduate school she had been filling out, Shaerl got to her knees and with a sigh, arched back into a yoga position. Her dark, fashionably spiked hair, thick with mousse, touched the carpet as she said, "What's for dinner?"

Dissatisfied with the look of the page, Mrs. Dambar was resetting her margins. "Huh?"

"Are you going to let me try your boat?"

"I, uh . . ." She saw a typo in her heading and corrected it.

"You know, you ought to let me do your hair."

"Mm."

"I see you as strawberry blonde. It would soften your face. Why don't you like the Philippines?"

Mrs. Dambar looked around at the girl, whose face was red from the position she had assumed. "Does it sound like I don't?"

"That letter, yeah. Sounds like you're mad at them."

The girl had struck a nerve. Mrs. Dambar was very sensitive about the Philippines. "I'm angry at Mrs. Marcos—not the people."

"Then why did you have tea with her?"

"I didn't know she was going to be there," Mrs. Dambar replied with a twinge of conscience. She had known, of course, and she had hoped to say something stinging to the woman, who was then at the height of power. But her courage had failed. On a personal level it was very difficult for Gretchen to be mean or vindictive. And also, it would have embarrassed her friend Amanda, the hostess, who did not share Gretchen's political views. After Radcliffe, Gretchen had spent a year in the Philippines with the Peace Corps and some time later published two articles critical of McKinley's imperialistic policies. The editor of the respected left-wing journal that had printed the articles—and since folded—had encouraged her to expand them into a book. Over the years she had compiled hundreds of pages of notes on the U.S. suppression of Filipino patriots at the turn of the century, a bloody foreshadowing of disastrous imperialistic policies in the Far East, but she had not yet gotten down to doing the actual writing. There had been so many distractions in New York—too many friends, relatives, friends of relatives, relatives of friends, all with claims upon her time. And then there were those emotionally draining affairs, all of which had to be discussed at length with various analysts. It was no wonder she hadn't been able to do anything but research. Here in Louisiana, though, things would be different. She had reduced her life to a bare, almost conventual minimum: a husband she loved above all else—and that was it. Now, finally, she would be able to concentrate on what was important and get the book done. It disturbed her greatly to think she was already forty-two and hadn't accomplished a thing with her life—and such a privileged life at that.

"What do you think now?" she asked after making a few revisions in the letter to the *Times*.

Shaerl reached up and took it from her.

"It's clear now, don't you think, that it's Mrs. Marcos I'm mad at? And by the way, it doesn't sound too self-righteous, I hope."

"You misspelled *embarrassed*. There's two *r*'s."

"Don't look at things like that, Shaerl. Just the general tone. Do you get the drift of what I'm trying to say?"

"Yeah, it's OK. But I still think you ought to let me do your hair."

"Leo, will you say grace?" Mr. Dambar requested after everyone was seated.

Mrs. Dambar held out one hand to Shaerl, the other to Mrs. Howard, the housekeeper and cook. Although Gretchen found this practice of joining hands somewhat childish, Mr. Dambar had been doing it for years, and out of respect for him, she kept her peace.

"Now shall we all, together, reflect upon the infinitude of existence," Leo began with an earnest quaver in his voice. With his unwashed hair gathered in a ponytail and full graying sideburns, the handyman had the pseudorustic air of a refugee from the sixties. He reminded Gretchen of the effort she and her peers had taken in Cambridge to look nonmaterialistic, at one with the earth.

"Life is a paradox," he went on, "one too profoundly anomalous for human comprehension and attainment. Consider the ways of the quarks and—"

"All right, dat will do, Mr. Leo," Mrs. Howard put in, and the circle of hands was broken. In her late seventies, Mrs. Howard was a buxom, vigorous woman who had devoted all of her adult life—except for a brief, unfortunate marriage to a phone repairman—to the service of the Dambar family. It was she who had stuffed little Frankie full of gingerbread men after school, who had tucked him into bed and lulled him to sleep with the same tales of enchanted castles, trolls, and talking spoons that her own beloved mother had told her in Düsseldorf. More than grateful for so many years of dedicated service, Mr. Dambar had offered to pension her off when his parents had died and he had sold the old cypress house in town. But Mrs. Howard had insisted upon working for him and his bride and was soon installed in her own room in the new house in the country. All of which proved to be fortunate for Mr. Dambar, who did not know how he would have gotten along without her after the tragic car accident that cut short the life of the first Mrs. Dambar. When the new Mrs. Dambar arrived some fifteen years later, there was another attempt to help the old woman enjoy her last years in peace and comfort, this time by offering her a condominium in an elegant retirement village on the Mississippi Gulf Coast. But Mrs. Howard would have none of it. She did not want to be surrounded, she claimed, by a bunch of has-beens.

"Here look," Mrs. Howard said, spearing a pork chop and holding it aloft for all to see. "I wait for the cousin—and now, ruined. Everythink ruined."

"Oh, it's good, really good," Mrs. Dambar exclaimed somewhat fatuously. "You've outdone yourself tonight, Mrs. Howard." She was anxious to have the housekeeper like her, since Mr. Dambar thought so highly of the old woman. But at the same time Gretchen was aware that there was something faintly ignominious about her behavior. Twice Gretchen had escorted distinguished boyfriends to the White House for dinners with Ford and Carter; she thought nothing of telling a film star or celebrated writer how his work could be improved—and yet here she was trying to curry favor with a cook who didn't understand the first thing about proper nutrition. Every meal had enough cholesterol in the heavy Teutonic fare to kill a horse. And Mrs. Howard was always urging Frank to have seconds, thirds, and looking hurt if he refused. As soon as Henry left, Mrs. Dambar thought she might have a little talk with the woman about the wonderful things that could be done with dill and fresh tuna.

"Do you think he's all right?" Mr. Dambar asked.

Mrs. Dambar smiled absently.

"Angel?" he said, cutting into another creamed chop.

"Yes, dear?"

"You think he's all right?"

"Henry? Oh, Frank," she added, looking over at his gilt-edged plate, "do you think there'll be enough for him if you eat all that?"

"He can have mine," Shaerl said eagerly, shoving her plate away. Though she had a lovely figure, the girl was unable to walk without a slight hitch, caused, she had informed Mrs. Dambar, by arthritis. When it was acting up, she often lost her appetite and would subsist on cashews.

"Shaerl," Mr. Dambar said firmly, but gently, "don't worry about our guest. There's plenty for him, if he ever shows up."

"Where is dat cousin?" Mrs. Howard demanded.

"He's out exploring," Mrs. Dambar said evenly. "Henry just loves to explore."

"But he knows we eat at six," Mr. Dambar said. And he was about to add something when Mrs. Howard started to scold Shaerl about her untouched food. Throughout the meal Mr. Dambar had been wondering if he should come right out and ask his wife when Henry was planning to leave. But this interruption gave him time to reconsider. Perhaps it was better to let sleeping dogs lie. Gretchen was, after all, so sensitive about her cousin; the least criticism of him made her bridle. Mr. Dambar had to admit that once Henry was gone, life would become much easier. He would like to spend some time alone with Gretchen. But now it seemed that whenever he looked up, there was Henry. And if he wasn't there physically, he was always in her thoughts. "Henry said . . ." she would begin every other sentence; or "Do you think Henry would like to . . ." When you got right down to it, they would have no peace until this aging boy wonder headed back up North, where he belonged.

"It's good food," Mrs. Howard was saying to Shaerl. "Dat's what will fix you up. You eat the nuts all day like a mouse and den you say to the world, 'I can't walk mitout I limp.' Oh, my darling, you must listen to Mrs. Howard. She knows."

"Pass the gravy," Leo said.

"Gut, gut." Mrs. Howard's florid face was beaming as she handed him the silver gravy boat adorned with two gaping dolphins. "See, Mr. Leo knows too."

"Uh, Frank, listen, I was wondering, dear." Mrs. Dambar held up her hand as the boat was aimed at her. "Do you think it's a good idea to invite the Keelys over tomorrow?"

"What do you mean, angel?"

"Well, with Henry here, you know . . ." she began, thinking of the staid, silver-haired Mrs. Keely, the wife of one of Frank's army buddies. Henry would be bored to tears by her. And since Gretchen hadn't made any effort to cultivate friends down here, she did not want him to think this was the type of woman she would socialize with.

"Maybe you're right. Yes, maybe so." Mr. Dambar tried not to look too relieved. He had been dreading this dinner with the Keelys, an invitation made a week ago, before Henry's unexpected arrival. Mr. Dambar had no idea how he would explain the cousin to them. And Henry had a way of bringing out the worst in Gretchen, an adolescent cynicism that often degenerated into plain four-letter crudeness. It was so important that the town got the right idea about her, that she was a real lady, a solid, thoughtful choice for a wife and not, as many people seemed to suspect, some sort of adventuress who had taken advantage of a momentary weakness on his part.

Of course, he had ruffled many feathers when he, the town's most eligible bachelor, had overlooked the excellent women ready and willing to tie the knot and chosen instead this dark horse, a Yankee, no less. Mrs. Keely, in particular, had been wounded by this choice. For years she had been grooming a widowed friend of hers to take the place of the late Mrs. Dambar. Frank and the widow, Mrs. Bill Anderson, had actually been lovers off and on—though in a highly discreet manner—for the past six years. As a matter of fact, he had been on the verge of giving in to her, resigning himself to a safe, comfortable marriage, when Gretchen had yanked him off the floor of the souvenir shop and asked him if she could buy him a cup of coffee. He had never met a woman like her before, so forthright, even challenging. After that cup of coffee, Mrs. Bill Anderson, who was actually much prettier than Gretchen, seemed too artificial, like a hothouse orchid. He was exhilarated by the discovery of a new species of woman, one who could thrive in any climate, a hardy perennial that might be a bit thorny around the edges, but that could survive on its own. Gretchen hadn't seemed at all ashamed or self-conscious when she told him she had never been married. It was the first time he had been with a woman who didn't, even if ever so subtly, cling, or worse, pretend to cling. As a matter of fact, she insisted on paying for the coffee and *beignets* at the Café du Monde, and when later they had dinner at Gallatoire's, she took care of her share of the bill.

"Will you call them and explain?"

"Me?" he asked, wondering what she meant by explain. He couldn't very well ask the Keelys not to come because his wife's cousin was loony. "Darling, I think that's your job, isn't it?"

"They're your friends, Frank. I don't really know them at all."

"Well . . . Leo, what's that you're writing?"

Leo sometimes wrote at the table, a habit Mr. Dambar didn't approve of, but tolerated. It turned out to be a letter to one of his pen pals at Angola, the Louisiana state penitentiary. Leo belonged to an organization that corresponded with convicts on a nationwide basis, offering them guidance and advice in specific areas. In Leo's case, it was philosophy. "I'm trying to explain Böhme to him."

"Oh, Böhme," Mrs. Dambar said agreeably, "yes, he is a little knotty."

"There's like one passage here"—Leo peered at the text beside his gold salt dish " 'Thus the compunction willeth upwards, and whirls crossways, and yet cannot effect it—' "

"Leo," Shaerl interrupted, "I changed the sheets on your bed today, so don't put them in the wash tomorrow."

"Thanks, man. ' . . . effect it, for the hardness, viz., the desire, stays and detains it, and therefore it stands like a triangle, and—' "

"Shaerl, you didn't happen to see my jeans?" Mrs. Dambar inquired.

"Huh?"

" ' . . . transverted orb, which (seeing it cannot remove from the place) becomes wheeling, whence arises the mixture in the desire, viz.—' "

"Viz., Leo, why did you leave the Catfish Chow open?" Mrs. Dambar smiled and winked at Mrs. Howard, who appeared distressed by the book on the table. "Mr. Dambar found it all soggy, ripped open. He's asked you to be careful. If you want to raise fish, then you should do it properly."

"What? I didn't—"

"I'm only asking you—we're only asking you to please accept a little responsibility."

"Listen, man, I'm sorry," he said, getting up from the table. "I just can't take these vibes. Too hostile."

"Leo, please, I didn't mean to—"

"I got to finish this letter. It's been on my mind," he muttered as he gathered up the book and his stationery.

"What about your vegetables!" the housekeeper demanded. "You didn't have no green and yellow."

"Let him go," Shaerl said. "He doesn't like carrots."

"I think it's so wonderful, the way he takes time for those prisoners," Mrs. Dambar put in. "It seems he would make a wonderful counselor of some sort. Don't you think, Frank?"

"Huh? Oh, right, yes. Shaerl, why don't you go talk to your uncle, see if you can get him back?"

"Really, he *hates* carrots. I mean it."

"Frank, was I being hostile to Leo?" Mrs. Dambar asked casually some minutes later when it seemed that Mr. Dambar had finally had his fill of pork chops and white bread.

"No, dear. But really, it's not important, the fish stuff."

"But you said yourself, in the shed . . . Well, I guess I was a little too . . ." She stood up and began to clear the table while Mrs. Howard lit a Newport, using the pink candle in front of her plate.

"Have one," the housekeeper urged, thrusting the pack at Shaerl.

"Mrs. Howard," Mrs. Dambar warned as she set the dishes on a filigreed serving cart with ivory handles.

"You only live once," Mrs. Howard said, beaming genially as Shaerl, with a defensive look on her soft, appealing face, plucked out a cigarette. "Live and let live, dat's what I say. I been smoking a pack a day since no bigger than Shaerl." She swept an ash from the bosom of her canary yellow dress, which had a bold collar printed with irregular triangles.

"What about Henry?" Shaerl asked, taking a deep drag, her large doe eyes glazing over with satisfaction.

"He can eat air," Mrs. Howard pronounced with a flourish of her cigarette. "See how he like dat, ha!"

"I'll heat up some leftovers," Mrs. Dambar stated more reasonably, with an edge to her voice. She was looking at her husband, wondering if he was going to let Shaerl go on smoking like that. And just the other night, after making love, he had promised to forbid Shaerl to smoke in the house. Of course, nothing could be done about Mrs. Howard's habit. But Shaerl, barely twenty-one, ruining her health like that and filling the house with that God-awful stench . . .

"Frank."

"Yes, dear?" Seeing the look in her eye, he thought he had better come to her defense. "Of course, yes, Henry can eat leftovers when he comes in. Right, Mrs. Howard? We don't want all that good food going to waste. Now, what's for dessert? I left plenty of room."

CHAPTER TWO

"What time did you get in last night?"

Henry seemed not to hear this.

Mrs. Dambar cleared her throat, said something inane about the weather, took a bite of a cucumber sandwich—they were having tea on the patio while Mrs. Howard napped—then despite herself, knowing that he might get annoyed, added, "I waited up till midnight. I was going to heat some leftovers for you. Frank was really upset. He was afraid you'd gotten lost or something."

Still wearing the same khakis, a shade darker now after his dip in the pond, Henry tossed a lemon rind into a potted ficus. Beyond hearing range Leo was busy planting turnips and onions in the garden, while farther out Shaerl was occupied with a neighbor's bay mare. An inconstant roar of traffic from the highway just beyond the pasture mixed with the sounds of a tennis match going on next door behind a redwood fence. It seemed a hard-fought, bitter match. Groans and curses filled the air.

"Where were you?"

Raising an eyebrow, he regarded her for a moment as if through a monocle. By a mere look, a certain intonation, Henry could make one feel so bourgeois. Though not conventionally handsome, his sleek, thoroughbred lines gave him a distinction that was all too often missing in the landed gentry on his mother's side of the family, Englishmen who could easily be mistaken for Sear's auto parts salesmen. "Where was I? I was asleep."

"In the middle of the woods?"

"In the bedroom. I was exhausted, didn't feel like eating. So I went right to bed. You realize, of course, that you're throwing your life away here."

Even though Mrs. Dambar was used to her cousin's abrupt transitions from one subject to the next, one continent to another, she was not quite prepared for such directness. Earlier, when she and Henry had discussed her move to Louisiana, he had seemed, if not exactly enthusiastic, at least agreeable. She laughed in a forced way, uncertain if he was just parodying her friends. "Oh, come on. I've never been happier in my life." As an afterthought, she added, "You mean all that time I was waiting up for you, you were asleep? That's nice."

"You know Molly's pissed at you," he said, not to be side-tracked. "She invested a lot of time and money trying to get that jewelry business off the ground; then you leave her in the lurch."

Mrs. Dambar colored. She had thought Molly was the one friend who had supported her marriage. To learn now that she was unhappy with her was disquieting. "Well, I can only blame myself. I was a fool to have let her talk me into it. And I don't really understand why *she* should complain. I never asked for a cent back. Three thousand down the drain. The funny thing is, I don't really care about jewelry at all. But Molly was so convincing. She made me think that I really was interested in garnets and opals. And seaweed."

"Seaweed?"

"Oh, some design we had cooked up. Actually, I am interested in seaweed. I guess that's how she hooked me." Mrs. Dambar glanced anxiously over her shoulder. She thought she had heard a noise in the kitchen. Could Mrs. Howard be up already?

She wasn't—a good thing. The tea dishes must be done before the old woman awakened. While Henry videotaped Leo planting onions—Henry kept a diary on videotape, from which he culled material for his performance art—Mrs. Dambar swiftly and quietly washed up, leaving no evidence of the healthy tea that allowed her to pass up the cholesterol at dinner.

"Did she tell you that herself?"

"Who? What?" Henry asked after his cousin had rejoined him in the backyard. His camera was aimed at the beige mobile home that stood, wheel-less, in a corner of the adjacent pasture. A picket fence laced with roses and sweet-potato vines hid the cement blocks upon which the deluxe establishment stood. The camera hummed as Henry zoomed in for a close-up of the picture window, custom-designed by Leo and fitted with vertical miniblinds.

"Molly—that business about being mad at me."

His face taut with concentration, he did not reply until he had put down his camera. "It was some friends of hers."

"Who?"

"I don't know. People who used to work with her or something."

"Must be the Hornbys. Was it the Hornbys?"

"Kyss and Walter, yes."

Kyss used to be a reasonably good friend of Gretchen's before she married Walter. Now all Kyss could talk about were her children and the co-op on East Eighty-fifth Street they had just bought. It was like that with most of Gretchen's friends. One by one they had become preoccupied with nannies, stepchildren, schools, so that it was impossible to talk to them about anything important. They couldn't listen for more than thirty seconds to a word she had to say about the Philippines or Third World economies, and when Gretchen had tried to get them to march against apartheid, they had made her feel like a naive college girl. Of course, none of them would admit they were drifting toward the Right. They were beyond politics, they insisted. They were into reality.

"You know, Henry," she said a few minutes later as they were sitting in the Jeep, waiting to drive Shaerl into town, "I was wondering if you remember who it was who stood up for you when—"

He reached over and beeped the horn in front of her. "Yes?"

"When you quit your job at Ogilvie and ran off to Africa? I was the only one who stood up for you and explained you to the family. I made your mother see just how right it was for you—and

22

burns, which were almost a beard, and black twill shirt, there was something sectarian about the handyman that made his employer feel uncomfortably fashionable. Mr. Dambar was not sure, but he thought it not impossible that if his letters were ever published Leo might turn out to be a modern-day Thoreau. Mr. Dambar had read many of them, at Leo's request, and although half of what Leo wrote was too deep for him, he was nonetheless impressed by the serious tone. Leo kept up a correspondence not only with intellectual prisoners in Louisiana, Oregon, and Rhode Island, but also friends on the faculties of Millsaps College, UCLA, and Peru State College in Peru, Nebraska. In any case, even if the letters were never published, Mr. Dambar couldn't help respecting his handyman's intellect. Probably, if it were not for the shock of his father's suicide, Leo would have written his thesis and won tenure in the philosophy department of some first-rate university. Mr. Dambar did genuinely feel for Leo and still had hopes of seeing him established one day in a position more commensurate with his abilities. Indeed, that was the reason he had taken Leo's money. At that time it seemed Leo stood a good chance of quadrupling his initial investment. Living off the interest on this amount, and perhaps with a teaching fellowship or student loan, Leo could have gotten a Ph.D.

"So what's the story? Is she hard of hearing, or what?"

Mr. Dambar's handsome face, the strong, chiseled features mellowed in a kindly way by Mrs. Howard's generous fare, seemed to cloud over. He was sensitive to any criticism of Gretchen and thought Leo could make more of an effort. "As I was saying, she probably doesn't realize—"

"I heard you tell her it was mine."

"Well, yes. But she could have interpreted it in the sense that it was something I was letting you use, that it really belonged to me."

Leo had bought the Jeep from Mr. Dambar's older son, a Shreveport veterinarian. His other son was in law school at Tulane. Both, for some reason, had been unenthusiastic about their new stepmother. It was something their father preferred not to think about.

While Leo went on about the Jeep, Mr. Dambar's eye was

Grandpa, he listened to me. I made him listen to me. I wasn't going to let him bully me . . . All the time I spent sticking up for you—and this is what I get when I could really use a little support and encouragement. I don't think you realize what a difficult thing it was, how emotional and all, to just uproot myself like this from my friends and family and end up here in the middle of nowhere. It was a terrible risk I was taking and . . . What?"

His shoulders were heaving with that odd, silent laugh of his. "I'm sorry, Gretch baby," he said, patting her on the head. "I can't help it. You move to New Jersey, Morristown, or no, Parsippany, and you expect me to admire the risk."

"This is not New Jersey, Henry."

"No, you're right. This is Africa—and you're Baroness Blixen, fighting off alligators, keeping the niggers in line. Ah, there she is, finally."

Shaerl had emerged from the oversized double front doors and paused beside a thin pillar to adjust an earring. Her long legs were sheathed in leather slacks that seemed a size or two large, as if she were trying to be both sexy and respectable at the same time.

"Did you ever notice how some women make a lot of unnecessary movements with their hands and head?" Henry observed, his cold, appraising eyes upon the girl. "It must be evolutionary, like pretending to have a broken wing or something, little spastic gestures. And the way she blinks, totally gratuitous. Oh God, she is great. I can't stand it."

Henry's delight did not rub off on his cousin, who was brooding about his New Jersey remark. To think that he saw her as a typical suburban housewife—it was so unfair. And all this time she had viewed herself in such a romantic light, running off to the Deep South with a perfect stranger, sacrificing everything to begin anew, to find real values in this remote hamlet where everyone wasn't caught up in all the hype that had made her life in New York such a burden. What was the matter with Henry? Why couldn't he see how different this place was?

Shaerl groaned as she hoisted herself into the backseat. Her arthritis must have been acting up, for she had walked a little more stiff-legged than usual to the Jeep. Mrs. Dambar glanced anxiously at her as she backed out of the driveway. "You OK?"

"Fine. Now I hope y'all don't mind if we stop at K Mart first before we go to the mall. They're the only place that have this tweezerlike thing I've been looking for."

Henry looked over at his cousin. "I love it."

"Henry, please," Mrs. Dambar muttered.

"Love what?" Shaerl asked.

"Never mind," Mrs. Dambar said as she turned onto the highway that led into town.

When Mr. Dambar pulled up in his Buick Riviera he noticed that Leo's Jeep was gone. With the best of intentions Mr. Dambar had planned to march straight over to the trailer and lay everything on the line; but now that Leo wasn't here, it would have to wait.

Right from the beginning Mr. Dambar had had an uneasy feeling about taking Leo's money and investing it for him. Leo had insisted, though, thinking nothing of the possible risks Mr. Dambar had carefully outlined for him. Three years ago Mr. Dambar had been invited to join a consortium of developers who were building luxury condominiums on the north shore of Lake Pontchartrain. Leo had given him almost $20,000, money he had saved from a frugal life-style and a small inheritance from his father, an English professor at St. Jude State College who, during an MLA conference at the Hilton Hotel in New York City, had taken his life. The economy had been booming in Louisiana when the condominiums, The Antibes, had been in the planning stage, and Mr. Dambar was going to derive added benefits by contracting the roofing and plumbing out to his own firms. Then, with the condominiums almost completed, the price of oil had plummeted, meaning disaster for Louisiana. In a ripple effect, one North Shore business after another had failed, and as the oil prices continued to remain low, house after house went up for sale. It was now a buyers' market with property values at a new low, and Mr. Dambar was lucky to have a third of the condominiums sold by the end of the fiscal year. After several days of internal debate, Mr. Dambar had come to the conclusion that the time had come for Leo to pull out and save what he

could of his investment. With some personal sacrifice, M. was going to be able to return twenty cents on the dolla refused this offer, it was highly possible that he could lo thing. Indeed, Mr. Dambar himself anticipated a loss of ove thousand this year alone on the venture. Of course, for him i be a tax write-off.

"Oh, you're here," Mr. Dambar said as he wandered in library with a bowl of chocolate chocolate-chip ice cream tha Howard had thrust into his hands as he passed through the kit Leo looked up from the boulle desk, where he was painstaki copying a letter in calligraphy.

Disconcerted, Mr. Dambar stood there a moment, unsure w to do. He had been relieved by Leo's supposed absence and v planning to watch the free videotape of NFL Bloopers that h come with his subscription to *Sports Illustrated*. The late Mrs. Dan bar had allowed only one TV in the house. Along with a stereo an a pinball machine one of their sons had bought and restored, this TV had been relegated to the library, which was stocked with all the Great Books and everything by Will and Ariel Durant. With a sigh Mr. Dambar realized that the NFL would have to wait.

"Leo, there's something I must—"

"She took it again."

They had both begun talking at once. Mr. Dambar deferred. "What?"

Leo wrote a few words before replying. "The Jeep. Didn't even ask me. Just barreled off."

Without being fully aware of it, Mr. Dambar ingested a spoonful or two of ice cream. Then, thoughtfully: "Perhaps I'm at fault here, Leo. Maybe I haven't made it clear to Mrs. Dambar who owns that Jeep."

Although there was never any question of Mr. Dambar's sounding phony, as a successful businessman he had developed the habit, almost unconsciously, of adapting his manner to the person at hand. With Leo he was perhaps more formal than he would be, say, with Mrs. Howard. Indeed, just a moment ago in the kitchen, he had used "ain't" in the most natural manner.

Leo regarded him with a stern, heavy face. With his full side-

caught by something he had just noticed through the French doors. Two well-dressed ladies in high heels appeared to be deep in discussion in the middle of the vegetable garden.

"Leo?"

"Speak."

"That looks like Mrs. Keely out there. And Mrs. Anderson. What are they . . ."

He was writing again and took a moment to reply. "They came for the lawnmower."

"Pardon?"

"Bums me out. I told them I'd bring it back myself. In the Jeep. Then I look and the Jeep isn't there, and Mrs. Anderson's huffing and puffing, all in a swivet."

"Why don't you go help them?"

The two ladies had moved to the edge of the garden and, both shoving at once, were trying to roll the mower through a patch of thick, unruly grass.

"I told them I'd do it myself as soon as I got my Jeep back. But no, they got to have it now."

A slight arrhythmia, distinct but not too painful, caused Mr. Dambar to pause before opening the French doors. He had not seen Mrs. Anderson in months, not since the supper at Isola Bella, when he had told her that he was planning to marry Gretchen Peabody Aiken–Lewes. There hadn't been a scene, not so much because Mr. Dambar had thoughtfully chosen a public place to make his announcement, but rather because Mrs. Anderson was not an excitable woman. She had even offered him her best wishes for a happy life. Their affair, after all, had been losing steam in the last few months; much of the early attraction had been replaced by routine and comfort. More important, though, he had never lied to her, promising more than he could deliver. From the very beginning he had made it clear that he did not have marriage in mind. In fact, as she had reminded him at that supper, he had often said, "I'll never get married again, ever. I'm too set in my ways." Of course, how could someone predict a Gretchen swooping into his life? he had tried to explain. He had gone on to extol Gretchen's unique and marvelous qualities at some length before he realized this was hardly the time

27

to do so. Supper had ended on an awkward note of apology when he tried to make up for praising Gretchen by praising Mrs. Anderson even more.

"You borrowed her lawnmower? Why, Leo? We have a perfectly good riding mower."

"It's no good for tight spots, edging and all."

"You should have told me about this. And when? When did you borrow it?"

"Long time ago."

The doors opened with a jerk and a squeak. Mr. Dambar was about to step outside when he had second thoughts. Why did *he* have to help them? Perhaps it was better if he stayed out of sight. There was no good that could come of trying to be helpful in this situation. And besides, he didn't feel right about facing Mrs. Keely so soon after dis-inviting her and her husband to dinner. The phone conversation that morning had been awkward. He was not adept at telling white lies. "Gretchen has come down with a touch of the flu," he had explained to Mrs. Keely. Not satisfied with this, he had made the amateur's mistake of supplying additional excuses. "And then, you know, we've been having trouble with the sink." "The sink? I'm sorry to hear that, Frank." "Oh, yes. It's been backed up and Mrs. Howard, she's been worried about her neck, those kinks . . ." Realizing that he was beginning to sound like a nursery rhyme, he quickly changed the subject and asked after Leon, Mrs. Keely's husband. "Did he ever get that stole patched?" "What stole?" Mrs. Keely asked, sounding a little annoyed. "Your mink."

Muttering under his breath, Mr. Dambar carefully pulled the doors to, and, forgetting the ice cream, which he had set down on a brocaded ottoman, left Leo in peace.

A shot or two of Wild Turkey during a soak in his round, emerald green tub with the Jacuzzi going full blast helped restore his equanimity. Steam obscured the lush profusion of remarkably lifelike plastic ferns and philodendrons that Gretchen had watered for a week before realizing her mistake. Remembering this with a smile, he dozed off on a massage table under a tanning lamp.

Twenty minutes later a ping from the preset lamp awakened him. He sat up, and as often happened when he was in this groggy state, forgot he was married. But when he couldn't find any under-wear in his chest of drawers, his memory revived. In one or two little ways, Gretchen had upset the smooth efficiency of Mrs. How-ard's household. Both Shaerl and Mrs. Howard had taken him aside from time to time with minor complaints. "She took my wash out before it was done," Shaerl would say. Or Mrs. Howard: "I iron my heart out and den she smush all the shirts in the closet. They must have the air between dem. Let dem breathe!" He had tried to speak to Gretchen about this, but it was amazing how sensitive she was to criticism. Yes, while in many ways she seemed so robust, any mention of laundry and her eyes would fill with tears.

With a towel around his waist he went to check the laundry room on the other side of the house, but only got as far as the brightly lit kitchen. Swinging open the door, he had taken an iner-tial step or two before freezing like a deer in the glare of onrushing headlights. Mrs. Anderson, Mrs. Keely, Mrs. Howard, Mrs. Dam-bar, and Henry looked up from the painted oak table they were congregating around.

"Oh, Henry, do please put something on," Mrs. Dambar said as the visitors' eyes darted about the room in modest confusion.

"Henry?" Henry said after Mr. Dambar, smiling hard, had made his retreat.

"I meant—"

"Frank—that guy's name is Frank."

"Anyway, as I was saying, it's the last straw, keeping your mower like that. Mr. Dambar and I knew nothing about it, and I just can't imagine—six months, you say. Well, that man really has to go. To tell the truth, I don't understand how Mr. Dambar can put up with him." Mrs. Dambar was talking very rapidly and some-what forcefully, as she was in the habit of doing when she was uneasy. Coming home from town, she had been a bit perplexed to find Mrs. Keely and her friend struggling to load a lawnmower into the rear of a shiny subcompact. Henry had given them a hand, securing the hatchback with a rope from the garage while Mrs. Keely had taken Gretchen aside to tell her how sorry she was to intrude on her like this.

"I had no idea that Dot was coming over here," Mrs. Keely had explained. "I thought we were going right home from the Colonial Dames meeting, but then Dot asked if I wouldn't mind helping her with something and the next thing I know . . . I tried to tell her how ill you were, dear, but she said she really had to get that lawnmower back. You see, her sister-in-law's nose is a little out of joint. It's really her brother's lawnmower, Dot's brother's, and she shouldn't have loaned it out in the first place. Only, seeing how it was for Frank . . . I mean, well, I told her just to . . . Anyway . . ."

While Mrs. Keely continued to explain she avoided looking directly at Mrs. Dambar, who was confused about her illness (Had Frank said she was sick? Oh, what a childish excuse to make . . .) and self-conscious about the way she looked. In her jeans, smudged sweatshirt, and sneakers, Gretchen couldn't have made more of a contrast with the sedately coiffed and powdered older woman. Sloppy dressing was a habit she had gotten into in New York, a kind of protective coloration that made it easier to get around in a city of leering crazies. It used to be that, if there was a crazy within ten blocks he would by some sixth sense find Gretchen and assail her with ludicrous propositions. But simply by looking the slightest bit off-center herself, she was given a wide berth. Sometimes, seeing a crazy in her path who looked undecided, she would start muttering to herself. That always did the trick.

Appearing around the side of the house with some freshly snipped calla lilies, Mrs. Howard, without consulting Mrs. Dambar, had invited Mrs. Keely and her friend in for a cup of coffee. At first Mrs. Keely had demurred, but Mrs. Howard would have none of it. "You don't like my coffee, that's it, huh? You think, 'Ach, that coffee Mrs. Howard she makes . . .'" Herding them inside, Mrs. Howard had asked everyone to walk on the newspapers she had laid down while the wax dried on the kitchen floor.

"I'm Mrs. Bill Anderson," Mrs. Keely's friend said, nodding in Mrs. Dambar's direction.

"I'm sorry," Mrs. Keely said, a hand patting her silver chignon, "I thought you'd met."

After exchanging a few stilted comments about the weather and reassuring Mrs. Howard about her coffee, the ladies were joined by Henry. "Go ahead," he said, swinging a bare leg over the back of a chair. "Just pretend I'm not here."

Mrs. Anderson, Mrs. Keely smiled uncertainly.

"Henry," Mrs. Dambar said as he raised the video camera in his hand. "Not now, please."

Caught between the urge to explain her cousin to the ladies and the equally strong urge to explain the ladies to Henry (They were not really her friends, she wanted to say. This was not a typical way she spent her day), Mrs. Dambar wound up commenting about Mrs. Howard's floor. Why was Mrs. Howard waxing a no-wax floor? Mrs. Anderson enlightened her on this score, explaining that one did have to wax a no-wax from time to time. It was the new never-wax tiles that one did not have to wax, supposedly. A tall, comely woman with a carefully tended beauty mark, Mrs. Anderson only glanced furtively at Mrs. Dambar while addressing her remarks to Mrs. Howard, who was not listening. The old woman was preoccupied with the coffeepot, which was acting up again. "It knows when I got company," she was saying, giving the pot a hard stare. "Oh, yes, don't tell me it don't know." Mrs. Howard leaned closer to the spotless perculator: "I hate you."

"Oh, it doesn't matter, Mrs. Howard," Mrs. Keely said in a warm, gentle voice. "I had far too much coffee at the Dames." She glanced somewhat doubtfully at Henry, who seemed on the verge of raising the camera again, and for Mrs. Howard's benefit went on to explain about the lawnmower in elaborate detail. While Mrs. Dambar learned about Mrs. Anderson's sister-in-law's difficulties with her fuchsia, she pondered whether she should make some effort to appear ill. Should she cough—or would that seem too histrionic? Perhaps if she appeared weary or listless—or talked through her nose . . .

"Well, all that aside, I told Mrs. Anderson that it probably would be best if we called Leo first," Mrs. Keely was saying when Mr. Dambar appeared, clad only in a towel.

"Oh, Henry, do please put something on," Mrs. Dambar called out fondly, somewhat distressed for him.

"Henry?"

"I meant—"

"Frank—that guy's name is Frank."

"Anyway, as I was saying . . ." Glancing at Mrs. Anderson, she noticed the lady's violent blush, apparent even beneath the many layers of Kabuki-like makeup. With a sure instinct, Gretchen scented danger. Her heart began to pound. ". . . it's the last straw . . ."

After peering out the window to make sure Mrs. Anderson's car was gone, Mr. Dambar emerged from his room and walked a few steps down the hall, when he remembered that Mrs. Dambar did not like cologne on men. Retreating to the bathroom, he scrubbed thoroughly and reemerged a few minutes later, his neck pink and raw. Looking for Leo, he passed the den and hesitated a moment. The door was ajar, the typewriter clattering furiously. He wanted to ask his wife if she really thought it had been such a good idea to invite Mrs. Keely and Mrs. Anderson in, but it was probably not wise to disturb her while she was working on the Philippines. Oh, and yes, he also wanted to have a word with her about the Jeep. It was very important that, from now on, in order to preserve domestic tranquillity, she ask Leo's permission.

Mrs. Dambar was aware of someone hovering just outside the door, Frank probably. She almost called out to him, but she did want to finish this letter to Molly. Molly must be made to understand how happy she, Gretchen, was in her new life down South, what a wonderful man Frank was. Knowing this, Molly couldn't help forgiving her friend for backing out of the jewelry venture. "I know it might have seemed precipitate," Gretchen wrote in a P.S., "the way I decided not to go on with our little business, but honestly, Molly, I think in the long run I was doing you a favor. You need a real expert, someone who cares passionately about such things. I'm just not enough of a materialist to . . ." She paused, wondering if Molly would think she was calling her a materialist. Of course, Molly was. But Gretchen had long ago forgiven her for that. While she thought of a way to rephrase her explanation, she began to worry about Mrs. Anderson again and found she could not sit still.

"Oh, hi."

"Hi."

She had left the study and found him out on the patio with an old broom, half its bristles missing.

"What are you doing?" she inquired, giving him a peck on the cheek.

"I thought I'd sweep."

She watched him take a swipe or two at the pine straw that had fallen onto the blue and pink stones. "Oh."

For a while she stood there, debating whether to bring up Mrs. Anderson. Sometimes it was better to let well enough alone. After all, except for today, the woman had kept her distance. Yet at the same time, she felt she had a right to know. Had he been involved with her? Not that it really mattered—except for the fact that Mrs. Anderson wore so much makeup. Was it possible that he found that sort of getup attractive? She would really like to know.

Sweeping around his wife—he was getting used to the momentary spells she seemed to succumb to in the midst of her routine—Mr. Dambar wondered if he should say something about his near-naked entrance into the kitchen. What could she mean by asking those women in with Henry around? And her in jeans. "Dear, I was—"

"Yes?"

"I was going to ask you about the Jeep," he said, suddenly veering away. What good would it do now? It was too late.

"Ask me what?"

"Well, you know that's Leo's Jeep. I don't think he likes it when you take it without asking."

"I have to ask *him?*"

"That's the general idea, when something belongs to someone—don't you think?"

Mrs. Dambar plopped down onto a redwood chaise longue, cushioned in a floral pattern. "Oh, Frank, you realize, of course, dear, that you're going to have to let that man go."

"Pardon?"

"It can't go on any longer. No one can understand how you put up with him. Mrs. Keely was just saying she thinks Leo takes advantage of you. And Mrs. Anderson, I think he hurt her feelings. She is a very attractive woman," she added. "Don't you think?"

"If you like the type." He kicked a pine cone off into a bed of forsythia. "Anyway, it's none of her business. Leo works hard. He's got the vegetable garden going now so we never have to buy tomatoes or squash, anything like that."

"Frank, I really don't like him. There's something funny about him, so hostile. I don't understand why I have to eat with him every day. And why you let him use the library when he's got his own trailer."

"Now, dear, he's been with me for years, and I have all this space. Why should I coop him up in that . . ." He gestured toward the beige trailer beyond the lawn. "Besides—"

"You're not mad at me?"

"No. But I do resent those women telling you . . . Leo is a fine young man."

"Young? He's forty if he's a day."

Mr. Dambar resumed sweeping, his wife's eyes upon him. He supposed he would have to let her know now about Leo's recent financial embarrassment. One could hardly fire someone from a five-dollar-an-hour job after losing his life's savings. As a matter of fact, this might be a good opportunity to talk about finances in general. She should know that they were going to have to tighten their belts. If she objected, then she would have to be a little more forthcoming about her own state of affairs. He knew nothing about her personal assets, which were managed by an uncle of hers in Connecticut. It struck him as being somewhat childish, this refusal to be up front about her worth even after they were married. If he didn't love her so much, he would have felt hurt. It was almost as if she didn't trust him.

He cleared his throat. "You know, I'm glad you brought Leo up, because there's something . . ." he began just as Mrs. Howard called out the kitchen window.

"What?"

"Phone! Schnell!"

*

When he returned to the patio a few minutes later, Mrs. Dambar was not there. The call had been from a member of the Men's Bible Study group he belonged to. Was it his turn to bring the soft drinks that evening? Mr. Dambar had consulted Mrs. Howard, who got tense and red in the face as she in turn consulted her kitchen calendar. Details like this were taken very seriously, and she was apt to raise her voice and wave her hands about if there were any discrepancies. "Nein, it is Dr. McFlug's turn. Why do dey ask you for the soft sodas when it is *his* turn, I would like to know."

He was about to go in search of his wife when it occurred to him that perhaps it would be better if he first informed Leo about the condominiums. Afterward, he would talk to her.

Flushing the toilet, Mrs. Dambar worried that she had sounded too bossy about Leo and resolved to let her husband make up his own mind. On the way to the patio she rehearsed how she would introduce Mrs. Anderson into the conversation again, giving him another opportunity to share his past with her. It did seem important to her that she learn a little more about him. Love was all well and good, but it would be nice to know just exactly what it was she was clasping to her bosom. Unlike her thoroughly analyzed male friends in New York, Frank rarely talked about his past or his feelings. At first this had been a refreshing change, to deal with someone who wasn't so self-conscious. In fact, it had been positively charming. But charm, like sugar, left one craving something more substantial. To know the real Frank, that was her goal.

"Henry, have you seen Frank?" she asked, stepping out onto the patio. Standing on one leg, Henry was sketching in his notebook.

"Can you take me to the airport?"

"You're not leaving?"

"Got to."

"Oh." Mrs. Dambar stood there a moment, wondering how she felt. Was it relief or a slight panic? Surely she should be able to tell the difference. "What are you drawing?"

He snapped the notebook shut. "Nothing."

"Was it the backyard?" she asked hopefully. How nice it would be if Henry immortalized the backyard. Friends might see it in a Soho gallery, one of those fascinating collages of drawings, photos, and rubber dolls he used to do before he got involved with video.

"I want to leave in an hour."

"So soon? Oh, Henry . . ."

From the picture window of the beige trailer Mr. Dambar watched his wife gesturing to her cousin on the patio while Leo went on about his Jeep. "Yes, yes," Mr. Dambar said absently, "I told her it's yours. She must ask."

"Bums me out, man."

Letting the curtain fall over the miniblinds, Mr. Dambar was about to broach the topic of certain investments when Leo, with that peculiar sixth sense of his, said, "So how long you going to let that dude hang around here?"

From the Eames chair he was sitting in, it was impossible for Leo to see out the window, and yet he seemed to know not only whom his employer had been contemplating, but also what.

"Henry is a fine young man, Leo. Very fine."

The trailer creaked as Mr. Dambar walked over to the Castro convertible beneath a portrait of Fichte, the dogmatic idealist philosopher Leo's father had specialized in. "You remember what I told you about The Antibes, Leo? How those condominiums might be something of a risk?"

"Why do you change the subject, Mr. D? Seems to me like that cousin makes you pretty uptight." Leo smiled and shook his head, and for a few moments both men stared blankly at the soundless TV. A Colombian soap opera was playing, the walls of the set shaking whenever one of the stars shut a door. Leo was hooked into a neighbor's satellite dish in exchange for a monthly supply of beans, basil, and catfish.

"Here he is, eating up all your food, just hanging around taking home movies." Leo switched channels by remote control. "You know why he's filming us?"

"I understand it has something to do with his art," Mr. Dambar said, semimesmerized by a Ping-Pong tournament on the screen.

36

"Mr. D, he's making fun of you. He thinks this place is quaint, cute. You should have heard what Shaerl told me, the things he says to Gretchen. He thinks he's in New Jersey."

"What?"

Leo stretched his robust frame. "You're too nice a guy, Mr. D. You don't see what's going on right under your nose. There he is sitting right next to you three meals a day shoveling in your good food and like not one thanks. Have you ever heard him say, 'Hey, thanks, man. That was good'?" With a sigh Leo flicked to another channel. "Ok, he's her cousin and it's Relative City, we all got to be nice. That's fine. But I tell you, Mr. D, you've done your duty. You've leaned over backward. She has nothing to complain about. It's time you showed him the door."

"You think?"

"Oh, man." Leo ran his fingers through his thick, graying hair. "You should have heard what Howard told me. She was there when Mrs. Keely and all had coffee. Howard said she nearly died, she was so humiliated. The dude had on those hot pants of his and he kept on trying to like video the dames and—"

Mr. Dambar interrupted. He could not bear to hear any more details. "Say, Leo, how would you like to have dinner one night, just you and me? I thought maybe we could go to Isola Bella. They got a new dish on the menu I think we should try out."

The handyman's eyes lit up. "Far out."

"Maybe tomorrow night."

"Right, I need to get away. Change of scene and all that."

Mr. Dambar was gratified by his response. Underneath Leo's gruff exterior he could see the small lost boy, searching for some foothold in life. Leo had loved his father so much, Mr. Dambar knew, and had never really gotten over the suicide. It was nice to think that he was able to offer the boy a helping hand.

"So Mr. D, we got a date?"

Mr. Dambar, at the door, gave him a thumbs up.

"By the way, you were saying something about the condos."

"Condos? Oh, it's nothing. It can wait."

*

"I thought you were Episcopalian," Mrs. Dambar said as her husband dressed for his Bible study.

"I am."

"Then why are you going to a Baptist Bible class?"

Propped up in the high canopied bed, she was writing checks—the rent for her apartment on West End Avenue (it was sublet illegally to a cousin of Molly's), Con Edison, Lord & Taylor, Altman's, Oxfam America, Tiffany's, Hammacher Schlemmer, the Fresh Air Fund. It always amazed her how little she had to show for the amount she spent. She barely had a dress to wear or a decent cup to drink tea out of. Mainly it all seemed to go for gifts, an endless round of social blackmail in the form of weddings, birthdays, anniversaries, and dear friends' favorite charities.

Dawdling in front of the wardrobe mirror, Mr. Dambar tried to decide which trousers to put on. "I joined as a favor to Mr. Keely. He's a Baptist."

"Oh, I see. Business."

"I like the Bible. It's fun."

"A barrel of monkeys."

Pricked by her cynicism, he said what he had managed not to say for so long: "Hon, you have any idea when Henry is planning to leave?"

"In about half an hour or so. Why?"

"Oh, what a shame."

"I'm devastated, Frank. Absolutely devastated." She took the pen out of her mouth and scribbled her signature on a check. "By the way, I'll have to take the Jeep. I'm driving him to the airport."

"The Jeep?"

"Yes, will you ask Leo for me?"

"Well, I . . ." He opened the crested wardrobe and put back the blue trousers in favor of yellow. "Why don't you take the Buick, dear? I'll take the Jeep."

She frowned and bit the pen. Why should he be afraid of borrowing the Jeep for her? But she decided to ignore this for now. She was determined to do everything in her power to make his life smooth and easy. "I really don't like driving the Buick. It's so big and ugly. But never mind. Now get over here."

"What?"

She patted the counterpane that Mrs. Howard had instructed Shaerl to scent every day with a few drops of Chanel No. 22, a fragrance that Mrs. Dambar could do without. "I said get over here, you. I think you're just too cute in your shirt and tie and little underpants—I can't stand it."

As he tumbled semiaccidentally onto the bed of bills, he felt a hundred pounds lighter. Henry was going. He was finally going.

Mrs. Dambar spanked him lightly for looking so pleased, then kissed him all over his sweet, year-round tanned face.

CHAPTER THREE

With Henry gone Mrs. Dambar spent less time thinking about what was wrong with the house. The royal blue of the carpeting didn't seem such an eyesore after all, or at least she wasn't noticing it as much. And the flocked wallpaper, the gilt scrolls and paws and curlicues of the furniture began to seem less of a personal affront. Indeed, during a quiet moment with a cup of tea, she actually felt the stirrings of a fond amusement.

Yes, with Henry gone, Mrs. Dambar found herself breathing easier. Even Mrs. Keely did not seem quite as old and prim when she ran into her at the stationer's, where she was looking for a particular onionskin for her work on the Philippines. And she herself did not feel as self-conscious as she thought she would when, in order to please her husband, she began to upgrade her wardrobe with a few purchases from the mall just across the state line in Mississippi. She was glad Henry hadn't seen the mall, for it was exactly the sort of thing one might find in New Jersey. Probably Africa itself had malls like this—she wouldn't be surprised. After all, hadn't Baroness Blixen's farm been turned into a suburb? Karen, was it called? How hard it was nowadays to really get away from it all.

Putting on a new outfit from the mall, clothes that made her feel somewhat bourgeois, Mrs. Dambar would endure butterflies until he had assured her that yes, he liked it, he liked it very much.

It was odd what love required one to do. If she had not been so crazy about Mr. Dambar, she would have laughed at herself making such a fuss over clothes. The thought of losing him, though, was unbearable, and she knew that if the marriage was going to work it would have to be by her own efforts, her own painful adaptation. He was too set in his ways to make any real changes. And so, with the help of Shaerl, she began experimenting with makeup, trying out a bolder look that was still soft and feminine. Shaerl even managed to talk her into a rinse, a surprisingly natural light red that, unfortunately, turned a little brassy in the sun.

"You sure this is the one you bought?" Mr. Dambar asked as he tugged on her zipper. The Keelys were due any minute to take the Dambars to a play in Baton Rouge, and Mrs. Dambar was having some difficulty with the new dress she had bought at D.H. Holmes in the mall. For some reason it wouldn't zip all the way up in the back.

"I don't understand. It's the size I always buy."

"But didn't you try it on, dear?"

"I was in a hurry. Just pull, Frank. Pull hard." She exhaled as the dress tightened about her. "I put in some herbs today, fennel and oregano."

"Oh, good."

"While I was digging, I noticed something odd, Frank. I put them in right by the side of the house, and it seemed the bricks felt so smooth. I've never . . . Got it?"

"Wear something else. This won't go, Gretch."

"Oh, but it must. Anyway, the bricks . . ."

"It's brickface."

"What can that mean?"

"Well, they're bricks, sort of. I had it done awhile back. We were spending a fortune painting this place every other year it seemed. So I got it brickfaced." He tugged a final time. "No way, Mrs. Dambar. This won't work."

"Well, I don't have time to change. And I like this dress so much," she added, going to the closet. A shawl that a former boyfriend had brought back from Peru, where he had worked with the Quechuans, would cover the zipper that wouldn't close. "There.

How's that? Frank, why aren't you dressing? They'll be here any second."

"Who?"

"The Keelys."

"Oh, but hon, I already told you. I can't go tonight."

"What?"

"Don't you remember? I've got a call coming in from Vancouver—really important. I've got to be here."

"But . . . I don't . . . Did you? What about . . ."

"The Keelys? I already phoned them. They know. It's fine."

Mrs. Dambar sank onto the absurdly low, flounced dressing table stool and pondered this. Had he told her? Was it possible that she did not listen carefully enough? Jeremy, her most recent boyfriend, the one she had met not long after Zeke had returned from Peru and started drinking so much and eating Fruit Roll-Ups for dinner, Jeremy had broken up with her because of this. He claimed she never listened to a thing he said. Oh, she must be careful from now on. She must attend. God, how Jeremy had hurt her, just as she was beginning to trust him. And then, out of the blue, he had stormed into the apartment one day—"You never listen to a thing I say!"—and Jeremy was usually so sweet and docile. Oh, the shock and pain of his abandonment. In a way, she knew she would never fully recover. There would always be a part of her broken, wounded.

Mr. Dambar had gone back to the collection of miniature cars his late wife had given him when they were married. Every anniversary she would buy another car, custom-made by a firm in Islip, New York. As he rearranged them in the display case, he began to wonder if he had indeed told her. He was sure he had spoken to Mrs. Keely about it, and Mrs. Howard. Shaerl and Leo, too. But Gretchen? Could he have forgotten to tell her?

"Well, I—"

"I mean, I—"

They both waited for the other to go on.

With a sigh Mrs. Dambar took off one of her earrings, a sapphire surrounded by diamonds that her grandmother had left her. "Don't worry, Frank. I really didn't want to go tonight anyway. It'll be nice to spend the evening here. What would you like to do? You want to play Scrabble?"

"Hang on a minute. You're going."

"No, I can't. Not without you."

"But you got to. I already told the Keelys. They're expecting you."

"Oh, Frank."

"Angel, think how it would look if you backed out now. We can't go on making up excuses to them, pretending you're sick. Now come on, you'll have a ball."

It took a moment for Mrs. Dambar to reply. A small but surprisingly bitter rebellion had to be quashed in one of the remoter outposts of her heart. "Well, I guess it would look sort of unfriendly, dear."

In the backseat Shaerl sat between Mrs. Dambar and Leo, who was massaging the girl's right leg, which was acting up again because of the humidity. Up front Mrs. Keely was driving while her husband stared straight ahead, brooding over a recent injustice. There had been a slight contretemps between Mr. and Mrs. Keely over who was to drive to Baton Rouge. Mrs. Keely claimed that her husband had no "night vision" and that she wasn't going to risk a young girl's life because of Mr. Keely's silly pride. Mrs. Dambar, who was still trying to reconcile herself to the presence of the handyman—Frank could have at least told her that he was coming along, too—was perplexed by the repeated references to the "young girl's" life, as if Shaerl's was the only one worth saving.

"I think it's so nice the young people can come," Mrs. Keely said at the first traffic light. "It always depresses me seeing all those gray heads at a cultural event."

Mrs. Keely was saying this into the rearview mirror, where her eyes met Mrs. Dambar's. Though she had made up her mind to be agreeable tonight, for Frank's sake, Mrs. Dambar refused to respond. She did not know what Mrs. Keely could possibly mean by "the young people," as if Leo were to be included in this category. It had only been with the strictest self-discipline, a Puritan suppression of almost every natural instinct, that Mrs. Dambar had been able to countenance this man's presence in her household. She realized she had no choice, though, after Mr. Dambar had informed her of the unwise investment he had made on Leo's behalf. As for Leo, he had taken the news of his financial ruin philosophically. He had let everyone know that he didn't give a damn. He hated money. Money was what was rotting the moral fiber of this country, turning all those yuppies into a bunch of pansies. And with this scorn, Leo gained a certain moral leverage over his employer. Mr. Dambar seemed to defer to his every whim with guilty affability. Even Mrs. Dambar, who was of course entirely blameless in this affair, couldn't help feeling guilty by association and perhaps criticized the handyman much less than she felt entitled to.

Not being naturally a moody man, Mr. Keely was unable to sulk for more than a mile or two. Soon he was twisted around in his seat, trying to spark up a conversation in back while his wife, with solemn concentration, attended to the dark country road.

"Now tell me again who you are," he said to Shaerl. An officer in a savings and loan company, he had the weary, defeated look of a junior college football coach, his weathered face kind in an apologetic way, as if he felt kindness a weakness.

"Shaerl Blackburn." The girl sat erect, her eyes avoiding Mr. Keely's while her uncle gently rubbed the painful leg. Forgoing spikes this evening, she had slicked her hair back like a matinee idol of the twenties, her ears prominent. The effect was striking and made the girl look much more mature and sophisticated. Beside her, with her thick peasant shawl and beaded dress, Mrs. Dambar felt quite dowdy.

"So you're Leo's girlfriend?" he ventured.

"That's his niece, sugar," Mrs. Keely put in.

"Shaerl's been helping Mrs. Howard out," Mrs. Dambar said, wondering if she should add something about the girl's arthritis. Surely some explanation was in order for the uncle's groping. "You see, she's—"

"It's only part time," Shaerl said in the carefully modulated voice of a beauty pageant contestant. "I'm fixing to go to graduate school."

"Oh?"

"I'm going to get a degree in business administration. I'd like to teach business administration someday." With her manicured nails she fingered the high collar of her black, mandarin-style dress. "That's why I like working for Frank. I feel like I can learn so much being around a successful businessman. I admire his abilities so much. That's enough, Leo," she added, removing the stepuncle's hand. "Leo, too, is helping me out. I always like to be with people I can learn from. He's teaching me how to cope with pain, mentally and psychologically."

"You're not feeling well?" Mr. Keely asked.

"I suffer from arthritis. Leo's the only one I know who can make it go away, the pain. I used to go to all these doctors, but you know . . . My mom got so stressed out. She'd get real, um, and then she started getting sick, migraines. That's when I figured I'd be doing her a favor if I lived with him." Still not looking at Mr. Keely, she nodded in her uncle's direction and then, as if remembering to, smiled.

"Well," Mr. Keely said, turning his slack, lined face toward Mrs. Dambar, "you must be proud."

Not quite sure what he could mean by that, Mrs. Dambar shrugged deferentially. They were passing through Tula Springs now, and she turned her head, feigning interest in the dimly lit streets. Fresh out of Radcliffe, during her Peace Corps days, Mrs. Dambar had spent seven months in a town about this size an hour north of Manila. What a bitter disappointment it had been, to travel to the very ends of the earth and there find everyone obsessed with America. She had struggled hard to master Tagalog, but no one wanted to speak it with her. Instead of learning more about their own rich heritage of ancient tribal customs, everyone was anxious to copy the latest American fad. Mrs. Marcos epitomized this whole mentality with her coterie of male starlets, her film festivals and townhouse discos. This was the point Mrs. Dambar had been trying to make in her still-unfinished letter to the *Times*—that Mrs. Marcos had no soul of her own. In that tasteless palace of hers, a monument to vulgarity, she revealed her true self.

"Oh, he's gone all right," Leo was saying in response to a question from Mr. Keely concerning Henry's whereabouts. Mr.

45

Keely had been looking forward to meeting him, it seemed. "A real space cadet."

Mr. Keely looked thoughtful. "He went back to New York City?"

"Yes," Mrs. Dambar said, anxious for Mr. Keely to get the right impression, "you see, he got an invitation to redesign a space in—"

"Did you hear what he did?" Leo interrupted. With his gray tweed suit, string tie, and ponytail, he reminded Mrs. Dambar of the American Studies instructor at Yale she had dated in the late sixties, a fortyish man who, untenured, had thrown his plate of beef stroganoff out a Saybrook window in support of the striking dining-hall workers. "He's got all his clothes on, see, and it's like thirty degrees out." He had leaned closer to Mr. Keely, in a confidential manner. "I mean it was cold, man. So he's out by my pond where I raise my cats—"

"Speak up, Leo, please," Mrs. Keely put in. "I always hate it when Mr. Keely mumbles. I don't want him getting a bad example."

"Yeah, so anyway," Leo went on, his voice a little higher, "this Henry is all dressed up, right? Well, God strike me dead if he didn't jump in my pond with all his clothes on. Nearly scared all my cats to death. I swear, it's the truth. You ask Mr. D, he'll tell you. The dude gave me the creeps. Wouldn't have surprised me if he didn't pull out a machete at dinner and hack us all to death. I could hardly eat with him around."

"Oh, Leo, really," Mrs. Dambar said a little shrilly. Then, controlling herself, she added, "Such nonsense."

"Am I right, Shaerl?"

"Well, he was sort of weird. He told me he knows Morgan Fairchild."

"Ah, Miss Fairpiece," Mr. Keely said. "Hasn't she moved to those new apartments near the elementary school, Mother?"

Shaerl shifted her leg; Mrs. Dambar moved her own out of the way. "No, this one's on TV. She's real famous and beautiful. I thought it was sort of sad that he had to lie about her."

"Well, it just so happens to be true," Mrs. Dambar said firmly. "Henry is one of the most desirable bachelors in New York, and I do hope you're not going to smoke."

46

Shaerl had taken out a Merit. "You're kidding," she said with a blink or two. The cigarette lay ambiguously in her lap. "Henry? Your cousin Henry?"

"Of course," Mrs. Dambar said with quiet, simple pride.

The girl gazed at Mrs. Dambar with newfound respect as the car crossed the bridge that marked the end of the city limits.

An hour later they found themselves in a cloverleaf that made Mrs. Keely unhappy. She was sure the mall where the Baton Rouge Little Theater was located was west because she remembered having the sun in her eyes the last time she drove there to buy a particular style of lampshade that was nowhere to be found in Tula Springs or the mall in Mississippi. Leo and Mr. Keely were reading aloud the green signs over the exits and realized this couldn't be the way, since it would head them out of town toward Hammond. Shaerl and Mrs. Dambar were hunched over, patting blindly at the floor carpet trying to find one of Mrs. Dambar's sapphire earrings. Shaerl had been the one to notice Mrs. Dambar's right ear was bare, and no one could remember if she had had two earrings on when she got into the car. They made a complete circuit of the busy cloverleaf, executing two figure eights, before Mr. Keely insisted on his way, which turned out to be correct.

As soon as she was settled in her seat and Albee's *Tiny Alice* had begun, Mrs. Dambar turned her attention to Leo's uncalled-for remarks about her cousin. It suddenly occurred to her that Leo hadn't even been there the day Henry had taken his dip in the pond. That meant only one thing, that Frank had been discussing the incident with him. What could dear Frank mean by telling Leo such a thing? It was almost like tattling. Very childish. And it showed a lack of good judgment. As a matter of fact, it did seem that Frank was spending an awful lot of time with Leo. He was always finding some excuse or other to go out back to the trailer. "Leo wanted to see the paper when it came," he would say. Or, "Leo asked me to bring him these screws."

With furtive, mouselike hesitancy, a woman beside her in shot silk opened a cellophane wrapper. Mrs. Dambar gave her a look, and then continued with her worrying. What could have happened to that earring? She would die if it was lost. Irreplaceable. In fact, it had survived the burning of Washington, D.C., by the British—and now she loses it on the way to a play. Of course, not being a materialist, she shouldn't be *too* upset. But still . . .

Looking hard at the stage, Mrs. Dambar tried to get involved for a moment or two in the action. But for her there was something deeply silly about plays and movies, grown people pretending to be who they weren't, expressing emotions that they didn't feel. The only art she appreciated was visual. Yes, she considered herself to be primarily a visual person. And perhaps this was why she had let herself become enmeshed in that thankless research that had nearly ruined her life. A friend of Henry's had needed help in his study of Piero di Cosimo's *Discovery of Honey.* Feeling that a short vacation from her research on the Philippines might do her some good, Gretchen had volunteered to assist him, and after six months of research Jeremy, the art historian, and she were officially in love. The monograph he had planned on the single painting was not enough, Jeremy decided, and Gretchen found herself struggling with obscure German and Italian dissertations on *Perseus Freeing Andromeda* and *Death of Procris.* Two years later a slim volume appeared in which there was not a single mention of Gretchen in either the acknowledgments or footnotes. Jeremy and she had quarreled and separated in galleys. Even today Mrs. Dambar could not bear the sight of honey on the breakfast table.

She was wondering about brickface, how anyone could feel right about living in a house that looked like brick but really wasn't—and to think she hadn't noticed how regular the "bricks" were, a dead giveaway—when the curtain came down.

"Oh, yes, it was wonderful," Mrs. Dambar said as Mrs. Keely pulled up in the driveway beside the Jeep. She had dozed off on the way home, her head on Shaerl's shoulder, and felt a little groggy and embarrassed. "Just great."

"No, Mrs. Dambar, I was talking about your earring. It worries me so."

"Oh, that. Well, if you find it, let me know."

Mr. Keely set down the banana daiquiri he had bought at a Daiquiri Hut, where drinks were "to go," and shook Leo's hand.

Leo had had a guava, Shaerl a strawberry, which Mrs. Dambar, who had ordered a double passion fruit, had helped her finish. As she got out of the car, she felt a damp spot on her leg. Something must have spilled.

"Thanks so much," Mrs. Dambar called out as the Keelys' car pulled into the street. "Well, I think that was fun," she added brightly to Shaerl, who had already disappeared around the side of the house with her uncle.

In the morning Mrs. Dambar drove Shaerl to town so that the girl could pay a visit to her aunt, who was in bed with a virus. If it weren't for a hangover, which made it impossible to concentrate on the Philippines, Mrs. Dambar wouldn't have played chauffeur. The night before she had tried to talk to Mr. Dambar after the play, but he was remote and withdrawn and soon fell back to sleep. Feeling keyed up, she had nursed a glass of wine or two in the study to help her relax. It was the mixture of passion fruit and wine that had given her the hangover. And strawberry.

"I can't believe Mrs. Keely stopped in that place," Mrs. Dambar said as she slowed for a large, tawny dog that was lying in the middle of the road. Not budging, it gave her a look as she pulled to the right with a honk. "The only reason I got something was because of the earring," she went on as she nosed the Riviera out onto the Old Jeff Davis Highway. Because of the trees it was hard to tell if any cars were coming, and there was no traffic light. "And all the time it was sitting on my dressing table. I was so relieved."

"I really don't care for daiquiries myself."

"Neither do I."

Shaerl's face was pale and puffy. On her lap was a present for her aunt, three frozen catfish. Mrs. Howard was defrosting.

"This was where she was killed," Shaerl said as Mrs. Dambar lurched out in front of a red Nissan.

"Who?"

"Frank's wife. They were going to put up a light after that, but then people still didn't think there was enough traffic from our road, so that was that."

A tractor trailer approached, and as it whipped past advised them to DRINK MILK. "Shaerl, I meant to ask you. If we get in an accident, will you mind saying that you were driving?"

"I don't know. Why?"

"I don't have a license. See in New York, there was just no reason. I never had to drive."

"Oh, OK." Though she had a license, Shaerl didn't like to drive because she couldn't tell where the car left off, especially a big one like the Riviera. "I just have the feeling I'm scraping everything I pass," she had told Mrs. Dambar one day when she was vacuuming.

"Did you ever meet her yourself, Gretchen?"

"Who?"

"Morgan Fairchild."

"God, no."

The aunt's house turned out to be surprisingly large and attractive, almost the size of the Dambars'. Anthropologically speaking, Mrs. Dambar found it curious that one's maid's aunt could live in such style. Granted, one side was glassed in with solar panels that did not quite jibe with the Colonial feel of the rest of the house. But overall a certain taste and substance were apparent, especially in the neatly manicured lawn. If only Leo could see how level the grass was around the pines and with what care the hedge was trimmed. While she waited for the girl to pay her respects, Mrs. Dambar dozed off in the car, her head tilted at an uncomfortable angle.

After the visit, a short one, they drove across the railroad tracks to the Sonny Boy Bargain Store. While Mrs. Dambar searched for a staple remover Shaerl bought a different brand of hair rinse for Mrs. Dambar, one that they hoped wouldn't turn so brassy in the sun.

"Everyone looks at me as if I'm crazy," Mrs. Dambar said when they were back in the car. "They've never heard of a staple remover. I'm always breaking my nails trying to get them out."

"Why do you want to get them out?"

"One does from time to time."

The next stop was a health-food store located in the defunct railroad station. While Shaerl looked for the bee pollen she had to get for Leo, Mrs. Dambar made conversation with the clerk, a nice-looking young man with a prominent aristocratic nose.

"Did you hear that, Shaerl?" Mrs. Dambar asked when Shaerl walked up to the counter with the pollen. She repeated a few of the interesting facts the clerk had told her. "There's no railroad here anymore, no trains, and it's all because of air conditioning."

"That's right," the clerk said. "People used to come up here to get away from the heat down in New Orleans. All the pine forests made ozone, and they used to have these ozone resorts along Tula Creek. Then when they cut down all the pines—the lumber companies from up north, Chicago and Minneapolis—the ozone went away. Now I'm not so sure just how bad all this is, since someone came in yesterday and said ozone was dangerous. And my wife told me pines don't make ozone anyway."

"Isn't there some sort of ozone hole over the Antarctic?" Shaerl asked, taking her change.

"And maybe one here," Mrs. Dambar mused aloud. "How strange." She appreciated the clerk's taking the time to be so friendly and repeating everything for Shaerl. It reminded her of the native elder she had met in the Philippines's Sulu archipelago. He had sat and repeated his family's genealogy to her, twenty minutes of nonstop names.

As a token of her gratitude, Mrs. Dambar bought an expensive jumbo bottle of stress vitamins and some aloe face cream.

"Isn't it awful how people came in from Chicago and exploited the natural resources?" Mrs. Dambar was saying as they climbed back into the turquoise Riviera. "It's a very colonial type of thing to do, like the English did to India, Spain and America to the Philippines. It gets me so mad."

"That's why I like the Germans. They minded their own business."

"Shaerl, the Germans are the worst, the very worst of all. How in the world can you possibly—"

"Left."

Mrs. Dambar turned left. "Can you possibly think . . ."

"I mean aside from the Jews."

"Oh God, you've got to be kidding. Don't you realize that they are sick? I had a terrible fight with my mother last year. She wanted to go to Bayreuth, and I reminded her that Wagner was a—"

"Frank's German."

"What?"

"His grandparents are from Germany. That's how they got Mrs. Howard. Her mother worked for his grandparents in Düsseldorf. Are we stopping here?"

"Yes, I have to buy a broom."

For a moment before pulling open the rusted screen door of Ajax Feed and Seed, Mrs. Dambar worried about having married a German. In her mind there had never been any connection between Louisiana and Germany. Mrs. Howard had just seemed an anomaly, like a Turk among the Eskimos. Still, even if Frank had mentioned his ancestry, she knew this wouldn't have affected her decision to marry him. No, not one iota. It was silly to even think about it. And probably she should ask Shaerl not to mention anything she had said to Frank. Or maybe she shouldn't, because then she would be underlining the incident. Best to just let the girl forget.

After picking out a sturdy push broom for the patio, she decided on impulse to purchase two dozen chicks that weren't really for sale. The store manager explained that someone had left them behind a couple days ago. " 'Spect they be back for them any day now," he said, eyeing the cardboard box that cruelly housed the unfortunate poultry. He himself with his starched white shirt and pressed overalls did not seem anything but good-hearted, but still, Mrs. Dambar could not get over the feeling that if the owner did not return that day, the chicks would be suffocated or drowned or at the very least, die of hunger and thirst. With much shrugging of his round shoulders and many *Well, I don't know*'s, he finally sold the whole lot to her for forty-five dollars plus tax.

"They ain't even mine," he said as he loaded the chicks into the backseat. "How can I sell you stuff ain't even mine?"

"Thank you very much, Mr. Guest. That will be all."

Mr. Dambar emerged from the Bessie Building and stood for a moment on the pavement, looking off into nowhere. This latest meeting with his lawyer, Mr. Herbert, had not gone smoothly. According to Mr. Herbert, it would not make sense for Mr. Dambar to use any of his personal funds to pay Leo back at twenty cents on the dollar for The Antibes debacle. Rather, he should wait until the money was provided by the corporation itself. But Mr. Dambar was afraid that if he waited, Leo would wind up with nothing. Surely, some token payment to Leo now could do no harm. Although Mr. Herbert commended the impulse behind the idea, he could not approve of such irregular business dealings. It was sure to throw everything out of whack.

Wedged between a toddlers' outlet and a store that specialized in Western clothes and saddles, Mr. Dambar's own office was part of a mini-mall on the outskirts of town. The play-school architecture, in primary colors somewhat reminiscent of a children's zoo, was perhaps too whimsical for most businesses; half the space was still unrented. Mr. Dambar didn't really remember driving there in Leo's Jeep. He wasn't ever fully conscious of being in transition. Either he was in one place—downtown at Mr. Herbert's in the Bessie Building—or another. His mind was too preoccupied to notice much else, and besides, he could probably drive anywhere he wanted in Tula Springs blindfolded. It was the goal, the destination, that mattered. If he was sent to the A&P by Mrs. Howard, he would go on automatic pilot, turning at the right intersections without having to think where he was.

Mrs. Sklar, his partner, looked up from a word processor when he walked into the narrow office. She was breaking in a new assistant, a bright girl with an M.B.A. from St. Jude State College. "Can I see you a minute?" she said in a hoarse, no-nonsense voice after giving the girl a few operating instructions. Mr. Dambar nodded, and she followed him into his modest cubicle of frosted glass.

Although she was seventy-two, Mrs. Sklar looked in her fifties. A sturdy woman with dark, bushy eyebrows, she managed the lumber and creosote companies she had inherited from her father, Mr. Dambar's grandfather. For nearly twenty years they had worked side by side, aunt and nephew, gradually expanding their interests into contracting and building supplies as well as a stab or two at real estate. Mr. Dambar had started off as an assistant to Mrs.

Sklar's husband, and when that gentleman had succumbed to cirrhosis, the nephew had found himself a full partner and built his wife the house of her dreams.

"Well?" she said, hands on broad hips, her legs firmly planted as if for a huddle. "How'd it go?"

"Didn't really see anything I liked."

He had told her that he was going to Florida Parishes Olds-Buick to scout out a car for Mrs. Dambar so that they wouldn't have to rely so much on the Jeep. It wasn't that he had anything to hide. After all, it was his own money that he wanted to advance to Leo. But Mrs. Sklar, having invested a substantial amount of her own money in the project, was very touchy on the subject of The Antibes. She had a stubborn notion that eventually all the condos would be sold, oil glut or no oil glut.

"Good. Keep him hanging." She was referring to the Buick dealer, a friend of her late husband's. "Let him think you can do without. Then when he makes you an offer, you send me in and I'll talk him down another grand, I guarantee. Jack's a real marshmallow when you come right down to it and . . . What?"

"I'm sorry," the new assistant said, standing in the doorway. She was a plain-looking woman, as all the staff tended to be, with a weak chin and nice figure. "Your wife's on line two."

"He's not in," Mrs. Sklar volunteered.

"Thank you," the girl said, backing away with almost Oriental deference. Though she paid them well, Mrs. Sklar ran a tight ship and kept the three secretaries and five assistants in a constant state of anxiety. Not infrequently they would seek out Mr. Dambar for consolation, sometimes weeping in his office while Mrs. Sklar was out inspecting a shipment of plywood or pine. He felt sorry for the office workers and did everything he could to bolster their confidence. When Mrs. Sklar fired them, he would treat them to a lavish meal at Isola Bella, male and female alike. He was good, too, at sincere and expert letters of recommendation.

"Mamie, I wish you wouldn't—"

"You can call her back later, Frankie. It's setting a bad example for the others. I don't allow personal calls, you know."

Months ago Mrs. Sklar had made it clear to her nephew that he was making a big mistake by hitching himself to that girl from out of state. In an effort to get his aunt to change her mind, Mr. Dambar had arranged a dinner for the three of them at Mrs. Sklar's favorite restaurant, the China Nights. Gretchen seemed to like his aunt quite a bit and always wondered why they didn't get together more often. But Mr. Dambar hadn't the heart to tell her what Mrs. Sklar had said to him after the dinner: Gretchen was handsome perhaps, but could stand to lose a pound or two; she seemed bright perhaps, but didn't seem to know the first thing about manners. "How many times did she interrupt me?" his aunt declared. "I hate to be blunt, Frankie, but she just didn't strike me as being very ladylike."

Mr. Dambar had taken this barrage with equanimity. In a way he was proud of himself for having defied his aunt with this marriage. And he suspected that deep down, she admired him for having the gumption to stick to his guns. It showed he was a man with a mind of his own, just the type of person Mrs. Sklar respected most. To be fair, once she had gotten Gretchen out of her system with a few pointed remarks, she had taken no more potshots at the marriage. As far as she was concerned, it was almost as if Mrs. Dambar didn't exist. And this was fine with her nephew. He saw enough of his aunt at work and didn't really miss the occasional dinners they used to have together. In fact, he was relieved. Those dinners had always been something of a chore. All she ever did was wonder aloud why such a handsome, successful man like him refused to get married again.

"I'm really sorry." Francine, the new assistant, was at the door again. "She says she's just got to speak to him right away."

"Who says?" Mrs. Sklar frowned at her Rolex. "I thought I told you to tell her—"

"I'll get it, Francine. Thanks." He punched the blinking light on his green phone. "Hi, hon."

"Love, hi. I'm at the Rexall downtown. Do you want to have lunch? I drove Shaerl in to see her aunt and she's having lunch with a friend and I don't really want to eat alone. Say yes, please."

"Well, I told you—"

"I know you're busy. But we didn't get a chance to talk last night and it'd be fun, don't you think?"

Mr. Dambar glanced over at his aunt, who was unwrapping the sandwiches she had made for their lunch today. "I'd love to, but really . . ."

"You took Leo out to dinner the other night. A fancy restaurant. All I want is a little bowl of soup. Please, sir, a tiny bowl?"

"Now, Gretch, I told you why I took Leo." His voice had become hard. "That was business."

"Oh, all right. Can't blame me for trying, can you?"

"What? No, no, fine. Look, I really got to go."

"All right, it's OK. I love you."

"Me, too."

Mrs. Sklar was talking even before he had hung up. "Here, try this out on your piano, boy. This is my Salmon Surprise, the kind you like so much."

Actually, it was good, her salmon. She really knew how to make canned salmon taste good. And she had told him that salmon lowered your cholesterol; that should make Gretchen happy.

CHAPTER FOUR

Any good?"

Mrs. Dambar looked up from the book she was reading, *Raising the Family Cow,* and smiled back at her husband. As he leaned closer for a glimpse of the title, his smile faded.

"Do you think it's wise, Gretchen, buying a book like that?"

The twenty-four chicks Mrs. Dambar had purchased last week had dwindled to three as a result of an unpleasant disease and six or so getting lost on a walk she had taken them on to strengthen their leg muscles. The three were now kept in a box in the laundry room next to a portable electric heater, an arrangement that upset Mrs. Howard, who feared the disease might be communicable.

"I didn't buy it. I ran over it."

He regarded her calmly. "You ran over it."

"It was in the middle of the street. Can you imagine someone throwing a perfectly good book in the middle of the street? I think it says a lot about this country's literacy, and well, I wasn't going to let it just lie there. So I pulled over and went back and picked it up."

"Oh. Well, I got to get going."

"Bye." She grabbed his hand and gave it a firm squeeze.

When he got home from the office that evening he noticed the book lying on a patch of yellowed grass near the sundial. Picking the swollen volume up—it had been left out in the rain, apparently—he examined it for tread marks before dropping it into a plastic garbage can. There were none.

"Hon, did it ever occur to you how strange it is?" he said after dinner as they walked hand in hand past the neighbors' homes. She was a little apprehensive about meeting up with the large dog who often lay in the middle of the road near the highway, but he had reassured her, telling her he had known the dog for years. Wouldn't harm a flea.

"How strange what is?"

The houses were all on one side of the road, mostly older homes of wood and brick, stolid, unpretentious. Across the road was a patchwork of untended fields returning to the wild. Dirt bike trails crisscrossed the grassy furrows on which saplings sprouted, skinny irregular trees with broken limbs, scarred trunks. "What I mean is," he went on, "doesn't it seem odd that we never discuss finances?"

A gentle wind stirred his iron gray hair, bringing with it a faint scent of wildflowers. "How can you say that, Frank? That's all we ever seem to talk about."

"You don't mean that, do you?"

"You're always telling me how bad business is, how we got to tighten our belts."

"No, hon, I'm talking about you." He yoked an arm over her shoulder. "Let's face it, Gretchen, I don't have a clue what's going on with you—financially. Doesn't that seem strange to you?"

She stiffened so that his casual embrace became awkward as they walked along the road. "I already told you, I'm not even sure myself." Her voice had become high, girlish. "You know my uncle handles everything for me. All I do is sign on the dotted line."

"Good. But what are we talking about here—a few thousand, millions, two bucks? Give me a ballpark figure."

"Oh, Frank, really."

Mrs. Dambar's reluctance to disclose her net worth was perhaps understandable. Jeremy, the art historian, had actually come to resent her for loaning him the eleven thousand he needed to complete his book. From time to time she would get a check from him for a couple hundred or so—just a check, no note, no word of thanks. And of course, there was that terrible mess with Henry that still wasn't straightened out. When her Uncle Laeton, who managed her portfolio, refused to let her help Henry out with a rather large no-interest loan, Henry had sued and taken him to court. Since Gretchen genuinely liked her uncle, who had just gone through considerable trouble to divest all her South African holdings, she had found herself in an awkward position, almost as if she were testifying for both sides. No matter what she said in court, she couldn't help sounding two-faced, even to herself. She simply had had no idea how complicated her affairs were, tied up with grandparents' trusts, disputed wills, tax shelters, and joint ventures that involved various uncles' and great aunts' approvals. Even though she had a million or two in her name, she could hardly lay her hands on a cent. And, of course, in this day and age a couple million meant nothing. Indeed, most of her friends considered her a virtual pauper. Gretchen figured she had just about enough to get her through old age without having to be a burden to anyone—and that was about it.

"Look, let's put it this way: I've got a few dollars of my own, OK? But it's nothing really."

"So how much is nothing?"

A branch nippled with delicate, fleshy buds blocked their path, and they were obliged to detour into the street. "Look, I'll be glad to show you everything. But Uncle Laeton will have to mail it down. It's all up in Cos Cob now, my statements and things."

"Why can't you just tell me?"

"Because I don't know for sure. It's all so complicated and I just hate thinking about it. Besides, I have a bone to pick with you." She felt justified in bringing up a matter that she had been afraid to discuss before, out of respect for his feelings. "You know, when we went to the play the other night, Leo really got out of hand. He was making fun of Henry, telling the Keelys about the time he went swimming in the pond. It's so easy to misinterpret Henry, especially if you're not very sophisticated. I just wish you hadn't told someone like Leo what happened. He doesn't see things in the same light you and I do. Henry is too subtle for someone like Leo."

59

"What are you talking about?"

"When Henry dove into the catfish pond, did you have to tell Leo about it?"

"It was so subtle I couldn't resist."

"Oh, Frank."

"Take it easy, Gretch. Don't be so sensitive."

"But it shows such poor judgment on your part. And you're supposed to be such a great businessman. I just can't understand how you can spend so much time talking to that man. There's no reason he's got to know everything that happens."

"I tell him one thing and you say . . . Where you going?"

Mrs. Dambar had turned around, anxious to put as much distance as possible between herself and the dog that had ambled out from beneath a neighbor's van, the same large dog that often hogged the middle of the road. The February air was soft, cool, and inviting, and yes, she would have liked to continue the stroll—but there was something about that beast she didn't trust, as if suddenly, with no warning, he might go off his head.

"Come on, Grank. It's getting dark. Let's go inside."

"Grank?"

"Oh, come on, hurry, before that animal . . ."

"Moll, hi, it's me."

"Huh?" a groggy voice came over the wire.

"It's Gretch the Wretch. Don't you recognize . . . Just thought I'd see how things were going. Is everything all right? Henry was down here, you know. I hope you'll keep an eye on him for me."

"It's three. Three A.M."

"Oh, God, is it really? I thought . . . And the time change. We're on Central."

"Gretch, you sound funny. What's going on?"

"Nothing. I'm fine. Great. Listen, I'm going to hang up. You go back to sleep. I'm really sorry, didn't realize the time change and all. Call me, Moll."

Mrs. Dambar hung up. She was in the study, nursing a glass of wine or two which she hoped would put her to sleep. Suddenly it occurred to her that the French doors might be open. They felt open. Leaving the wine half finished, she turned off the type-writer—she had written half a page at one-thirty on the Philip-pines—and went into the library.

The doors were securely bolted, it turned out. And the trailer in the pasture was dark.

Once a year Mrs. Howard shampooed the royal blue carpet, every square inch of it from the sitting room to the utility closet. Mrs. Dambar had offered to help with the machine they had rented from the A&P. She was afraid Mrs. Howard might overexert herself, especially since Shaerl wasn't around to give a hand. Shaerl and her Aunt Myrtice had driven to St. Jude State College, where they were attending a three-hour seminar on how to program your mind to think like a millionaire. "Couldn't that have waited?" Mrs. Dambar wondered aloud as she untwisted a knot from the orange cord. "Of all the days for Shaerl to go out."

"Careful mit my little man," the old woman scolded. Mrs. Dambar had accidentally bumped into a rosewood end table and upset a statuette of an epicene cavalier. "I buy this myself," she said, admiring the porcelain as she set it upright again, "for the anniversary. Mrs. Dambar she cries when she sees it. It's so beautiful, my little man. Oh, and the house, too. You should have seen the house then. Not a spot. Mrs. Dambar she was so clean and so quiet. You hardly know she was here."

"Was she good-looking?"

"Good-looking? Ha, she was a dream, a walking dream. Never have you seen a lady with such fine skin. And her hair so blonde."

"They should have put up a traffic light, don't you think? At the corner."

"Oh, I hate them," the old woman said, her eyes bright with emotion. "I hate the city elders, yes I do! And I hate Mr. Ford for inventing the cars that kill everyone in sight. Yes, right this second, a young person, a wife, is being murdered."

"Well, but we need them, don't we?"

"Oh, yes, of course, my darling. Like we need the bombs and the bazookas." As Mrs. Howard leaned closer Gretchen caught a strong whiff of the old woman's Chanel No. 22. "I tell you a secret, my dear. He has never recovered. You ask me, he is not the same from that day. He don't laugh the way he used to laugh. See, he used to be a card, a real card. Everyone loved Mr. Frank. His jokes—my goodness, you never hear such jokes. And tell me, darling, when was the last time you ever hear him tell a joke?"

"Mrs. Howard, this was fifteen years ago. I'm sure by now—"

"Eh, fifteen years—nothing. Nothing at all." She switched on the shampooer. "The heart has its own . . ."

"What?"

The machine seemed louder, on a higher setting. Mrs. Dambar could not stand such decibels. Hesitating, for she did want to help the old woman, she finally decided to go check on Rob, Lily, and Dwight. After all, Mrs. Howard didn't seem to really need her that much. And she would just as soon not listen to any more nonsense from her about how happy Frank used to be.

"Come here, you baddies," she crooned, leaning over the cardboard box next to the washer and dryer. "Don't you dare run away from Mommie, Lily, you hear?" It was always a comfort to kiss and pet the surviving chicks whenever she felt unhappy. She was so glad she had saved them from the hands of that man at the Feed and Seed. And despite the fact that Leo had thrown her book away—she was sure he had, for she couldn't find it anywhere—she was not giving up on the idea of purchasing a cow. It wasn't the milk and butter that interested her, but the animal itself. To enter into a relationship with something so basic and primeval was bound to do her good. She really wished to care for something large and mute like that.

"Wha's wrong, Wob? Yes, sir, I means you, little pooh—Oh!"

Like the prow of the Vineyard ferry one foggy morning when she was out sailing alone, Mr. Dambar loomed up on her without warning, the rumble of the washing machine covering his entrance into the laundry room. "Oh, hi, Frank, I didn't . . . What's the matter? I thought you were at work."

Mr. Dambar considered his wife a moment, then plucked a bit of fuzz from her chin, relieved that it was not some sort of growth, as he had first thought. "Mamie had to go to Baton Rouge to see about some siding," he explained. "I gave everyone the afternoon off. She's been driving them pretty hard, you know."

The washing machine shuddered as it segued into its spin cycle. "Well, I'm glad you're here. You can help me move my scull." She put down the large, whitish chick she was fondling. "Somebody scraped it when they put the Jeep in the garage. There's a horrible scratch that just makes me ill."

Mr. Dambar accompanied her through the doorway to the garage. While she shined a flashlight he gazed attentively at a hairline scratch that at certain angles didn't seem to be there. "Mm," he commented thoughtfully.

A row of shovels and hoes was rearranged, and then the sawhorses on which the scull rested were pushed farther toward the wall. While they did this, Mrs. Dambar mentioned that Shaerl had taken off for a lecture leaving Mrs. Howard all alone to do the shampooing, which she was sure was going to give the poor woman a stroke. "You realize, of course, how ridiculous wall-to-wall carpeting is anyway," she added. "No one has wall-to-wall carpeting. It's just not done."

"I don't know about that. Jane had damn good taste."

Jane was the first Mrs. Dambar. Noting well the warning look in his eyes, the second Mrs. Dambar beat a hasty retreat: "What I mean is how much trouble it is. Look at all the work it is to keep clean. I just don't know what people would think if Mrs. Howard keeled over while shampooing that thing. Imagine. They would think we were exploiting—Careful with those oars, darling."

Her eye lingered fondly on the sleek varnished curves of her pride and joy. "Such a shame, poor scull."

"Huh?"

"There's no place to row; I can't get out. I used to row two, three times a week. Sometimes I'd have to chop through ice. There's nothing like it, Frank. It's utterly exhausting; you feel wiped out. You can barely walk when you're through. You're a dishrag, you know . . ."

"By the way, have you asked your uncle about those . . . Oh, there you are, Leo. I was looking for you."

Mrs. Dambar kept her back to the handyman while she ran her fingers over the scull's subtle lines. Instinctively, Mr. Dambar maneuvered Leo out of the garage.

"You let her call you a dishrag?" Leo asked as they strolled around the side of the house.

"What? Oh, no, she didn't mean that. Anyway, I got something for you." Reaching inside the vest pocket of his plaid sports jacket, he pulled out a beaded cowboy wallet that his younger son had given him ten years ago. Inside was the check neither Mamie Sklar nor his lawyer knew anything about, a personal check for $4,213. This was the amount due Leo once The Antibes went into receivership—but who knew how long this process would take? As far as Mr. Dambar was concerned, Leo should have his own share as soon as possible so he could start earning interest on it.

"Oh, man, no, I can't take this," Leo said after Mr. Dambar had handed it over. "This is your own money, Mr. D."

"It's all right. When you get your check from The Antibes, you can pay me back."

"No, it's not right. You shouldn't have to lay out bread like this."

Mr. Dambar laid a hand on Leo's shoulder. "You'd be doing me a favor. I feel just awful about the whole thing."

"Yeah, but it's not your fault. How could you know that everything was going to get screwed up by oil." Deftly folding the check with one hand, he slipped it into the pocket of his lumberjack shirt. "I'm not going to cash it."

"Please, Leo, put it in the bank."

"No, man, I'd rather play by the rules. This is like some sort of shortcut. I took a risk—so I ought to pay just like everyone else. No one should be exempt."

Mr. Dambar took an uncertain step or two around a kumquat bush Leo had planted the week before. As always, when talking with the handyman, he had the funny feeling that Leo was referring to something other than the matter at hand. That's how it was with intellectuals, he figured. They could talk about two or three things all at the same time. Very economical, but somewhat trying for the average brain.

"I think I'll go give Mrs. Howard a hand," Mr. Dambar said after trailing Leo to the garden. "It's her rug day, you know."

"Did you talk to her?"

"Mrs. Howard?" he said innocently, even though he knew full well whom Leo meant.

Leo bent over and yanked up a flowery weed. Though the garden looked bedraggled, the stalks gray and bent, fat leaves dry, begrimed, the yield had been good on the fall crop, the last of which was coming in. In a farther section, near the pasture, Leo had already begun spring planting.

Mr. Dambar cleared his throat. "Listen, I've thought about it, what you were saying the other day, and, well, I don't think I have a right to ask Gretchen that. It's too personal."

"Personal? What's more personal than a wife?" Squatting now, he kneaded the earth with his powerful hands.

"To tell the truth, I don't think much of psychiatrists."

"But Mr. D, I already told you, she's not a shrink. She's just a therapist. See, there's no messing around with childhood traumas and all that crap. This is real businesslike—behavioral stuff. She defines the problem, right? Then she comes up with suggestions on how Gretchen can improve herself. No hocus-pocus. In and out, four or five sessions at the most." Leo rose and presented his employer with a small turnip. "There. Now let's be real about this. There's hardly anything wrong with Gretchen, right? Just a few kinks that got to get worked out. It's more like preventive therapy, nipping a little neurosis in the bud."

"But I'm not sure she's done anything really neurotic."

"What about those chickens?"

"Well . . ."

"First it's chickens, next it's cows. You want dead cows all over the lawn?"

"I suppose she's just trying to be rural."

"Is it rural to wear one earring to a play and then make a big fuss that it was gone—implying that someone in the car had taken it? Mrs. Keely was really bummed out, I can tell you. She made us all feel like common thieves. And what about those cracks she's been making about Germs."

"You mean what Shaerl told you?"

"Yeah, how Gretchen can't stand the Krauts."

In themselves none of these faults troubled Mr. Dambar very

65

much. But seen in conjunction with Gretchen's neurotic refusal to talk about her own finances, they did cause him some concern. The overall picture was worrisome.

"And then, Mr. D, there's the way she goes on about that cousin of hers. Now, like you weren't there, but I got to tell you, man, it was embarrassing. You should have seen the look Mrs. Keely was giving me in the car. Mrs. Keely knows this dude, remember. She's met him. And to hear Gretchen praising him to the skies like that, saying how Henry knows all these movie stars, dates them, how brilliant he is . . ."

Mr. Dambar sniffed the turnip, turning it over in his hands. "Well, relatives, you know how that is."

"Right, everyone's got relatives they got to stick up for. Course when you start shelling out dough, that's another thing."

"So he had a few free meals, Leo. Don't you think you're being a little hard on the guy?"

"Yeah, maybe so." He hugged himself as if he were suddenly chilled. But it was mild out, the sun temperate and genial. "What's fifty thousand bucks after all."

Being a veteran of financial shocks, Mr. Dambar did not betray his unease. After all, Leo could be misinformed. If he wasn't, then how foolish Mr. Dambar would appear if he had to question his handyman about his own wife's finances. "Now who told you that?" he asked nonetheless, unable to resist.

Leo shaded his eyes, looking beyond the garden to his trailer. "Henry."

"Henry?"

He nodded.

"But that can't be . . . I mean . . ." Mr. Dambar found himself gazing into the distance for a moment or two, a hand shading his eyes. At the far end of the pasture a Pepsi Lite billboard proclaimed its glad tidings of fewer calories, more fun. "Oh well, Mrs. Howard, I better see about her. And Leo, I hope you'll be around when the Roto-Rooter man comes. I want you to show him where to go in, the drain right under the kitchen window."

*

"Whenever I'm in bed, it's very hard for me to relax," Mrs. Dambar was saying to her husband that evening as they lay side by side in the matching striped pajamas she had picked out for them. "I'm almost afraid that someone is going to burst in on us."

She did not mean this literally, for she always locked the bedroom door before retiring. But it did express the feeling she had that there was nothing sacred in Mr. Dambar's house, no place that was off-limits. And she hoped to get him to agree with her. It might help him feel less responsible for this recent little bout of impotence.

"Who can function when they're thinking any minute someone could barge right in?" she went on. He took her hand and removed it from his belly, which she had been gently massaging.

"I've always felt that way, Frank, ever since I moved in."

"What are you talking about? A thief?"

She frowned. "No, darling. I'm talking about the help. Everytime I sit down to write, Shaerl comes in to ask me a question or Mrs. Howard wants to dust. And Leo, you know the way he wanders around the house." Propping herself up on one elbow, she looked right at him, her eyes moist with love. "Sweetie, I know men don't like to talk about dysfunction, but really, it's nothing. Almost every man I've been with, at some time or other . . . It happens all the time. Maybe if we could go someplace together, just you and I, get away from all this. I feel so cramped, like there's no air in this house. It's almost as if we were being watched all the time, every move we make."

Mr. Dambar was glad Leo could not hear this. It would only confirm his ideas about her need for therapy. And he wished she wouldn't talk so foolishly about dysfunction. Just because he didn't feel like making love to her tonight . . .

"Why don't you and I go away this weekend?" Mrs. Dambar gaily persisted. "We could fly to New York and see some of my friends. I'm sure you'd have fun. And I want you to get to know Molly. She's so nutty, I love her. People used to call us Mutt and Jeff because I'm so much taller. We went everywhere together. I even taught her how to row. Come on, what do you say?"

Mr. Dambar muttered something about a meeting and turned over on his side. Before getting into bed, he had asked her once again, calmly and rationally, about her finances, with particular emphasis on Henry. And again she had equivocated and even giggled, behavior that he found very disappointing. Yet he did not want to confront her with the information Leo had given him that day. He still wanted to give her the chance to be direct and honest with him. And furthermore, if the information was not accurate, how would that make him look in her eyes? As if he were taking Leo's word over her own. No, that would never do.

Reaching out tentatively, Mrs. Dambar began to stroke his smooth, lovely back. If she were still seeing Dr. Stone, the kindly psychiatrist on East Ninety-sixth Street who had approved of this marriage, she would have reported to him how fiercely loving and protective Frank's impotence made her feel. It was a shame, she thought, that there was no Dr. Stone in Tula Springs for Frank to see. Of course, even if there were, she knew well enough that he would never let her make an appointment for him. He would regard it as a sign of weakness, so unmanly.

"Hon?"

"Yes, Frank?"

"I've really got to try and get some sleep."

"I'm sorry." She stopped stroking the skin, which was as tanned and supple as one of Henry's starlets'.

The idea that a trip might be good for them stayed with Mrs. Dambar even after several rebuffs. She asked her husband if instead of New York he might want to visit one of his sons. When he said no, she was somewhat relieved. She had met both sons and did not care for either. They were arrogant creatures who did not seem at all sympathetic toward the poor and dispossessed. In fact, Robert, the younger, had actually taken a *vacation* in the Philippines once. It was simply beyond belief.

"What about if I asked Molly to come down for a visit?"

"I don't understand."

"It might be a nice change, don't you think?"

"Gretchen, I've got all the change I can stand for now," he said rather obscurely. They were driving in the Riviera to a dinner party that he didn't really want to go to. For the past few days he had seemed listless, a little down. Seeing new faces might cheer him up, she thought, which was why she had urged him to accept the invitation.

"Well, actually, you're right, Frank." She touched her earrings to make sure they were both there. "It's a little too soon for Molly to visit. I'd like to get the house fixed up first."

"Fixed up?"

"I'm just not that wild about Louis Quinze. Unless it's done absolutely right, you wind up feeling you're in Vegas." Jane, she suddenly remembered. He was going to think she was criticizing Jane. "Of course, I've always thought there was something quite wonderful about Vegas," she hastily backtracked. "It's so exuberant, so totally naked in its aspirations. I feel sorry for people like Molly who just can't appreciate it."

The Fuzzbuster atop the white leather dash gave off a warning beep. Mr. Dambar, who had been steering with one finger, a puzzled look on his face, became alert and drove the rest of the way craning his neck from side to side, prepared to slow down.

"Yes, it was almost like a mystical experience. I don't know how else to describe it," Mr. Dambar heard his wife say a little later in the evening when they were seated for dinner. In bits and snatches he had gathered that she was talking to Mr. Herbert, who was seated across from her, about how she had met him, Mr. Dambar, in the souvenir shop on Bourbon Street. Somehow he couldn't help feeling that this was neither the time nor place for such a story. And of all people to tell it to, his lawyer.

Mrs. Jonsen, the hostess, went on with her critique of a Finnish tenor's performance at the New Orleans Opera while Mr. Dambar nodded appreciatively, straining to hear more of what his wife was saying two guests apart. Gretchen was wearing the dress that wouldn't zip all the way up, the Peruvian shawl hiding the result. He had asked her why she must wear this of all outfits, and she had explained that there was soy sauce on her other good dress. Plainly, that shawl simply wouldn't do. It looked like something a barefoot coed would have worn at Woodstock.

"Has anything like that ever happened to you?" Mrs. Dambar wound up her Bourbon Street narrative.

"I'm afraid not," Mr. Herbert said, avoiding the direct gaze leveled at him from across the table.

For no good reason Mrs. Dambar giggled. Something about Mr. Herbert tickled her, his precise, fussy mannerisms, his reserve. She had chatted with him before dinner and learned that he handled some of her husband's legal and financial affairs. Now at the table she found herself opening up to him, saying things that she really hadn't intended. She was like this with very reserved people. They seemed, in their vacuumlike way, to draw her out.

"I'm so excited to be in the South," she went on after taking a bite of white asparagus. "Of course, it doesn't seem as Faulknerian as I had hoped. People don't seem really weighed down by the Civil War and all that. But I must admit there are some characters. Did Frank ever tell you about our handyman? He lives out back in a trailer and talks like wow, like cool, man, what a gas. I mean it's a scream. He makes me feel like I'm in some sort of time warp."

"Leo, you mean," Mr. Herbert said quietly.

"Right on." She took a gulp of her white burgundy. "What really gets me, though, is that he's all screwed up, politically. He actually contributed to Reagan's campaign, can you believe?"

"So did I."

"Yes, but my dear Mr. Herbert, you don't have sideburns and listen to Pink Floyd."

The lawyer's thin nose gave a distinct twitch. "Your husband seems to think a lot of Leo. He was just in my office not long ago."

"Oh?"

"Gretchen," Mr. Dambar put in somewhat loudly, two guests away, "why don't you tell Mr. Herbert something about your book? She's an expert on the Philippines."

"Oh, Frank," she protested, secretly pleased. It was so nice of him to give her a chance to shine, she thought as she launched into a few facts and figures on the plight of that wonderful, abused archipelago. Many of her remarks were addressed diagonally to her host, Dr. Jonsen, who seemed a particularly egregious specimen of white, heterosexual male sexism and racism. The minute she had been introduced to him, she had taken an active dislike. His hand was soft and clammy, his domed forehead bulging with what seemed an overdeveloped neocortex—that cool, rational part of the brain that could call a massacre of innocents a "preventive troop deployment." How quickly she had turned away from him during cocktails.

"And then when I had tea with Mrs. Marcos," Mrs. Dambar went on, "I couldn't help being struck by how vulgar her jewelry was. It was like something you'd see at a Wayne Newton show."

"Wayne Newton?" Dr. Jonsen asked with a polite smile.

"He's a stand-up comic in Vegas."

"I'm afraid I've never been there."

"Well, of course, I haven't myself, either. But anyway . . ."

"Didn't you and Leo go there a couple years ago, Frank?" the lady to Mrs. Dambar's left said.

"I believe so, Eleanor."

"Anyway, I said to Mrs. Marcos, I was going to ask her about that new cultural center. So, fine, she would have a pretty place to take that marvelous man, George Hamilton. But what about the cardboard shacks the people have to live in?" Mrs. Dambar was on automatic pilot; fervor was lacking in her voice. She was too depressed by what she had just heard: Leo and her husband in Vegas. Could he possibly have done such a thing, brought his handyman to Vegas?

Hearing the familiar litany of shame, Mr. Dambar's mind began to wander and soon he was worrying about his urine. Four months ago Mr. Dambar had been referred to a urologist because of traces of blood in his urine. Dr. Jonsen, the urologist, had seen no cause for alarm, but continued to monitor Mr. Dambar every month. In the meantime they had met socially on one or two occasions at Mr. Herbert's, which had led to the invitation for this evening. Mr. Dambar had been reluctant to accept; being around Dr. Jonsen made him worry about a trace of pink in the toilet water. But Gretchen had seemed so eager to go, for some reason. Well, if it made her happy, he was willing to endure the mental discomfort, the distinct chill of mortality that the doctor's presence evoked. What had Dr. Jonsen meant when he had told him not to worry?

Why couldn't he just come right out and say, "No, this is not a sign of cancer"?

"We'll have dessert in the studio," Mrs. Jonsen announced when they had finished the veal Milanese. Earlier, when the cold cherry soup had been served, the lady to Mrs. Dambar's left, a widow on the board of the local hospital, had informed her that the doctor's hobby was painting. He had built a studio in his backyard, where he worked every morning from five-thirty to eight, six days a week.

As they trailed the other guests through the living room, with its spartan yet elegant arrangement of teak chairs and tables, all custom-made from Chinese originals, Mrs. Dambar took her husband's hand. "Having a good time?" she asked softly, giving the hand a squeeze.

"Don't you think you overdid the Philippines?"

"What? But you asked me to."

"I didn't mean for you to give a lecture."

"That's unkind, Frank. I wasn't lecturing."

"I know, but . . ."

"You hurt my feelings."

"I'm sorry, dear, but . . . Oh, for heaven's sake, don't be so sensitive," he said, wiping a tear from her rouged cheek.

At the back door, Mrs. Jonsen called out cheerily, "Coming?" and the Dambars hurried out.

Prepared to murmur some vacuous compliments about the paintings, Mrs. Dambar was somewhat taken aback when Mrs. Jonsen had adjusted the display lights in the studio to reveal what seemed like scores of landscapes, one more interesting than the next. Although she was certain that they could not really be good—surely Dr. Jonsen would be known if they were—Mrs. Dambar couldn't help being moved by the real feeling for nature that was expressed in such a fresh, naive manner. The sheer volume alone was impressive to her. In wooden vertical shelving were what must be hundreds of canvases, unframed, and upon the built-in counters lay notebooks thick with pen and ink sketches. These were humble landscapes, slanted views, glimpses from the corner of the eye. She recognized the halfhearted woods of adolescent pines, scrub oaks, the idle fields strewn haphazardly with sumac and dandelions, jarring bits of plastic or metal, a tire submerged in ditch water complete with minnow. The studio itself was so orderly—not a brush out of place, and drawer after drawer filled with everything an artist could want. The cumulative effect was extremely depressing. Mrs. Dambar, abashed in the face of such energy, such creativity, was ready to go home.

"We haven't had dessert yet," Mr. Dambar whispered back to her when she told him she would like to leave. He, too, was depressed by the paintings. They were some of the dullest landscapes he had ever set eye on, drab as dishrags, with no sense of design or balance. But just because it looked as if the good doctor had the talent of an eight-year-old, one couldn't simply run away like Gretchen wished to. It would be so rude.

"I'm really impressed, George," Mr. Dambar said as the doctor handed him a thin slice of Key lime pie. "Didn't know you were a Van Gogh underneath it all."

"Well, Frank, still got my ear," he said, beaming with pleasure.

One afternoon not long after the dinner party Mr. Dambar happened to comment on Dr. Jonsen's landscapes as they were strolling through the mall. Walking past a display of arts and crafts from the local school for special children, he made a disparaging remark about the doctor's comparative ability. If only Frank had liked Jonsen's landscapes, then Mrs. Dambar would have had more room for doubt concerning her own initial judgment. But now she was sure the paintings must be good.

"Gretch, hon," Mr. Dambar said a few moments afterward, when they were seated at a tray-sized table provided for the mall's Chick Fil-A customers, "did you give Henry fifty thousand dollars?"

Mrs. Dambar readjusted herself on the molded seat that cut cruelly into her derriere. "Oh, before I forget, would you please remind me to look for a staple remover?"

"Gretchen." He took a bite of his fried sandwich.

"What?"

"Henry."

A gaggle of barely pubescent girls shuffled by on the brickwork linoleum, their knee-length sweatshirts emblazoned with arcane ads for German nightclubs, French sodas, and what seemed to be a luncheon meat, pink and gelatinous. "Have you been going through my desk, Frank?" she asked, keeping her eyes on the girls, who appeared to have an irresistible need to clutch and shove one another.

"Can't you give me a straight answer, dear? I think I'm entitled to know." He regretted having to ask her point-blank, but Lord knows he had given her enough opportunity in the past few days to volunteer the information herself.

Mrs. Dambar sucked stubbornly on her soda. Ordering a Diet Coke had given her some satisfaction, a way of protesting the horrid billboard in the pasture.

"Gretchen, I didn't look in your desk."

"It's a family matter, Frank. I don't think it has anything to do with you one way or the other." Perversely, an urge arose to press her mouth against his, to smother him with all her love. But first things first: "If you didn't look through my things, just how did you find out?"

"Then it's true; you did give him fifty thousand."

"No, I didn't say . . ." Unwrapping her sandwich, she added, "Is that Shaerl?" thinking she saw the girl by an unenclosed jewelry store. It was Mrs. Howard's birthday, and they had driven in with Shaerl to buy gifts. Mrs. Dambar had found a porcelain shepherdess at a Hallmark card shop on sale for six dollars. Mr. Dambar had enrolled the housekeeper in a Cheese of the Month club and had also picked up something that was supposed to be from Leo.

"No, afraid not," Mrs. Dambar replied to herself once she had put on her tortoiseshell glasses, which she used for distance. "I wish she'd hurry." Leaning over the slick table, she pressed an arm against her husband's side as she reached for his shopping bag.

"What are you doing?"

"I want to see what you got. Oh, Frank!" she exclaimed as she examined the sales slip. "A hundred and eighty-two dollars?"

He took the bag away from her. "It's not me. It's from Leo. He wanted to get Mrs. Howard a water purifier."

"But dear, it's so much for a birthday present. How can he afford such nonsense?" She smoothed the wool tartan skirt that she had bought fifteen years ago and still used for everyday wear. "I don't understand what's going on, all this fuss about gifts. You take him to Las Vegas two years ago—now he gives Mrs. Howard a two-hundred-dollar gadget."

"Gretchen, I told you before, he took *me* to Vegas."

"Well, that's even worse," she said, vaguely remembering their conversation after the doctor's dinner party. "How could you allow him to do something like that?"

"It didn't cost him a cent. He won a contest at Winn-Dixie, guessing the weight of a pumpkin. And as for the purifier, we're all going to use it. It'll be good for the house, so I'll pay for some of it, of course." He moved his long legs out of the way of an oncoming Chick Fil-A waitress. "Now about Henry . . ."

"OK, I did try to lend him fifty thousand a long time ago, before I ever set eyes on you. It's all tied up in the courts still and it's not something I like to think about. It's been a horrible experience, and everyone in the family is furious with me. So, please, Frank, if you don't mind"—she reached out and took his hand—"let's don't talk about it."

Mollified, he gave her hand a tender squeeze. "Fine, love. I understand."

She blinked back a tear. "So how did you know?"

"Let me see." He freed his hand to finish his chicken. "I think someone might have mentioned it to me. Leo, maybe—I don't know."

"Well, it looks like I'm going to have to get a lock for my desk."

Tapping his fraternity ring against the table, he smiled that devilish smile that made him so irresistible. "Come on, now. Henry himself told Leo."

"No, I don't believe he would tell Leo such a thing."

"How else would Leo know?"

"As I said, Frank, I'm going to have to get a lock."

"Don't be ridiculous."

Mrs. Dambar put down her sandwich, only half eaten. "Here

75

she comes now," she commented as Shaerl trudged toward them, hugging an ungainly gift-wrapped box. "I suppose she bought Mrs. Howard a garbage disposal."

"You're grouchy today, huh?"

"No, Frank," she said wearily, "it's just the air, all that recycled stuff, ugh. Come on, sweetie, let's get out of here before I scream."

CHAPTER FIVE

Sometimes it's good to have an outside, objective person to discuss things with. It's so hard to find anyone who is truly disinterested, who doesn't color everything with his own needs and illusions. Do you agree?" Mrs. Dambar looked appealingly at her new therapist, who did not reply.

Dr. Lahey was a sober woman in her midthirties with thick ankles and a sallow, pockmarked face that somehow managed to be not unattractive. A maternal quality radiated from her tired, stocky body and made Mrs. Dambar feel immediately at ease. Already she had convinced herself that Dr. Lahey was better than Dr. Stone in New York, far more intuitive and less eager to please. Last week, though, when she had reported enthusiastically on her first session to her husband, he had sounded so doubtful. Why did she want to start up with therapy again? he had asked with a troubled look. Of course, she wasn't able to tell him the real reason yet, which was to eventually lure him into joint sessions with her, to work out the kinks in the marriage. Although he had resumed making love to her, she sensed a difference, a lack of spontaneity, some sort of reserve on his part. He seemed to be drifting away emotionally, and she wanted to know why. It was a terrible thing, to love someone as much as she did, to stake everything on this love, and then to feel it wasn't as secure as she had imagined.

Resuming her outpouring without the benefit of a supportive

comment, Mrs. Dambar said, "I believe I told you last week a little about the house. It seems to me everything would be all right between me and Frank if it weren't for Mrs. Howard and Shaerl. And Leo."

"The dog?"

"The handyman."

"Go on."

"As far as I can see, and I may be wrong, but trying to be objective"—Mrs. Dambar eased back a notch or two on the La-Z-Boy so that she was almost horizontal—"Frank has developed what I would term an unhealthy relationship with these people. He's a very successful businessman, you know; one of those quote pillars of the community. I've gone out of my way to be agreeable to his friends. OK, I'll admit that at first I wasn't too thrilled with them and wanted to spend time alone, getting to know him. But recently I've noticed how much time he spends talking to the help, and so I've made an effort to socialize him, get him out with his friends and business associates. It hasn't been easy, either. I really believe he'd be perfectly happy just sitting around with Leo or Mrs. Howard. I just can't figure it out. The other day was Mrs. Howard's birthday, and I can't begin to tell you all the Sturm und Drang that went into it. Shaerl put up balloons all over the house like it was a six-year-old's party, and then she cried at dinner because she was so happy— or so she said. I think it was the helium. Then Leo—"

"Take your time. Breathe."

With a tissue from her purse Mrs. Dambar dabbed at her eyes and gave her nose a hearty blow. "Leo gives Mrs. Howard a three-hundred-dollar water purifier. Now, Dr. Lahey, can you tell me that sounds right? A handyman who makes a few dollars an hour? I would really like to have your objective opinion on this, if you don't mind."

From behind the door seeped the unctuous strings of piped-in music for the mall's parterre, where the doctor shared a suite of offices with a dentist and an electrologist. The therapist leaned over and tied a loose lace of her mannish Oxfords. "Money seems to trouble you," Dr. Lahey said with a crimson face.

78

"Misuse of money. But actually, I never give money a second thought."

"I see."

"It's just too vulgar the way some people are obsessed with money. Those dreadful yuppies that have infested New York, well, at one time there were standards. Anyone quote in trade was, you know. As a matter of fact, I think we can date the decline of Western Civilization quite precisely. It was when the Church caved in regarding usury, when they decided it was no longer a sin to make money off of money."

"Are you a Catholic?"

"Good God, no. As far as I'm concerned the Church—and Christianity as a whole—lost all moral authority when it did its convenient little volte-face regarding usury." Noticing Dr. Lahey's eyes stray to the square digital clock on the wall, Mrs. Dambar sped up, anxious to get her point across. "The only hope for mankind, as far as I'm concerned, is to turn to the East. I suppose you could call me a Mahayana Buddhist, if you need a label." Jeremy had been more deeply into Buddhism than she. He was the one who had awakened her to the moral outrage of compounded interest, dead money regenerating itself as if it were alive. "What is this country based on—the economy, I mean? It's the dead come to life, the dead not being properly dead but parodying life and creativity and productivity." As she was saying this, she realized she was trying to compress too much meaning into a few seconds and that this might make her sound a little weird. Yet Dr. Lahey's face betrayed nothing, not the slightest sign of disapproval.

"Anyway, I suppose it's time to go." Mrs. Dambar yanked the bar on the side of the chair and returned to an upright position. "By the way, do you think I could start coming twice a week? I really feel I'm not getting enough time the way it is."

A somewhat protracted discussion followed during which the two women tried to decide on the best day of the week for a second visit. The electrologist, with whom Dr. Lahey exchanged services, was going away on a two-week singles' cruise, and Mrs. Dambar might be able to use her time slot while she was away. Mrs. Dambar commented that she could not imagine anything worse than being cooped up with a boatload of desperate women, all vying for the attention of divorced aluminum-siding salesmen. "It's my idea of hell."

"Indeed," the doctor replied blandly.

Mrs. Dambar stood there a moment uncertainly. She hated to leave. There was something so comforting about this woman's presence. "By any chance, would you like to come to dinner?"

"Pardon?"

"One evening, if you're free, it might be nice if we could get together."

"My husband usually has dinner waiting, Mrs. Dambar. Besides, do you think it's a good idea to socialize with one's patients?"

"Actually, I do, I think it's a great idea. But, of course, no one seems to agree with me." Here she had finally met a woman who could be a real friend, someone to take Molly's place, and yet she was only allowed to see her twice a week. "I'm just joking."

"Joking?"

"I realize you're not supposed to socialize."

Dr. Lahey went to the door, where Mrs. Dambar, unused to the new high heels Shaerl had persuaded her to buy, bid an awkward farewell, tottering a bit as she exited backward. "Next Tuesday, right, Dr. Lahey?"

"Correct."

The Roto-Rooter man was making frequent entrances and exits through the French doors while Mr. Dambar, in his army coveralls, dug in the garden. For the past week or so Roto-Rooter had been dealing with long-neglected drainage problems, the most recent being the pipes to the emerald green tub. "Why does he keep going in and out like that?" Mr. Dambar asked Leo, who was passing by. It was Leo who had decided to get all the pipes tended to; he and the Roto-Rooter man had gone to high school together.

"What?" Leo said, continuing on his way to the trailer.

Mr. Dambar shrugged and, still on his hands and knees, went back to digging. He had already put in a few hours at the office that morning, but found himself unable to return directly after lunch.

Mrs. Howard's creamed chipped beef was not agreeing with him. There was a burning sensation in his chest—heartburn, no doubt— that he refused to let frighten him. What with the pink in the toilet water this morning, he could easily become a regular hypochondriac.

On his way back from the trailer, pipe wrench in hand, Leo was hailed from the garden again. Shading his eyes, Mr. Dambar looked up at the handyman, whose head only partially blocked the sun. "By any chance, Leo, you never talked to her, did you?"

"Who?"

"Mrs. Dambar."

Mr. Dambar was still puzzled by his wife's decision to see a therapist so soon after Leo had made the same suggestion himself. And Mr. Dambar had never mentioned the idea to her.

"You talking about the shrink, Mr. D?"

Nodding, he avoided Leo's coal-black eyes. The handyman had a tendency to stare when he talked, without a single blink. It was a curious, disconcerting mannerism that one normally associated with Byzantine emperors.

"Never said a word to her."

"But Leo, how did she . . . Why?" He was looking at him now, raising himself up a little to hear better, but still on his knees.

"Love is not powerless," Mr. Dambar heard, or thought he heard. For when he said, "What?" Leo replied, "Said 'better lug this on over,' " and walked off toward the French doors with the heavy wrench.

Later in the afternoon, when his stomach had settled, Mr. Dambar sat in his frosted glass cubicle at work, mulling over the incident in the garden. It had all happened so fast, and yet what he had seen in Leo's eyes—a disturbing combination of pain, anger, and compassion—had made such an impression on him that Mr. Dambar felt very small. But after all, the whole thing must have been a coincidence, he reasoned. Gretchen had been in therapy in New York, hadn't she? Well then, it was only natural that she would want to continue working out her personal problems in Tula Springs. Leo had had nothing to do with it.

"You all right?" Francine asked as she breezed in with the mail.

"Huh? Fine, sure."

"You don't look so hot." The assistant placed a cool hand on his forehead. "No fever."

He smiled wanly. The chinless face that he had once thought so homely now seemed warm and comforting, suggesting a certain inner strength. Francine was turning out to be worth her weight in gold. A myriad of details that he hadn't the heart for these days, from The Antibes' problems to a sharp decline in profits in every one of his businesses, she attended to cheerfully and responsibly. And with her as emissary, he was able to spend as little time as possible consulting with Mrs. Sklar about the condos. His aunt was still determined to breathe new life into The Antibes, which as far as he was concerned, were dead and buried. Leo had his money—only Francine was in on this—and the case was closed. All this fancy wheeling and dealing Mrs. Sklar was engaging in was just not his style. Like his good looks, success was something he had never had to think about before; it just came naturally. Through his father, his uncles, cousins, second cousins, he had met all the right people. Anyone who was too pushy, too eager to succeed—well, that was definitely a loser. But now it seemed there was a new set of rules. "You got to get out there and *make* them take notice," Mrs. Sklar would urge. And all he could think was no, this was not right. This was not how things were supposed to be.

Mrs. Sklar having left a few moments ago to check on her cat, who was recovering from surgery, Francine was in less of a hurry than usual. "Mrs. Anderson called twice," she said as she watered the cyclamen she had brought in last week to cheer up his cubicle. "I told her you were in Baton Rouge."

"Oh, good."

"I can't believe that she still calls you. She ought to know better."

At lunch one day in the office Mr. Dambar had opened up to the new assistant, telling her about Mrs. Anderson and how he had married Gretchen instead. Francine was a wonderful listener, tactful and soothing, and made him feel much less guilty about Mrs. Anderson.

"Anyone can see how deeply you love Mrs. Dambar," Francine

said, perching on the edge of his desk. Her mousy brown hair was pinned up modestly like a schoolmarm's, and her shapely legs were covered by patterned white hose. "It's ridiculous that Mrs. Anderson would waste her time trying to call."

"Well, I'm sure she just wants to be friends or something."

"I'd watch it when old flames try to be friends."

Mr. Dambar found himself grinning. Francine tittered in a quaint, old-fashioned way that broadened his smile. "What is this, high school?" he said jovially. " 'Old flames,' I like that."

"I had gone to New Orleans, I forget why," he was saying awhile later in reply to a question from the assistant, who was still perched on the desk. "Oh, yes, something to do with those condos."

"The Antibes?"

He nodded. "This fellow was interested in taking them off our hands, a Brazilian. So I had lunch with him in the Quarter. He was representing a syndicate that was buying up a lot of real estate all over the country. Spoke perfect English, didn't seem at all Latin. I was surprised, you know, expecting something a little more colorful. He had even worked for Chase Manhattan in New York a few years back. In any case, I liked him OK. The only trouble was, he was a jerk. What he proposed to me wasn't really illegal. It just wasn't ethical. I could have saved my ass on those damn condos if I had just shaken hands with him. Instead I told him I'd think about it, which was the same as saying no to him. Either you fish or cut bait. He walked out, polite as could be, and I went to a bar and had myself a couple martinis, then found myself in some sort of souvenir shop."

"She was there?"

"I didn't see her, no, not at first. I had leaned over to pick up some change, and the next thing I know I felt this terrible pain in my ankle. She had accidentally kicked me or tripped over me or something. It really hurt, too."

While she listened Francine deftly slit open the mail and, with a glance at each piece, sorted it into three piles. "In other words, you were drunk. Come on, Frank, admit it."

"Potted, my dear child," he said, mimicking the tone Gretchen sometimes lapsed into with Leo or Mrs. Howard. "I had gone in to get Shaerl a birthday card, a present, something funny—only it wasn't her birthday." It was odd how the pain in his ankle came back to him. He had forgotten about it, mainly because he was used to hearing Mrs. Dambar's version of their first meeting. He had never told it himself before now. "And if I'm not mistaken, the little woman had taken a nip or two herself."

"Does she drink a lot?"

"Oh no. Just a glass or two in the middle of the night."

Francine's pale eyebrows went up.

"She has trouble sleeping," he explained. "So she gets up and has a belt. Sometimes she reads, works on the Philippines." For some reason the last word he had spoken brought to mind the pink in the toilet. He would have to report this to Dr. Jonsen when he saw him next week for a check-up.

"You know she's writing a book on the Philippines," he went on, trying to cover his anxiety. "She really has a lot of concern for the poor."

"Nice," Francine said, skimming a letter. With a red pen she made checks in the margin as if she were grading it.

"That's right. She gave her cousin fifty thousand dollars."

"He's a Filipino?"

A dim smile softened his face. "Lord knows what that guy is. She's actually only trying to loan him the money."

"You mean he doesn't want it?"

"Not exactly. See, an uncle of hers handles all her assets, and believe me, it's a mess. They just don't seem like they know what they're doing. I tell you, Francine, I'm afraid Gretchen's being screwed. She's just not responsible when it comes to finances."

Still marking the letter, she said after a short silence, "Seems to me you should be helping her more."

"Like?"

"Advising her, helping her with her investments. Why should an old uncle be in charge? After all, you're the husband."

The nicked swivel chair creaked as he angled it away from the desk. Stretching out full length, he yawned, his hands locked behind his head. "I don't know. My grandmother was the one who got my grandfather going. He didn't have a cent. I think he was a tanner or something in Düsseldorf. It was her money that got them over here and set him up in business."

"Why would they come to Louisiana?"

"They didn't. Milwaukee was where they went. And after a few years, they got into the lumber business. The Illinois Central put out a lot of propaganda about how wonderful Louisiana was, you know. So . . . Anyway, when my mother told me it was my grandmother who really got things going, I felt funny. I never did like the idea."

"That's pretty sexist."

"You think?"

"Very."

"I was always a little afraid of my grandmother. Whenever I saw her, I had to wear my Buster Brown suit, and my hair, it had to have a real even part. If it wasn't right, she'd snap at my mother. Funny, she never did learn English very well. Half the time I didn't know what she was saying, my grandmother, I mean. 'So cute, Herr Frankie, I vant to eat you,' " he added in a thick German accent. " 'Eat you all up.' "

The assistant tittered at her boss's antics.

"You think it's sexist of me?" he asked, looking over his shoulder at her. "I mean about my grandmother's money and all."

"Très sexist. Now I better go and finish those letters you got to sign. And please don't put gum wrappers in my poor plant," she said, plucking a bit of foil from the cyclamen on her way out.

"That wasn't me," he called out. "It was the Dragon Lady."

Try as she might, she could not dispel the image of her husband on his knees before the handyman. Mrs. Dambar had just returned from her therapist's when she happened to peer out the bathroom window and saw them conversing in that odd, though presumably explainable, pose. Then she had gotten into a discussion with the Roto-Rooter man about the emerald tub, and the next thing she knew, Mr. Dambar had left—back to the office, according to Mrs. Howard.

"Just between you and me, what do you really think of him?" Mrs. Dambar asked, sitting down with the housekeeper, who had invited her into the kitchen for a cup of coffee. Of late Mrs. Howard had let down her defenses around the new Mrs. Dambar and had even seemed fond of her at times. What friction remained between them in the matter of household affairs was minor. Mrs. Howard insisted on the Chanel No. 22 in the bedroom, Gretchen on the chicks in the laundry room. As far as cholesterol went, Gretchen was wise enough to know when she was beaten. After making a few polite suggestions, which were met with a look of horror and outrage, Gretchen resigned herself to a hardening of the arteries.

"Frankie? Very fabulous."

"I'm sorry. I meant Leo."

"Mr. Leo? Also fabulous." Mrs. Howard urged a slice of coffee cake upon her guest, a thick, frosted slab lopsided with nuts.

"Did you ever think he might be just a little . . ." Mrs. Dambar tapped her head and then took a bite of cake.

"Oh my, yes, he's brilliant, a brilliant boy. Frankie told me he could be a professor. Now when I was a girl, I work for a professor in Düsseldorf. Oh my, it is so marvelous to be mit the brains around." Her blue eyes twinkling, the old woman clapped a dimpled hand to her breast. "He knew everything, Herr Doktor Voss. Anything you ask him, he has the answer just like dat. Oh, darling, it was fabulous." Leaning closer, she confided, "Of course, it is not always easy to live mit the smart people. They are never no good with the everyday life, no? I never let my Herr Doktor Voss near my kitchen. It would be like a bomb, everything ruined! All mixed up!" Her eyes wide with amazement, she looked about her spotless kitchen as if Doktor Voss had paid a recent visit.

"Doktor Voss sounds very smart. But Leo, now, it's curious how he—No, no, please," she interjected, holding up her hand. Mrs. Howard had another too generous slice of Jane Parker cake on her serving knife.

"Come, eat!" the old woman urged, the slice hovering before the hand. "You mustn't eat only one. You must sweeten yourself up, darling. The gentlemen they like this. Oh, yes, I know. They want to gobble you right up."

"Well, just a bite."

A dusting of powder gave the old woman's plump white face a glazed look reminiscent of the porcelain glow of the lads and lasses who adorned her walls. As they talked, Mrs. Dambar's eyes would stray to these dimestore oils, the paint as thick and cloying as the sentiment—lambs, hayricks, bluebirds, and furtive prepubescent kisses between figurinelike innocents.

". . . and he bring home with him the dirtiest books from the library," Mrs. Howard was saying one slice later, "black with filth. I tell Herr Doktor Voss I am not to allow such germs in the house. So each book I take and put in the oven—yes?—and I bake out all the germs. Dat is me. I am the enemy of all germs. We can't stand each other."

A tune going through her mind, Mrs. Dambar nodded abstractly for a moment or two until she recalled herself to the matter at hand. "But Leo isn't a professor. I just don't understand why everyone thinks he's so smart. Am I missing something, or what?"

The old woman's face clouded over as she swallowed a dainty bite. "Sweetheart, no, you must not talk like dat." She reached across the butcher-block table and took her hand. "Many times it happens to me, I'm thinking to myself, Oh, Mrs. Howard, how you need the Cascade automatic dishwashing powder. What will become of my poor dishes without the Cascade! Then you know what happens?" She gave Mrs. Dambar's hand a powerful squeeze. "In walks Mr. Leo and he hands to me a box of Cascade. There now. You see!"

"Well, it doesn't take a genius to know when you're low on detergent."

"No, no. I don't have to say nothing to Mr. Leo. He just knows. Underneath it all, he knows, he sees. There are no secrets from Mr. Leo. You must never think bad things around him, darling."

The bright Mondrianish pattern on the old woman's rayon dress seemed to blare out painfully loud as Mrs. Dambar experienced a rush of sugar and caffeine. Freeing herself from the viselike grip of the creamy soft hands, she said, "Really, Mrs. Howard, I never thought you were so superstitious. I've always admired you for having such good common sense."

Ignoring the comment, the housekeeper got to her feet. "Now I say to myself, 'What's the matter, Mrs. Howard? Don't you know the roast is waiting? It's time to pop it in the oven.'"

"Besides," Mrs. Dambar added on her way out, "I don't know what you mean by bad things. I don't think bad things."

"Good, I'm so glad, darling."

In the study Mrs. Dambar tried to concentrate on 1899 in the Philippines, but she found herself distracted by the stylized birds decorating a potpourri jar. And behind the jar on the paneled wall, veneered C-scrolls, S-scrolls, palmettes, and foliage seemed to crave attention. The house was simply too busy; there was no rest for an attentive eye. Even the candelabrum vase had a scene painted on it, a dainty lady upon a swing. Was it any wonder she had made so little progress on her book?

"Oh, yes, that's it," she said aloud, and after reaching for a scrap of paper on the desk, wrote: "Now I lay me down to sleep, fourteen angels round me keep." It was the tune that had been going through her head earlier while Mrs. Howard talked. She would like to mention this to Dr. Lahey on Tuesday. Humperdinck. "Gretel gingerbread house gobble me up." Musing, she added some filigrees around the edges and inadvertently a jagged line, when Shaerl suddenly appeared.

"Rob's loose," the girl said, peering over Mrs. Dambar's shoulder. In her arms were a stack of freshly laundered towels; a hot comb dangled from her neck. "He got out of his box."

"Why didn't you put him back in?" She covered the pink sheet with a hand.

"What's that?"

"Nothing."

"It looks like my stationery."

Mrs. Dambar slid it under her manuscript. "Let's go get him, Shaerl," she said, rising from the gilded chair that made her back ache.

"Mrs. Howard told me not to touch him. They're diseased, you know. They got all sorts of germs."

Already on her way down the hall, she called back, "You guys are such babies. Afraid of a little chicken, good God."

*

After dinner that evening, Mr. and Mrs. Dambar took their accustomed walk—this time, however, in the pasture behind the house rather than along the road where they might encounter the large dog Mrs. Dambar disliked. "You see how it looks like sunset now?" he was saying. In the distance the grass that was so rough and tawny about their feet seemed transformed by the dusk to an almost lime-green shag carpet. A shaft of light dissolved the belly of the bay mare grazing near the Pepsi Lite billboard, giving the beast a weightless, impressionistic aura. But with each step the couple took, the lime became less green and the mare more substantial.

"What do you mean, 'looks like'? It is."

"No, Gretch, it's not. What you don't realize is that the sun has already set—it's gone. But the sky is acting like a huge crystal, the curve of the earth, reflecting the light back up." He paused, a little lost. Leo had explained this to him yesterday, but he wasn't sure he was now telling it right. "That's not the sun over there. It's just a reflection of the sun, which is really invisible."

"Are you sure? I never heard anything like that before."

They walked on in silence for a while, Mrs. Dambar's arm resting lightly on her husband's.

"Hon, I notice you don't seem to have any protective things."

"What?"

"Jellies and all." He avoided looking at her, seeming more interested in the mare by the sign. "Never can be too safe, you know. I mean you're really not too old to have something happen."

"Gee, thanks." Somewhat resentfully, she added, "Besides, would it be so terrible?"

"No, not at all. Except that at your age, a baby, well, it has a chance of being . . . Whatever . . ."

Tears welled up in her eyes as she pulled a little away from him. Though he was certainly one of the kindest men she had ever met, he could sometimes be so cruel, in an offhand way. "I told you before, Frank. You don't have to be concerned about that."

But she had never told him why he needn't worry. This was a secret between her and Dr. Stone. And Molly—and yes, the two psychiatrists before Stone, Dr. Firshein and Dr. Harvis. In the

Philippines Gretchen had fallen in love with a student activist, a handsome Filipino who several times had risked his life opposing the Marcos regime. When she had found herself pregnant, she had agonized for weeks about what to do, finally ending up with an abortion in Manila, a botched job that had damaged her tubes and left her unable to conceive. It was something she had been afraid to tell Frank because he seemed so conservative. As for Dr. Lahey, it wasn't necessary to tell her since she, Gretchen, had already settled the issue once and for all with Dr. Stone. Yes, it had been a tragic mistake, one that she would have to live with for the rest of her life. But there was no use dwelling on it. One had to go on living, somehow.

"You making any progress with Dr. Lahey?" he asked, side-stepping a crawdad mound.

"I like her, if that's what you mean."

He waited for her to catch up and put an arm around her shoulder. "But is she helping you out with your problem?"

"What problem?"

"Let's face it, hon. You're pretty neurotic about money. I thought she was helping you come to terms with it."

"Me? Angel, money is the very last thing we discuss."

Her freckled face glowed with peasant health, an effect that was reinforced by her extreme and undoubtedly honest naïveté. Unable to resist such a combination, he planted a wet kiss on her forehead. "You're a doll."

Pleased, but puzzled, she rested her head on his shoulder. "We spend most of our time discussing Leo, if you really want to know."

"Huh?"

"I think you would find it very interesting, what she says about him. Dr. Lahey thinks the whole relationship between you and him is a little cockeyed, to say the least." Of course, Dr. Lahey hadn't come right out and said anything about Leo yet. Mrs. Dambar had been too busy explaining the situation to give the therapist a chance. Yet she knew very well what Dr. Lahey must think. And the sooner Mr. Dambar was aware of this outside, objective opinion, the better.

"What do you mean, cockeyed?"

"Sweetie, surely you must realize by now that you have a very peculiar relationship with him. In fact, it verges on the neurotic. I just don't know what you would have done if I hadn't come along. But don't you worry. I'm going to think of something."

Catching wind of them, the bay mare, which belonged to their neighbor's daughter, a homely child who idolized Shaerl, moved off at a nervous trot. Mr. Dambar had stopped walking for a moment, but now, his eyes still on the mare, headed on. "Gretchen, I really don't know what you're talking about. You ask me, you should spend less time discussing Leo, who really is of no concern to you at all, and more on your own problems. In fact, I've been giving this matter a good deal of thought recently. Maybe it's time you considered making a few changes in your life."

"What sort of changes?"

"Well, to begin with, I never have liked the idea of that uncle of yours handling all your finances. Seems to me we should keep it in the family."

A vague panic made her smile brightly. "But Frank, it is."

"No, this is your family—me."

"Oh, but love, you can't possibly mean . . ."

"I mean that if I, we, were in charge, well then, you would know just exactly what was happening to your investments."

"But I don't want to know. I don't care about money."

"That's wrong, Gretchen. That's seriously wrong to think like that. You're not a child anymore."

"I know, but even if I tried to get it away, it would be such a mess. Legally, I don't know if it's possible. It's a great big block of family money. Mine isn't really separate."

"Nonsense. You've got your rights. Besides, I'd like to know how much this uncle is making for you. To tell the truth, I have a feeling he's not doing such a great job. Boy, if Mrs. Sklar invested for you, or me, why you'd be raking it in hand over fist, I guarantee." The look on her face, the acute distress, made him back off. "Now, hon, it's only a suggestion. I'm not going to make you do anything you don't feel is a hundred percent right. I just want to look out for your best interests, you see. It's an insult to my honor," he added in a playful drawl, like an old colonel in white, "to have my wife being taken advantage of. No sir, I will not tolerate such dastardly conduct."

"Oh, Frank, stop." She giggled nervously to cover her dismay. So hollow, she felt, as if he had reached inside and scooped out all that was precious. Why did he have to even think about her money? Why did it have to be an issue at all?

When they reached the billboard by the highway, they turned back, walking along the perimeter of the field, which led past Leo's trailer. Mr. Dambar tried to cheer her up with silly songs he had made up for his college fraternity years ago. Some of the words he had forgotten, but he was amazed at how much he did remember. Though she smiled, Mrs. Dambar did not seem to really appreciate the humor, which made him a little sad. He wished she were not so serious all the time. Life, after all, could be fun.

". . . and so Dingo Dilly with his Wingo Whacker," he sang as they made a detour around a puddle bright with algae.

"I can't believe it."

Mr. Dambar smiled and continued to sing.

"Look, Frank. What is he doing?" she said as the face in the window disappeared. She had happened to glance back at the trailer and seen him there in the picture window.

"What? Who?"

She didn't bother to answer. It was Henry, plain as day. Apprehension and joy left a metallic taste in her mouth as she hurried through the damp, feathery grass. What could he mean by suddenly appearing like this again, without the slightest warning? Oh, well, that was Henry for you. But what was he doing in that man's trailer? Probably just biding his time, waiting for her to get back to the house so that he could fling open the door and give her a big surprise. But she was getting a little too old for such childish pranks. They could give one a painful jolt.

Puzzled by the sudden retreat, Mr. Dambar watched her plough through the grass, her arms swinging in a somewhat rigid, military fashion. When the door to the trailer opened, after she had stood for some time knocking, it reflected an almost lurid orange from the sky. With a tentative step or two he started in that direction, but something in him prevented him from going all the way. He could not bear the thought of a scene between her and Leo. Why couldn't she leave the poor kid alone?

"What were you doing?" he asked when she came out awhile later to rejoin him. "Why did you go back there?"

She held the barbed wire apart as he gingerly crawled through the fence to their backyard. "I just . . ."

"Watch, my leg."

She pulled them wider, the two strands, her mind still troubled by what had just occurred. Leo had let her search the trailer, but there had been no sign of Henry. And the look that man had given her, the patronizing grin when she had flung open the closet and discovered how tiny it was, barely enough space for a broom, much less a man. Well, how was she supposed to know? In any case, she would rather not have to explain all this to Frank. It simply wouldn't do. And yet she was so sure she had seen Henry. Certainly she could tell the difference between Leo's fuzzy, bewhiskered mug and Henry's cleancut, chiseled features.

It was her turn now, Mr. Dambar holding the strands apart. "I just wanted to ask him about Rob."

"Who's Rob?"

"One of the chickens. His left eye seems a little milky."

"Oh."

"Maybe Leo could build a pen." She was on the other side now. "Your shoes are soaking. And look at mine—a mess. We better not wear them in the house. Mrs. Howard will kill us."

Chapter Six

She called again," Leo said as Mr. Dambar strolled into the library, where the handyman was making a list of various odds and ends that Mr. Dambar was to pick up on his way home from work.

"You mean . . ."

Leo nodded.

Unable to get past Francine at work, Mrs. Anderson had been calling the house recently. Fortunately, Leo had answered every time. Once she wanted to say that she was sorry about the lawnmower, although what she had to be sorry about, Mr. Dambar wasn't sure. Another time Leo had reported that she wanted to ask him to join the choir at the Episcopal church. They needed baritones desperately.

"What is it this time?"

Leo yawned and stretched as the lion-pawed chair tilted back on its fragile legs. "Rock of ages cleft . . ."

"For me," Mr. Dambar took up, singing in a clear light baritone, "DA de da da . . . You know, it might be fun."

"Not a good idea, man." Leo was shaking his head.

"Singing would be good for me."

"Yeah, but this dame—I don't know."

"Mrs. Anderson is as proper as they come, believe me, Leo."

"That's just the kind you got to watch out for."

"Hey," Mr. Dambar said, suddenly realizing why Leo seemed

a little different today. "I like it. Very snazzy." He fingered the striped shirt Leo had on, something a lot less somber than what he usually wore.

The handyman went red in the face, a touching, somewhat boyish embarrassment that made Mr. Dambar keep his fingers on the shirt longer than was necessary. "You really like it?"

"Where did you get it? It's real nice."

"Shaerl, she made me buy it. She says she's worried about me being a bachelor all my life. She made me promise I'd start going out when she moves."

Turning to his video library, Mr. Dambar made a noncommittal little grunt. It was the first time the handyman had ever brought up the subject of his personal life, something his boss was content to leave a mystery. The fact that the boy didn't have a girlfriend, much less a wife, Mr. Dambar attributed to psychological problems stemming from Leo's father's suicide. It had happened back in 1970, just when Leo was beginning to feel his oats as a man, and had probably stunted him in some Freudian way. A Rams quarterback had once mentioned Freud on "The Tonight Show," which had made Mr. Dambar think about subscribing to *Psychology Today*. But for one reason or another he never got around to it. Instead he adopted a policy of live and let live. If Leo was maybe just a little bit queer—this had occurred to his boss more than once—well, Mr. Dambar was cosmopolitan enough to accept even that, as long as the boy kept it a secret. In fact, it made him feel even sorrier for him. Poor guys like that, they deserved a little extra kindness in life, the same as Catholic priests did. Though he was not a Catholic, Mr. Dambar had had his men reshingle the roof on the rectory of Our Lady of the Flowers at cost.

The double doors of the library were veneered with seals emblematic of the Seasons, Poetry, Commerce, and Gardening, all of which looked pretty much alike to Mr. Dambar, who had never quite recovered from the artisan's bill. Jane had been talked into them by a young mason whose work was popular in the Catholic cemeteries of Ascension and Assumption parishes. A good friend of Leo's, the mason had grown tired of headstones and was trying to branch out in another medium when he was imprisoned for failure to pay child support to a vindictive ex-wife. It was through the mason that Leo had developed an interest in prison correspondence.

"What are you doing?" Mr. Dambar asked as Leo pulled these doors to and with a discreet click secured the lock.

"There's something been bothering me," Leo said, returning to the boulle desk. "You mind if we talk?"

Idly fiddling with the pinball machine, Mr. Dambar felt dimly apprehensive. "Sure thing. Get it off your chest, Leo. It will do you good." A bell clanged as a mermaid's eyes lit up.

"OK, so it was like the other day after supper and I was in the trailer straightening up for Shaerl. Her hip was hurting pretty bad, and anyway the next thing I know there's this banging on the door and before I can open it Gretchen busts in. She didn't even wait for me to put something on. I was in my underwear and Miss Storm Trooper demands to know where he is. 'He?' I say, and she says I know damn well who she's talking about. It turns out it was Henry she was looking for."

"What?"

"Her cousin. She thought I was hiding her cousin or something. Can you believe? Then she starts searching, going back into Shaerl's room, the closets." He smiled wanly, his hands making a helpless gesture. "I wasn't going to tell you at first. I didn't want to freak you out. But then when I thought about it . . ."

Mr. Dambar tried to think of something casual to say, but all he could manage was a shrug while he jerked the flippers about without a ball.

"Look," Leo went on, his dark eyes wide with pity and concern, "I'm sure there must be some sort of explanation. Something logical," he added without much conviction.

"Well, of course there is."

"She talked to you about it?"

"No, but I'm sure it was just some sort of mix-up. Now, where's that shopping list? I better get going."

With a gentle stir the desk drawer opened, and after rummaging about in it Leo produced a pink sheet of stationery, which he handed over.

"I hadn't planned on stopping at the Feed and Seed," Mr.

Dambar said, glancing down at the sheet. "What's this? This isn't . . . Leo, you gave me the wrong whatever. This looks like a letter of Shaerl's."

"Correct."

"Well, we shouldn't be reading her stuff. Here."

The handyman did not take it back. "Turn it over."

"What?"

"Go ahead."

With a frown on his handsome face Mr. Dambar examined the other side, and as he did, the lines about his eyes became more distinct.

"I don't understand," he said finally, laying the pink sheet on the desk. "What is this?"

"It's her handwriting, isn't it?" Leo picked it up and began to read, " 'Now I lay me down to . . .' something."

"Sleep."

" 'Gretel gingerbread house gobble me up' and then this mark, whatever that means." Leo scratched the dull receding hair above his prominent forehead while he mused aloud. "It could have something to do with the letter here—that might explain it. Oh, it's cool," he interjected, seeing his boss was about to protest, "Shaerl gave it to me herself. She said she had found it in the study, on Gretchen's desk. Maybe Gretchen had picked it up when she was searching the trailer. The only thing is, there's not much going on in this letter."

"What's it say?"

"Not much. It's to her mother. 'Aunt Myrtice and I didn't enjoy the seminar too much because there was nothing really that practical about how to invest and it was more like all this psychic willpower stuff.' Then there's something later on: 'I've already bought Frank a going-away present with the money you sent, so please can you advance me some more. It's Giorgio men's cologne that I know he likes, only Gretchen won't let him wear any, so I think instead I'll hold onto it and give it to Uncle Blue at Christmas.' "

"Well, I don't see what that has to do with what's on the back."

Leo put the letter back in the drawer. "Neither do I. Except that she could be getting a little jealous."

"Of Shaerl? Don't be ridiculous. I know for a fact Gretchen really likes the girl. Besides, there's nothing to be jealous of."

"Yeah, you're right. I was just trying to think of some way to explain that crazy stuff on the back of the letter."

"It's nothing, just some . . ." He faltered, avoiding the handyman's steady gaze. "Just some notes for her book probably."

"Frank, what do you know about this woman?"

The "Frank" gave Mr. Dambar pause. Leo had never called him that before, and he wasn't sure that he liked it. "All I need to know—I love her."

"Yes, wonderful. But aside from that."

"Look, she comes from a very fine family. They're in the social register, very distinguished."

"I don't doubt it. Just look at her cousin."

"Well, in any case, she's a brilliant woman, very caring and sensitive."

Pressing his fingers to his temples like a medium attempting to tune into the next world, Leo shut his eyes. "Frank, you and me," he said after a moment's silence, his eyes still closed, "we've never really talked before. I think it's time I told you how much I, how I feel about all you've done for me. If it weren't for you I don't think I could have made it after Dad . . ."

The tears that strayed into the boy's graying sideburns were both embarrassing and gratifying to his employer, who stood uncertainly beside the desk, hoping the speech was at an end.

"That's very nice, Leo. I—"

"What I want to say, man, is, well, I'd give my life for you. Goddamn straight, Frank, I'd die for you any day." His eyes had opened again and were bearing down on Mr. Dambar, wide and unblinking. "And I think you know that, too, Frank."

Mr. Dambar could not avoid a maidenly blush. "Well, I don't imagine that will be necessary. Leastways, I hope not," he added with a chuckle.

Leo had turned his head toward the French doors. The soft morning light made his wiry hair seem almost blond.

"Leo?"

"Huh."

"Will you do me a favor? I want you to make an effort to try to understand Gretchen—for my sake. I really believe that once you get to know her you and she will end up being great friends. She loves philosophy too, you know. I feel like my mind is always being challenged when I talk to her. Half the things she says are over my head, but still I always feel I'm somehow growing in her presence. She's a very unusual woman, one of a kind. If she seems a little odd at times, scatterbrained, it's because her mind is on more important things."

"Like what?"

"Her book, for one thing."

"Would you mind telling me how someone who spends like a year in the Philippines ends up being the world authority on the subject? It's classic, Frank: delusions of grandeur."

"She never claimed to be the world authority. And she *has* talked to Mrs. Marcos in person. Besides, she has a lot of girlfriends in publishing. They've all been encouraging her." Mr. Dambar sounded so sanguine no one could have guessed the effect Leo's doubts were having on him. They were so close to his own firmly repressed misgivings that it was almost as if the boy were reading his mind. "Now what about that shopping list? I've got to get going."

"It's in here somewhere," the handyman said, rooting about in his desk.

On the other side of the double doors Mrs. Dambar debated whether to knock and demand entrance. Seated at her desk a moment ago, she had come across a letter from one of Leo's philosophical convicts. Tucked inside this same envelope was an uncashed check made out to Leo for $4,213, signed by her husband. Envelope in hand Mrs. Dambar had sought out the handyman, intent on getting an explanation. But as she stood there, hearing the murmur of voices on the other side, it occurred to her that a private conference with her husband might make more sense. If she marched in there now with the evidence, Leo might think she had been going through his things. It would give him the upper hand.

Returning to the study, she placed the envelope under her

notes on McKinley's secretary of war, who happened to be her great-great-uncle. Then she walked down the hall to the master bedroom, where she had glimpsed Shaerl making the bed. She wanted to ask her to please not scent the sheets.

"But Mrs. Howard always checks," Shaerl protested softly when the request was made. "She comes and smells."

Taking an end of the fitted satin sheet, Mrs. Dambar began to tuck it over a corner that was awkwardly close to the carved painted headboard. She grunted as her fingers strained to make room for the sheet. "Please ask her."

"You don't like it?"

"No, never did. And I don't like satin sheets either. They're too slick. I almost slid out of bed the other night."

"We got some regular sheets." She winced as she leaned over. "You want me to go get some?"

Seeing that the girl was in pain, Mrs. Dambar had her sit down while she finished the bed herself. "What do you think of this headboard?"

Massaging her hip, Shaerl glanced over at the carved grapes and cupids. "Well, it's not exactly what I'd choose for myself."

"Can you imagine anyone who would? It's not that I'm one for interior design or anything like that. I can live with almost any-thing—or at least I thought I could. But this . . . Louis Quinze is a very dangerous period, Shaerl. It's got to be done just right or not at all. And even when it's done right there's always this creepy feeling that the dimestore is just around the corner." Somewhat exhilarated by being able to say exactly what she felt, she simulta-neously experienced a twinge of guilt. Was this being disloyal? "Of course, these are wonderful reproductions. I wonder where she got them."

"Who? You mean Jane?" An elusive rainbow, barely there, played over the girl's face as a chandelier tinkled softly. Mrs. Dam-bar had shaken out the counterpane, disturbing the crystal. "The stuff in the living room, that's from the funeral parlor."

Mrs. Dambar regarded the girl a moment, wondering if she had heard right.

"Jane's father was a funeral director, and when he died she

inherited a lot of his good pieces," Shaerl explained. "Least that's what Leo told me. She designed the house and all around them."

"You can't be serious."

"Sure, Leo helped her plan it. He'd drive all over the state looking for the right pieces, but then they had this big argument over the rug. Leo told her it was too tacky, and she got mad and tried to fire him. Frank stood up for Leo, though. But Jane got to keep the rug."

A vague anxiety made Mrs. Dambar fuss with the bed longer than was necessary. "She was very pretty, I hear. Of course, I agree a hundred percent with Leo about the rug. He and I must have similar tastes," she ventured, hoping the girl would forget about her criticism of the furniture. It was hard to tell just how close Shaerl was to her uncle, whether she could be trusted with any confidences. Though she was still cautious, Mrs. Dambar hadn't given up the hope that one day Shaerl would let down her guard and tell her what she truly thought of Leo, that he was really a little nuts. Then what a valuable ally she would have gained.

"By the way, I think they're in the library together," Mrs. Dambar said casually, as if she hadn't, just a few minutes earlier, walked outside to the French doors and seen them there. And as if she hadn't tried the handle to the double doors themselves and found them locked. "Frank and Leo, I wonder what they can be talking about."

"They talk all the time."

With the door locked? she almost said, but checked herself. It made her sound too suspicious. If there was one thing she prided herself on, it was being open and aboveboard. In fact, most of her friends back East found her too forthright. She was never one to curry favor by hiding her true opinions. Blunt and direct were the words most people applied to her.

"It would be nice if Leo had a good woman to look after him," she was saying a few moments later as she picked up a sock Mr. Dambar had left on the royal blue carpet. "Did he ever have someone he was interested in?"

Sitting stiffly in a tapestry chair, her face drawn and pale, Shaerl managed a smile. "If you only knew what I've been through,

Gretchen, trying to get him to go out on a date. All he needs to do is cut his hair and shave off those stupid sideburns. He's not bad-looking at all really. A little intense, but not bad-looking."

"Oh, no. He's got a nice build."

"You think? My mom told me he almost got married once." She fingered one of the three earrings, a miniature church key, that depended from a triply pierced ear. The other ear was bare. "There was this girl in college he went steady with. Mom said she was the intellectual type, only it didn't work out because she was too posses-sive. She used to cry and make scenes in the cafeteria and threaten to kill herself. Some sort of liquor . . ."

"What?"

"Her name, like Bourbon or Brandy. She graduated with a four point oh."

"No one since then?" she said, then added, "Must you?" as the girl drew a cigarette from the pocket of her black cotton shirt.

"I got to," she said, lighting up. "It gets my mind off my hip." She drew deeply, the cigarette quivering between her thin fingers. "I'll go outside if you like."

"It's all right. Oh, look—there goes Frank." Through the window they could see the Riviera pulling out of the drive. "I wanted to talk to him."

With a hard smile Shaerl flicked her ash into the cup of her hand. "He's late today. Well, I guess I better vacuum the canopy this morning."

"What canopy? You mean this thing over the bed? Don't bother. I'll tell Mrs. Howard you did it, OK?" Reaching into the girl's pocket, she brought out a cigarette. "You mind?"

"You smoke?"

"Used to, awhile ago."

"Oh, Gretchen, you shouldn't start up again."

"It's all right. Just one. Here, give me that ash. I'll dump it."

Back in the study Mrs. Dambar was unable to write a single sentence about the secretary of war. Her mind was too preoccupied with the check—and the furniture in the living room. There was no doubt about it now; she would never be at peace until she had convinced

Frank that it was in his best interest to redecorate. She didn't care what style, anything he liked, Danish Modern, Early American, Goodwill, anything but these scrolls and swirls and lion's paws. How could he be aware of the source of all this ornamentation and not be uneasy? And what sort of woman had he married, this Jane, who would see fit to decorate her entire house around such an inheritance?

"Oh, hi," Leo said from the hall.

She tensed, putting her hand over the notes on the secretary of war. Leaning casually against the door jamb, he went on: "I've been meaning to say, Mrs. D. Anytime you want to use the Jeep, just go ahead. There's an extra set of keys in the emergency cupboard."

"I thought you didn't like . . ." she began, but realized she should take advantage of this peaceful overture. "As a matter of fact, Leo, that would be nice. I sometimes feel sort of trapped without a car. Frank and I are going to have to do something about it."

"I know he's looking. In the meantime, feel free, Mrs. D." His hand strayed down to his crotch, as if to make sure his zipper was closed. She pretended not to notice.

"I know at first it bugged me, Mrs. D, but that's only because I needed it myself. Anyway, you know the emergency cupboard. It's where Howard keeps the first aid kit and Spam in case of nuclear war."

"I do appreciate it. And Leo, that shirt, it's really nice."

The blush on his face made her regard him a little more closely. It was true what Shaerl had said; he was not that bad-looking. His bone structure was very nice, a firm jaw, and he even had a dimple in his chin. "By the way, Leo, speaking of Mrs. Howard, I'm so concerned about her health. She works herself so hard."

He fingered his sideburns, staring noncommittally at the space just above her head.

"Last time she did this carpet—you know how she feels she has to shampoo every inch—well, I was so concerned she might keel over with a stroke. And Shaerl, all the vacuuming she has to do. I was just wondering, between you and me—what would you think if we took this thing up." She dug her toe into the royal blue carpet, making a somewhat comic face of distaste.

He shrugged.

"Please don't ever mention this to Frank, but honestly, it's just too much. When I first saw it, I thought I'd die. Can you imagine anyone installing such a thing?" Worried at first that she had gone too far, she was relieved to see his face light up with a boyish grin. In fact, it was the first time she could remember seeing an all-natural, honest-to-God smile on his face. For a moment he actually seemed human.

"Don't you worry, Mrs. D." He winked at her. "I think we'll be able to stuff this thing where it belongs. It'll just take a little psychology. He's sort of attached to it, if you know what I mean."

"Oh, Leo, do you think we could? I'd be so happy."

"You go get the keys now," he said, heading into the hall. "I won't be needing the Jeep."

As she was headed for Frank's office, where she planned to surprise him with an invitation to an expensive lunch, her treat, she had some difficulty with the Jeep's gears. At a traffic light she checked to see if maybe she was using the four-wheel drive, which could have been interfering with the regular shifting. As a result of this distraction she must have ended up heading in the wrong direction. The mini-mall where he had his office was not far, just on the outskirts of town, and yet it seemed she had been driving for a good while. Making a sharp U-turn, she headed back, feeling uneasy because now she was going toward the mall in Mississippi, which she knew for sure was the wrong direction.

Back in Tula Springs she nosed around, certain she could find her way without having to ask for help. After all, the place was so small, the population no larger than some apartment complexes in New York. Yet she soon found herself on streets she had never seen before, vaulted in by massive live oaks that lent a gloomy charm to the spare, grimly proper frame houses beneath. The transition from middle class to dirt poor was abrupt: Three blocks of unpainted shotgun shacks, some with soda or cigarette advertisements gummed to their sides, came without warning on the same street, as if a time warp had transported her from the fifties to the height of the Depression. Thinking this might prove somehow useful for her thoughts on the Philippines, she paused in the middle of the street and jotted a note to herself on the back of a handy parking ticket—"A colony is always time warped"—and then scratched it out and substituted "stove cleaning." Jeremy had once complained to her that nothing in her apartment was really completely clean and that this was a sign of mental slovenliness. Chastened, she had set to work on the stove and discovered that there were more angles and nooks and surfaces than seemed possible; in fact, it defeated her before she was halfway through. After "stove cleaning" she added, "Up close, nothing is as simple as it seems."

Going in what still seemed the wrong direction, she finally spotted the dulled primary colors of the mini-mall on the other side of a field of clover or alfalfa. Flipping on the four-wheel drive—or maybe flipping it off, she wasn't sure by now—she cut right through the field and over an asphalt hump into the parking lot. Before getting out she checked her makeup and hair in the rearview mirror. She had to admit that to herself she looked a bit garish. The blush Shaerl had bought her last week was a little much, and her rinse was not just brassy but—if she were not mistaken—slightly green. Could that be for real or just the way the light filtered through Leo's windows? For a moment she hesitated, wondering if she should go in. It would be nice to have a loving, thoughtful lunch with Frank where she could clear up all the things that were bothering her. And she knew she couldn't phone him; Francine, the assistant, would be sure to put her off. But what if her hair *was* really green? Tilting her head at an angle, it didn't look so bad actually. And surely Shaerl would have said something to her this morning. No, it must be the tinted windows.

Once inside the waterproofed knotty-pine door, slick as glass, she was surprised by how cramped the office space was. Secretaries and assistants were elbow to elbow in what seemed like half-size, beginner desks, on each of which were a word processor and a multi-buttoned phone. The voices were tense, subdued, and the faces that looked up at her entrance were either wary or sheepish.

"May I help you?"

"Oh, hi. It's so good to see you." Mrs. Dambar reached out for the older woman's hand, which proved to be elusive.

"Right, uh, could I do something for you?" Mrs. Sklar asked in a gravelly voice that was not unfriendly. Then in an aside to a spindly young man seated directly behind her, she added, "Make it seventeen and a half, babe."

"It's me. Your niece." It was not the most helpful identification, but Mrs. Dambar didn't feel like being too considerate. She let the old woman squirm a bit before supplying, "Frank's wife."

"Oh, of course, sugar. How are you? We're a mite busy this morning. I think he's in conference."

"If you don't mind," Mrs. Dambar said genially, edging past her toward one of the glass cubicles. There were no names on the doors, so she was not sure where to knock. When she turned to ask Mrs. Sklar, she saw that the woman had disappeared.

"How are you, Gretchen?" a warm voice greeted her.

"Hello," she said to the young woman who had come up beside her. Her own smile was uncertain.

"I'm Francine. We've talked on the phone." Leading the way into the last cubicle she held out a hand as if she expected Mrs. Dambar to take it, like a child. "I know Frank will be delighted to see you. Please come in."

Perhaps it was the fluorescent lights that made her husband seem a little different as he looked up from behind his metal desk, a cheap piece of furniture scratched and dented like something from a public school. "Hi," she called out with a cheery, idiotic wave that she wished she could take back. Leaning over the desk to give him a kiss, she missed the hand he held out. In a moment of confusion she switched to shaking hands, he to a kiss, and they ended up with a slight bump to nose and forehead.

"It's so good to see you," Francine prompted.

"Yes, dear, what brings you to this neck of the woods?"

"I thought I might take you to lunch. Would you like that?" She put on a big smile to match the assistant's. From speaking to her on the phone, Mrs. Dambar had imagined Francine to be much older, a gray-haired matron. But she was relieved to see how homely she was—except for that bust of hers.

"Lunch?"

"I thought it'd be a nice change to get away from the house, just the two of us."

Regarding her with a helpless grin, Mr. Dambar feared for a

moment that his wife was going to do something to embarrass him, perhaps start a scene with Francine, or worse, demand to see Henry. But then he realized how ridiculous this was. She was just trying to be friendly. "Lunch, well . . ."

"Why don't you let me cancel the Kiwanis luncheon for you?" Francine put in. "I'll tell them you've got a cold."

"Kiwanis?"

"You're supposed to introduce Mr. Heflin. He's going to talk about a health-care program, remember?"

"That's today? Well, I'm sure, Gretchen, you'll understand. I am the vice president, after all."

"Frank," the assistant protested, "go with her. You'll have fun."

From the way he was looking at her, she feared the worst about her hair. Oh, she wished she had never let Shaerl talk her into it. "That's OK," she said, anxious to leave him in peace. "We'll try it some other time, love. I really don't mind. I had some errands to do around here anyway, and I just thought I'd toodle on over."

On her way out of the cubicle, after having made some face-saving small talk with Francine, she overheard her saying to Frank in a subdued tone of voice, "She's so lovely, really striking. Oh, you're so lucky . . ."

Back outside Mrs. Dambar scanned the signs of the stores adjacent to her husband's office but saw nothing that might have the things Mrs. Howard had asked her to pick up when she had gone to get the keys from the emergency cupboard. As she turned on the ignition, she wondered why her husband would have chosen such a place for his office, a childish pseudo-cottage with a false gabled roof in the midst of a cement-block castle and what must be a large shoe that sold children's apparel. The whimsy seemed so at odds with the grim, cool interior. As she headed for the exit to the parking lot, she caught a glimpse of Mrs. Sklar standing by the window of the cottage. Plastic tulips from the window box obscured everything but her head, which seemed to float above the magenta blooms, unmoored to any body.

Reluctant to drive all the way to the mall in Mississippi, Gretchen was pleased when she came across a Wal-Mart on a strip of land that seemed strangely remote for such a large chain store. Good-sized pines shadowed the parking lot, which was virtually empty save for a few cars clustered to one side. Unsure if the store was open, she peered in and still couldn't tell, it was so dimly lit. Finding the door unlocked, she decided she might as well go in.

Although there were at least six or seven checkout counters, only one was manned, by an idle clerk jerking spasmodically to headphones. The cavernous space almost immediately sent Gretchen into a state of sensory overload. After only a few moments of cruising up and down the long aisles, looking for cashews, Newports, yellow yarn, and Super Glue, she found herself staring hard at socks or underwear to make sure they weren't nuts or cigarettes. Of course, there was no clerk to direct her to the right aisle; the few people she encountered seemed insulted to be mistaken for one. And when she did finally come upon the real thing, a genuine clerk, he informed her that he was not in that department.

"So maybe you could tell me where the nuts are?"

"Pardon? Oh, hello, Gretchen."

It was Dr. Lahey. She had been examining some Porky Pig videos when Mrs. Dambar rounded the corner. The very sight of the therapist seemed to revive her, though Dr. Lahey herself seemed to take it all in stride without seeming the least surprised or pleased—or dismayed, for that matter.

"My day off," Dr. Lahey commented as they strolled past racks of old B movies—Sidney Toler, Ida Lupino, Ronald Reagan, Helene Thimig. The polyester sweatpants the therapist was wearing, emblazoned with a famous tennis player's name, had the curious effect of making her look less athletic, more out of shape than she did in the office. Without any makeup her face seemed fresher, but less distinct, the eyebrows mere suggestions.

"I don't like shopping in the mall, so I come here," she went on, pausing to inspect a cassette head cleaner. "The only reason I got my office there is so I could get some Mississippi clients. I used to work out of our house here in Tula Springs, but it was hard drumming up business. And besides, my husband wants to use the house himself now. He used to be a stockbroker, but he quit so he could devote himself to architecture."

Usually so laconic in the office, Dr. Lahey seemed less guarded, more relaxed, and even agreed to share a cup of coffee at the store's lunch nook.

"In a way, Brenda, I'm kind of proud of myself," Mrs. Dambar was saying after they had given their orders to the waitress. Dr. Lahey had suggested they move on to a first-name basis, especially out of the office. "Dr. Stone in New York, just before I left, he was working with me on my paranoid tendencies. Of course, it's really hard to think of myself as paranoid. I'm not at all secretive, and I'm pretty good at calling a spade a spade. I guess it might have something to do with when I got mixed up with this FBI agent in college. He was questioning me about a friend of a friend, someone who was supposed to be a Weatherman, and I had this violent attraction to him, the FBI man. He was so horribly Irish, and then when we finished making love I couldn't get it out of my head that maybe it was all part of his plan—although he swore up and down it wasn't. Anyway, I'm trying to be very conscious of any paranoid feelings. The minute I spot them, they get busted."

Dr. Lahey rearranged herself in the booth so that they weren't looking directly at each other. "We're all paranoid to a degree, wouldn't you say?" Her stubby fingers picked at the unappetizing yellowish vinyl, the color of overcooked lima beans, while Gretchen lit up a cigarette she had borrowed from Shaerl.

"Sure, Brenda, but if I let myself go . . . I mean if I started thinking about it, there's so much I could worry about. Shaerl, for instance. She's a doll, right? And I can't help feeling the only reason she's playing maid is because of Frank. But I know if I ever said anything to him, it would only alienate him. And Leo, look at all the nasty things I've said about him to you. This morning even, I wanted so bad to come see you—only I made myself stay put. I wasn't going to call. I forced myself to get ahold of myself. You see what happened, I wanted to talk to Frank and I discovered he was in the library with Leo, and they had locked the doors. I think only awhile ago this would have set off all sorts of alarms. I would have been hyperventilating. But I forced myself to be rational. You know, actually, when you get right down to it, it's very self-centered to think that people are talking about you. I hate narcissistic types like that." Taking a long drag, she moved her elbows so the waitress could set down the coffee and Dr. Lahey's doughnut. "And it worked. Leo came to see me and he was so nice, offering to let me use his Jeep. I really felt sort of good about him, like there was hope for us. And I think I'm ashamed of all those things I said about him."

Dr. Lahey commended her, but Gretchen only gave her half an ear. It suddenly dawned on her: How had Leo known she had wanted to use his Jeep? Why at that particular moment had he come by, as if he could somehow tell she was dying to talk to Frank? As a matter of fact, wasn't she going to ask Shaerl to ask her uncle if she, Gretchen, could borrow the Jeep? Upset by these thoughts, Gretchen cut in on the therapist's gentle praise: "It's really childish to be so afraid, don't you think? There's this Mrs. Anderson, I used to worry about her a lot, but why? So I've heard Leo talking on the phone with her—big deal. And Francine this morning, Frank's assistant. You'd really be proud of me, the way I can see her as just a person, although she was a little too nice. What it comes down to is that I've got to trust Frank. There's no other way. I mean I've invested so much in this marriage. I really think if this didn't work out, I'd . . ."

"You've invested. Back to money."

"Brenda, please let's not get onto that again." She turned her head to exhale. "When I tell you I'm not concerned about it . . . I'd rather talk about important things. Don't you see what I'm saying? I've had a breakthrough. When I first came to you, I was blaming everything on other people, Leo, Shaerl, Mrs. Howard. I thought if only Frank would learn to wean himself from them, everything would be fine between us. But now I see it's a very immature way of thinking. When I feel like I'm not connecting with him, that we may be drifting apart a little, I can't blame it on anyone but myself. I've got to learn what it is in me that's so afraid of intimacy. I suppose it all goes back to how remote my father was, how like I said before, he thought he was a failure and drank himself to death. I think I might have to talk to you more about that, the feelings I had when I was twelve and he died. Mother had just taken me and my younger brother to see *Hänsel and Gretel* in New York, a special treat, and when we got back to the Westbury there was a mes-

110

sage . . ." Tears welled up in her eyes. She didn't care that the waitress, at a nearby table, was staring: It had been awful, hearing that news in a hotel room.

Dr. Lahey was so soothing and gentle that Gretchen would have hugged her if she could. When the check arrived, she was eager to pay for the doughnut, but Dr. Lahey was firm, insisting they go Dutch.

"Well, then you ought to let me write you a check," Gretchen said lightheartedly, dabbing at some mascara that had run. "This was really a session, I guess."

"If you like."

Somewhat taken aback, Mrs. Dambar looked up to see if she could be joking. But there was not a trace of a smile on her full, pale face. "Well, I . . ." she fumbled. "I'll have to . . . My checkbook is at home." Dismayed, she couldn't help thinking how unfriendly Dr. Lahey suddenly seemed. And yet the woman did squeeze her hand and hold it when they got to the electric doors.

"I'm so glad I ran into you," Mrs. Dambar said, trying to retrieve some of the good feelings she had had before money was mentioned.

Digging in her handbag, Dr. Lahey rambled on pleasantly about all the errands she still had to do. "It's funny how I never seem to get a thing accomplished on my day off." An unwieldy key chain was finally produced. "I ought to stay in bed all day, just give up entirely on getting anything done."

After the therapist had gone to her car, Gretchen wandered back into the store for the cashews and the cigarettes Mrs. Howard had asked her to pick up. For a moment the key chain had given her a turn. She had thought when Dr. Lahey had tugged it out that the gold-plated cursive letters spelled out BRANDI. But, of course, it had to have been BRENDA. Brenda, after all, was her name. Yet since when did A's have dots over them? She was sure she had seen a dot over that last letter.

Chapter Seven

Something about the room was different that evening, though as far as he could tell everything looked the same. On the shelf behind the window seat were the calla lilies Mrs. Howard brought in fresh every day. The Exercycle had been stowed in the walk-in closet, his robe and shaving tackle laid out on the walnut valet at the foot of the canopied bed. Perhaps it was the humidifier—but getting out of bed to check, he found that it was on. Every room in the house had at least one, supposedly to keep the furniture from cracking. Although he had little faith in their really doing any good, Jane had believed, and it was his chore every evening to make sure these lares and penates were filled and properly steaming.

Dimming the light in the adjoining bathroom, Mrs. Dambar emerged in the striped men's pajamas that she had worn when they were first married. Recently she had been experimenting with more glamorous outfits, flimsy negligees, skimpy lace nighties that embarrassed both of them. Not wanting to hurt her feelings, he hadn't said anything until the day before, when he had tried to get across to her that this was just not her. Yet even tonight she was still not the same as she used to be. He could tell that she had been worrying over her makeup and hair in the bathroom—as if it made any difference in the dark.

When they were lying side by side on the high bed, whose

springs needed oiling, he waited a moment before reaching over to let his hand sneak in between the buttons of her pajamas. It was now understood that he liked to be the one who initiated things. Whenever she had seemed too eager, it never worked as well—or sometimes not at all. Yes, this was probably sexist. But he was an old dog, not that anxious to learn any new tricks.

"Frankie," she whispered as he stroked her belly, "you do believe me about that letter of Shaerl's? I didn't take it. It just somehow got mixed up with my things."

After dinner that evening, on their walk, Mr. Dambar had brought up the letter, asking her if she thought it was a good idea to violate Shaerl's privacy that way. She had eagerly explained to him that she wasn't even aware that it was a letter, and somewhat less eagerly, what the notes on the back of the stationery were supposed to mean. "Dr. Stone used to encourage me to write down all the stray thoughts that occurred to me, the unimportant things," she had said, holding tightly to his hand. "He was a firm believer that it's the fleeting thoughts, the three- or four-second daydreams, they hold the key. Everything that you think is so important, like, you know, if your mother used to walk over you in spiked heels when you were a kid, that's never the real story. The real, uncensored story goes on out of the corner of your eye."

The bed creaked as Mr. Dambar turned on his side and nuzzled against her. When he was aroused, he couldn't seem to help thinking of her as a maid, a rustic serving girl from good peasant stock. It was a favorite fantasy of his that had been squelched for the most part during his first marriage. With her fine bones and porcelain skin Jane was too delicate. The freckles on Gretchen, the moles and ruddy complexion, everything she complained about, seemed to him so liberating. But, of course, he would never dare mention his little fantasy. "I got to admit, hon," he said, prying her legs apart with a knee, "when Leo showed me that pink sheet this morning, it did give me a turn."

Her legs stiffened, resisted. "Leo? Frank, you never told me it was him who showed you."

"Well, I . . ." Relaxing the pressure on her thighs, he began to

113

unbutton the pajama top. "Take it easy, sugar. He just thought you might have picked it up when you went through his trailer that day."

"What are you talking about?"

Her fingers pressed against his, but he continued to undo her. "Little Wretch, when you went in there searching for Henry. Remember? I wasn't going to bring this up. It's not that important really. I'm sure Leo exaggerated—so don't worry, sweetie pie. You're my sweetie pie, ain't you?"

"He told you I was looking for Henry?"

"Forget it."

"No. I want to know what he said."

"Just something about you coming into his trailer and wanting to know where Henry was. And searching through things."

"I never searched through anything. God, I'm sure he made me sound bananas."

"Honey, I think you did upset him. He's very big on privacy, you know."

They were both sitting up now, leaning against the silk bolsters. For the time being he kept his hands to himself.

"I don't know, Frank. I thought I had seen Henry in the window. It must have been the light, some trick it played with the reflection."

To be so near her husband and not touch him was difficult, especially when he had nothing on like this. Never before had she known a man with such enviable skin, small pored, with hardly a mole or a blemish, and hairless as a woman's. It seemed she never could get enough of him, the nights were too brief. Jeremy, though she had truly loved him, had stiff blond hair all over his chest and upper back. He was bony, knotty, sinewy, and she had to overcome a faint repulsion in order to make love to him. With Frank, the more she studied his body, memorizing its graceful lines with her fingertips, the more helpless she felt, almost addicted. Yet she forced herself to remain apart until these doubts of his were cleared up.

"OK, Gretch, it was the light. No big deal."

"Besides, you know I miss him terribly. I was probably just hoping a little too much that he would come and save me. I mean"—

she quickly added, noticing his frown—"not save, I didn't mean that. Just, you know, it gets kind of lonely around here. It would be nice to have someone who really understood me, a friend. I'm used to being much more sociable."

"But I thought you didn't want to be bothered? The book."

She leaned over, against her will, and traced his eyebrows with her little finger. "I know. Only it's so much harder than I thought. Sometimes, Frankie, I wish I could go to work in a glue factory or something, nine to five, have a job I didn't have to think about all the time. Come home, lift a couple brews, knowing I had to work to survive. I think I'd be happy then."

He took her finger and kissed it. "You keep your money with that uncle of yours and you might end up happy yet." Tickling her gently he made her squirm.

"Stop that—stop." Thinking this would be a good time to counter with a remark about that check of his to Leo—What sort of money manager are you, sir, forking over four thousand of your own personal funds to a handyman?—she nevertheless restrained herself. After his suspicions about Shaerl's letter, it would be too much to admit that she had found a check inside one of Leo's.

"Well, you gonna give Daddy your money?" With a silly grin, he threw a leg over her.

"Oh, Frank, really. Of all times to discuss such a thing." The intensity of her desire made her ears sing, almost as if she had a shell, a pink conch, pressed to each. "You is a bad boy, you know."

He had unbuttoned her pajama top so that his tongue could probe her nipples, large and erect. She was glad she had removed the two little hairs around the left one before coming to bed.

"Bad Frankie."

Knowing that she should probably wait, she went ahead and yanked the pajamas down below her knees. It was cruel of him to make her keep them on for so long. "Oh, Frank, my love . . ."

"Have you scrubbed hard today?"

"Huh?" She tried to kick the pajamas loose, but they were tangled in the satin sheet.

"You been on your knees scrubbing?" he whispered to her navel. He had just realized what was different about the room. It was the sheets. Shaerl had forgotten to scent them with the Chanel, Jane's favorite cologne. "You been doing those floors, girl?"

"Yes, yes," she murmured, not quite sure if she was hearing right, but determined to keep him happy and off the subject of money.

"I saw you scrubbing, babe. I got a good look at that ass today, soaking wet, huh? You be good and I get you a new mop."

"A new what? Oh, darling, please don't talk anymore. Just let me have it—hurry."

Though she had some misgivings about what she was about to do, Mrs. Dambar went ahead the next morning and summoned Leo to her study. Actually, it wasn't much of a summons. "Do you mind dropping by for a minute, Leo?" she had said into the phone after dialing the trailer from her study. "Anytime you're free. I don't want to disturb you, though, if you're busy." At this point her resolve had wavered. "In fact, don't bother now. You must have more important things to do. I'll talk to you some other time."

"I'll be there, Mrs. D."

She was on her hands and knees when he arrived a few minutes later. "Leo, I was just wondering if we could maybe pull back a bit of this carpet to see what's underneath, if you think . . ." Her voice trailed off as she turned and reviewed her brief first glimpse of him. Had he a new outfit on? Was that what made him look so different? But no, it was the sideburns. He had shaved them off—and the ponytail? No, the ponytail was still intact. "Oh, you look nice," she added briskly. "Anyway, do you think we might take a peek?"

Without the sideburns his face seemed more open, vulnerable; a sadness that she had never noticed before was now apparent. It was hard not to stare even though she knew it was discomforting to him. Muttering something she didn't catch, he sidled out the door. And in a moment he was back again with a claw hammer.

"I don't know," she said, her doubts reviving. "Frank might not like this."

"Won't hurt to take a look." Dropping to his knees he instructed her to watch the hall. "In case Howard comes by."

"You can put it back again, right, so no one can tell?"

Without answering he pried back a much larger section than she had intended. Underneath was well-preserved blond oak-block.

"Nice. No more, though, Leo. That's enough."

But he went ahead and exposed more of the flooring, stopping only at the paws of an ivory-inlaid side table. She reached for one of Shaerl's cigarettes.

"What do you say, Mrs. D, as a sort of experiment . . ."

Lighting up, she shook her head.

"Just this room. See how it looks without it." He narrowed his eyes as he surveyed the perimeter. "Then we can put it back before he gets home from the doctor."

"The doctor? I thought he was at the office."

"Had to stop by Dr. Jonsen's for a checkup first, Mrs. D. You know, the old blood."

"Oh," she said, somewhat distracted by the decision about the carpet. "What old blood? Is anything wrong?"

"The blood in the urine."

Alarmed, but ashamed to admit that Frank had never mentioned this problem to her, she sank down into the hard, cheap desk chair she had recently purchased to replace the overstuffed one that tended to induce naps. Of course, she had known that Dr. Jonsen was a urologist, but she had assumed the acquaintance was purely social.

"Don't worry, Mrs. D. It'll be fine." A jade deer toppled over as he shoved the side table out of the way.

"Careful, Leo. Let me give you a hand."

Lethargic at first, finding it difficult to even rise from the chair, she soon felt her blood pulsing as she helped him with the bookcases, a credenza, two heavy armchairs, and a floor lamp. The old exhilaration of strenuous rowing in the Harlem River was dimly recalled as she exerted herself to the utmost, groaning under the awkward weight, beet red in the face. Before long she was thinking how considerate it was of Frank not to worry her about the blood. If it were important, surely he would have said something. But she was going to give him a little spanking nonetheless—for telling Leo.

Moving the furniture was the hardest part. Taking up the carpet itself proved to be relatively easy. A hidden seam at the door

117

gave a clean break with the hall; she had feared they might have to use a razor blade or scissors. When they had finished she stood with folded arms admiring the new look. "It's so much nicer in here, don't you think? What a difference." For the first time in a long while she experienced the satisfaction of having actually done something, some real work.

"You have a key?"

"What for?"

"We better lock up in case Howard looks in. She'll raise a stink. I want to show you something now."

"I don't think there is a key."

But there was. Leo reached behind the desk and produced one, which he used after they had rolled up the carpet as neatly as possible and stashed it to one side.

"You sure Frank won't mind?" she asked, following him to the library. "Maybe we should have discussed it first."

"Don't worry. I'll fix it for you. And if he's bummed out, we'll put it back. I'll tell him it was my idea."

"Oh, no. If anybody should get the blame, it's me." He held open the French doors on the other side of the room. "Where are we going? I hate surprises."

"Come on, Mrs. D."

Hunched over slightly he walked a few steps ahead, skirting the garden where grimy turnip leaves drooped, lustrous with dew. The strap on her left sandal was broken, something she had been meaning to get fixed; she had to tense her toes to keep it on through the untrimmed grass. By the time they reached the pasture her feet were chill and wet.

"Where we going?" she demanded with a nervous laugh as he stretched apart the barbed wire for her to crawl through. She hoped it was not to the trailer. It reminded her of that unfortunate scene over Henry, something she had been on the verge of apologizing for when they had been taking up the carpet. But then she had remembered that Leo had shown Frank the pink stationery, something he should apologize to her for. In effect the two incidents canceled each other out, and she was willing to let bygones be bygones.

"Leo?"

He trudged ahead toward the trailer but did not enter the gate in the knee-high picket fence. Through a window Mrs. Dambar could see Shaerl folding clothes inside. And if she were not mistaken, the girl had on the black nightie that Frank had requested her, Gretchen, not to wear. Could Shaerl have just taken it without even asking? And really, was it right to fold clothes in such an outfit?

Preoccupied with these thoughts, Mrs. Dambar was not prepared for what greeted her in back of the trailer. With a shy grin Leo patted the brindled flank of a malevolent-looking cow tethered to the rear bumper.

"What's that?"

"A cow."

"Leo, I mean what is it doing here?"

"I thought you'd like one," he said casually, as if he were offering her a piece of candy.

"Me? This is for me?"

The supple hide twitched as she regarded the beast doubtfully. Somehow it seemed more like a bull than a cow, but she did not want to display her ignorance in front of the handyman. "Oh, I see. You mean Frank, he got this as a present for me?"

"Not really."

"He knows about it, right?"

"Not exactly."

"But Leo . . ."

"It's from me."

The beast's tail flicked, disturbing some hovering flies.

"Well, you'll just have to take it back. I'm sorry, but Frank will never allow something like this."

It was almost as if she had struck the handyman; the blood drained from his face, the hurt plain as day. Seeing this, she felt compelled to add, "It's lovely, Leo, really I do appreciate it. I'm very touched. But don't you think Frank should have been consulted?"

"Look, Mr. D doesn't like anything changed around here." The hurt had already soured a little; his smile was bitter. "What you got to do when you really want something is go for it. Do it. And stop worrying. He'll get used to the idea eventually."

She stood there uncertainly, her eye drawn to a large crack in one of the hooves, something that might have been natural or could have been the result of an accident; she wasn't sure. "But do I really want a cow?" she heard herself say aloud.

"Isn't that what you've always wanted?"

"I was thinking about it once. It was just an idea."

"You bought a book on cows."

"Oh, that. Well, you know I didn't exactly buy it." Remembering what had become of most of her chicks, she felt her doubt increase. How dreadful it would be if something this large got ill or went mad. Was the grass it was munching on now the proper thing for it to eat? Didn't it need some sort of vitamin supplement? And what if it didn't get along with the neighbor's horse? Perhaps the best thing to do was say nothing now to Leo, but when Frank returned, explain that she felt Leo might want to return the surprise to wherever it came from.

"It's just so thoughtful of you, Leo. I can't get over it." A few ants trickled up her leg as she headed back to the house. She slapped herself in midstride. "Really, I can't tell you how much I appreciate—damn things! I really—Christ. So nice."

Stepping inside the French doors, she looked around to make sure he was still in the garden, where he had lingered to adjust a few tar paper collars around the turnip stems. The top drawer of his desk slid open easily. From a pocket of her khaki trousers—they actually were Frank's, but she liked to wear them around the house—she took out the letter with the four-thousand-dollar check and slid it under the papers in the drawer, toward the back. She hoped Leo would come across it here in a natural way and think he had just overlooked it before. For a moment, after closing the drawer, she wondered if the check could have something to do with the cow. Did a cow cost that much? But Leo had said Frank didn't know about the animal. It began to trouble her again, what her husband could mean by writing such a large check. Somehow she would have to think of an excuse to bring the subject up.

"Oh!"

Mrs. Howard had given her a start as she hurried out of the library. The old woman was standing by the door using Windex on a candelabrum.

"Why is the door locked?"

"Good morning, Mrs. Howard. Pardon? The door? What door?"

"To the den. I got to get in dere and clean."

The harsh modernistic zigzag design on the old woman's dress, tiny collapsed swastikas, seemed to flicker as the yellow and red competed for the eye's attention. Looking a little to the side Gretchen told her not to worry about cleaning. "I'll do it myself."

"I see." Mrs. Howard regarded her doubtfully.

"The book, you know," Mrs. Dambar explained with a sudden twitch—another ant, "I've got to be so careful. If any pages got lost . . ."

"You think I steal your pages, me, Mrs. Howard?"

"Heavens no. I was just . . ."

"I work for this family since before you was alive." The jet collar hitched beneath her creamy double chin rode up and down as the old woman talked, her voice thick with emotion. "Never before has no one trusted me. Never before has a door been locked. Better you take one of the knifes from the kitchen and plunge it right here through Mrs. Howard's heart." She demonstrated with the Windex bottle.

"I didn't even know there was a key, honest. It was Leo." Gretchen couldn't believe how childish she sounded and wasn't surprised when, with a look of disgust, the old woman padded away over the thick carpet, shaking her head.

Dr. Jonsen explained that he wouldn't even need general anesthesia. A local would do the trick, and if Mr. Dambar liked he could be in and out of the hospital on the same day. *Polyp* was the word he used. A small benign growth in the bladder. Absolutely nothing to be concerned about.

Though the doctor was smiling, his voice was distant, cool, and somewhat weary, as if he had given this talk a hundred times. Avoiding his eyes, Mr. Dambar glanced around the office, at the bonsai on the desk, a Sierra Club calendar by the scales, and opposite, an impressionistic rendering of a culvert draining into a muddy ditch.

"Any questions, Frank?"

"No, sounds great."

"You want Jeannie to make the appointment for you? How about the end of next week? Sound good?"

"Terrific. When she's got it all set up, have her phone Francine. She'll put it on my calendar."

"Fine."

"Great."

After putting on his jacket, Mr. Dambar hesitated at the door. "Say, doc, how much would one of those run me? Like that one there." He nodded toward the painting of the ditch.

"You like it?"

"What is that, Busch Bavarian?" he asked, approaching the landscape for a better look. The beer can in the ditch was bluish.

"That's it, Frank, Busch Bavarian. I wanted to get in a veiled tribute to the Krauts, especially Kirchner. You familiar with his work? He was greatly influenced by black art, you know, and Munch. I've always thought he's been underrated. Now come stand over here. This is the best place to see it. No, a little to your right." A hand guided Mr. Dambar to the optimal viewing spot. The doctor's voice had come alive and his small eyes shone. "Do you see what's happening here? Everybody sees sights like this all the time, neglected, mundane views that they never really look at. Right away a label appears in your mind when you see a ditch: Ugly. Dirty. And so you really don't see what's there before your eyes. Sure, anyone can take a waterfall and make it seem gorgeous. But do we need a painting to do that? No, we can look at the waterfall itself. But a ditch, the seeming lack of design, one thing discarded beside another, totally unrelated lives like the man who threw the beer can away next to the doll's leg over there peeping up through the water. What little girl threw that out? And the crawdad there, a really remarkable creature, millions of years old, enduring in its fixed form through so much evolutionary change around it—a real mystery."

"How much, doc? You've sold me."

"Well, this is a favorite of mine. But hell, you want it, you got it. Two hundred even, including the frame."

With the landscape under his arm, Mr. Dambar heard the

doctor say as he showed him to the door, "Don't you worry, Frank. It's first class for you all the way. We'll have that polyp out in two shakes of an aardvark's tail." He clapped Mr. Dambar on the shoulder, as if they had been old friends for years.

When he got home that evening he left the painting in the garage, tucked beneath the seat of the scull. It was too depressing and amateurish to hang in the house, of course, but maybe he could give it to Shaerl as a going-away present. In any case, it was a small price to pay to insure that everything would go right in the hospital. Dr. Jonsen seemed a little lackadaisical at times, the type who might sew up a sponge inside you. He still hadn't told Mr. Dambar if he had cancer or not, even though Mr. Dambar really didn't want to know—except if the answer was no. Which was why Mr. Dambar hadn't come right out and asked him. The whole issue was something he would rather not think about.

"What an odd question," Mrs. Dambar said as she scrubbed the emerald green tub. Mr. Dambar had come into the bathroom to get ready for dinner. "But yes, as a matter of fact I have. At Yale."

His shirt off, Mr. Dambar scraped meticulously at his five o'clock shadow with a brass razor, a Father's Day gift from the veterinarian. "Yale?"

"When I was dating an American Studies professor. They were having some sort of solidarity thing with the campus workers and he signed on as a part-time janitor for the spring break. And I guess you could call me a maid."

"What did you wear?"

"Wear? Just old clothes. This must have been sixty-nine or seventy. He was a Marxist, my boyfriend, but then he got into Jesus and we split."

"Did you actually have to scrub floors?"

A weird feeling came over Mrs. Dambar as she sprinkled more generic cleanser into the sunken tub. She was happy enough to share her past with her husband, but somehow he was not asking the right questions. Wanting to get off the subject, she reverted to the polyp, which he had just told her about before asking her, out of the blue, if she had ever been a maid. "I'm still a little mad at you, Frank, for not telling me sooner."

"There was nothing to tell till today."

"But Leo was told."

"Angel, he's known for a long time."

Rinsing off the cleanser she was pleased to see the tub's drain working so well. The Roto-Rooter man had done a fine job. "By the way, I've got a surprise for you after dinner. Will you come see what I've done with my study? I know you'll love it. Oh, Frank, what are you doing? Stop that." He was rubbing against her, pressing her belly hard into the emerald green.

"Sorry, hon. You just look so good, you know."

Vaguely ashamed of himself, he retreated to the sink to finish shaving. What with the operation coming up, he should have his mind on Jesus, he knew, asking for forgiveness for any sins he may have committed. Yet his body seemed more alive than ever, joyful in a way it never had been with Jane or Mrs. Anderson. The resurrection of the body, he thought. The words had never meant anything to him, an empty formula, until now.

She was scrubbing the tiles above the tub. The lush green from the profusion of plastic ferns and philodendrons gave the carpeted room a steamy, tropical feel as hot water gushed from the gilt faucet, beading the leaves. Lulled by the warmth, he admired her furtively in the mirror between strokes of the razor.

"Now here's the news of the day," she said, bearing down hard on some mildew. "You won't believe what Leo's done. I was writing this morning and the next thing you know he comes by and asks me to go back to his trailer. So I go. And what do I find? A cow. I'm not kidding, Frank. There's a cow out there, just standing around. Of course, it's got to go back."

"I thought I told you I didn't want any cows around here. It's ridiculous, Gretchen."

"Hey, don't blame me. It was Leo. I had nothing to do with it."

"I thought I made it clear . . . You know what happened to those chickens."

"For Christ's sake, Frank, stop acting like it was me. I didn't want a cow."

"You told me you did, several times."

124

"That was only a thought. I wasn't serious about it."

He rinsed off his face, then patted it with a fluffy apricot towel. "It'll have to go back."

"That's what I said. Didn't you hear?"

"I won't be bullied into having a cow, understand. I'm going to put my foot down on this one."

"Bullied? Oh, Frank, that's so unfair. You know I'd do anything for you."

"Yes, but you always seem to get your way, don't you?"

He slapped the towel down on the massage table Leo had given him for Christmas two years ago. Leo had been planning to take a course in massage but then seemed to have second thoughts about it. "You could have consulted me first, you know. But to just go ahead like this . . ."

Fear got the better of her anger. She had never seen him so openly hostile. Why couldn't he listen to her? The whole thing was so simple; it was Leo's fault. But her instincts warned her that this was dangerous territory. Putting the blame on Leo would get her nowhere now. "Darling, please." Tentatively she reached out for his bare shoulder.

Though he still looked glum, her gentle strokes seemed to appease him. "So the little maid thinks she can put one over on the boss, huh?"

"I'm so sorry, sir," she said, picking up on his mocking tone.

"You promise to be good from now on?"

"Oh, yes, sir."

"You've been a bad little maid, huh? Come here. Put down that rag."

Her heart wasn't in it, but she was eager to mollify him. After all, she still had to explain the study to him that evening. So when he lay down on the royal blue carpet, beside the tub, she took off her sandals and snuggled up beside him.

"What if someone comes in, Frank?"

"Don't worry, babe."

"Can't we go in the bedroom?"

"Take it easy, girl."

Unzipping her khaki trousers, he reached inside. "Not too

hard, Frank," she whispered. He had never been so passionate with her before, though maybe a little rough. She knew she should rejoice, and probably would have, if she hadn't been upset about the cow.

"Frank, I love you so much, dear."

"At Yale, huh?"

"What?"

"Hug me, girl, tighter, tighter. I'm going to make you rich."

CHAPTER EIGHT

The raw cold startled her when she went outside, but she didn't bother to go back for her ski jacket. After all, it was only a week or two before spring officially began. In an hour or two it was bound to warm up. Besides, she didn't have much time. Frank was due at the hospital that afternoon, and of course, she would drive him there and help him get settled. In the meantime, though, she wanted to keep the appointment she had made on Tuesday. If she rescheduled it, she was afraid she might have to wait another week—and by then she might have lost her nerve.

Although there was a space in front of the Bessie Building, she decided to park two blocks away at the Leon, a movie theater that showed horror films on Fridays and on Mondays and Wednesdays served as a Tae Kwon Do studio. Aside from an elderly black man yanking wiring from a gaping hole in a pet shop, she found herself to be the only person using the sidewalks downtown. Perhaps it was the cold keeping everyone indoors. But even so, she couldn't recall ever seeing many people walking. Anthropologically speaking, there must be some significance to this, which she would have pondered if she wasn't so cold. Hugging herself while she tottered along as fast as her too-tight high heels would allow, she passed the dimly lit window displays that would have looked right at home in a Third World country. In one, unmatched shoes were arranged in a semicircle around a cardboard poster. Another had a toy dump truck sitting somewhat existentially among an array of "finer lingerie." And yet on the corner, to her surprise, was a tasteful arrangement of Lenox china with the same tureen she had given Sydney Renfrew when she married that awful Dalmatian count. Poor Sydney didn't realize what she was letting herself in for. Anyone could have told her he was a dreadful lech—and penniless to boot. The last she had heard, Sydney was optioning Silhouette romances for a cable TV production company that no one had ever heard of.

"He'll be with you in just a minute," the receptionist told her after she had climbed two flights of stairs in the Bessie Building, which was not sufficiently heated. Despite the recent exertion, she felt on the verge of literally trembling as she waited on a settee, thumbing through a copy of *U.S. News and World Report.* It was a choice between that and *Prevention* on the cherry mahogany coffee table.

"No, Burma," the receptionist, a weary-looking man in his early forties, was saying to someone who was apparently a trainee or replacement. "The brown mug is Mr. Herbert's, the blue is Donna Lee's, and that one with the mice is Eddie Jo's. You can keep yours in the drawer here where I got the Equal."

A few moments later she found herself in Mr. Herbert's office admiring his hand-benched shoes. "I would love to get Frank a pair like that. They're English, I bet. Frank has a pair of blue shoes that I would give anything to throw out. He thinks they go with the rug in our house—can you believe?" She laughed merrily as her eye swept the prickly office; it seemed Mr. Herbert was fond of cactuses. A surprising variety adorned every ledge, with some in bloom, others bloated or twisted into shapes you might expect on another planet, but not here on earth.

"By the way," she added as casually as possible, "you won't mind not mentioning this to Frank—my visit. He's going into the hospital this afternoon and I'd just as soon not have him worrying, you know."

"Mrs. Dambar, I—"

"Gretchen."

"I think you're putting me in an awkward position. He is my client, after all."

"Oh, but this isn't business really. Just a social call. That was fun the other night," she added lamely from the oxblood chair she had settled into. He remained standing, neat, compact, with a muddled part in his thin, shiny hair.

"The other night?"

"At the Jonsens'."

Hardly the other night, she realized, trying to keep from trembling in the dank chill of his office; she wasn't thinking straight. Her mind was preoccupied with how to bring up the subject of Leo. Now that her faith in Dr. Lahey had been shaken, she was casting about for some other outside objective opinion. Her first impulse had been to call Molly and tell her everything, all her fears, including the fact that her therapist had admitted that she had known Leo in college. Disturbed by the name on the therapist's keychain, Gretchen had asked her about it during a session following the chance meeting at Wal-Mart. Dr. Lahey had calmly explained that, yes, her nickname used to be Brandi, something only her mother still called her. And, yes, maybe she had gone out with Leo once or twice in college. "But don't you think that was something you should have told me?" Gretchen had demanded, though in what she hoped was a reasonable tone of voice. Dr. Lahey claimed that it was totally irrelevant.

"And now? Are you friends with him now?"

"Should I submit a list of my friends for your approval, Gretchen?" she had said. Or was it: "This sort of grilling, it's not healthy at all. It worries me, Gretchen, to hear you talking this way. You've been doing so well up to now." Whatever Dr. Lahey had said, it had put Mrs. Dambar on the defensive.

"Look, I don't mean to be paranoid about this, Brenda. Really, it's fine if you did see him in college. I just wonder if maybe you could have told me earlier." She didn't want to lose Dr. Lahey. She liked her far too much already. If only Brenda could come up with some reason, some excuse, she was ready to let the matter drop. But for the rest of the session Dr. Lahey had obstinately refused to say a word about Leo. All she wanted to do was examine Gretchen's lack of trust, which was now completely out in the open. The transference was evident beyond a shadow of a doubt. "Just look at the pattern you've set up with me, Gretchen. Does it sound familiar? An initial rush of enthusiasm, a willingness to give yourself up completely to this new arrival on the scene—and then? You tell me the rest."

Later, as she sat musing in the study, on the verge of calling Molly, she had remembered something about a dog. In one of their earlier sessions, hadn't Dr. Lahey seemed to confuse Leo with a dog? But how could she have done that if she had known who Leo was? Could it have been deliberate, a smoke screen? Or had Dr. Lahey actually said that about Leo? Could it have been about Shaerl? No, it was Leo. And she remembered that when Dr. Lahey had said dog, she had thought immediately of that big ugly beast that lounged around the end of the road, where it met the highway. Tawny, without a collar, a shaggy unkempt mane of hair, the animal should really be reported. It might harm one of the children on the street.

Molly had not picked up. Her answering machine started and then seemed to become confused, for the outgoing message suddenly speeded up and there was no beep. It gave Gretchen time to reconsider. Sure, it would be a relief to pour out all her anxiety. But what could Molly do for her? She would only think that she, Gretchen, had made a terrible mistake moving to Louisiana. In a few days everyone else in New York would know, too. Molly had a way of letting people force things out of her. "I swore to Gretchen I wouldn't say a word . . ." was the standard boilerplate preamble.

Remembering how much fun it had been talking to Mr. Herbert at the Jonsens', she had decided to give him a try. Her idea had been to bring up the matter of the $4,213 check, which was still a mystery to her. Perhaps this could lead to a more general discussion about Leo. Finding out about him and Brenda had put her on guard again. Thinking back over his recent friendly overtures, Gretchen had begun to wonder if the handyman had not deliberately set a trap for her. After all, Frank was quite upset about the carpet being taken up in the study. As in the cow incident, all the blame seemed to fall on her. Whenever she tried to protest to Frank, it simply seemed as if she were trying to get Leo in trouble.

"Lucius, I know you don't have time for small talk. I'll get right to the point." There was a quaver in her voice, from the cold, of course, the chill. She clasped her hands together. "The other day I happened to run across a check my husband had made out to our handyman. It was for a considerable amount, four thousand or so. I thought that, seeing as how you advise my husband on financial matters as well as, you know, that maybe . . ."

Still standing, he glanced down at some papers on his desk. "Why don't you ask him yourself, Mrs. Dambar?"

"Frank? Well, you see, we really don't discuss finances." Goose bumps stippled her bare arms; she was shivering. The Peruvian shawl, a sweater, anything would have helped. "It's sort of an un-spoken agreement between us. So many marriages have come to grief over this issue, you know. Frank and I, we're determined never to let it come between us."

"I see."

She rambled on for a while, anxious to give the impression of being a loving wife. She wanted him to see how much she cared about Frank, how she would think nothing of throwing herself in front of a speeding car for him. But she was having trouble getting this across. She feared she might seem somewhat conniving, going to her husband's lawyer behind his back. Somehow Mr. Herbert must be made to understand her special circumstances.

". . . and I guess I was wondering if somehow, maybe, the check was related to the cow," she wound up, some minutes later.

"You mean, perhaps Frank paid Leo for it on the sly?"

"Something like that."

Mr. Herbert glanced at the streamlined pocket watch chained to his vest. "I can assure you, it has nothing to do with the cow. If I were you, Mrs.—Gretchen, I just wouldn't worry about it." Holding open the door, he said, "Leo was involved in some financial venture with your husband . . ."

"You mean the condominiums?"

"I really don't feel at liberty to say."

131

"Oh, but I know all about that." She had gotten up and followed him to the door. In her heels she towered over him and, somewhat daunted by his bespoke elegance, felt so outsized, so bulky, like an ill-wrapped appliance on Mrs. Howard's birthday. "Frank told me about The Antibes. Oh, Lucius, I'm beginning to feel so much better. It's probably something to do with that, isn't it?"

"Well now, I'm not saying it is, you understand. I'm just saying it probably has nothing to do with the cow."

She took his white hand and squeezed it heartily. "I know you're busy. It was so kind of you to let me go on like this. Sometimes I get to feeling so . . ."

"Here, please."

She took the handkerchief he proffered and used it to dab at the tears, which had sprung up so unexpectedly. He was a good man, Mr. Herbert. She felt it in her bones. Good—and sane. "I'm sorry, Lucius." She handed back the silk handkerchief. "I guess I'm sort of wrought up about the hospital. Frank is having some work done on his penis."

"Oh." He stood there uncertainly for a moment, his pale neat face looking for the first time a little lost. "Is there anything I can do?"

"It's not serious, really. Dr. Jonsen says he does this all the time." She had spoken euphemistically of the bladder, which somehow seemed too vulgar a term for Mr. Herbert. "I'm going to have to get ahold of myself. It's too foolish to be so upset. You must think I'm a real idiot."

"Y'all want me to make some fresh coffee?" the trainee called out from the reception desk.

"That won't be necessary, Miss LaSteele. Mrs. Dambar is in a hurry, I believe. Please give my best wishes to Frank," he added as he extricated himself from her grip. "Perhaps I'll stop by the hospital."

"She's on loan."

"Well, then, send her back."

"Can't without a truck." Leo slapped the cow's flank. "Next

week this guy's supposed to come over with a livestock rig. He'll help me get it back to the farm."

"Shaerl says it's keeping her awake, making all sorts of noises. Can't you move it away from the trailer?"

Leo considered this a moment. "I suppose I could tie it to the Pepsi sign at night. I just don't want it getting loose and wandering out onto the highway."

Mr. Dambar shrugged, scratched his head. He was ready to go to the hospital, but Gretchen hadn't returned yet. To pass the time he had strolled out to have a look at the garden—and the cow.

"I thought it was something she'd like," Leo said, apologizing for the nineteenth or twentieth time. "I could've got a real deal on her. Moss Hanley said the old girl is about to kick the bucket anyway—got some sort of kidney infection. 'Course she wouldn't last long, but she'd do as a sort of beginner's cow, something to let Mrs. D get a feel for them. I was going to count it as a birthday present for her."

"Yes, of course," Mr. Dambar said wearily, for the handyman enjoyed giving this little speech whenever there was a lull in the general conversation at lunch or dinner. "I appreciate the thought. And I'm sure Gretchen does too. But . . . Why is it moving its head like that? Is that normal?"

The beast was twisting its enormous head from side to side, spasmodically, as if there were something it was trying to dislodge from its ears. Both men peered intently at it for a few moments until it settled down. "I really don't know much about cows, Mr. D. There was one at the parish fair this year that they put a funnel in so you could like see into its third stomach. Didn't exactly turn me on to them."

Leo was bundled up in one of Mr. Dambar's old hunting jackets and a scarf Mrs. Anderson had knitted. Mr. Dambar himself was wearing the down hunting jacket Leo and Mrs. Howard had given him for Christmas two years ago. As if with the same thought, they both turned and looked toward the house. "I wonder where she is," Mr. Dambar muttered. "Got to get going."

For a moment they both regarded the not very interesting prospect of the back of the house, their hands in their pockets, their heads covered by identical khaki hunting caps, the earflaps lowered. Mr. Dambar began to ask, "Did she say where she . . . ," while Leo simultaneously said, "Did she say what . . ." Leo then answered: "Don't know. She just took the keys to the Jeep."

"But she asked you, didn't she?"

The handyman stroked his graying ponytail. "It's OK, Mr. D. No big deal."

"How many times have I told her to ask you? Good Lord."

Leo's Earth Shoes made a squish as he avoided a sudden side-step from the cow. "So why don't I drive you? Doc wants you to check in, right?"

"Gretchen said she wants to come."

"Well . . ."

An unpleasant bovine odor wafted to his nostrils. "Maybe we better get going, Leo. She can always drop by later. I don't want Dr. Jonsen to be kept waiting."

"Well . . . Sure you don't think we better give her more time?"

"No, come on."

When they got to the driveway, Leo opened the door on the passenger side for his boss. Not wanting to be treated like an invalid, Mr. Dambar told Leo to get in and went around to the driver's seat himself.

"Hey!"

"Huh?"

"Mr. D!"

"Oh."

Mr. Dambar had not been consulting the rearview mirror as he backed out of the drive. Looking over his shoulder he saw Mrs. Howard and braked just in time. "She coming too?"

The old woman had not budged, perfectly confident that the Buick would come to a halt in time. Leaning over the front seat, Leo unlocked the back door for her. As she crammed herself in, with what seemed a monstrous handbag, Shaerl came hobbling as fast as she could around the side of the house. In her hands was a paisley scarf, which she used to flag them down before placing it over her head.

"My hair," she wailed after slamming the car door behind her. They pulled out of the drive. "You didn't give me time to finish."

"You don't have to come," Leo commented.

"Of course, she comes," Mrs. Howard said, giving her a pat on the hand.

For a sixties dance that Mr. Dambar's Episcopal church was giving that evening, Shaerl had rinsed her hair blond and teased it into a beehive. To get the full effect Mr. Dambar asked her to take the scarf off. She protested at first, saying she wasn't done with the back. When she finally gave in, he found the change disturbing. She looked so unlike herself, so much more feminine, more mature—and yet at the same time somewhat familiar. That shade of blonde, wasn't it exactly the same as Jane's? It was uncanny.

"Mr. D?"

"Yes?"

"I think we're on the shoulder."

Making a small adjustment he put the Riviera back onto the asphalt road.

"Turn up the heat," came Shaerl's voice from the backseat, "I'm freezing."

"Don't you think you ought to put on the wipers, Mr. D?"

A tenuous drizzle had just started up. Mr. Dambar reached out to the controls and knocked against Leo's hand. "You got it?"

"What are you wearing tonight?" Shaerl asked, thrusting herself forward, her head only inches from the driver's. "Leo."

"What? Where?"

"Where? How can you say where?" She thumped her stepuncle on the head. "The fundraiser at the church, cutie. You're going to be my date."

"Forget it."

"You promised." Another thump. "Don't be scared. You'll have fun."

"How can you talk about a dance when Mr. D is headed for the hospital?"

Mr. Dambar squinted; the drizzle had picked up. "Go ahead,

Leo. I already bought the tickets. Fifty bucks apiece. And that goes for you too, Mrs. Howard. You can chaperone."

"Nonsense. I stay with you at the hospital tonight. See, I have my overnight." She patted the handbag—which was actually a small suitcase—that Mr. Dambar had been wondering about when she had gotten into the car.

"Look, I appreciate it, Mrs. Howard, but it won't be necessary. Not at all."

"That's right," Leo said in the loud tone of voice he used for Mrs. Howard, who could hear perfectly well. "I'm staying with him tonight."

"What?" Grabbing his ponytail, Shaerl gave it a yank. "I swear I'll murder you if you don't come tonight. There's going to be all these divorced women you can meet, really nice chicks."

"Lay off."

"Listen, I don't want you to stay." Mr. Dambar fumbled for the higher speed on the wipers. "I'm fine by myself."

"I already checked with the hospital, Mr. D. They're going to get me a rollaway bed."

When they got into town they were still going on about the dance, Shaerl insisting that she would not go without Leo. In this she was supported by Mrs. Howard, who had made up her mind once and for all that she was spending the night at the hospital. Leo was free to go to the dance. She was reiterating this at a four-way stop on Flat Avenue, just across from the railroad tracks, when Mr. Dambar caught sight of a familiar car.

Gretchen was wondering who was supposed to go first; there were four cars, one at each stop sign. Probably it was the one who had gotten there first, which was the lady opposite, who was just sitting there with a blank look on her kind, grandmotherly face. "Well," Mrs. Dambar said, venturing out herself, and almost immediately being honked at, rudely. Discombobulated, she hesitated in the middle of her turn. Another impatient honk. "Well, I'm sorry," she commented to herself as she continued with the turn, "but if you insist on such stupid signs in this town. Why not just put up a light and be done with it? So it costs a few bucks . . . Besides, I'm in a hurry. My husband is going to the hospital and I've simply got to get home."

"What are you doing?" Leo asked as he switched on the defroster. The front windshield was misting over. "The hospital's not this way."

"That's Gretchen, see? I want to catch her. Save her from going all the way back home."

"Leo, I swear I'll never speak to you again if you don't go." Shaerl had wedged herself between the bucket seats in front to make him pay attention. At such close range her Chanel No. 22 was overpowering. "What is it? You afraid of girls?"

"Now, Shaerl," Mr. Dambar cautioned.

The rain was heavy now, and Mrs. Dambar was having difficulty with the Jeep's erratic wipers. Worse yet, she was still being honked at. The rearview mirror was not adjusted for her height, and besides the back window was clouded over. Probably some cracker upset because she had gone out of turn at the corner. Well, tough luck, buddy. "Honk all you like, baby. I hope it makes you happy, you little redneck." So here she was, once again attracting all the crazies, just like she used to in New York every time she walked out of her apartment.

"So Mr. Leo, you go meet a nice sweet girl tonight, someone with some meat on the bones. Dey always work out to be the best, no?" Mrs. Howard was clutching the overnight bag on her lap, as if it were in danger of being yanked from her grasp. For the occasion she had donned a trapezoidal cocktail hat, chartreuse, with a half veil of tulle. "I know Mrs. Anderson is expecting. She calls this morning to make sure all were coming."

"Did she?" Mr. Dambar mused aloud.

"She is so grateful for the donation. There are high hopes for the renovation of the Fellowship Hall. And she say she have a good vibration about the seal bid you put in, Frankie."

"See, you got to go, Leo." Shaerl reached out and smoothed her stepuncle's hair, her cologne making Mr. Dambar feel both hopeful and sad. It had been a good while since emotions came to him unadulterated. Even now anger and frustration were added to the

137

pot, a regular mulligan stew. Why didn't Gretchen pull over? What was the matter with her, speeding down a side street in this pouring rain?

"I already told you I'm staying with Mr. D tonight and I don't care how good Mrs. Anderson feels, I'm not—Mr. D!"

"Watch!"

"Dummkopf!'

Mr. Dambar felt his arm tangle with Leo's as the Buick skidded across the rain-slicked road in the direction of a two-hundred-year-old live oak, the roots of which had shelved the sidewalk like a geologic fault. He heard someone laughing, a man's voice, and wondered for a brief moment if it could be him.

Having made an extremely sharp turn at the last possible moment, Mrs. Dambar breathed a sigh of relief. She had eluded her tormentor and could now drive home at a more reasonable speed. Southern men, she knew, were very touchy about their driving. It was all bound up with their masculinity—the vehicle itself, as anyone familiar with Lévi-Strauss' reading of Durkheim might surmise, being both an extension of their own bodies and an embodiment, with its voluptuous curves, of the female. Mauve Livingston, Molly's stepsister, said she had a friend who was driving through someplace like North Carolina when she passed a van in the breakdown lane. The van chased Mauve's friend for twenty miles on the interstate and took a shot at her tires with a sawed-off shotgun. Mauve said her friend, who had known Henry at Yale and thought he was a bore (sour grapes, of course), well, her friend was too scared to go to the police. She just knew the police would take the crazy lunatic's side. It was a cultural thing, like in the Sulu archipelago, where in some tribe or other the brother-in-law was traditionally allowed to strangle an unfaithful wife.

For a hospital it had a decidedly hopeful atmosphere, such as one might find in the student union of a Bob Jones-type college, where bright vinyl furniture set amid a bewildering variety of vending machines invited one to linger and perhaps make a new acquaintance. The volunteer at the main desk was helpful and considerate and even emitted a distinct cluck or two when Mrs. Dambar explained what had happened. "Yes, looked all over the house, not a soul there, so I figured he must have gone ahead and checked in without me. I told him I'd be home in plenty of time, but he couldn't wait."

"So where's the fire?" the volunteer said, punching out the name on his computer. He was a pleasant-looking young man gone prematurely gray, except for his eyebrows, which were quite yellow. "Here we are, 6KE. That's down the hall to your right, then hang another right at the tamale thing, through the door, the green, not red, and up three steps, veer left."

As Mrs. Dambar wended her way through the clean, well-lit corridors, she made up her mind not to be bitchy and complain. If she resented Frank a little for taking off without her, she could live with it. There was no reason to make him feel guilty at a time like this. Loving, supportive, selfless—this was the role cut out for her now.

"Frank?" she said, peering into his room, her voice interrogative for no good reason, other than that people might tend to add question marks in hospitals. "Frank?" He was lying there plain as day, a starchy sheet covering the lower half of his hospital gown.

"Come in."

"Angel, how are you?" There was another bed in the room, unoccupied and nearer the window. "Why don't you move over to that one, Frank? You'd get more light. Here, let me . . ."

"Don't. Just . . . You can't go rearranging . . ."

"I'll talk to the nurse about it. Has the doctor been to see you yet?"

"He won't be in till midnight."

"Well, I won't say I told you so. But really, there was no big rush to get here, was there? I did want to drive you, honey." She really didn't like that word *honey* at all, and wondered why she had called him that. "Are you sure you don't want to move over to the other bed? No? Well, here, let me fix your pillows."

"It's all right."

He seemed oddly distracted, almost to the point of rudeness. In any other man, such behavior would not have been tolerated, bladder or no bladder. Giving the pillows a couple of whacks, she replaced them under his head. "There. Well now, here we are and we've got till midnight—though I hope he doesn't expect you to wait up for him. In any case, how would you like me to read to you? That would be nice, don't you think?" Reaching into her canvas tote bag, she came up with a stained copy of *The Princess Casamassima*. "It's one of those books one never gets around to. I suppose sometime before I die I should . . ." The stony look he was giving her made it hard to think. "Did you ever notice how many so-called educated people say 'Princess C' and leave off the 'The'? You won't believe, but the *Oxford Companion,* they actually have *Portrait of a Lady.* I swear, that's how they have it, without the 'The.' "

"What do you think you were doing?"

The flat, affectless voice, the strange syntax, stopped her cold. She wasn't quite sure what he meant. "I told you I had a few errands to run," she tried out. "I got back in plenty of time."

Gingerly he felt the bruise on his chest where the steering wheel had banged into him. "Gretchen, do you realize you could have—"

"You won't believe, but I saw a tureen exactly like the one I had given Sydney Renfrew. I told you about her, didn't I? She married the Dalmatian, and everyone was so upset."

"What?"

"Of course, some of us tried to tell her what a big mistake she was making, but there's some people who are just so willful that— Oh, Leo."

The handyman had wandered into the room, his left eye swollen shut in an unobtrusive way, with little discoloration. At first she thought he might be squinting, but another look canceled out this notion. "What happened to you?"

Walking right past her, he muttered something to Mr. Dambar, who had raised himself to a sitting position. "Come here, son, let me see how it's doing."

Leo complied, perching on the edge of his bed. Neither one bothered to answer Mrs. Dambar's anxious questions as Mr. Dambar peered intently at the handyman's eye. Finally, the examination completed, Leo glanced over at her, a dim smile of forbearance on his doleful, clean-shaven face. "It's nothing, Mrs. D. Don't worry. The doctor thinks I'll be able to see out of it—eventually."

"Were you in a fight?"

"Gretchen, please. Enough."

"Frank, I'm only trying to find out what happened."

"Oh, for heaven's sake."

"Now Mr. D." Leo placed a hand on his employer's shoulder. "It's really not her fault."

"My fault!" she exclaimed, reaching out to him. "What are you talking about?"

Mr. Dambar visibly shrank from her touch. "Why did you turn like that, going so fast? For God's sake, woman, why couldn't you pull over and see what I wanted?"

"Well, the rain, Mr. D."

"Leo, please, the rain is no excuse. She heard me honking."

"Yeah, but . . ."

"That was you?" Despite herself Mrs. Dambar couldn't help smiling. How ridiculous she must have looked, running away from her own husband like that. "Oh, Frank, what a scream."

"Yes, this poor boy's eye, it's a riot. And Shaerl in the Emergency Room—"

"They're examining Mrs. Howard now," Leo put in respectfully, in a hushed voice. "But I'm sure it's not Mrs. D's fault. There must be some explanation. After all, the rain . . ."

"Well, of course there is." She had risen to her feet, anxious to get over to the Emergency Room to find out how Mrs. Howard and Shaerl were doing. "See, I thought you were some sort of . . . That corner there where everyone was stopped—and I couldn't see out of my mirror. But what happened, Frank?"

"We skidded," Leo supplied after a pause during which Mr. Dambar kept his head turned away. "When you turned so fast we skidded across the road and like hit this tree."

"Tree? Oh, my God. Is everyone OK? Listen, I got to go see how they're doing. I'll be right back. Oh, Frank, I'm so sorry, angel." She looked anxiously at the handyman, who smiled benevolently upon her evident discomposure.

The water was dark, still, and in the shallows the cypress knees offered a gratifying challenge. Maneuvering through them, the oars

141

feathering like the deft, probing limbs of a water strider, she rode lightly over the sleek surface with hardly a wake. To have discovered this place on her own, without any planning, no maps, simply following her instinct down one country road after another, always choosing the most neglected, the least likely to lead anywhere—this gave her a sense of accomplishment. Of course, the bayou or creek or whatever it was must have a name, but not to know it gave her a furtive thrill as if she were trespassing on a genuine wilderness that even Henry would approve of. Oh, if only she could have shown him this. She had been rowing for half an hour and hadn't seen a sign of human life, not one. He would have had to be impressed, whether he showed it or not.

It was still cold, but she had come prepared with a parka and a thermos of hot tea. Letting herself drift for a while, she poured herself a cup. The blue heron that had preceded her from bend to bend, evidently annoyed by her intrusion, was preening itself at a safe distance. Outsized and angular, it had a prehistoric look to it, a proto-bird of sorts. It made her worry a moment about alligators, until she reasoned with herself that being cold-blooded they would be in no mood to give chase.

A muffled thud and the heron, with amazing grace, mounted into the hard teal skies. Hunters, no doubt, deep in the woods that lined the bayou. At dinner the other night Leo had taken her side about hunting. She was hoping to cure Frank of the need to kill. "What sort of contest is it between an unarmed deer and a man standing twenty, thirty yards away with a goddamn blunderbuss? Only a sissy and a bully would think that was manly. If you got to kill, then you ought to have the guts to go in there and strangle it with your bare hands." Frank—this was before the operation—had asked her what she was eating. Of course, it had been steak, and he did ask why she hadn't gone out and strangled Leo's cow for supper. The damn cow. She wished he would take it back. It was looking strangely bloated, and the sounds it made did not seem very cowlike to her. In fact the moos were positively embarrassing. She had been out back chatting with Marge Tilly, the banker's wife, when the cow let out a groan that made Mrs. Tilly glance at her as if somehow *she* were at fault.

As she stowed away the thermos, her hand happened to knock against something wedged between one of the struts. Wondering what it could be, she yanked it loose and discovered a framed painting. What in God's name was a landscape doing in her scull?

"OK, so it's good," she said aloud after studying it a few moments. One of Dr. Jonsen's, she knew right away. "What am I supposed to do, kill myself?"

She thought with despair of her book. If only she could hold it in her hands, like this landscape—if only it were something real, solid. But she knew she would never finish it, much less get it published. Who was she trying to fool? So she had spent years researching the period, what did it amount to? She had nothing original to say about the Philippines, nothing that hadn't already been said before hundreds of times in one scholarly journal after another. And to think she had only been there once in her life. Good God, she must be insane. She really couldn't blame Leo for giving her that look the other day after she had shown him a chapter she had written.

"It's good," he had said, but his eyes betrayed him. They were saying just the opposite—and deep down she knew he was right. This is bullshit, the dark, piercing gaze let her know.

Of course, she never would have dreamed of showing him anything if he hadn't asked her several times. Feeling in need of his support, though still leery of his motives, she had given in finally. Ever since the accident he had seemed to go out of his way to be nice to her, which made her, admittedly, a little uneasy. She knew Frank was still blaming the mishap on her. Yet even if she accepted the blame, which she didn't, was it such a big deal? OK, so Frank had a bruise on his chest, practically invisible. What did it matter when the bladder operation had gone so well? A small benign polyp had been removed, and he had gone home that same day. As for Shaerl and Mrs. Howard, not a scratch on either one of them. Why they had been examined in the Emergency Room, she couldn't say. The only one who had a right to complain was Leo, who had gotten a shiner when his eye had somehow come into contact with Frank's elbow. Leo wasn't complaining. And the Buick had only a small dent in the fender where it had hit a root. She had offered to pay for that, hadn't she? It just wasn't fair of Frank to act as if it had been a big tragedy. So he might not refer to it often, but the way he looked at her from time to time, she knew he was brooding about it. He was upset because she didn't feel guilty enough about it. Yes, her apologies might sound a little glib. But it was extremely hard to apologize for something you didn't do—and that was that.

Suddenly she found herself looking into a pair of eyes. A sleek brown head had emerged only a foot or two from her scull. Almost as a reflex action she hurled the landscape at it while letting out a girlish scream that, a moment later, she was thoroughly ashamed of. Imagine, being frightened like that by a beaver—or no, was it a muskrat, or what? She had never seen anything quite like it before. In any case, she was getting cold. Maybe it was time to head back. As for the landscape, it had sunk.

The Ferry Queen Lounge at Ozone's Ramada Inn had an all-you-can-eat buffet on Wednesdays from noon till three. Mr. Dambar had loaded his plate with stuffed flounder, lasagne, pork chops, and oysters. Francine had a modest mound of shrimp salad—for the same price, her boss pointed out. "Not very economical," he added with a wink. Aside from an elderly lady in a pants suit who was seated next to a large paddlewheel, they were the only customers in the dimly lit room, probably because it had just turned twelve. Mr. Dambar believed in an early lunch.

"Charlotte says she's getting some definite nibbles," Francine commented, referring to The Antibes, which they had driven down to inspect. Charlotte was the agent showing the condominiums; they were just down the road from the motel.

"Sure, but we're talking twenty percent below our original estimate. What sort of profit margin does that leave us with? You want a drink?"

A waitress was hovering.

"Perrier."

"I'm sorry. We don't carry Perrier—I don't think." Attractive, middle-aged, the waitress looked as if she would be more at home playing golf at a country club than working in a motel lounge. "Want me to check for you?"

"That's all right," Francine said. "Club soda. And he'll have a Johnnie Walker Black on the rocks with a splash of water."

"Listen, if we have Perrier, I'll bring that instead, OK? And I tell you what, I'll bring the water in a separate glass because last time I tried to put in a splash the customer got upset, said it was too much. So now I let people please themselves, if you know what I mean."

Francine nodded somewhat curtly, which made Mr. Dambar feel he should say something polite so the poor woman wouldn't feel bad. After all, she was going out of her way to make sure Francine had what she wanted. "Oh, yes, sir, you wouldn't believe the type of people who come in here," she was saying some moments later, after having verified that Francine would take a twist of lime, not lemon. "And I'm not talking about rude, I'm talking down-right . . . well, you know." Before she went away to place the order, Mr. Dambar had learned that the waitress used to teach at a Montessori school, which had closed down three and a half weeks ago because there was too much lead in the wall paint, and that her husband, a helicopter pilot, was in the hospital for an inner-ear disturbance that made him dizzy all the time, and that her mother-in-law, who was the lady sitting over by the paddlewheel, never left a tip.

"I don't understand why you have to encourage people like that," Francine commented once they were alone again.

"Well, she's a human being, isn't she?"

She took a bite of salad. "Anyway, I've plotted some graphs. They're here in my . . ." As she leaned over to pick up her leather attaché case Mr. Dambar asked her if that could wait.

"Sure. But what you'll see, Frank, is that there is a good chance we could do something with The Antibes. Charlotte says that every-body just loves the private boat dock underneath the L units. She's sure things are beginning to move, and with a refinancing plan— well, I've come up with a suggestion about how this could be done with only a minimal capital outlay. In fact, it's funny that you never thought of this before. It's so simple."

Whenever Francine prefaced any idea with "simple," he knew she was about to make his head swim. He liked things to be straight-forward: If you were going bankrupt on a venture, then you bailed out and saved as much as you could. But with Francine and her fancy M.B.A. theories, when you were going bankrupt you were actually about to make money hand over fist. No wonder Mrs. Sklar thought the world of her. "Look, Francine, I'm sure your graft is just wonderful and—"

"My what?"

"Graphs and all, the figures, but you know, we can have a thousand nibbles a day and it doesn't mean a thing. What has Charlotte actually landed? So I'd rather . . . See . . . For now, let's just eat. I really can't deal with it over food."

Francine's knee accidentally brushed against his. Instinctively, he moved his out of the way. "You're still upset about the accident, Frank. I can tell."

"No, not really. It's not that."

"You've been looking pretty out of it. What's going on? Come on, kid, level with me."

Though she was half his age, every now and then Francine would adopt a big-sister attitude toward him, her plain face lit up with gruff affection. Mr. Dambar found himself confiding in her more and more, but not without feeling a little uneasy about it afterward. Promising himself to take a more businesslike attitude toward her, he would be somewhat cold and remote for a few days. Unfazed she would perform her own job with her usual cool efficiency—until she turned into big sister again. What puzzled him was that he was not at all physically attracted to her, so there should be no reason for him to feel guilty. Yet he did.

The waitress brought their drinks just as he was about to complain to Francine about the cow that was still hanging around in the pasture. And he wanted to ask Francine about the carpet, which they had already discussed—whether he should make Leo put it back in the den. He was afraid that if he didn't, one day he would come home and discover that the entire carpet had been ripped up. It would be like a desecration, something he was not sure he could bear. The den, yes—but the entire house? No. Although he had told Francine about the accident, he had not yet mentioned the two things that disturbed him most, Gretchen seeing Henry in Leo's

146

trailer and the strange scrawls on Shaerl's letter. Ever since the accident, Gretchen's explanations for these two things had come to seem less satisfactory. They worried him more than they worried Leo, who appeared much less concerned these days about Gretchen's mental health.

"The check, please," Francine cut in abruptly as the waitress was explaining to Frank how important a variety of sensory stimuli was to preschoolers.

"Don't you think you were a little rude to her?" he asked as they walked outside. Sucking on a breath mint, he was feeling a little proud of himself for not discussing Gretchen at lunch. Proud and frustrated, for he still had so many nagging questions on his mind, like whether he should press Gretchen about her finances. She still had done nothing to get her portfolio away from her uncle in Cos Cob.

"Frank, please, I'd rather not talk about it."

"But she's a human being."

"Your eyes were shining."

"What?"

"Your eyes were positively shining when she talked to you."

"I was just trying to be polite."

"Don't make me laugh—polite."

"Francine," he said, taking her arm and leaning close, "don't be mad." He meant this as mock affection, to humor her out of this grouchy spell. But for a moment he wondered if she got the joke; so he repeated himself to make sure she did. "Aw, honey, don't be jealous of her. You're much prettier."

"You mean that?" she shot back.

It was then that he noticed the eyes upon him. As Mr. Dambar and Francine were walking past the motel office, he glanced over and saw a man inside who looked very much like Leo. Letting go of Francine, he continued a few paces before glancing back over his shoulder. With the reflection on the plate glass he couldn't tell for sure whether it was the handyman or not. The only way he would know for certain would be to go back.

"Frank?"

"Go on," he said, catching up with her. He had decided not to return. But he wished he had had more sense than to just stand there for a moment or two, as if he were paralyzed.

"What's the matter with you?"

"Nothing." He waited for her to unlock the passenger door of her Nissan.

"Hi there," he heard just as he was opening the door.

"Oh, hi," he said to a woman who did not look familiar at all. She was walking past the front of the Nissan on the way to the motel.

"Cold, huh?" She smiled and hugged herself, still walking. A chubby woman in a pink jogging outfit, she could have been one of his son's high school friends. The women sometimes changed so much that he had a hard time keeping them straight.

"Freezing," he said with a wave. She waved back, dangling a large gold key chain from her hand.

"Who was that?" Francine asked as she pulled out of the parking lot.

He shrugged. "Don't know."

"If we see any more strangers, you want me to pull over so you can chat? Really, kid, you're too much."

With a sigh he quieted the red bleeping on the dashboard by fastening his seat belt. He realized he had eaten too quickly, and he probably had not needed three drinks for lunch. It was odd, but ever since getting married, he seemed to be eating and drinking so much more than normal. Was it any wonder that he had that goddang heartburn again? Someday he should speak to Dr. McFlug about a good prescription antacid. Maybe at the next Men's Bible Study.

"Francine, mind if I grab forty winks? I'm bushed."

Chapter Nine

Hi, it's me."

"Morgan?"

"Morgan?"

"Come on, Fairchild. I know it's you."

"Henry, it's me, Gretchen."

"Oh. What's up?"

Mrs. Dambar had been trying to reach him for weeks, but he was never in. Now at three A.M. she had finally gotten through on the phone in the study. A wave of embarrassment passed over her; it seemed so dramatic calling at this hour. Henry hated family drama.

"Oh, nothing. Just thought I'd see how you were doing."

"Been real busy. Actually I'm in the middle of some editing right now."

"Oh, well, I won't be long. I was just wondering if maybe you could come visit sometime. Soon."

"Sure, Gretch. Matter of fact, I got to go up to Broadway and Ninety-second tomorrow to pick up some prints, so I'll just drop on over. We could grab a bite."

"Henry, I'm in Louisiana, remember?"

"Oh."

"I really have to talk to someone."

"Louisiana? Oh, wait, don't tell me. You got married, right? Yeah, that's it."

She was determined not to be too discouraged. It always took Henry a moment or two to get his bearings. After that he was fine.

". . . and I just have this feeling," she was saying not long afterward, when Henry had been reminded of Leo, Mrs. Howard, Shaerl, Frank, "like someone's out to get me. I have these anxiety attacks, like something is about to happen, like I'm not safe. And you know me, Henry, it's not like me. I'm not naturally paranoid, I don't think—although Dr. Stone did think I displayed some tendencies that way. Actually, sometimes I wish I *was* paranoid, that I was imagining all this. Then I wouldn't have to worry. All I'd have to do was cure myself, so to speak."

"It isn't Frank, is it?"

"What?"

"It's that gardener."

Yes, once he was in gear, Henry cut right to the bone. He knew exactly what she was talking about. She didn't have to explain. "You mean Leo, the handyman."

"There's something about him, Gretch. I—oh, right, yeah, I was splicing him by the trailer the other day. He was bringing in some turnips and when I looked at it, there was the weirdest light."

"You mean on the videotape, your diary?"

"Yeah." A long pause.

"Henry?"

"The thing about it, I couldn't remember who he was. See, I had a huge stockpile from Quito and Fez, and I thought at first he was this Berber I had met in Fez."

"What are you saying, Henry?"

Another pause. "There's some people who do something with light. The Berber, he comes across—it's hard to describe. I mean you see him on the street, in Western dress, and you don't give another look. But with the camera. Leo's that way too."

"What way?"

"I'm not sure. I guess the only word that comes close is, well, uncanny. Look, Gretchen, all I can say is, I wouldn't mess with people like that, not me. I give them a wide berth. There's some-

150

thing they know . . . I mean, I didn't realize it about Leo until I saw the tape. But when I saw you down there, I could feel something was cockeyed."

The phone, like a seashell, seemed to magnify the rush of blood in her ears—or was it just a bad connection making that distant rush of surf? "But Leo has been kind to me. He's changed. I don't know what to think now. And what do you mean by uncanny? It's a stupid word."

"OK, maybe so. But I can't help thinking the guy's in tune with something—like the Berber."

"Oh, come off it, Henry. Leo is just a mixed-up, overgrown adolescent."

"Then why does he bother you so much?"

"Well . . ."

"You're afraid of him."

"No—I mean, I do get this feeling. But I'm not going to be intimidated. It's not right. He may think he can drive me away but hell, he's met his match. I won't—Let me call you back. Bye, dear."

Hanging up quietly, she watched the door open another inch or two. Her heart seemed to have swollen to painful proportions, and yet with only a sluggish, feeble beat, like that of a clumsy animal in hibernation. "What do you want!" she whispered savagely. "Get out. Leave me—"

"Hon?" It was Frank. "You all right?"

Relief got her pulse back to normal. "Oh, darling, why did you open the door like that? You gave me a real turn."

"I thought you might be asleep. I didn't want to wake you." Hugging his bare chest, his toes curled on the oak block, he felt too vulnerable and wished he had put on a robe. "I saw the light on," he added, hoping to appease her. Her voice, when he had walked in, had been chilling. Never before had he heard her sound like that. It was almost as if she were a different woman.

She took a sip of the wine beside the phone.

"What are you doing?"

"Nothing."

He had heard her on the phone. Standing outside the door he had tried to make out whom she could have been talking to, but her voice had been too guarded, indistinct. "Working on your book?"

"Yes. I mean, no." She could not lie to him, no matter how convenient it might be. "Frank, there is no book. I've been fooling myself all along. No one's going to want to publish anything I write about the Philippines. I mean, why aren't I in the Philippines if I'm such an expert? What am I doing here?" She glanced at the almost empty wine glass, hoping he wouldn't think she had been drinking. It was only her second glass that evening.

"You're too hard on yourself, honey."

"Please don't call me that," she put in hurriedly, before she forgot. It was something she had been meaning to tell him for a long time.

"What?"

"Hon, honey. I hate that word. And I wish Mrs. Howard wouldn't insist on having it at breakfast."

With a puzzled shrug Mr. Dambar asked if maybe she would like to come back to bed. "It's after three, you know."

"No, Frank. We got to talk." She was determined to communicate with him, to find out what it was that was making him back away from her. Was he really that upset about the carpet, the cow? Was it the dent in the Buick? Just what was the problem between them?

"Maybe it would be better when you've . . ." His eye was on the wine glass.

"One glass, Frank. That's all—one and a half. Now listen, we have got to talk."

Mr. Dambar feared the worst. Leo must have said something to her about seeing Francine and him at the Ramada Inn in Ozone. He should have talked to the boy after the incident, explained to him how they had just been eating there, taking advantage of the all-you-can-eat buffet. But he was afraid that too many protestations of innocence, too many explanations, would have aroused the handyman's suspicions. And he had hoped at the same time that it had not been Leo standing in the motel office—just someone who looked like him.

"Let's talk in bed, Gretchen. Come on, darling."

She was tempted. The look in his eye, the soft, tan, naked torso were hard to resist. Their lovemaking was still highly charged, as if whatever happened during the day were an entirely different life, happening to different people. No matter how angry or resentful he might be because of the cow, the accident, it seemed to have no bearing on his passion. By now, without any explanations from him, she had caught on. Feeling a little degraded, but desperate for this bond between them, she would go along with his requests. They were modest, after all, nothing beyond an innocent fantasy that he would have blushed to talk about.

"How long have you been working here?" he might say.

"A week."

"Yes, I saw you polishing the scones the other day."

"You mean the sconces, sir."

"Are you being impertinent? You realize who I am, don't you?"

Of course, if it ever got out of hand, if he made her dress up or bring a mop to bed, then she would draw the line. But these stories they played out, usually with little variation on the script, surely they couldn't be doing any harm. As a matter of fact, she herself was beginning to respond to them in a furtive way, perhaps as a vent for frustrated leftist sympathies. It was something of a relief to escape the burden, for an hour or so, of being overprivileged.

"Darling." He had approached the desk. She felt the warmth of his arms around her pajama top. "Bed."

"No, Frank. Not yet, please. Oh, don't." It was so difficult to push him away. Yet she had to, she knew. "Sit over there, angel, please. We must talk. Frank, if we can't communicate, if we can't be completely honest with each other, then . . . We've got to try."

Rubbing the goose bumps on his arms, he sat down on the edge of the brocade chair, from behind which a little cloud of steam rose—a humidifier's. "By the way, you know the other day when you went out rowing," he said, stalling for time, "did you happen to notice a painting in the boat?"

"Yes, as a matter of fact."

"Oh good, I've been looking for it."

"One of Dr. Jonsen's, right? What was it doing there, Frank?"

"I was hiding it from Shaerl. I thought it would make a nice present, sort of a going-away gift, you know."

More gifts, she thought. Not even the Trobriand Islanders went this far with such elaborate exchanges. And at least their gift-giving had a sacred meaning, helping them to get over some sort of ritual guilt for being alive. "She's not going for another month, right? Anyway, why a Dr. Jonsen? I thought you didn't like him."

He shrugged.

"Well, you'll just have to ask him to give you another."

"What do you mean?"

"I accidentally . . ." She was about to say "lost it." But there must not be any more lies between them, white or otherwise. "I guess I threw it."

"Pardon?"

"I threw it at some sort of animal. I was scared. I thought it might try to get in the scull with me." He regarded her for a moment uneasily, before saying, "Let me get this straight. You say you threw Dr. Jonsen's landscape at some sort of animal?"

"A beaver or rat or something. I've never seen anything like it before in my life. It was awful. Anyway, that's not what I wanted to discuss."

Sensing a moral advantage, Mr. Dambar was loath to change the subject. He asked her if she realized how much the landscape had cost. He wondered how she would feel if Dr. Jonsen had thrown her book on the Philippines at a rat.

"It wasn't a rat."

"Well then, what was it?"

"What does it matter what it was? It was some sort of in-between mammal, like it might have been a member of the rodent family. Only it was big, and stop looking at me that way. I've only had one and a half glasses, that's all."

It was probably a nutria that she had seen, a common enough animal in these parts. But he wasn't sure if it would be wise to give her the name right away. It might encourage her to pass on to other topics that he wasn't up to discussing at three in the morning.

"Where are you going, Frank?"

He had gotten up and was padding toward the door. "I'm sorry, hon, but I don't have the strength to stay up discussing strange mythical beasts. I'm tired and I've got to go to work in the morning. Now come to bed."

There was enough wine left for one healthy gulp. She took it, closing her eyes as if it were bitter medicine, and followed him into the other room.

After the accident Mrs. Dambar had become a little concerned that she had no license. Shaerl had told her that Mrs. Howard wanted to make an official report to the sheriff's office. She was afraid it was illegal not to. But Shaerl had reasoned with her. "I explained that the sheriff would probably want to see your license, you know, since she was going to report you, too. And I remembered you told me once you didn't have one. Well, Mrs. Howard fussed and said how she wasn't going to go to jail on account of you. I didn't realize how scared of the law she is. Anyway, I calmed her down and told her I'd clean all the tanks in the humidifiers for her. She hates to do that, see." Mrs. Dambar thanked her for her intervention, and one day, not long afterward, Shaerl accompanied Mrs. Dambar to the Department of Motor Vehicles.

"They really could use a light here," Mrs. Dambar commented as they were about to pull out onto the highway. Waiting for a break in the traffic, she glanced doubtfully at the large, tawny dog that was lying in the road beside the car. Someone should really do something about that beast, she thought. It was a real nuisance. "No one ever slows down to let you in."

"Hm?" Shaerl, who had decided to keep her hair blonde for a while, was engrossed in a book of essays. She had been accepted at L.S.U. in the M.B.A. program and was determined to get a head start on the reading list for the summer session.

"It would really help, a light."

"Oh, here? Yeah, I know. Leo tried when he was in the hospital." She was able to talk while reading, it seemed.

"Last week?"

"Hm? No, I mean years ago, after Jane was killed."

155

"But what do you mean, in the hospital?"

She looked up from the book. "Hm? Well, he was all banged up, in pretty bad shape. Least that's what my mom said."

"What happened?"

Shaerl looked perturbed. "What do you mean, Gretchen? Jane was killed, that's what happened. And Leo was almost killed."

"He was in the car with her?"

"Of course."

"Driving?"

"What? No, she was."

"But he was there—Leo?"

"Didn't you know?"

Mrs. Dambar's knuckles were white on the steering wheel. She was going to try to cut in after the dump truck that was barreling past the Pepsi sign. "I—no one told me, no." She pulled out onto the highway.

For the rest of the way into town Shaerl read, leaving Mrs. Dambar to her own thoughts. She had a session the next day at the mall with Brenda and was planning how she would calmly and rationally explain that she did not wish to continue with her. Brenda, of course, would assume it was because of the Brandi incident. Failing to see the larger implications, she would simply accuse her, Gretchen, of giving in to paranoid feelings, letting them control her life. Gretchen felt she had to make it clear that it had nothing to do with paranoia. Dr. Lahey had made an error in judgment by not being up front with her about Leo. It was ridiculous for Brenda to pretend that her own personal history had nothing to do with Gretchen's present concerns. As a matter of fact, Gretchen saw it as a sign of mental health that she herself was not taking the blame for the break-up. How many times in the past when she had found it necessary to leave a therapist had she loaded herself down with guilt? Those had been such agonizing decisions. But this one seemed so clear-cut. Of course, she would give Brenda a chance to apologize and come clean about Leo. If Brenda did, then Gretchen might possibly reconsider her decision. But otherwise, she had made up her mind.

"Look, the Jeep," Shaerl remarked when they were downtown

156

opposite the Tchefuncta Bank and Trust. The building was drab save for a curious miniature temple atop the tarred roof, the Doric columns casting their shadow over the Jeep's hood.

"I thought Leo was seeing about the cow today."

"Frank," Shaerl said, returning to her book. "He's got a board meeting at the bank."

"Oh."

Two blocks later she was still hurting from this slight. Why couldn't Frank have told her he was coming to town? Well, it was ridiculous to brood about it, she knew. She had to stop being so self-centered. "What's that you're reading?"

The maid didn't answer.

"Shaerl?"

"Hm? Oh. Keynes, something called 'Economic Possibilities for Our Grandchildren.'"

"Oh, John Maynard Keynes, how nice."

"Kanes, not Keenes," Shaerl corrected.

Mrs. Dambar blushed. "Is it good?"

"No, it's weird. Listen to this: 'There is no country and no people'—better signal, we're turning left here—'no people who can look forward to the age of leisure and abundance without a dread.' Why does he say weird things like that? It's so stupid."

"Shaerl, he happens to be one of the greatest—"

"I don't care how great he is. He doesn't have an ounce of common sense. I mean, what he's saying is, if I inherit a million dollars I'm going to be scared or something? What is this? I'm so tired of being the only one around with any common sense."

Not knowing quite how to take this outburst, Mrs. Dambar decided the girl didn't mean "only" in a literal sense. Surely there was one exception in her mind. "I know what you mean. The way people have been acting around the house, sometimes you have to wonder. You know, Shaerl, I often think about your uncle."

Plucking a loose thread from her Italian hand-knit sweater, Shaerl remained noncommittal.

"What is he doing with his life, anyway? He seems like a bright enough person, yet all he does besides putter around the house is write these ridiculous letters to inmates."

"He has a good heart. He feels sorry for them."

"That's all well and fine. Everybody should be involved in some charity or other. I used to read for the blind, you know. I made tapes of the classics—'The Beast in the Jungle' and all that. But still . . . Has he ever been institutionalized?"

"What?"

"Does he have a history?" She had decided to be blunt. It was a risk, but she was not one to be afraid of risks. "Tell me, Shaerl. I want to know the truth. I would rather not wake up one day with an axe in my skull and . . ." The look she was getting from her made her backtrack a little. "I'm just joking, of course. But I mean, Leo does display some interesting character disorders, you have to admit."

"You know, you can be sort of mean, Gretchen."

"What?"

"Just because Leo doesn't fit into your preconceptions of what a person should do—like just because he doesn't have a nine-to-five job and he lets his hair grow long . . . You really hurt his feelings about the cow, too. He knows you don't like him, but he thought that if he did something nice for you, you might somehow overcome your prejudice and accept him. That's all he wants, to be accepted."

"Shaerl, that's so unfair. I've leaned over backward to accept him, to welcome him." Even as she said this, she knew it was not quite true—and it disturbed her.

"How? What have you ever done for him? You've never given him a single present and you gave Mrs. Howard that shepherd thing, remember?"

"But it was her birthday."

"How do you know it's not Leo's birthday? Have you ever bothered to ask him when it is? And he didn't wait for your birthday to give you the cow. And now you're making him send it back."

"But it makes such strange noises. You yourself said it was keeping you awake. Is this it?" she added quickly, seeing the Wal-Mart sign.

"Yes, turn."

The Department of Motor Vehicles was directly in back of

Wal-Mart, where Shaerl would do some shopping while she waited for Mrs. Dambar. Very considerately Mrs. Dambar pulled right up to the main entrance and let her out before driving around to the barracks of the state troopers. "Shouldn't they see me driving you up?" Shaerl asked as she got out. "You're not supposed to be driving yet, right?"

"It's all right. If they ask, I'll just say you did."

A few minutes later, after parking in back of the giant store and checking her makeup and hair, which was no longer greenish thanks to a new brand name Shaerl had discovered, she pulled open the screen door to a Quonset hut that had the state seal upon it. Although she didn't like to think in stereotypes, Mrs. Dambar couldn't help recoiling at the sight of a beefy state trooper with a florid face and mirrored sunglasses, the epitome of Southern racism. He looked at her as if he could tell what she was thinking.

"Ma'am?"

"I'm here to get my license."

"This here's hunting and fishing. Motor vehicle's next door."

She could see two of herself in the reflecting lenses, which had grotesquely foreshortened her. It was so sexist of him to assume she would not want a hunting or fishing license. Of course, she deplored both activities, but this was beside the point. About to turn and go, she had second thoughts. She was not going to let herself be bullied by this Neanderthal.

"I would like a hunting license."

His powerful jaw moved with stereotypical insolence as he chewed his cud. She braced herself, waiting for his refusal. But before he could manage to say anything, a lanky, pot-bellied young man—not in uniform—had strolled up to him. "What's up, Mel?" the trooper asked.

The young man, college-age it seemed, pointed toward a shapely blonde trooper, who had just emerged from an office. "Desirée said I should ask you first about that CB and—"

"Hold on a minute. Let me take care of this here lady. Ma'am, you want a hunting license, you go to the counter there and Judy will be right with you. Now Mel," he said, turning to the young man, who had very awkward posture, "I don't care what you and Desirée cook up so long as I don't have to do no explaining, hear? I'm through with the explaining, son."

Mrs. Dambar was hoping they would join the blonde trooper in back so she could leave without actually having to apply for a license at the counter. But it was just her luck that Judy had overheard. The black woman beckoned her from behind a counter decorated with magazine photos of sunfish, oysters, and a Hudsonian curlew. "Step over here," she said in a no-nonsense tone of voice.

Mrs. Dambar complied.

On the way home from the board meeting at the bank, Mr. Dambar made a detour onto the Old Jeff Davis Highway to see how Leo was doing. As he was pulling up to the handyman's regular spot, about a hundred yards down the road from the doughnut trailer, he was glad to see there were customers. Leo often sat for hours without selling a single catfish, though it didn't seem to bother him. Slouched in his lawn chair, his feet propped up on an ice chest, he would mull over Böhme or Fichte while the cars whizzed past. Later the unsold fish would be buried in the garden, as fertilizer.

"Frank."

"Frank."

He was already upon them; too late to pretend he hadn't seen them. Mrs. Keely had spoken first as Leo handed her a fish. Mrs. Bill Anderson echoed her. Her fish was in the scale.

"Well, I see Leo is doing a land-office business today." He winked at Mrs. Keely, whose silver chignon was unperturbed by the gust from a passing recreational van. Mr. Dambar patted his own straying locks.

The business of paying for the fish preoccupied the women for a few moments while Mr. Dambar fiddled with the bar of soap dangling from a nearby branch. Zest, the punctured wrapper proclaimed. Leo hung these bars to ward off deer. A St. Jude College Extension Wildlife Specialist had recommended this practice on TV, though why Leo felt it necessary to keep deer away seemed unclear. Perhaps they ate the leaves.

"Deer hate soap, you know," he commented, turning to the ladies.

"Oh?"

"I wonder why."

Mr. Dambar shrugged. "It's just one of those things, I guess."

Her alligator purse slung over her shoulder, Mrs. Bill Anderson clutched in both hands the plastic bag with her beheaded fish. Though she was smartly dressed and fully made up, she looked tired and unfocused. "I was just saying to Leo how sorry I was he couldn't make it to the sixties dance—and he told me about the accident. What a shame, Frank."

"Accident?" Mrs. Keely said as she opened her car door.

"Yes, Mr. Dambar was run off the road—nearly killed."

"Oh my." On the verge of dipping into the driver's seat, Mrs. Keely paused and gave him a searching look. "Are you all right, Frank?"

"Fine, actually—"

"They all had to go to the hospital," Mrs. Bill Anderson went on, "and Mr. Dambar was operated on."

"Who is they all, Dot?"

"Leo and his niece and Mrs. Howard."

"Well, actually, see, I was—Dr. Jonsen had scheduled me for a look at my . . . thing."

"Are you sure you should be up and about?" Mrs. Keely was talking from the car now, the window rolled down. "Your what? Oh, I'm so sorry to hear. These dreadful maniacs they let drive. Why, just the other day, Wednesday I believe it was, Dot and I were coming home from the most wonderful luncheon in Ozone, all professors, very distinguished, you know, so well preserved, and this perfectly awful man in a red something or other pulled right out in front of me with no warning. You remember, Dot. I so much wanted to give him a piece of my mind."

"You should have. Oh, Frank," Mrs. Bill Anderson added from the passenger side, leaning toward Mrs. Keely's window, "you heard about your bid? I phoned Mrs. Sklar yesterday. It was very kind of you to . . ."

"Participate," Mrs. Keely supplied.

"Yes, I just wanted to thank you personally on behalf of the Building Fund Committee."

The bid had not been accepted, Mr. Dambar had heard from Mrs. Sklar. In a way, he was glad. Though they really needed the business, it would have meant frequent consultations with Mrs. Bill Anderson, which was why he had estimated the labor costs a fraction on the high side.

"Well, better luck next time," he called out glibly with a wave—and instantly regretted it. He had meant better luck for *him* next time, but the way her face had fallen, he was afraid she had interpreted it as better luck for her. What a stupid thing to say! And Mrs. Keely had already pulled away. He couldn't explain now.

"Gee, Leo, do you really think you should have told them about the accident?" Mr. Dambar had wandered back over to the ice chest.

The handyman looked up from his book. "She asked me about my eye. What was I supposed to say?" Though the swelling had gone down, his eye was still discolored by some yellowish marbling.

"Well, I hope you didn't say anything about Gretchen. And you didn't have to make it sound so dramatic." With a faint smile he reined in his peevishness. This was not what he had come to talk about. There was no sense in putting Leo on the defensive. "Anyway . . ." Grit from the highway made him cough. "How are sales going?"

"Eleven dollars and thirty-two cents."

"Well, you haven't been out here long, right?"

"All morning."

"But I thought you were seeing about the cow?"

Leo stroked his ponytail. "Moon gave me a buzz. Said he couldn't make it till next week. He's having problems with a feeder."

"Moon is the guy with the livestock truck?"

"You got it."

Mr. Dambar settled down onto the ice chest, but rose when Leo asked him not to sit there, please. The hinges were loose and might bust. "Well," Mr. Dambar said, trying to look casual and relaxed while standing up. There was nowhere else to sit. "You didn't tell Mrs. Anderson it was Gretchen, did you?"

"Gretchen what?"

"Who caused the accident."

"Why should I?"

"Well, good. See, sometimes people can get the wrong impression. Appearances can be pretty deceiving sometimes, wouldn't you say?"

With a hand shading his eyes Leo continued to regard his employer disinterestedly, as if Mr. Dambar were a dubious philosophical proposition.

"Like the other day, for instance. Here I was taking advantage of the all-you-can-eat at the Ramada Inn in Ozone, a real bargain. And it's so close to the condos, too, right down the street. That's where we had been, my coworker and me. You know Mrs. Sklar is questioning the Chapter Eleven reorganization, and I'm concerned about foreclosure proceedings on The Antibes that might be filed in U.S. District Court. And wouldn't you know that my coworker has convinced Mrs. Sklar that there's still a way for us to come out on top." Here he was telling the exact truth, and he sounded, even to himself, as if he were covering something up. It was unfair. "So we stopped to have a bite to eat and I'll be darned if there wasn't a guy that looked just like you, only I wasn't sure and my colleague was in a hurry to get back to work so anyway . . . She's not really very attractive, is she?"

"OK, Mr. D, so you saw us. Big deal. I mean, like I'm not supposed to have any friends? And great, so she's not Miss America. At least Brenda's for real."

"Brenda?"

"She's just a friend. We just happened to be . . . She had a meeting in Ozone and I, you know, those tiles. I was checking out some tiles for the back bathroom."

"Tiles? Oh, right." Slowly it dawned on him: Leo must have a sweetheart. And all these years he had been thinking there was something not quite right about the handyman. What a sly dog he was.

"All I meant to say, Leo . . ." Mr. Dambar struggled with a

smile. It was such a relief to find out that the boy was normal, that he knew how to have some fun for himself. "I didn't see a thing."

Leo picked up his book. "Neither did I, Mr. D."

"What? You mean me? But there was nothing to see."

"Just what I said. Didn't see a thing."

His good humor was fast dissolving. It wasn't fair for Leo to put this slant on things. After all, Mr. Dambar was completely innocent. Why should he find himself in the same category with Leo and his secret admirer, whoever she was? He hadn't been sneaking around. Francine was just a colleague. He didn't even find her attractive. "Leo, maybe you don't understand what I was trying to say. I—"

"Hey, relax, man. Don't get so uptight. Nothing happened, right? We're fine, you and me."

Though he wanted to protest, Mr. Dambar knew that any more plain honest truth would only make him seem more guilty. In any case, there was only one thing that really mattered—that Leo hadn't said anything to Gretchen.

"You didn't happen to . . ."

"What? Mrs. D?" Leo completed while Mr. Dambar got back into the Jeep. "Say something to Mrs. D? Do I look insane or what? Come on, Frank, relax."

"Well, I, you know." He started the engine in what he hoped was a nonchalant way. "So wait a minute, how did you get out here? Didn't Shaerl and Gretchen take the Buick?"

"Got a lift from that kid down the street. His dog was messing with the cow this morning."

"Oh. What time are you calling it quits?"

"Come get me around five, OK?"

Mr. Dambar eyed the oncoming traffic. "You know, we really ought to get another car. Someday I got to make up my mind to do it." Glancing over, he saw he was talking to himself. Leo had returned to his Böhme.

Mrs. Howard loomed into view at the other end of the pasture while they were out inspecting the cow. The housekeeper had put on galoshes to make the trek out to the barbed-wire fence, from where she could yell, "Phone!"

"Me?" Mr. Dambar pointed at himself.

"The other one!"

Mrs. Dambar rolled her eyes—and unwittingly caught sight of a swallow flicking batlike in the dusk. "I'll just be a minute."

When she returned, Mr. Dambar had wandered away from the cow, who had been induced to eat a special mash that Marge Tilly, the banker's wife, had concocted. Marge was good with animals and played a mean game of tennis.

"She's looking a little better, don't you think?" Mrs. Dambar slapped at a mosquito on her husband's neck. He winced. "Poor Lurleen."

"I wish you wouldn't call her that."

"Leo told me that's her name, Frank."

"I know. But you shouldn't get attached. And by the way, who is Mel?"

"Mel?"

"The person you were just on the phone with." Mrs. Howard had called out the name to him before she had trudged back to the house.

"Oh, him. I don't know. Just someone I met at the state troopers."

"What?"

"I was there getting my license."

"Oh, right." He regarded a clump of papery wildflowers for a moment before plucking a stem for the bouquet he was collecting. A vase in the foyer always held blooms from the pasture year-round. "Why was he calling?"

"Who? You mean Mel? Well, you see I failed the eye exam because I brought the wrong glasses and he . . ."

"Wait, when you got back you told me you got your license."

"I got *a* license, yes. It just didn't happen to be a driver's license." She glanced over at Lurleen, who was beginning to grow on her. The poor beast no longer seemed so menacing, and her noises had become somewhat more conventional.

"What other kind of license is there?"

"Oh really, Frank, it's nothing." She had hoped he would drop the subject so that she wouldn't be forced to be honest again. "Just an alligator hunting license."

He had leaned over to pick up a trial-size sample of a feminine hygiene product, no doubt dropped by the horse's teenage owner. "Hold on, you got a license for—"

"It's really easy to get one. If you'd like to borrow it sometime, dear . . ."

"Gretchen," he said, handing her the sample, "all I hear is how much you hate hunting and the next thing I know you go out and get yourself a hunting license."

"Yes, I know. But alligators are different, wouldn't you say? They're not at all like deer. And besides, I have no intention of using it. I'm going to send it to Molly as a little souvenir. She'll get a kick out of something so indigenous." She glanced at the packet in her hand, wondering what he meant by giving it to her like that, as if she were some sort of walking trash bin. With a sigh she tucked it into the pocket of her khaki trousers. "Frank, you know last night when you came into the study? Well, we never did have our talk, did we? Do you feel like talking now, maybe?"

Still trying to digest her explanation for the hunting license, he stood mutely before a clump of spiky white flowers. She repeated her request.

"Well, what is it, Gretchen?"

"I want to know, A, if you regret marrying me and—"

"No."

"B, if you still love me."

"Yes."

Though the answers were correct, they were not eminently satisfying. Taking his arm, she aimed him toward the billboard, a distance that should give her enough time to get her point across. "If you'll bear with me, Frank, just let me try to explain how I've . . . How recently there seems to be some sort of breakdown in communication between us. Sometimes, to tell the truth, I feel so alone, more alone than I've ever felt in my entire life. That can't be right, can it? I mean, that wasn't exactly my intention when I got married, to see if I could die of loneliness."

"Why do you exaggerate like that?"

Here would be an appropriate place for tears, yet none were forthcoming. And yet they flowed so freely whenever there was a squabble over Mrs. Howard's ironing or the way she folded towels. "I'm not really exaggerating. Maybe just a little," she amended as a concession to her goal of total honesty between man and wife. "The point is, Frank, that I think you owe it to me in some way to listen to my views on certain subjects. And if you don't agree, well, fine. But at least give me a fair hearing."

He switched his bouquet from one hand, which was getting sweaty, to the other. "By certain subjects, you mean?"

"Leo, for instance. Why should I be afraid to tell you what I really think of him? I'm tired of hiding my feelings from you."

"Why do you?"

"Because I'm terrified that you'll get mad at me, that you'll leave me."

"Don't be ridiculous. I won't get mad."

"All right, then. The truth is, Frank, I feel threatened. I don't know why or how or by what or . . . All I know is that deep down, I feel very insecure. And I think it's your duty as my husband to protect me, to make me feel safe."

He paused to remove a burr from his suit pants. "How can you—"

"Please, Frank, let me talk. I'm not saying I know anything for sure—except deep down inside. Something's going on. Now the next thing you're going to say is how wonderful Leo is, how sensitive, how wounded and brilliant. Fine. I've heard that over and over again and I've done my best to see things from your point of view. There's only one problem: It doesn't work. I don't buy it. Something inside me is saying, No. I've tried to smother this voice, but I can't. And I think if you have any respect for me at all, you should begin to at least ask yourself if you are totally one hundred percent right. Is it possible that I may see something you don't? Like a blind spot when you're driving. From your perspective everything may

167

look just fine and dandy, but maybe from where I'm coming from, well maybe I can see things from a slightly different angle, and spot the lion's tail behind the bush. I mean, what's the sense of two people going out hunting together if only one of them is allowed to see?" Her tropes were a little heavy-handed, she realized, but she knew he liked hunting and wanted to maintain his interest. In any case, exhilarated by so much honesty, she could not stop herself. "And another thing, Frank. I'm simply going to have to tell you about that house. It's the ugliest thing I've ever seen. Now don't get upset. I'm not criticizing you. I'm talking about that structure back there"—an arm gestured in the general direction of the house—"that totally material pile of wood and stuff that has nothing to do with what a wonderful, loving man you are. I'm perfectly willing to live with it, but I want you to know that it offends me, my aesthetic sensibility. Yes, I wanted the carpet out of the study. And by God, if it were up to me I'd like to see everything royal blue out the window, and the furniture, too. But I can live with it, Frank. I don't care if it did come from a funeral parlor—if that's what you like, then fine. But I just can't help wondering if you've ever noticed a place like Dr. Jonsen's, how tasteful the furnishing is, so spare and simple, yet real quality. Look, I'm not a materialist, so all this doesn't matter. I probably could adjust to living in a cave. In fact, it'd probably be easier for me to adjust to rocks than to all those scrolls and paws and paste flowers and . . . Anyway . . ."

He had stopped walking and was regarding her with a face that looked strangely similar to that of the master she worked for in the bedroom. "Anything else, Gretchen?"

The look convinced her that they had had enough honesty for one day. "No, that's it for now—" She caught herself from adding, "sir."

"Shall we go back?"

"Yes, Frank, dear—the mosquitoes are . . . Hold still, there's another one on your neck." And she slapped him ever so gently.

Chapter Ten

He was twenty-seven, but his awkwardness took off a good five years. Without the potbelly he would have had a pleasant, lanky build, but the mound, which was abrupt, seemed to throw his whole body out of kilter. His large hands, bony and sensitive, were in constant motion while he talked, probing the air about him like antennae. Mrs. Dambar was not sure she had done the right thing by hiring him, even if it was, as she hastened to point out, only on a very temporary basis. "You understand, Mel, there can't be anything official about this. I still haven't made up my mind if I like the idea."

Mel Tempel lived at home with his stepfather and Mr. Ames, his stepfather's uncle. His office, on the second floor of the frame house, had its own private entrance, an outdoor staircase, just over the kitchen. While Mrs. Dambar and he talked, the smell of frying was accompanied by occasional grunts from the uncle downstairs, who did all the cooking. Mel had befriended Mrs. Dambar at the barracks behind Wal-Mart, easing her through the application for the hunting license. He seemed to enjoy a privileged status there, the clerk allowing him behind the counter to borrow Scotch tape, the troopers themselves bantering with him as if he were a kid brother. From what she could gather, Mrs. Dambar speculated that he must run errands for them and from time to time assisted in unofficial ways with the routine legwork in various investigations.

In the evenings he drove to the Lewis Mason Career Academy in Baton Rouge, where he was taking courses in weapons theory, baton and teargas, search and seizure, powers of arrest, self-defense, and first aid and CPR. During the day, when there was nothing going on at the barracks and he had put in his two-hour stint of dispatching for Tula Springs' Citizens Patrol, Mel would drag himself to his office to earn his keep. He was a C.P.A., but his heart wasn't in it.

"By the way, would you like me to do your taxes? I'm not very expensive."

Mrs. Dambar declined this offer.

"How about investment strategies? If you have a couple thousand you could spare, I could really make it go to work for you—medium to low risk."

"Mel, if you don't mind, I'd rather concentrate on Mr. Vogel. Now, as I was saying, do you think it was a good idea to call the house like you did the other day? My husband is beginning to wonder who you are. And Mr. Vogel himself could easily pick up the phone."

Fingering his Adam's apple, he appeared to consider this. "What should I do then? How do I talk to you?"

"Well . . ." Somehow it didn't seem quite fair to her that she had to think of this. After all, he was the one studying in Baton Rouge. "Why don't I call you at a certain time every day?"

"But suppose I have to ask you an urgent question, something that won't wait?"

"Well, then say you're from the public library or something. Like a book I wanted has come in. But for God's sake, don't just say 'it's Mel' and act so mysterious."

"How about if I pretend to be a relative? I mean that way I could come visit you, check out the place, see how Mr. Vogel . . ."

Leaning toward the sofa Mel was stretched out on, she placed a finger over his lips. "Cease. Desist, Mel. You must not come to the house. And I don't want you to be a relative. Are you listening? No relatives. I'm from New York, and my husband knows I don't have any relatives down here."

Mel winced as he tried to sit up. His back was bothering him, a pinched nerve.

"Stay still. Don't get up, Mel."

He sank back onto the faded corduroy. "Well, I would like to have a go at that trailer he lives in."

"Listen, I'm going to call this whole thing off if I hear you say that again. You can't sneak in there. Not only would Leo—Mr. Vogel—know you'd been there, but it's against the law. I'm not going to have anyone breaking and entering on my account."

Despite his awkwardness, Mel had a charming, open face that was enhanced by a warm, caring, yet very manly and competent-sounding voice. Hearing him on the telephone, a woman could easily conjure up fantasies of movie-star good looks. All this, combined with a totally unself-conscious manner of pure, unadulterated friendliness, had quickly broken down any defenses Mrs. Dambar might have had at the barracks. After a few minutes of small talk it was as if they were already old friends. Having helped her get the alligator license by talking the clerk into bending a few rules for her, he had accompanied her to the other Quonset hut for the eye test. Though she failed it, he made her laugh by telling her something personal about the woman who had administered the test. The next thing she knew they were involved in an intense discussion about Leo. "I could tell something was troubling you the minute I saw you," he would say from time to time as he refilled her Styrofoam cup with coffee from the pot the Motor Vehicle clerks used. To tell her story to this outside, objective person was even more exhilarating than telling the complete truth to her husband. There was no skepticism in Mel's eyes, no faint smile, no prejudices to overcome. And what was most gratifying was that Mel believed her. He said that he thought it highly possible that the handyman could be up to something. The evidence was in her favor. And he was so kind and considerate in regard to Frank. This was what had really won her over. "I've seen it over and over again, Gretchen. The closer you are to someone, the blinder you can be. Frank is a good guy, right, so all he sees in other people is good, too. He's so used to Mr. Vogel that Mr. Vogel could probably chop up Mrs. Henry right before—"

"Howard, Mrs. Howard. Henry is my cousin."

"Mrs. Howard right before his very eyes and still believe Mr. Vogel was innocent."

Bit by bit she had pieced the story together for him, at least as much as she could before Shaerl had waved to her from the door. She was through shopping in Wal-Mart and anxious to get home.

"Oh, here's an expense item," Mel said now as his hand strayed to the coffee table beside the sofa. Mrs. Dambar looked at it—$3.75 for catfish.

"I had to buy something to make it look real."

"That's fine, Mel." She dug in her purse and found the exact amount. "Anything else?"

He shook his head.

"No information? What about that woman I told you about, Brenda Lahey?"

Though she had determined several times to stop seeing the therapist, Mrs. Dambar kept on putting off the actual confrontation. Every time she got in the office she would let herself be swayed by Dr. Lahey's opinions—that it really was wrong of Gretchen to pry into her personal life. Brenda took a firm stand about answering any questions about her relationship with Leo, and for fifty minutes the stand would seem eminently reasonable. But once Gretchen had left the office, her doubts would return with a vengeance. She hoped Mel could in some way substantiate these doubts. In the meantime, she knew she would have to stop seeing the therapist. At the next session—or maybe the one after the next—she would inform the woman that their relationship was terminated.

"Uh, Lahey, the doctor, right? Yes, I called on her house and ascertained that she does have a husband living there."

"What do you mean you called on the house?"

"I pretended to be lost and asked for directions. He was home alone, and I was able to pick up a bit of info that may come in handy. In the meantime I plan to pay a visit to the mall. Probably tomorrow."

"To her office? But you can't do that."

"I can't?"

"What are you going to say?"

"I thought I might pretend to be a patient—have a session or two with her."

She closed her eyes and rubbed her forehead. "Now, Mel, you don't seem to understand. The whole point is for you not to be noticed. If she keeps seeing you—and her husband . . . That isn't really how you follow someone around." Distressed that, yet again, she was giving him advice about his job, she thought seriously about calling the whole thing off. He had seemed so much more competent in the Department of Motor Vehicles. And he had told her he had had years of experience. Brooding over this, she was unable to make up her mind, mainly because on a personal level he was such a fine young man. If she fired him now, surely she would destroy his confidence in himself. She really did like him and hoped that one day he would get on in the world.

The interview concluded on this unsatisfactory note. He promised to be more discreet in the future. And he refused to accept the six dollars she offered him for the hour he had spent in the sheriff's office looking for the report on Jane Dambar's accident. If he had found it, he would have taken the fee for the hourly rate they had agreed upon. Mrs. Dambar tried to insist, but got nowhere with him on this score.

Later that day Mrs. Dambar reviewed the notes she had made for her appointment with the therapist. "Be firm, not militant. Professional responsibility. Don't make issue of Leo. Do not protest, deny. Be positive." She was working up the courage to tell Dr. Lahey that she no longer wished to see her. Earlier, in the morning, she had thought that she might need another week to prepare herself. She knew that Brenda would accuse her of giving in to paranoid feelings, which really wasn't the case at all. It was simply a matter of trust. Of course, she still liked the woman quite a bit. Brenda would have to understand that this wasn't easy for her, that the decision had come only after a long struggle with herself. But Mrs. Dambar was feeling clear-headed. Being honest with Frank the other day had helped restore her confidence. Perhaps she still wasn't quite sure how Frank had taken her outburst in the pasture concerning Leo and the house. He tended to be guarded these days, hard to read. But at least he hadn't yelled at her or called her crazy. That was something.

When she walked past the electrologist's office she saw Dr. Lahey standing outside her door. It made her apprehensive. Brenda always waited inside for her clients, who were buzzed in. With a sinking feeling, as if she were the one who had something to feel guilty about, Mrs. Dambar avoided the therapist's eyes as the door was held open for her.

"How are you, Gretchen? I couldn't wait to see you today."

It wasn't just the words, but the tone of voice that gave Mrs. Dambar pause. She sounded so warm, so personable. Taking her accustomed place in the La-Z-Boy—not reclining this time, however—Mrs. Dambar could not help noticing the soft glow that seemed to transform the therapist's face. She had never looked so peaceful, content. And the habitual neutral gaze had been replaced by something Mrs. Dambar could not really identify.

"Brenda, what is it?"

"You can tell?"

"I don't know. You look so . . . So happy?"

Dr. Lahey wiped away a tear that had suddenly welled up. "I just got back from the doctor. Gretchen, you have no idea what I've been going through these past few years. I . . . Oh, what am I saying. I shouldn't be talking like this."

"No, please, go ahead."

"But this is your session." She sniffled like a little girl. "We can talk afterward."

"Brenda, please. You can't leave me hanging like this."

The therapist pulled up her black vinyl chair so that their knees were almost touching. "OK, you asked for it. I probably wouldn't have been able to listen to you anyway, not today. Oh, this is so unprofessional. I really should be ashamed, but . . ." She threw up her hands in mock resignation, a somewhat stiff, self-conscious gesture. "We didn't know what was wrong, Gretchen. We did everything possible to make it right. I even went to Oshner's for an operation on my tubes. They thought it might be that, a trauma that goes way back to a bike accident I had on a Girl Scout trip. But it didn't seem to do much good, the operation. Sid and I had charts,

174

when to do it, optimum time for intercourse, temperature. He was such an angel to put up with it, too. He never complained. And it was becoming so mechanical for us, like we were some sort of breeding animals. Gretchen, you have no idea how depressed it made me. And every year I was getting older and older—thirty-nine now. Just last week we had gone to Ozone to see about this Vietnamese girl. I already had a name picked out for her. And then, just today, during my lunch hour . . ."

Gretchen let out a little involuntary cry. "No!"

"Yes, he told me . . . He said it was definite. No doubt about it. This kid has finally got herself pregnant."

"Brenda!"

They were hugging each other, Gretchen surprised at the ache in her heart that didn't seem to quite match the happiness that she thought she was feeling. But she did understand now that affinity she had always had with Brenda. Somehow, subconsciously, she had picked up on Brenda's yearning, her despair over her barrenness. This was the first time Brenda had ever said anything about it, yet all along Gretchen must have known. Her instinct had been proven right.

Although Dr. Lahey was willing to proceed with the session, Gretchen insisted that she go right home and celebrate with her husband. Obviously grateful to be released, Brenda gave her a peck on the cheek before hurrying down the hall past the electrologist's.

It was only when she had settled at a table outside the Chick-Fil-A counter that a sense of shame dimmed her spirits. Could she have really asked Mel to check up on Brenda? Well, she would just have to give him a call as soon as she finished her chicken biscuit. Mel could forget about Brenda and concentrate solely on Leo and the accident records. In the meantime, surely she could go on seeing Brenda. How could she have ever doubted the woman?

Mrs. Howard had driven in with her to do some shopping. Glancing at her watch, Mrs. Dambar saw that she would have to wait another half hour for the housekeeper. With a shrug she got up and ordered herself another chicken biscuit, and then opened *The Princess Casamassima*.

*

When Mr. Dambar got home from a Boosters' Club executive meeting, where plans had been made to lure the Southeast Christian Handgun Association convention to Tula Springs, he asked Leo if he wanted to go to a movie. It was only three in the afternoon, but he could not bring himself to return to the office. The idea of projecting numbers, percentages, all sorts of calculations into the future—it was estimated tax time—seemed too wearisome to contemplate, especially with The Antibes financing still not settled. Let Francine and Mrs. Sklar hash it out. Neither one of them seemed to mind.

"What's on?" Leo wanted to know.

Mr. Dambar shrugged. "Let's take potluck. Come on. My treat."

"Not the Leon."

"OK. We'll check out the Quad."

While they talked Shaerl sat on the trailer's loveseat mending a pair of Mrs. Howard's huge, delicate lace panties.

"You want to come?" Mr. Dambar added casually in her general direction. Ever since she had turned blonde, he had found her presence somewhat disturbing.

"Huh?"

"We're going to the movies."

"Oh."

She looked off into space. Leo yawned. Mr. Dambar scratched his head. It was about this time that a synapse occurred in his brain, making it possible for him to see what was right before his eyes: a maid. A real live genuine maid.

Aware that he might have been gaping, he quickly brought himself under control. This was only a very temporary maid, after all—soon to become a student. "I guess you're busy, Shaerl. Come on, Leo. Let's go."

"Bring me back something," Shaerl called out as Mr. Dambar held open the door for the handyman.

During the drive to the mall neither man said much. "Is that new?" Mr. Dambar asked as they passed a Taco Bell that had been there, as Leo pointed out, for at least ten years. A fanciful zigzag on the drive-in's eaves brought to mind Gretchen's comments on the house, something he had been brooding over for days. At first he had angrily rejected everything she had to say. Any woman who went around in unironed khaki trousers, whose dresses wouldn't even zip up the back, had some nerve making comments about style and taste. Yet the very fact that he felt so defensive about Jane's furniture had begun to trouble him. If it really was in good taste, he probably wouldn't feel the need to apologize for it. Why did he feel so protective of it? The truth was, he knew very little about interior decorating. And Gretchen, back in New York City, must have been exposed to a wider range of taste among her friends, who might conceivably have more exacting standards.

At the concession stand that served all four theaters Mr. Dambar purchased a jumbo box of Milk Duds for himself and an Orange Crush and buttered popcorn with extra salt for the handyman. The movie in Cinema 3 had started a half hour earlier, and for a moment they were temporarily blinded when they walked in and tried to find a place to sit.

"Is that a threat?"

"I'm not just whistling Dixie."

"You piece of shit."

"Say your prayers, big boy."

Settling into a low plush seat Mr. Dambar watched a comely young woman with high cheekbones shoot a bullet through the eye of an attractive young man. He had already forgotten the title of the movie, which Leo had chosen. A few minutes later the woman was hacking the hand off another good-looking gentleman, this one graying around the temples. Although this was a comedy that had come highly recommended by all the reviewers on TV, his smile was still uncertain. Perhaps one had to see it from the beginning to get the humor.

Feeling Leo's elbow on his armrest, Mr. Dambar removed his own. It was probably wrong of Mr. Dambar to assume that he should be entitled to use the armrest in the middle just because he had paid for Leo's ticket and popcorn and soda. Even so, since his arm had been there first, Leo could have maintained the status quo.

"You piece of shit."

"Scumbag."

"You're so self-centered."

"So are you."

This was a love scene, but it made Mr. Dambar very uncomfortable. He couldn't trust those high cheekbones. The anticipatory smile had long since faded from his face. His mind had wandered from the screen to Gretchen again, what she had said about Leo. It was such a shame that they couldn't get along better. There was something almost instinctive about their animosity, like deer and soap. Of course, Leo had been making a real effort of late to be friendly. But Mr. Dambar could still sense the handyman's distrust of her. Jane and he had gotten along better, hadn't they? Of course, there was that incident over the carpet. Leo had threatened to quit if Jane installed the royal blue wall-to-wall. He had told him in private that Jane had absolutely no taste. But wasn't this what Gretchen had been telling him, too? Could they be right? And if Gretchen was right about the house, could she also be right, in some small way, about Leo? But then again, Leo had cause to complain. Hadn't Jane burst into his trailer looking for Henry? Jane? No, that was Gretchen. But Jane had done something similar once. She had gone through his drawers in the house, before Leo had moved out to the trailer. She was sure Leo was taking drugs. Oh, what a blow-up there had been when Leo found his socks and underwear rearranged. Jane refused to admit she had done it—though Mr. Dambar knew she had. She had told him so herself. But she wouldn't admit it to Leo. Probably he was not being a gentleman by remembering this not altogether admirable side of Jane's behavior. Mr. Dambar had made it a point, ever since she had passed away, to remember only her good qualities. Like her abilities as a hostess. Jane was very social and did his businesses a world of good. On the board of the Baton Rouge Symphony, president of the Ladies' Aid Society, a member of three or four committees at both the country club and the Episcopal church, she yet managed to find time for bridge parties, receptions, and seven-course dinners for twenty at home. It was like being married to a public figure. Her picture was in the papers nearly every week. Leo had taken advantage of this, clipping the photos and drawing in balloons from Jane's mouth with some not very nice quotations. Mr. Dambar had accidentally come across these one day but had never mentioned it to his wife—or Leo. They were in Leo's desk, where he had been looking for stamps. Leo, after all, was entitled to his private thoughts. The First Amendment applied to him as well as everyone else Mr. Dambar might disagree with.

Now it was Leo's leg. He could feel the material of the handyman's trousers against the light wool of his own. Looking down, he gauged that he was well within the boundaries of his own seat. There was no reason he should have to move his leg.

The pressure increased a fraction. Mr. Dambar held his ground. They sat this way throughout the almost-nude love scene, which ended in a broken arm. When it became more than material that he could feel, the actual pressure of the bony knee, Mr. Dambar gave in and moved his leg. But by then Leo's shoulder seemed to be beyond the armrest boundary, touching his own. Probably the boy was just unconscious of what he was doing, Mr. Dambar thought as he leaned away. Some people were like that.

"Well, that was interesting," Mr. Dambar commented when they were back outside the theater. The movie had ended, and Leo did not want to wait for the first half hour they had missed.

"Too predictable." Leo ambled toward the mall plaza where a fountain danced in colored lights. "The director deserves to be shot."

"What about the actors?"

"Hung."

Leo did not smile when he made these pronouncements. He was quite serious; art meant a lot to him.

At the fountain they stood for a few moments looking at the pennies and nickels lying at the bottom of the shallow pool.

"You want to like go look at stuff?"

"Huh?"

"Shop a little?"

"I don't know. Do you?"

Leo shrugged. "I don't know."

They stood there uncertainly. Mr. Dambar noticed that the coins had not been tossed into the pool for good luck. They were part of the design, fastened to the tiles with a deceptive symmetry.

179

"Well?"

They wandered off in the direction of the nearest store.

To Mr. Dambar there was something vaguely ignominious about grown men shopping. He and Leo should be out in the woods hunting. It was a shame that Leo had to equate hunting with murder. What he should do is ask Mr. Keely to go hunting one weekend. They used to go deer hunting together when Jane was alive. It had been fun talking about Korea before turning in for the night. Neither Mr. Dambar nor Mr. Keely had actually done any fighting there. But they had been close to the front, working at supply depots. Mr. Dambar had been shot at one night when he went to take out the garbage. It happened so fast that he didn't even have time to be scared. There weren't supposed to be any North Koreans around. The front was thirty-five miles away. And yet the bullet had nicked the garbage pail. He wished now that he had kept it, the pail.

"It's OK," Mr. Dambar said noncommittally when Leo showed him a skirt for a twin bed. They were in the linen department in J. C. Penney.

"You think Shaerl will like the ruff?"

Mr. Dambar was not sure what he was looking at. He did not understand what a skirt was, in regard to a bed. The whole idea depressed him. How could anyone be happy when they opened a going-away present and discovered it was a ruffed skirt for a twin bed? Which reminded him, since Gretchen had thrown his own gift at a nutria, he would have to come up with something else for Shaerl. "Do you think . . ." he began, meaning to ask, Do you think she'll ever visit us? But Leo had nudged him in the ribs, cutting him off.

"What?" Mr. Dambar asked, feeling crowded.

"Shhh."

"Why should I— Oh, look. There's Mrs. Howard."

Another nudge, and then Leo had taken him by the arm and led him farther from the aisle of towels, where Mrs. Howard was standing.

"Leo, what's the matter with you?"

"Keep it down," Leo whispered. "See that guy she's talking to?"

"The clerk?"

"He's not a clerk."

"What? How do you know?"

"Where's the name tag?"

Since the young man's back was to them, Mr. Dambar could not answer this. "Leo, I'm going to talk to her. This is ridiculous."

The sudden grip on his bicep was painful.

"Hey—all right, Leo."

Angered and puzzled, Mr. Dambar decided he had had enough of shopping. Without waiting for the handyman, he headed for the exit.

"I'm sorry, Mr. D," Leo said as he got into the Jeep. Mr. Dambar had sat in the parking lot a good ten, fifteen minutes before Leo showed up.

"What did you mean by grabbing me like that?"

"I'm sorry, really. It's just that I was like afraid you were going to say something."

"So?"

"So something's going on, man. That kid she was talking to— I've seen him before."

"Terrific." Mr. Dambar had pulled up to the traffic light that helped mall customers enter the highway.

"He always seems to be around. Like when I was at the Feed and Seed the other day, I'm sure he was there. It's weird, Mr. D. I don't like it."

"Just a coincidence."

Leo sat there shaking his head, muttering to himself. Mr. Dambar began to wonder. Could Gretchen be right about him? Was the boy all there?

"Did you get the dress?" Mr. Dambar asked, feeling guilty about his uncharitable thoughts. They were on the highway now, heading south to the state line.

"Huh? Uh, look, Mr. D, I'm really sorry. I didn't mean to make you mad and all."

"Well, I just hope Mrs. Howard didn't see us. She'd certainly think it was strange." Glancing over at the handyman, who really did look distressed, he found himself adding, "Now don't worry, son. Strange things happen in everyone's life, things you just can't explain. Did I ever tell you about what happened to me during the war?"

"The bullet, right."

"I was at a supply depot a good thirty, forty miles from the front . . ." And Mr. Dambar went on to fill in the details that he was sure Leo must have forgotten.

Dinner that evening was late. Mr. Dambar tided himself over with some ice-cream chocolate drops that Mrs. Howard had urged upon him when she returned home. These he brought with him into the library, where Shaerl had set out his accustomed glass of Johnnie Walker Black, fixed just the way he liked it. He had intended to watch the Brigham Young basketball game that had been on ESPN the night before at two A.M. But something must have gone wrong with his timer or channel selector on the VCR. The tape turned out to be a talk show on how women with large hips and thighs should dress. Before turning it off he learned that these women should never tuck in their blouses, but always wear them outside an unobtrusive belt.

"Where were you this afternoon?" Leo inquired after they had finished praying.

"Who—me?" Mrs. Howard fingered the lopsided gold triangle that graced her moiré collar. "I went to town."

Leo waited for Mrs. Dambar to set the split pea soup before him. Then he said, "Town? How did you get to *town?*"

"What?"

Hunched over his soup Leo commented between spoonfuls, "Mr. D had the Jeep, right? And Mrs. D the Buick."

"Leo, I took her," Mrs. Dambar said from the tureen, where she was filling her own bowl. "The soup looks delicious, Mrs. Howard."

"I thank you. Now sit down, darling. We can serve ourself."

"Just let me get the bread."

She hurried into the kitchen. When she returned with a basket of high-fiber, low-calorie Seven Grain, Shaerl was asking her step-uncle about Baton Rouge. "You can drive me tomorrow, can't you?"

Leo didn't reply.

"Why Baton Rouge?" Mr. Dambar asked. "What's up?"

"I want to look at a couple apartments. I'm going to live off campus if I can find something cheap enough." She blinked at her soup, then at the chandelier. Mrs. Dambar wondered if she had something in her eye. Then it occurred to her that the girl was just being vague, like a fifties blonde starlet. The truth be told, Mrs. Dambar would be happier with black hair on the girl. So much more sensible.

"What is dis?" the housekeeper said, dangling a slice of bread from two fingers. "Where is my bread, the bread I bought?"

"Sit, please. You're going to love this." Mrs. Dambar took a bite of the Seven Grain, nodding her head. "Mmmm. It's so good."

"It's not Wonder. Frankie only eats Wonder."

"Frankie's going to love this, aren't you, dear?"

"It's brown," Mr. Dambar said.

"Try it, please. It won't kill you." Mrs. Dambar took another demonstration bite. "Mrs. Howard, what are you doing?"

The old woman had plucked something from her bowl and transferred it to Mr. Dambar's.

"You don't give him any ham. There's no flavor without the ham."

It was fat, gristle, and knowing Frank, he would eat it. "Do you want Mr. Dambar to end up in the hospital again?"

The look she got from the housekeeper confirmed that this remark was ill-advised. She knew it as she was saying it, but couldn't help herself.

"What did you do in town?" Leo said, surfacing from his brief funk. "Mrs. Howard?"

"Oh, I shop. Always plenty to buy."

"I see."

"Leo," Shaerl said languidly, "you will take me tomorrow, won't you?"

Again he made no reply.

"Why does everyone hate me?" She sighed and patted the rather childish pink barrette in her teased hair. "Pass the duck please."

Mr. Dambar reached in front of the housekeeper to move the dish closer to Shaerl. He practically had to stand.

"Where did you shop?"

"What?"

"What stores did you go to, Mrs. Howard?"

Shaerl and Mrs. Dambar exchanged a look. "Leo, what is this?" the girl said.

"I just would like to know where she shopped."

"Leo, she isn't a child," Mrs. Dambar said with a faint, humoring smile. "I think she's old enough to spend some time alone."

"Gretchen, did I ever tell you about the time I went to take out the garbage and was nearly shot. Came this close." Mr. Dambar almost touched thumb to index finger.

Mrs. Dambar paused in mid-sip from the Waterford crystal. "What? When was this?"

"We never found out who might have done it, whether it was an accident or intentional."

"But Frank, that's awful."

"He's talking about Korea," Shaerl put in.

"Korea? The war? Frank, really."

"It's just one of those things. I suppose I could have been killed, and no one would have known why." For some reason this notion seemed to please him. He looked round the table. "Of course, they would have said it was the enemy. But it crossed my mind once or twice that it could have been an American. Think of that. Not that I had any enemies. I suppose I was pretty well liked. The fellas thought I was pretty regular. But you never know. There could have been some kook. A guy can look real normal, everyday, and turn out to be a kook. That's one thing you learn in the Army."

"Well, I don't know what else you can expect," Mrs. Dambar said, "playing around with guns like that. Someone's bound to get hurt."

"So what was the store?"

Mrs. Howard swallowed a bite of duck before replying. "I'm not sure, Mr. Leo. A lot. Dere was a drugstore, J. C. Penney's. I look at the latest offerings in shoe styles at the Fayva."

"Penney's? That's in the mall, isn't it?"

"Of course."

"But you said you went to town."

"Yes."

"But the mall isn't town. They're two different places. One's in Mississippi and the other's here."

"Leo, really, that's quite enough," Mrs. Dambar put in, adopting the tone of a rather formidable aunt of hers. "I really can't sit here and listen to you cross-examine Mrs. Howard like this. If you must know, we stopped in town on the way to the mall. I had a session with Dr. Lahey while Mrs. Howard shopped."

Mr. Dambar cleared his throat. All eyes turned toward him, but it turned out he had nothing to say. Somewhat worked up, Mrs. Dambar prepared for an assault from the handyman. But to her disappointment, he went back to his food. She was enjoying her role as protector so much that she even tried to goad Leo—in a veiled way, of course—to enter the lists. But he did not say another word till dinner was over when, with perhaps more feeling than was necessary, he asked to be excused.

"What do you think got into Leo tonight?" Mrs. Dambar asked her husband over dishes. Mrs. Howard had retired to her room to watch "The Hollywood Squares." Shaerl was in the trailer planning her school wardrobe while Leo was holed up in the library working on his correspondence.

"Don't know. Seems sort of wound up."

Mrs. Dambar jerked her hand out of the way of the faucet. The water she was using to rinse was hot. "I don't understand why Mrs. Howard just doesn't tell him to mind his own business. She's sharp enough with everyone else."

"Well, she, you know."

"Frank, I really wish you would make an effort not to speak in sentence fragments. My father did that, and it used to drive my mother wild." There was still a residue of the formidable aunt in her voice. She was unhappy about this and hoped that Frank hadn't been listening, as often he didn't. Lately, she could say something right to his face, and his reply would be "Huh? What?" Or simply a spaced-out, smiling nod.

"I, Leo . . ."

"What were you saying about Mrs. Howard?"

"Me?" He looked at the dish towel in his hand. "I suppose she's a little in awe of him. His intellect. But now you've made me forget—Oh, right. He was acting a little strange today, dear. We went to the movie this afternoon. It was a comedy, very contemporary modern stuff. I don't know if you'd like it."

"What were you doing at a movie? Frank, why is this water so hot?"

"Put in some cold. Anyway, afterward we happened to see Mrs. Howard at Penney's."

"You were at the mall? Why didn't you come say hello? I was at Dr. Lahey's."

"That's what I thought. But we were at the mall."

"Dr. Lahey's *is* at the mall."

"What?"

"Frank, I must have told you that a hundred times. Where do you think I go when I see her?"

He scratched his head, wondering if it was time for a haircut. "So Leo won't let me go say hello to Mrs. Howard. It was very strange."

"Why not?"

"There was some kid she was talking to, a clerk or something. I couldn't quite make it all out. Apparently, Leo's seen him around or whatever. I think he thinks he's being followed."

Being a basically honest person, Mrs. Dambar could not help blushing violently. She knew it had to be Mel. And she had asked Mel to please be discreet. But how in the world had he managed to hook up with Mrs. Howard?

"I don't know, Frank," she said, her face averted as she feigned interest in the dirty dishes. "To be perfectly honest, well, I've always thought there was something a little cockeyed about Leo. I've told you that. Now he thinks he's being followed. Next thing you know he's going to be seeing visitors from outer space."

"I admit, Gretch, I mean at first I thought, well, you know. I mean like you didn't like him. But after today . . ."

Though she had a troubled conscience, Mrs. Dambar could not help feeling a tingle of hope, as if something long anesthetized were coming back to life. It would be such a shame to clobber this hope with an overdose of honesty. Of course, one day she might tell Frank about Mel—maybe. But why? It seemed the boy was getting too careless. She must do something about him soon.

"My father, when his drinking had got out of hand—Frank, you listening? Anyway, he used to suspect my mother of being unfaithful. There were some awful scenes going on behind closed doors. At the time I didn't know what to think. They believed in keeping up appearances before the help and us children. So they would smile at dinner and be polite—but my brother and I knew that something awful was going on. The funny thing was that my mother really hated sex. She would no more think of having an affair than going to the moon. My father knew this, and yet he couldn't help suspecting her every move. It's a disease really, this frame of mind. And hard as it is for me to say, I'm afraid that poor Leo might be infected. Did you see the way he kept on looking at Mrs. Howard tonight? It's the same guarded look my father used to have—and I loved him so much, too. My father," she hastily clarified. "It hurt so much for me to see him torturing himself like that. I just wish there was something we could do for Leo—so we could spare him."

An unwiped plate in his hand, Mr. Dambar gazed off into space.

"Frank."

"What? Oh, yes, right. I was thinking, there's a credit union in Baton Rouge I've been meaning to visit. Maybe I could give Shaerl a lift tomorrow. What do you think?"

Mrs. Dambar looked in despair at the burnt-in grease on the duck pan. "Why not? No sense making two trips. You know, I think we'll leave this pan till morning. Let it soak."

"Oh, Gretchen, you know Mrs. Howard. She likes to wake up to a clean kitchen."

"I know. But then she shouldn't burn the grease. Come on, Frank, let's go for a walk."

"Can't you scrub just a little for me?"

"You bad boy," she said, catching the glint in his eye. "Oh, all right. Just a *little*—that's all."

CHAPTER ELEVEN

Sitting on a terrace of the L.S.U. Student Union, Mr. Dambar let her go on without interrupting. She was worried about what was going to become of her uncle once she was gone. He was getting so old, and he still hadn't found anyone to look after him. "If you could encourage him to get out of the house more often. He spends too much time at home."

Shaerl had bought him a double espresso to thank him for taking her to Baton Rouge. As he sipped it, he could almost imagine what it must be like to have the whole world ahead of you, as she did. He had felt that way once, back in college, when Jane had been elected Homecoming Queen and that same night, promised to marry him. Walking back to her dorm, they had paused beneath an oak with roots that humped the earth like half-submerged gators. Standing side by side, they had gazed up at the dark network of branches that seemed to encode some message of unlimited hope, the intricate outline of leaf and limb endless and varied.

"I've tried to talk to him about his father," she went on, wiping powdered sugar from her lips. She had ordered a doughnut with her cappuccino. "He's very closed off about it, though. It worries me, Frank. I wish there was some way he could open up. If he could just express his pain, then he could let go of it. And get on with life—find someone, you know."

Mr. Dambar nodded absently, momentarily distracted by a sudden flutter in his breast, an acute but painless arrhythmia.

"Like you have."

"Pardon?"

"Like you, Frank. I've always held you up as an example. Your grief had to have been as bad as his."

"What grief? Oh."

A minute frown dimpled her forehead. She touched the blonde hair that made her look so charming. Flipping through a college yearbook, he would smile at how cheap all the good-looking blondes looked now at a distance of twenty, thirty years. Yet at the time how stylish and sophisticated they had seemed.

"But you learned to let go. And when you did, you found someone. The same could be true for Leo."

"Yes, I'm very fortunate to have found . . ." His pant leg was touching something, either a leg of the table or her own leg. Whatever it was, it remained where it was. On a nearby ledge, annoyed by a hesitant squirrel, a sparrow hopped, seemed to shudder, then exploded into the air. "Very fortunate, someone like Gretchen. You never can tell what life is going to bring you. You've always got to leave yourself open to any possibility—don't you think? That's how we grow as human beings." His leg pressed a fraction closer; it still didn't move away.

"That's what worries me about Leo. He's not giving himself the chance. And he's such a good man. Honestly, Frank, I don't know what I'm going to do without him. It's a little scary. He's helped my arthritis so much. The way he can manipulate my leg."

"Listen, I wouldn't worry about Leo. He's a sly dog, really." He winked at her. Although it wasn't very appropriate, he realized that she had just made him jealous. Or at least it felt like jealousy. He wasn't quite sure. "Leo's doing just fine."

She leaned closer and for a moment he was lost in those brown doe eyes of hers that always seemed on the verge of filling with tears. "What do you mean?"

He increased the pressure with his leg. "I happen to know Leo isn't quite as lonely as you may think."

"You mean . . . ?"

He nodded. "I caught him once at a mot—restaurant. He was pretty embarrassed."

"That's impossible."

"Don't underestimate your uncle, Shaerl. He knows how to take care of himself."

"But where? When? He never said anything to me. He wouldn't dare . . ."

Mr. Dambar scrutinized her. Something seemed wrong, a little off.

"I mean, Uncle Leo is so shy about girls."

The "Uncle Leo" made him even more uneasy. She had never called him this before. "Shaerl, you should be glad, shouldn't you?"

"Glad?"

"That he's got someone."

She played with a sugar cube, pushing it around an ant that crawled weakly between the runnels of the concrete table. "I am. Except that I can't really believe it."

"You won't tell him I said anything, will you? It's just between you and me." He almost whispered this, leaning close in a conspiratorial way. Still looking straight at her, he furtively adjusted his penis, which had gotten caught at an odd angle as it became erect. "Just you and me, Shaerl. OK?"

She would not look back at him. Her face was dark, brooding. "OK."

Realizing that life was so terribly short, he decided to plunge ahead and press his leg even closer. He did so—and discovered it was a concrete leg he was so fond of.

"Come on, Frank. We better get back. What's the matter?"

He shrugged.

"You look so funny. No, bring your cup and saucer with you. We have to bring them back to the counter with us. Come on, hurry. I've got a lot of sewing to do when we get home. And Gretchen wants me to feed the chickens. They must be hungry by now."

Mr. Ames showed her the key to the soda pop machine at Tula Springs High, the key to the candy machine in the lobby of City

Hall, and the key to the vending machine in the men's room of the Shell station on the Old Jeff Davis Highway. Mrs. Dambar commented politely on each. The stepfather's uncle had seen her climb the outside stairs to Mel's office and followed her up. Mel, the old man had explained, was over at the Quick Stop for a quart of two-percent fat milk. He ought to be back any minute.

"I do plastering, too. I always say to Mel, diversify. That's how a man gets on in this world. A little bit here, a little bit there."

Though not a pleasant-looking man—Mr. Ames's features were coarse, and there were beige stains on his ribbed undershirt— his manner was neutral, neither friendly nor off-putting. In between each of his observations on life he inserted a longish pause, during which Mrs. Dambar would consult her watch.

"You sure Mel will be back soon?"

He rubbed the gray stubble on his chin and gave the many keys attached to his belt loops a good shake. "Store's two blocks."

Mrs. Dambar smiled and crossed her legs. She wished he would go away. It was hard to think with him hanging around.

He was at the screen door when suddenly he turned. "Who are you?" he blurted out as if he had just come upon her.

Somewhat taken aback, she didn't know quite how to reply. "I'm just . . ."

"You one of the boy's clients?"

"No, a friend, that's all."

The small pale eyes squeezed shut as if he were taking a bead on her. Then with an indistinct guttural sound, he returned to his neutral mode. "It's like I always say to the boy, friends is like smallpox. Can't live with 'em, can't live without 'em."

Mrs. Dambar nodded agreeably. Of course, one could live without smallpox quite easily—but she thought it wiser not to mention this to the old man. Instead, she made a vapid comment about the weather, how nice it was outside.

"Always nice this time of year," he said flatly, turning to the screen again. Bamboo and elephant ears stirred in the contrary March breezes. It seemed a noisy yard, with a fair amount of clicks, knocks, and rustling, some of this perhaps the work of songless birds rooting about for grubs.

191

"Listen, I could come back later," she said after another unsettling pause. She hated to waste time like this when she could be doing errands in town. The chickens and catfish needed some food from the Feed and Seed, and Mrs. Howard had run out of Fab laundry soap. "Tell Mel, will you, that I—"

"Hold your horses. Who do I remind you of?"

"What?"

The old man was blocking the screen door. "Guess."

"Mr. Ames, I really haven't the faintest idea."

Leaning over he unbuckled one of the leather sandals that he wore with black socks. A little worried, she watched him slap the sole against Mel's desk.

"Give up? Khrushchev!"

With his bald head there was perhaps a mild resemblance, she conceded to herself. "Oh, yes. Good."

"Everyone says how I ought to be on TV, make myself some commercials. I say to 'em, life is not supposed to be one big circus. That shuts 'em up."

Mrs. Dambar looked at her watch. Why was it that so much of her life seemed to be used up by people who had no point, no meaning for her? It made her so anxious. She couldn't help thinking of the hundreds of hours she had wasted in New York in equally pointless encounters—dinners with so-called friends who had never written to congratulate her on her marriage, charity auctions with friends of friends encouraging her to buy things she didn't need, receptions where she would chat for half an hour with someone whose name she had forgotten.

"Who are you?"

Mr. Ames, she felt like replying, you are rude and impertinent. But she composed herself enough to say civilly, "I just told you, didn't I?" And she would have left then and there if Mel hadn't walked in through the door that led to the hall.

"Hey, Gretch! I didn't know you were here." Slamming the door behind him he lumbered over and gave her an awkward hug. "I was watching TV downstairs. Why didn't you say something?"

She gave the old man a look.

"What about the milk?" Mr. Ames wanted to know.

"There was a whole half gallon in the back of the fridge. Behind the roast. Come on, sit down, Gretch," he added as he held open the screen door for the old man, who went out grumbling to himself.

Mel was wearing the same threadbare button-down shirt he had had on at their last interview, too short at the wrists. While he listened to her, he wiped a speck of mud from his well-polished wingtips. They looked too large, like hand-me-downs.

". . . and so you see you've just got to be more careful," she wound up after explaining her fears about Leo finding out who he was. "In fact, Mel, I'm afraid that I might have to—sort of terminate our relationship. I told you it was just temporary in the beginning, that I wasn't sure. Surely you understand that if Mr. Vogel ever found out that I had . . . Well, it would be the end for me."

"Oh, but Gretch," he said eagerly, "I'd never admit it was you. I'd die first. I mean it. No one will ever know I'm working for you."

"Mel, remember please that you're not really working for me. This is more on a friendly basis. You don't have your degree yet—so I can't really be an actual client. That's true, isn't it?" Mrs. Dambar still could not admit to herself that she had actually hired someone to follow Leo. It shocked her if she heard it put in such crude terms. "By the way, dear, just how did you manage to talk to Mrs. Howard?"

His face lit up with excitement. "OK, I was pretending to want to know about the rates at the electrolysis place so I could keep an eye on Dr. Lahey, and—"

"But I told you to forget about her."

"I know, but I was in the mall anyway. Dad wanted me to pick up a crowbar from Sears, so I thought I may as well give a routine sweep. That's when I spotted you and the old lady. From what you had told me, I figured it must be Mrs. Howard, so when you went into Lahey's, I trailed her into Penney's and struck up a conversation." His right hand mimicked talking to his left. "Hey, you have to admit"—the hands flew apart—"it wasn't bad, huh, not half bad the way you didn't see me. You know you walked right past me. I was squeezed against the corner."

"Dear, it's not me you have to hide from."

Dismay registered so clearly on his mobile face that she felt compelled to add, "Well, it wasn't bad, Mel. I really didn't know you were there. But I don't see why you had to talk to Mrs. Howard."

"She's a lead. There's very few leads in this case."

"Mel, please, dear, I'd rather you didn't call this a case."

"What is it then?"

"Well, it's more like a friendship."

"But I thought you didn't like Mr. Vogel."

"I meant between you and me."

He looked puzzled. "But . . ."

"You're someone I could talk to about a particular problem. I have other friends for other problems."

"What other problems?"

"Well, for instance, if I have a problem with my car, I go to a friend who knows something about engines."

"Otherwise known as a mechanic. Anyway," he went on, impatient to continue with his story.

"Mel," she interrupted as he was describing how he had ingratiated himself with Mrs. Howard by pretending to have a maternal grandmother from Germany, "please stop referring to her as a lead. I don't like that word. And I don't think it's a good idea to lie to the poor woman. That bothers me a great deal."

"It's not a lie. It's a modus operandi. So like I was saying, I told her how she used to talk Yiddish at home."

"Who?"

"My grandmother."

"But you said she was German."

"Yeah, right, a German Jew, just like Mrs. Howard. Of course, Mrs. Howard is only half Jewish."

"That's impossible. She cooks ham and pork all the time."

Mel raised his hands with a night-club comedian's shrug. "What can I say, Gretch? I guess she's not one of those practicing types. But all I know is she had to get the hell out of Germany. Stayed on till it was almost too late. Ended up on the wrong boat or something. Mr. Dambar's father went all the way up to Montreal,

Canada, to get her. Amazing story. I could have talked to her all afternoon."

"But how did you know she was half Jewish?"

"Didn't at first. But she started opening up when I told her about my grandmother. Anyway, what difference does it make? I'm not going to charge you for that conversation. We didn't have time to talk about Mr. Vogel. I got too interested in what she was saying about herself."

Having long suspected the housekeeper of an unsavory, Nazi-sympathizing past, Mrs. Dambar felt somewhat chastened. Though she was still hoping that Mel would come up with some objective evidence against Leo, at the same time she realized that it was time to rein him in. She could not have him spying on her household like this. It simply was not right.

"Speaking of money, dear, there's something I have to say. Now Mel, you know as well as I do that when money comes between friends, well, it's always bad news. I consider you a friend, a good friend, and if it's all right with you, I'd like to keep it that way. I'll be more than happy to pay you cash for any time you put in this week—including Mrs. Howard. But after this, well, like I was trying to say when we first started talking today, I think the professional side of our relationship should be terminated."

Mel looked stricken. "I could lower my rates, Gretchen. And you won't have to pay expenses."

"That's not the point. Don't you see, I just can't go through with this. Perhaps I didn't make myself clear enough on the phone the other day. When I called you back, remember?"

"About Dr. Lahey?"

"Yes, and asked you to stop following her."

"You're mad at me for that. I promise I won't do it again. I won't ever mention—"

"No, Mel, it's not you I'm mad at. It's more like I'm disappointed in myself, how I could have thought anything so ungracious about her. At my last session, well, it was like a revelation. I know now that she really cares for me on a personal as well as a professional level. And I'm ashamed of myself for harboring those doubts." Seeing that he still appeared downcast, she attempted to bolster his ego. "It's me, Mel. Not you. You really are great, you know. Here I've been living with Mrs. Howard all this time and never once managed to get her to open up the way she has with you. You have a real talent for friendship. Believe me, I'm a very picky woman. I know quality when I see it."

This seemed to perk him up. He flapped his hands, as if he were about to protest—but waited for more.

"Let me tell you, I've known some muckitymucks in my day. I told you, didn't I, that I've had dinner at the White House more than once—and I'm not one to waste time on just anyone. So listen. My husband is in Baton Rouge this morning. Would you do me a favor and escort this old lady to lunch—my treat? How about that nice place next to City Hall? I've always wanted to try it."

"Isola Bella?"

She nodded.

"The only trouble is, well, we might run into someone. Maybe we should try that new seafood place on the Old Jeff Davis."

She was searching in her purse to make sure she had enough cash to pay him off once and for all. Isola Bella would take her American Express. "Hm? What do you mean run into someone?"

He cleared his throat. "Well, I saw Mr. Vogel and . . . Just the other day."

"Mr. Vogel and whom?"

He had put his wingtips on the desk and was knocking them together in a distracting fashion.

"By the way, how is your back, dear?"

"A little sore. Dad's been rubbing it with Mineral Ice."

"What a shame." A hundred and ten dollars in her wallet and some change. Good. "You were saying about . . ."

"Dr. Lahey. He was there with her."

"Oh, no, Mel. It couldn't have been. Are you sure? Yes? Positive? But how could you not tell me this?"

"Look, Gretch, you've been telling me not to talk about her anymore. What am I supposed to do?"

"But . . . Oh, come on. Let's talk about it at that seafood place. Come on, dear. Get your jacket. And your list of hours you put in this week. You sure it was them? My keys, where are they? Oh, here. I hope they serve wine. Dear, there's a rip in your jacket, did you know?"

On their way down the outside stairs, they were hailed by Mr. Ames, who was mending a toaster in the yard. "Bring back some two-percent, Melvin. It's skim in the fridge. Can't use no skim in my coffee. I tole you that long time ago, boy."

In the days that followed her lunch with Mel, Mrs. Dambar could not get her mind off the handyman. She knew this was not a healthy state of affairs and did her best to distract herself with positive thoughts. Several times a day she would remind herself how lucky she was. After all, how many of her friends had managed to marry the love of their lives? When you came right down to it, not a single one. Cynthia Dobbs had married a man who was more like a brother. They had known each other since kindergarten and been engaged for eight years. Jo and Teague Small-Jones had both married on the rebound. Kyss, of course, had openly admitted that her second husband was a compromise, a steady, unimaginative corporate lawyer who made up for her passionate and jailed first husband. The list went on and on. Perhaps that was why she rarely heard from them. To confront the real thing, a marriage as deep and loving as hers, must be threatening. And probably they must resent the courage she had shown. To uproot herself so completely from her past in order to devote herself to the love of her life—well, it was positively romantic. Some women might enjoy reading about such romance, but few had the guts and stamina to actually live it. Yes, it was a little peculiar—she had to admit—how exhausting it was to live happily ever after. But nonetheless, she was doing it.

What disturbed her most about Leo was that he continued to seem so nice to her. In a way this was even harder to bear than outright hostility. It put her at such a disadvantage, emotionally speaking. For instance, he had kept his promise and removed Lurleen from the pasture. The minute the cow had gone, Gretchen couldn't help feeling a twinge of conscience. Had she been ungracious? Should she have made more of an effort to show Leo that she appreciated the thought behind the gift? As a matter of fact, she was even beginning to miss the beast, though in the comfortable way one can miss someone who is certain never to turn up again.

As far as the carpet went, Leo was pressing their small victory in the study. Day after day he would chip away at Mr. Dambar's resistance until finally one evening over bratwurst Mr. Dambar had laid down his gilded fork and said, "All right, give it a try, Leo. Take up the carpet in the living room and we'll see how it looks. But only the living room, understand."

And so one afternoon Mrs. Dambar returned from the A&P to find that the royal blue wall-to-wall had disappeared. After standing in the midst of the furniture, contemplating the effect, she hurried outside to look for Leo.

He turned out to be behind his trailer, working with grease-stained hands on what appeared to be an engine part.

"What a nice surprise. I'm thrilled, really. It puts the furniture in a whole new light. Some of it actually looks quite decent now. Oh, Leo, I don't know how you did it, but you did."

"Shaerl helped me out."

"No, I mean talking Frank into it. He never would listen to me. But you kept at him. And he's bound to see what an improvement there is. All we need to do now is get rid of some of the excess. You know all those little tables and those two commodes? If we take those away we could make two islands of furniture in the room, each centered around a sofa. There'd be space in between, and the room would look so much lighter and airier. That's the only way to make a rococo style work—you've got to give the furniture room to breathe." A few loud clanks of his pipe wrench punctuated these ideas. "The next step after that will be the molding around the ceiling. Do you think Frank would object if we stripped off all those swirls and flowers and replaced it with a clean line? I think you could talk him into it."

Leo grunted as he pried apart two strips of metal.

"Well, of course you could. But I suppose we ought to take it a step at a time, give Frank a chance to get adjusted." She regarded the handyman for a moment, feeling something was wrong. His profile seemed so different—and yet a little familiar. Then it struck her: "Your hair."

Looking intently at the dull metal, Leo shrugged. "Shaerl got to me."

"It's very nice, really. You look—nice." His ponytail had been lopped off, making his head seem somehow off-balance. It was odd, too, how this seemed to affect his features, making them sharper, more defined.

"What are you doing?"

"Got a new brake drum, Mrs. D. For the Buick. I dropped Mr. D off at work this A.M., then brought it back to fix."

"Shouldn't a mechanic . . ." Out of the corner of her eye she noticed something move in the pasture. Looking closer to make sure it wasn't Lurleen, she saw it was the overgrown mutt from down the street.

"Leo, are you sure the chickens are safe with him around? Don't you think you'd better shoo him away? I'd do it myself but these heels."

"Relax. He won't get inside the pen. I strung it with barb wire this morning."

Looking doubtfully at the dog, which seemed to move with an almost feline grace as it stalked some unseen prey, she was about to go back to the house when he said, "Mrs. D?"

"Yes?"

"Who is he?" he asked flatly, with no sign of emotion.

"What?"

"That man who's been following me."

Mrs. Dambar had positioned herself by the clothesline, where one of Shaerl's nightgowns, flapping conveniently at her face, hid her consternation. "Leo, dear, you must get that idea out of your mind. It really is not very healthy."

"The guy who was talking to Howard the other day, I keep on seeing him."

"Well, this is a small town. You're bound to see the same people from time to time."

"But he's—"

"Leo, really, this is too ridiculous. Frank is beginning to worry about you, you know."

"He hasn't said anything, has he?"

"As a matter of fact, he did think your behavior was quite odd at Penney's. I tried to reassure him, but, well, if you keep this up, I'm afraid he's going to start really wondering. If I were you, I'd not say anything more about it." She looked at her watch, as if she were late for an appointment. "Keep an eye on that dog for me, would you, dear? And stop worrying. Everything is going to be just fine."

Back in the house she tried to rearrange some of the furniture in the living room. But she was leaving scratches on the oak block flooring. If anything was to be accomplished, it was evident that she would require Leo's assistance. Yet she was in no mood to have him around her now. She was afraid of her guilty conscience, what it might make her say. It was a shame that circumstances forced her to keep him in the dark about certain matters, but after all, he had brought it upon himself. He should not be having lunch with her therapist. This was a shocking invasion of privacy. In fact, the more she thought about it, the more upset she became. She would like to go out and give him a piece of her mind. But if she did, she would be admitting that he was being followed—and, of course, he would tell Frank. What a horrible embarrassment that would be, trying to explain Mel. She really wished she had left well enough alone and never spoken to the boy, nice as he was. Except that he had provided her with information, valuable information. How else would she have found out about Leo and Brenda?

"Get under the covers."

"It's all right, Mrs. Howard," Mrs. Dambar said from the bed she had thrown herself down upon. "I'm just resting."

"You look ill."

"I'm fine." She was not in her own room. It was Robert's, one of Mr. Dambar's sons, where she had put the antique car display that seemed so out of place in the master bedroom. "I've got to get up anyway. I'm going to the mall."

The old woman placed a creamy white hand on her forehead. "No fever. Well, OK, you go. Everybody do what they want. Dat's our modern philosophy, nicht? Mr. Leo he takes up Mrs. Dambar's beautiful blue rug dat we all adore. Dat I break my back cleaning. Mrs. Howard don't care. No, you think she cares? She don't care. Everything is fabulous."

Since learning that the housekeeper had fled Nazi persecution, Mrs. Dambar leaned over backward to be more accommodating. But still she could not help considering these references to "Mrs. Dambar" as being somewhat thoughtless. "I might be a little late for dinner. But do please start without me. Don't make Frank wait."

Shortly before going into Robert's room, she had phoned Dr. Lahey to ask if she could squeeze in an emergency appointment. Reluctantly, Brenda had agreed to see her at four-thirty, which left Mrs. Dambar at loose ends for two and a half hours. Lying upon the bed, unable to doze off, consumed twenty minutes. Looking at the living room again—ten. A short discussion with Mrs. Howard in the hall ("I thought you were going out?" "I am, in a while. I'll have to take the Jeep, though. Leo's working on the Buick." "Ach, from the accident. He's looking at the brakes so no one be killed." "If the brakes really need checking, he should take them to a garage." "Fine, darling, but here we are not made of money. And by the way, please do not fold the socks from the dryer no more." "Why not, Mrs. Howard?" "They was damp, darling. No one likes to wear wet socks.") took up approximately two. Every time she consulted her watch, she wondered if the batteries were wearing out. Never had a couple hours seemed so impossibly long.

"Sometimes I wish you were not so nice and intelligent," she found herself saying, at long last, using the opening line she had brooded over at the house, revising and polishing it on the drive to the mall.

Dr. Lahey had been suffering from morning sickness, but there was no evidence of it now. Though she didn't look fresh—her first appointment had been at seven that morning—she seemed composed and at ease. The tennis outfit she had on would give her a chance to hurry to the courts as soon as they were done. She did not want to keep her husband waiting any longer than necessary, she had explained to Mrs. Dambar in the outer office when she had arrived.

"It would be much easier if you were a difficult woman, Brenda."

"What would be?"

Mrs. Dambar was sitting upright in the La-Z-Boy. She did not want to lean back and get too comfortable. "I've made up my mind. I just can't go on with this."

"Why is that?"

According to the script she had prepared, Mrs. Dambar was to answer coolly, in vague, roundabout terms. It would be ill-advised, she knew, to mention Isola Bella. Dr. Lahey would just think she was being paranoid. "I feel I've progressed as far as I can go."

"I see."

"And Brenda, I want to thank you for all you've done." She spoke steadily, her eye on the digital clock just behind the therapist. "You really are as good as anyone I saw in New York. I mean it. I want to wish you the very best with your career. I think it will be wonderful. And I want to say how really delighted I am that you're, uh, having a baby."

A long pause made Mrs. Dambar rather uncomfortable. She regarded the pompoms on Brenda's tennis shoes and tried not to look at the birthmark on her thigh.

"It's interesting," Dr. Lahey said finally, "interesting that you should decide to quit after learning about my baby. Don't you think?"

"It has nothing to do with that, Brenda. As a matter of fact, I would have quit long before if it hadn't been for that. I was so happy for you, I thought I'd give you another chance."

"Have you ever had a child?"

"Of course not. I would have told you."

"Do you want one? With Frank?"

"Heavens, no. It's all I can do to— To manage as it is."

The pleated tennis skirt exposed some cellulite that Dr. Lahey didn't seem at all concerned about. "Can you tell me how you feel about my joy?"

"It's totally beside the point."

202

"Not really, Gretchen. I've been thinking about how I behaved at our last session. I'm afraid it wasn't very professional—that it was some sort of breach. At the same time, I can't really regret it—or I didn't think I would. Until now. I think I might have been far too personal. And I think that this has affected you in an adverse way. Mainly because it's a subject that you and I have not spent any time on. And—"

"Oh, for heaven's sake, it's not that at all." Mrs. Dambar gripped the bar of the chair, her knuckles white. She was tired of this charade. "Brenda, you've forced me to leave by your . . . You know how I feel about Leo, your past history with him. How do you expect me to feel free talking about him when you're going around wining and dining him."

"Pardon?"

"It's no use, Brenda. I know the truth. You still see him, don't you? He's not just someone you used to know. You had lunch with him just last week."

The therapist's eyebrow went up, like Mr. Spock's. "I did?"

"At Isola Bella. Thursday."

"I'm afraid you're mistaken, Gretchen."

"It's an objective fact. I know." She tried to hold back the tears. It was so important to be dispassionate, to show Brenda that she was in full command of herself.

"You saw us?"

"I— A friend did."

"What friend?"

"Does it matter? The point is I know. And you never bothered to tell me."

"Your friend must not have very good eyes."

Mrs. Dambar twisted the diamond ring her husband had given her, the one she was afraid to ask about—if it had belonged to Jane or not.

"Because I've only eaten at Isola Bella once in the past six months. I usually eat here at the mall. And that one time was with a woman."

"But . . ."

"A friend of mine, Donna Lee. I can give you her number if you'd like to verify it. Yes, I believe it was on Thursday."

"But I can't . . . You must have . . ."

Dr. Lahey adjusted the Head tennis racket that was propped against her chair. "She did have to leave a little early, before I finished my dessert. And Leo, all right, walked by and saw me inside. He came in and had a cup of coffee with me. If I had known he was going to walk by, I suppose I would have reported it to you. As it was, I just didn't think that it was really that important."

A digit changed in the square clock. Mrs. Dambar preferred time to revolve in smooth circles, not to jump so unpredictably at discrete intervals. "But don't you see—even if it was just coffee . . ."

"She's at Herbert and Herbert. I have her number if you want to check it out. Her name is Donna Lee Keely."

"Keely?" She wondered if she was any relation to Mrs. Keely. And Herbert and Herbert—that was Lucius Herbert. Why did everything have to seem so connected? It made her uneasy. "Don't be ridiculous, Brenda. I'm not going to check anything out. The point is—I just find it far too stressful to know you know him in any way. This sort of thing would never happen in New York. I feel it impairs your ability to be objective about my situation."

"Maybe you're right about New York. Perhaps there you may never cross paths in any circumstantial way. But I doubt anyone in a town this size can live in a glass bubble."

"I'm not asking you to live in a glass bubble." Mrs. Dambar took a moment to make her left breast the same size as her right; a shoulder pad had slid down, giving her an excess bulge that she hadn't been able to figure out for some minutes. Setting things straight, she felt much better. "It's plain, though, that someone as important as Leo—you should feel you have a responsibility to me on that count. To fraternize with him in any way, it seems almost unethical. No, Brenda, I don't care if he had only a sip of coffee with you. I've made up my mind. I'm sorry it had to work out this way. But I just don't think I can carry on with our professional relationship."

Dr. Lahey crossed her legs so that the birthmark was no longer showing. "Gretchen, I think you're making a mistake. I think I'm able to help you. I've got an idea of what's going on, and I think if we work together you'd be able to see the pattern, too."

"Pattern?" It was such a condescending term, as if Gretchen were some sort of aborigine with interesting mating rituals.

"I don't like to do this, but let me tell you what I see. I see a woman crying out for help, someone who has tremendous difficulties establishing trusting relationships with other people. I see a woman who at the age of forty or so left all her friends and relations behind. Why? What was she afraid of? I think this woman is terrified of intimacy. The closer you get to someone, the more afraid you are. Your best friends are strangers—aren't they? You have this honeymoon period—like when you first met me. I couldn't do any wrong. You were praising me to the skies. But the longer you've known me, the more doubts spring up in your mind. To tell the truth, it's not your relationship with me that matters so much. I do care about you a lot, don't be mistaken. But if you leave me, well, my life is full. So is my schedule here at the office. But what worries me is that this pattern is going to be played out with someone else eventually."

"Who? Leo? Well, I'd like nothing better, Dr. Lahey. I'll draw my first real breath of fresh air when that man is out of my life. I can't tell you how good it will feel."

"I'm not speaking of Leo. It's your husband I'm worried about."

"Frank? Me leave Frank? You've got to be kidding." She decided right there and then that she was furious at Brenda. "I love him. He is everything to me. Do you think I left all my friends and relatives because I wanted to? It was hard—damn hard. But I had to make a choice. I sacrificed everything for love—my career, my home. And you have the nerve to twist it around like I was running away from something. It's so unfair, Brenda."

Dr. Lahey reached over and handed her a handkerchief. Mrs. Dambar pressed it against her eyes for a moment, then blew her nose.

"What are you running from?" Dr. Lahey asked as Mrs. Dambar handed it back.

"I forgot my checkbook," Mrs. Dambar said, ignoring the question as she got to her feet. "I'll have it in the mail this afternoon, your fee." She felt her left shoulder, to make sure the pad was in place. It was. "Good-bye, Brenda."

"You have my number."

"I won't need your number anymore, I assure you."

Francine regarded the check Leo had returned to his boss that morning, which Mr. Dambar had now handed over to her so she could make the proper adjustments in the books. "So he never cashed it?"

"Apparently not."

"And it was sitting in your checking account all this time, not earning a dime of interest?"

"Not only that, I paid myself back from D&D Building Supplies without telling Mrs. Sklar. What I'll do is make out a personal check to D&D for $4,213, which you can deposit this afternoon."

"That's going to look so strange. How do I explain all this to Mrs. Sklar?"

"I'm sure you can think of something."

"How about the truth?"

"Lord no, Francine. Mrs. Sklar will think I'm off my rocker handing out my money like that before the bankruptcy business is even settled."

"Well, why did he wait so long to hand it back—Leo?"

"What? Oh, who knows." Leo had told him that he had lost the check—and then it had mysteriously reappeared in his desk drawer. By "mysteriously" he made it clear that he suspected Gretchen of searching through his desk, something he would rather not have to try to explain to Francine.

"What did you call the $4,213 that you gave yourself from D&D?"

"Nothing. I thought I'd describe it later—maybe personal expenses or something. In any case, my personal check will cancel it out."

"Oh, Frank, really. From now on, just ask me first. You've made a real mess." The door closed a little harder than necessary behind her, leaving him alone in the glass cubicle. Ever since their trip to Ozone, Francine had seemed moodier, though just as efficient. He resolved to be more consistent with her in the future, to forgo the personal chats. Granted, he would remain pleasant and affable, but she must realize their association was strictly professional.

Francine was perhaps the first victim of the fallout from his recent trip to Baton Rouge with Shaerl. He was appalled at his behavior and could not think of their talk at the L.S.U. Student Union without wincing. In the past he had always taken a somewhat avuncular interest in the girl. He admired Shaerl's intelligence, her get-up-and-go. What then could have made him behave so degenerately? Well, it was a blessing that she hadn't responded. He could thank the good Lord for that. And also, she probably hadn't had the slightest idea of what was going on. So they could return to their normal everyday roles with no harm done except to his self esteem. To think that he had come so close to turning into a depraved old man—it made him shudder.

And it also made him think twice about what he was doing with Gretchen. He would have to cut it out. No more mention of scrubbing, scouring, mopping, or vacuuming. Everything from now on would be strictly normal, he promised himself. After all, what must Gretchen think of him? She was good to have put up with it as long as she had—or was she? Perhaps she could have discouraged him, not made it so easy. Doesn't it take two to tango? Of course, this was unmanly to try to shift the blame. No, he was responsible. And there he was, just last night, in Mr. Keely's living room, listening to a discussion of Philemon for the Men's Bible Study Group. How horrified those men would be if they ever found out how truly depraved he was. And yet he had been able to sit there so calmly, even somewhat proud of himself when everyone got mixed up about Onesimus and he had corrected them. "Onesimus was the runaway slave, Mr. Pickens, not Philemon."

After Mrs. Sklar had dropped him off on her way home from work, he saw for the first time his own living room, minus the carpeting. Everything looked so cheerless, so cold, without the royal blue, and with the furniture still in disarray, it felt as if they were in the process of moving out. He wondered if it had been such a good idea to let Leo talk him into this change. After all, the house was at one time considered a showcase. Jane had gotten it featured in a Sunday supplement twice, a four-color spread.

His Johnnie Walker Black, faithfully poured and mixed with just the right amount of water, was waiting for him in the library. After gulping half of it down, he felt a little better. What did it matter if he had wall-to-wall or not? He went to the phone to give Shaerl a buzz in the trailer. It would be nice, wouldn't it, to thank her for setting out the drink so thoughtfully.

"—it says ninety-nine and forty-four percents pure, no?" he overheard Mrs. Howard on the line. "So what I want to know is what is the fifty-six percents impure you puts in? Why you got to do that?"

He hung up. Mrs. Howard was in the habit of calling the toll-free numbers listed on the labels of household items. Apparently she was upset with Ivory soap.

The glass was empty soon, quicker than usual. After pouring himself a refill, he noticed that he had turned on the TV. Or had it been on, soundlessly, when he came in? With a shrug he wandered to the French doors and gazed out.

Leo was in the garden—but what was it about the boy? He looked so much younger, or was it just the light? Although his face was indistinct, the body itself seemed lithe, supple, even joyful as he toiled among the weeds. So many had sprung up—overnight, it seemed—a lush, tropical growth. Mr. Dambar had risen early that morning and pulled a few before breakfast. Maybe now he should go out and give Leo a hand.

He was about to, when he noticed the bottle on the desk. Chanel No. 22. Shaerl must have left it when she had come to pour his drink. He picked it up, thinking he might return it in case she was looking for it. Then he would help Leo.

The top was off. He should find the top before he went out. But for some reason his eyes were drawn back to the garden, those weeds. Never before had he seen such an intense green, the light dancing from the sheaves in Leo's arms to the more muted greens of the far pasture. And yet there seemed to be no distance, as if Leo could reach out and touch the billboard near the highway. It made his heart ache, this ragged emerald.

When he brought the bottle to his nose, the scent was a jolt, blurring his eyes and then burning a passage down to his lungs. Another sniff—out of curiosity—and the burning sensation again. Good heavens, he thought, there should be a warning on the label. This was the strongest cologne he had ever come across.

One final sniff and the burning spread from his lungs and down his left arm. Though it hurt something fierce, he felt the pure unadulterated joy of being scoured clean, once and for all. In the garden the boy raised his own arm—as if to urge him on into the green that was roaring in his ears like the phantom waves of a conch.

PART II

Chapter Twelve

After the funeral Frank, Jr.—the older son, a Shreveport veterinarian—moved into the house on a temporary basis with his wife and two children until all the legal and financial affairs connected with Mr. Dambar's estate were settled. As executor of the will, Frank, Jr., kindly offered Gretchen a room in the house for as long as she cared to remain. It turned out that Mr. Dambar had never gotten around to revising his will; Gretchen was not mentioned. When she was informed of this in a gentle, professional manner by Mr. Herbert, she felt strangely relieved. There was nothing more distasteful to her than ugly court battles among family members. For she was sure that if Frank had left her the house or any money, the sons would have contested the will. Neither one had ever approved of her, she knew. And though they were cordial at the funeral, they hardly offered the sympathy a widow had a right to expect.

Two weeks after the service at Frederik Episcopal Church she found herself installed in a rented farmhouse on the Old Jeff Davis Highway, eleven miles from the Tula Springs city limits. Mr. Herbert had taken care of the arrangements. She had been under sedation a good deal of the time, Dr. Jonsen's prescription supplemented by Molly's Valiums. Though Henry had an opening in Tribeca and couldn't possibly get away, Molly had appeared on the morning of the funeral looking dazed and discomfited after a hundred-and-twenty-seven-dollar cab ride from New Orleans's Moisant Airport. She proved useful as a buffer between Frank, Jr., and Gretchen, keeping a close watch on her friend's privacy. But once Gretchen made the move to the farm, it was a different story. Molly's solicitude began to seem a little bossy, and there was an edge to her voice that grated on Gretchen's nerves. Perhaps she had gotten used to a gentler, more Southern manner of speaking. In any case, Molly was at times impatient and willful. She could not understand why Gretchen did not fly back to New York with her.

"You've got to make a fresh start, put all this behind you," Molly would urge as they sipped Lapsang souchong in the farmhouse's modest living room. "You still have your apartment, right? I'll get rid of my cousin for you, and it will be just like the old days."

Gretchen could not put into words that the last thing she needed was another "fresh start." No, what she yearned for was a sense of an end, a completion. "The rug's been pulled out too quickly from under me, Molly. I need to get my bearings."

"What rug? Oh, you mean Frank."

Though Gretchen was sure Molly didn't intend to sound callous, the way she tossed off, "Oh, you mean Frank," wounded her. For Molly, Frank would always be just a name. She had never seen him, never known what a gentle, loving soul he was. And as a result, she could only put her own interpretation on events. "You realize you're in shock now, Gretchen. Once you come to your senses, I'm sure you'll be back in New York."

After three days on the farm Molly packed her battered Louis Vuitton suitcase. They parted with a hug, tears in their eyes. Perky and petite, though with considerable gray in her straight, unkempt hair, Molly was more like her old self as they waited on the porch for Mel, who was going to drive her to the airport. Gretchen had the feeling then that they were only playing at being older, like two high school girls onstage—that all her sorrow was something she had memorized in a night.

When she woke the next morning, she stared for a time at the pine dresser on the far side of the bedroom. As her gaze wandered to the cedar chest, the braided throw rug that with all the other furnishings had come with the house, it occurred to her: This was what she had always wanted. A simple room, straight lines, no frills. The irony frightened her. It was like one of those cruel fairy tales in which a poor child—a milkmaid, a tinker's daughter—learns to rue the day her wish came true.

That afternoon Bitsy Hayes-Broune, an aunt by marriage, called from her home in Aix to express her concern and support. She was only a year older than Gretchen and an accomplished harpist who had made a recording with the Orchestra of Radio Luxembourg. Gretchen had a hard time visualizing whom she was speaking to. It had been years since they had seen each other. Bitsy had a warm, matronly voice that kept on urging her to "open up the floodgates. Go ahead and cry, right now. Don't hold it in, love." Getting off the phone with her was an enormous relief.

The next day, around three A.M., she had a call from her mother, who was vacationing in Moscow with her third husband, a retired underwater photographer. She told Gretchen that she was planning to take the next direct flight she could find to Louisiana. But she was worried that she might need a visa. Gretchen thanked her for calling, but recommended that she go on with her vacation plans. There was plenty of time for a visit later. Not long afterward she received five calls in one day from various aunts and uncles, plus three from Foxcroft alumnae. It was too much. From then on she refused to answer unless there were two rings and a pause. This was Mel's signal.

Twice a week Mel would drive in from town with groceries. Without being asked, he began doing odd jobs around the place. In the barn he found a scythe, and before long the ragged border around the pond was tamed. Gretchen paid him six dollars an hour, though he was scrupulous about deducting the time he spent shooting baskets in the barn, which had a hoop. One afternoon he cleaned the algae and grime from a concrete watering trough, a task that wasn't really necessary, since Gretchen had no plans to buy any animals. A horse, a cow, a pig—they seemed too much of a responsibility.

Sometimes, groggy from the pills that knocked her out each night, she would bring her coffee down to the pond in the morning. Dragonflies hovered with mechanical ease among stems bristling with hair, while sharp-toothed petals and thick milky leaves harbored a porcelain translucence. At times the swirls and curlicues of violet or yellow would take on the air of painstaking reproductions, as if someone with infinite patience had worked in soft paste. Though minnows pocked the algae-green skin of the pond, she had never seen a fish of any size. Water bugs skated blithely in the warm shallows, the surface tension firm as a mattress beneath their legs. Cocking her head at a certain angle she could transform their drab brown shells into an intricate network of teal and orange.

"Now why did you get another pack of granola bars?" she asked one morning shortly after returning from the pond.

Mel had driven up with groceries from Winn-Dixie and was helping her put them away. "I thought you liked them."

"There's three boxes in the cupboard. I can't possibly eat all this."

She looked with despair at the package. They were chocolate-dipped with a peanut butter center. With a sigh she stuck them in the cupboard behind a bag of whole wheat flour.

"You're going to have to defrost. Look at this freezer," he commented as he tried to insert a package of tofu ice cream sandwiches between the swollen walls of ice.

"I suppose. How is Mr. Ames?"

The week before Mr. Ames had fallen off a ladder while trying to spray beetles in the attic of a retired schoolteacher's house. His ankle was sprained. "He's getting around OK now. I rented him a cane at the mall."

"You can rent canes?"

"Sure, why not? Hey, check this out."

Mel held up a blue and white teapot in the shape of a hen. It had come with the house. "Neat."

Gretchen smiled faintly.

"I like Mrs. Sanchez. She has my taste."

"Who's Mrs. Sanchez?" Gretchen asked, looking worriedly at the teapot Mel was flourishing.

"The lady you rent this place from. Her mother had a stroke, so she moved into the old lady's house in town for the time being—to look after her. Didn't Mr. Herbert tell you?"

"No, I let him take care of all the details."

When the groceries had been put away, they wandered out to the porch. Mel sprawled on the wooden swing, one foot pumping it up and back. Gretchen collapsed onto a worn, comfortable armchair that she had appropriated from the living room. Often when they were together like this, saying little or nothing as they stared off at the pines walling in the distant highway, she would start to cry in a quiet, unobtrusive way. At first Mel seemed embarrassed; his hands and feet would fidget while he served up platitudes. But after a while he seemed to grow used to it and would sit quietly until it was over.

"If you could have any car in the world you wanted, what would it be?" he said presently, after she had blown her nose and wiped away the tears. Her face felt bloated and raw.

"What? Oh, I don't know."

"Me, I'd take a Lincoln Continental, silver with black leather interior. Now that's class."

She rooted about in her handbag for more tissue.

He sighed. "There's just something about a Lincoln that gets me—you know, deep down." The chain creaked as he pumped a bit faster.

"Would you like some tea, Mel?"

He yawned and stretched. "Better not. I got to get rolling. Mrs. Lamarca is dropping by at noon for me to do her taxes, and I got to warn Mr. Ames to stay in his room. She can't stand him."

"Why is that?"

He shrugged. "Don't know. They never talk, don't even know each other. It's just instinctive, I guess." Looking back over his shoulder as he went down the porch steps, he added, "You all right?"

She nodded. "Just don't bring me any more of those granola things. They're beginning to depress me."

He smiled as he crammed his long legs into his stepfather's yellow compact. There was a crack in the windshield, and the grill was caked with bugs. As he sped down the half-mile-long dirt drive the car sounded as if it could use a new muffler.

217

One morning she woke up and decided she should drive into town for some Super Glue. It was probably not a good idea to rely entirely on Mel for everything she needed from town. And that day, she realized, Mel would not be able to come see her. He was doing taxes in the afternoon, and later he would have to go to Baton Rouge for classes. If she wanted to get the platter fixed that she had dropped the night before, she would have to do it herself.

Mr. Herbert had leased for her an olive Ford Escort, two door. Getting into it for the first time, she discovered it was a stick shift. After driving around in the oval in front of the barn, she felt more confident about using the clutch and headed for the highway.

At the end of the access road she looked both ways and saw she had plenty of space to pull out. A white Volkswagen coming from town at what seemed a slow speed was the only car in sight. Probably, though, because of the clutch, it would be better to let it pass. She would have to go up a sharp incline to get on the highway and she didn't want to stall.

After the white car there was a pickup, which she also let pass. Gravel spat out from under her wheels as she gunned the engine and nosed a little closer. But when she looked to her right, she saw a trailer heading for town. Probably she could have pulled out, but she decided to let it go by. Matching chintz curtains were hanging in all the windows, and she thought she saw an old woman inside putting on lipstick. Somewhat unnerved by the sight, Mrs. Dambar missed two more opportunities for pulling out.

Five minutes later she gave up and backed the car down the road to the house, where she left it under the shade of a chinaberry. She decided she really didn't need the glue that bad. Mel could bring it on his next trip from town.

"After all, she wasn't married to him that long, only a few months, wasn't it?" Robert, the younger son, had brought a friend to the funeral, a good-looking law school student who had made this remark in the kitchen just before it was time to leave for the church. Neither Conrad, the friend, nor Robert had seen her come into the kitchen, so it wasn't a deliberate cruelty. Nevertheless, she was stung. And from that moment on she thought she could read this thought in everyone's eyes and hear it in their whispers. For the service she had worn the dress that wouldn't zip all the way up the back, and the shawl. Molly had tried to find something else for her in the closets, but the few other dresses she had on hand seemed too casual. When Mrs. Bill Anderson showed up in black, with a veil covering her face, leaning upon the arm of Mrs. Keely, Gretchen felt for a while almost disembodied, as if she were watching herself go through the ritual of mourning. Feeling so unreal, with Molly beside her, she could not cry.

Only a few months. The platter was on the kitchen table, the break clean, and beside it a note reminding her to call Mel about the Super Glue. She was about to pick up the phone when she started making some computations on the note. Seven months in the Philippines; five months, one week, six days with Frank. She looked hard at these figures, hoping they would make sense to her. But the equation seemed to belong to a higher math, to a quantum calculation that would cover an entire blackboard.

"Hey, this is good."

"What? Oh, Mel, give it here."

Holding on to the onionskin, he read aloud. " 'The sensibility is that of someone nourished exclusively on made-for-TV movies. Mrs. Marcos is the apotheosis of the third rate, just as Mr. Reagan demonstrates the—' "

She snatched the paper from his hand. It was the letter to the *New York Times* that she had started in the winter during Henry's surprise visit. How foolish it sounded to her now; no one cared about Mrs. Marcos anymore.

"Where did you get it?" she asked, tearing it carefully to pieces.

"It was folded up here." He tapped her checkbook. "What's Altman's?" he added, examining one of her bills.

"A department store. I ordered a birthday gift for my mother last month."

Mel paid her bills for her now. For some reason the very sight of her checkbook made her slightly ill. She even allowed him to send her Uncle Laeton whatever information he required to do her taxes.

As for cash, Mel had helped her open an account at the bank he used. She and Frank had never gotten around to opening a joint account. If she needed spending money, he just handed it over, no questions asked.

"Did you bring the glue?" she asked after he had put her checkbook away.

"Let me see that platter. I got some good stuff right here in my pocket."

The kitchen table wobbled as he leaned over to examine the break. With a quaint border of faded pigs, the platter seemed old, possibly of some value, and not easily replaceable. She was annoyed with herself for letting it drop from her hands the other night as she washed it in scalding water.

"You think it can be fixed?"

His tongue between his teeth, he applied the glue. She noticed that he had on Shirt Number Three. Mel, she had determined, owned only three shirts, which he alternated throughout the week. Each was faded and threadbare, yet they were always freshly laundered and ironed, thanks to Mr. Ames.

"Mel?"

"It's coming. Move out of the light, OK?"

Last night before going to bed Gretchen had once again considered taking an overdose of Dr. Jonsen's sleeping pills. She realized, of course, that she had the strength to go on living. But the life that stretched out before her had no purpose, no meaning. Without Frank, every breath seemed an effort of the will. He was the linchpin, the love she had staked everything on. It was only with the greatest bitterness that she could think of Dr. Lahey. The gall of that woman to think that she, Gretchen, would ever have left him. Sometimes this anger would seep over into her dreams. Not infrequently she would wake with a cry from a vivid, realistic scenario in which Frank was very much alive—and happily divorced from her. Sitting up in bed she would experience the most shameful relief that this was not true, that he was only dead.

"Hold this." Mel reached for her hand and guided it to the piece of china to which he had applied the glue.

Perhaps it was the thought of Mel that had kept her from taking those pills. It would be so inconsiderate, making him deal with the body he would find upon the bed. But as the shock of Frank's death began to wear off, as she came to accept the fact that he was truly gone, that he would never return, the pills continued to be a temptation. And one day, she was afraid, Mel might not be enough.

She was in the backyard raking up some bits of shredded newspaper that Mel had run over with the lawnmower the day before, when the car pulled up. She heard someone go to the side door of the frame house and knock.

"Anyone home?" a voice called out, a woman's.

Unnerved by the thought of a visitor, Gretchen stood still, hoping whoever it was would go away. In her hands was a scrap of paper that had escaped the blades. "Louisiana Public Service Commissioner George Jenerette," she read, "said South Central Bell will begin mailing out $30 million plus interest in refund checks to it's customers. The refunds are part of an oder issued by the Commission on March 1 dealing with the telephone company's depreciation rates. The—"

"Oh, here you be." The woman had come around the side of the house, an older lady with sunglasses and wide heels that left hooflike prints in the soggy saint augustine. It had rained heavily only a few hours before.

Gretchen nodded uncertainly.

"When Frank, Jr., told me you were living out here—well, naturally I assumed you had gone back up North, dear. I was so mad at that sucker for waiting so long to tell me. Of course, I would have dropped by sooner. Lordie me, these forsythia. They hurt your eyes."

The old woman had pulled up her designer sunglasses for a better look at the brilliant yellow hedge beneath the kitchen window. When she did, Gretchen recognized her.

"How are you, Mrs. Sklar?" In her hands was a covered cake pan, which Gretchen relieved her of. "Here, let me."

With a gust of wind Mrs. Sklar's rayon print dress suddenly

blossomed about her waist, revealing a pair of sturdy legs. There was no Marilyn Monroe-like squeal as the aunt gave the dress a healthy swat.

"You're looking good," Mrs. Sklar said after she had invited herself in for a cup of coffee and a bite of the cake.

"It's nice out here." Gretchen put a slice of the homemade coconut cake on a glass plate for the aunt. She herself was not hungry.

"Nice enough for now, dear. But believe you me, in a couple weeks you'll be sweltering. I didn't notice any air conditioners in the windows. Why don't you let me get one of my boys to put one in for you? I can get it for you at cost."

"I don't like air conditioning."

"Can't live without it down here. The heat can be murder. And another thing, if I were you I'd get my car from under that china-berry. You're going to be cleaning up after those berries every time you want to drive." She took a sip of the instant coffee while Gretchen sat with a fixed smile on her weary face. "Listen to me, handing out advice like this. You got to take me with a grain of salt, you know, Gretchen. I'm just so used to running things, I can't stop."

An awkward silence followed. Gretchen tried to come up with some small talk to cover her resentment. It was a fine time for the aunt to visit now. Why couldn't she have dropped over just once when Frank was alive? She could have made a difference then, helped Gretchen to feel less like a stranger.

"Not bad," Mrs. Sklar said finally after taking a test bite of the cake. "Pillsbury. I always tell Ocea to use Betty Crocker. She swears by Pillsbury, though. Won't use no other. Ocea's been with me thirty-seven years now. She's quit for good six times and once tried to set fire to my hair. But we're still hanging in there. Why?—I don't know."

"Your maid?"

"That's right. Now look, Ocea's got a friend. She could come out here and give you a hand, Gretchen. Why don't you let me talk to her when I get home. It wouldn't cost you much, I guarantee."

"No thanks, I'm fine."

The gingham curtains over the sink stirred in a gust of wind. Both women turned their heads slightly and, for want of anything better to do, stared at them a moment.

With a sigh Mrs. Sklar reached for her handbag. "Gretchen, you'll forgive me, I'm sure, but there is one bit of business I'd like to clear up." Taking a piece of paper from the handbag, she gave it to her to examine. "Does this mean anything to you?"

It was Frank's handwriting on a check made out to Leo Vogel for $4,213. Gretchen's hand trembled as she handed it back to the aunt.

"No, nothing? I can't imagine what Frank could mean, doing all this behind my back. Francine at the office has some long involved explanation—but I thought you might know better yourself. It's a personal check, that's what I can't understand."

For the most part she had been able to suppress any thought of Leo. But now to be confronted with the dreadful memory, the misery that man had caused her—it almost completely ruined the picture she had been building up in her mind of the way things had been. Her only comfort these days was to cling to the memory of her joy, the perfect idyll that her marriage had been. She was not going to have this ruined.

"Mrs. Sklar, I'm sorry, but I've simply got to—"

"Of course, I'm in a hurry myself," the aunt said, getting up from the table as Gretchen went to the sink with the cups and saucers. "You let me know if you change your mind—about Ocea, I mean. Her friend."

"I don't want a maid."

"Yes, of course, dear. Well . . ." She hesitated at the kitchen's screen door. "Gretchen, I am so sorry. If there's anything I can do. We're all just devastated. Francine, you know, she didn't come back to the office for two weeks. Even now I catch her with tears in her eyes." The old woman had put on her sunglasses. "When Percy, my husband, passed away, well, it seems like just yesterday. Ocea called me at the office. I was sitting there doing the estimated tax and—Stop me, Gretchen. Here I am running on and I'm sure you got better things to do. Now you remember, girl, call me anytime you need something, hear? Don't be shy."

After she left Gretchen locked the screen door and pulled down the shade behind the gingham curtains. Then she went and lay down on the sofa in the living room.

"I never was so happy in my entire life. You know, before I met Frank, I really didn't have much faith in marriage at all. I always thought work was the key to happiness, for women as well as men—good, creative, productive work. That was the true expression of the self. Lord, what a ninny I was. It was Frank who turned all that around. When I married him, I suddenly discovered the truth behind all those clichés I had always turned my nose up at. Marriage for a woman—and for a man, too—a real marriage is the most fulfilling thing a person can ever experience in life. Someday you're going to meet your Frank, too. And when you do, grab onto him. Hold him tight. Don't let anything matter more than this relationship. Nothing counts, really, alongside it."

Gretchen poured herself another glass of white wine and was about to do the same for Shaerl, but the girl put a hand over her glass.

"No thanks, I got a lot of studying to do tonight."

It was a Sunday. Shaerl had driven in from L.S.U. to her aunt's in town, from where she had given Gretchen a call. She wondered if she might drop by on her way back to Baton Rouge. Instinctively, Gretchen had made up an excuse, saying something about the house being a mess and nothing to eat. But Shaerl didn't seem to get the hint. She was polite, but insistent. "I'll just stay a minute. And I've already had lunch at my aunt's." To prepare herself for the visit, Gretchen had poured herself two or three shots of Polish vodka that she kept in the freezer.

The first thing she noticed was that Shaerl's limp was much improved. She walked evenly, with only a slight hitch as she mounted the stairs to the porch, where Gretchen had set out the wine in a wooden pail filled with ice. The girl was well dressed, as usual, though in a more conservative style. Her hair, black again, was cut in a less ruthless fashion, with both sides the same length.

"I think I'm beginning to like Keynes," Shaerl said after Gretchen had refilled her own glass. For a moment Gretchen wondered if the girl was being rude. Surely what she had just said about marriage deserved some sort of comment.

Lighting a Merit in the flame of the scented candle that was supposed to discourage insects, Shaerl went on. "I have this old professor who actually met him once. He's making him sound less weird."

"Well, yes, Keynes is wonderful. And it's wonderful, too, that you're getting your master's. But I hope you're not going to be unrealistic about what a degree can do. Look at me, I didn't do badly at all at Radcliffe. And what doors did that open for me? I'll tell you: seventy-five hundred a year as a secretary at Ogilvie and Mather. My cousin Henry, he waltzes in a few months later at three times the salary. And they expect me to stay there? Everybody wonders why I went to the Philippines. Well, it's not that hard to figure out." They had been rather large shots of vodka. And now, after two glasses of wine, she was concerned that she might slur some of her words. So she was careful to enunciate, which made her sound prim, schoolmarmish. To compensate for this, she interjected a wink or two and slouched in the wicker chair.

"Last week, Wednesday, I think, I was in town," Shaerl began after a slight pause. "I went to see Mrs. Howard. She's got the nicest little house not far from the library. She told me how generous Frank was in his will. It was so like him, to remember her like that. He was the most considerate man I ever met. Anyway, she asked me to give you her number. I've written it here somewhere."

While she flipped through the pages of a looseleaf notebook, Gretchen said, "Please, don't bother."

"You really ought to call her, go see her. She doesn't have any real friends. Her whole life revolved around Frank, you know."

"I said don't bother," Gretchen repeated, a little roughly. Shaerl looked up, surprised.

It was amazing how naive the girl was. Frank had been struck down by a massive heart attack, losing consciousness in the library and dying in the ambulance on the way to the hospital. And what had brought this on? Years and years of Mrs. Howard's criminal indulgence—the pork, the ham, ice cream, Scotch, pies, whipped cream, strudel. It made Gretchen so angry that, were it not for Mrs.

225

Howard's having fled from Germany, she would have given the woman the tongue lashing of her life. As it was, she was being charitable by leaving the old woman in peace.

"How much did Frank leave her?"

"What? I don't know exactly. Enough so she'd never have to worry. Frank, Jr., was pretty upset when he found out. He said it was cockeyed for a young man like his dad to leave so much to an old woman. And he wouldn't let Mrs. Howard go on working for him. She offered to, you know."

"Well, good. It's high time she retired."

Gulping the rest of the wine in her glass, Gretchen felt the intense regret that she had kept at bay for so long well up inside her. She hadn't followed her instinct—and because of this Frank was dead. Hadn't her instinct told her, plainly and clearly, that Mrs. Howard was a danger? Hadn't her subconscious been warning her all along? She had even written it down and talked to Dr. Lahey about it. She was Gretel; Frank, Hänsel—and what did that make Mrs. Howard? The tune had been going through her head, the same tune she had heard just before her father's death. Her heart had known everything. But she wouldn't listen to it. No, she had to be swayed by reason—and fear of upsetting Mrs. Howard and displeasing Frank. And out of those petty motives—afraid of being disliked—she had ended up as an accomplice to the old woman. She didn't know if she could ever forgive herself for that.

"I'm sorry," she said presently, seeing the hurt look in Shaerl's warm doe eyes. "I don't mean to sound so . . . Anyway, it's too soon. I can't really deal with anything that has to do with Frank. It hurts too much."

"Gretchen, that's what I wanted to talk to you about. That's why I came here."

Looking out over the small civilized front yard, which ended abruptly in a field of weeds and dandelions that stretched to the highway, Gretchen propped her feet up on the railing and sighed. "Not now, please."

"But it's worried me so much. I don't think it's fair that you should take so much blame. You've got to realize that it's no one's fault really. Things just happen."

"What blame?" Puzzled, Gretchen turned to look at the girl.

"It's not your fault the ambulance took so long getting there. I had a big fight with Frank, Jr., about it. He said the doctor told him Frank might have lived if they could have got him to the hospital just five or ten minutes earlier."

"But I wasn't even there. It was Leo."

"That's just it. You had the only car that worked. Leo was fixing the Buick."

"And they're saying if he had only had the Jeep, he could have driven Frank much quicker—wouldn't have had to wait on the ambulance? Oh, Shaerl, that's so unfair."

"Well, they had heard about the accident, you know, with the Buick."

"But that had nothing to do with me."

"I know. But Leo had to redo the brakes, check them out after we went into that tree. In any case, I said to Frank, Jr., how could Gretchen know all this was going to happen when she went shopping at the mall? Isn't she allowed to shop? Is that a crime?"

"But I wasn't shopping. I had an emergency appointment with Dr. Lahey."

Shaerl carefully extinguished her cigarette in the candle holder. "I know. I left that part out."

"But why? It was important. I wasn't just going off to buy a new hat or something. They should know."

"Frank, Jr., is pretty conservative, much more than his dad. He doesn't really understand about shrinks. I think to him, only crazy people go—you know?"

Somewhat grimly, Gretchen reached for the bottle and poured herself another glass. Shaerl continued to regard her anxiously.

"Gretchen, I hate to pry. But I was wondering, I mean I've always wondered—why did you see someone? Am I being too personal?" She took the bottle and poured herself a half glass, as if to appease Gretchen, and then went on: "It always seemed so sad to me. There you were, married to one of the nicest, best-looking men in the whole world—and you had to have a therapist. I never could figure out why you seemed so miserable all the time."

"I was not miserable," she shot back.

"But you seemed so unhappy, really. I know the house bothered you, the furniture. But that couldn't have been it, could it? Sometimes, you know, I worried a lot that it was me you hated."

"Don't be ridiculous."

"Well, let me just talk now. Don't get mad. I have to get this off my mind. I know that Frank, like I said, was real good-looking, and I guess I'm sort of young and all and he might have sometimes looked at me a little too long or something."

"Do you think you might be flattering yourself, dear?"

"Well, OK, maybe so." The girl had stiffened and was sitting perfectly erect. "All I want to say is that we never, I never . . . I cared for him very deeply, but it was like a father. There was never anything at all wrong about our relationship. And I just thought you ought to know that."

"Why are you saying this? Not once did I ever suspect Frank. He was totally faithful, I know. The only thing I might have wondered about," she added after taking a sip from the wrong glass, "was maybe you and that uncle of yours."

Shaerl's face became cold, immobile. Gretchen realized she had gone too far. "Don't listen to me, Shaerl. I don't know what I'm saying. I'm sorry, really."

"It's OK."

"No, it was a stupid thing for me to say. Are you sure you wouldn't like some more wine?"

Shaerl had gotten to her feet. "I better be going."

"I was just upset by what you had told me, dear. You understand, don't you? It hurt me so, to hear what Frank, Jr., said about the car. How could anyone be so petty? You will forgive me, won't you?"

"I said it was OK."

As Shaerl walked back across the lawn to her car, it seemed to Gretchen that her limp was more pronounced. But the girl was learning to appreciate Keynes. That was something, wasn't it?

CHAPTER THIRTEEN

The Swamp Possum Resort was located within the city limits on a parcel of land that contained neither swamp nor opossums. A laminated sign over the entrance was enhanced by cartoon characters—each with a registered trademark—that promised competitive rates and a children's zoo. The zoo, upon inspection, consisted of three languishing alligators, one spider monkey, five squirrels, two raccoons, and a nutria. Nearby was a log cabin gift shop, the logs a veneer that looked real only from a distance of ten or fifteen feet. The few tourists who were lured with their campers for a weekend stay usually left after a single night since, aside from the zoo, there was nothing to do. Yet the advertising was so energetic—Swamp Possum was listed in several national guidebooks, thanks to Tula Springs's Boosters' Club—that word of mouth was effectively neutralized. The regular inhabitants of the trailer park coexisted peacefully with a steady stream of dazed-looking families who wandered fitfully in and out of the gift shop, the zoo.

Mr. Vogel's trailer was the most elegant among the permanent residents'. His neighbors, twin sisters originally from Fort Wayne, Indiana, had tried on several different occasions to strike up a conversation with Mr. Vogel in the hopes of being invited inside for a look at his decorating scheme. Erma Swann, a retired postal inspector, had peered in the picture window once when he was away and thought she had seen Early American. Grace Nan Rendozo, her widowed sister, had a feeling it was Danish Modern. But since Mr. Vogel remained standoffish, neither lady was ever able to settle the question to her satisfaction.

On Mondays, Wednesdays, and Fridays, Mr. Vogel rose at 6:30 in order to make an eight o'clock class at St. Jude State College in Ozone. He was getting a master's degree in counseling, having been awarded a fellowship that covered tuition and provided a modest sum for room and board. This Miss Swann and Mrs. Rendozo had ascertained from Carmen McMahon, who ran the gift shop and collected the rents.

"What about Tuesdays and Thursdays?" Gretchen asked.

Mel finished an entry in the checkbook before replying. "I think he might have a part-time job somewhere. But I haven't had a chance to follow up on it."

"Whatever you do, don't talk to those ladies anymore, the twins. They're bound to say something to Mr. Vogel."

They had just returned from town, Gretchen having driven in with Mel for a change of scene. She was afraid that if she didn't force herself to get away from the farm, she would become too attached and never want to leave. With the trunk loaded with groceries, Mel had pulled off at Swamp Possum, which was only a few blocks from the Winn-Dixie. He had mentioned the place to her before and thought that she might want to see it with her own eyes. At first she had protested, but when he assured her that Mr. Vogel was miles away, in Ozone, she let him have his way. The trailer was without its picket fence, and looked smaller than she remembered it. In the zoo she asked Mel to say something to the lady in the gift shop about the alligators' water, which looked none too clean. And when she saw the nutria—and the sign that said it was from South America, and was really "a coypu, extremely common in Louisiana wetlands"—she felt a small, but definite surge of self-confidence. "I'm not crazy after all," she told herself. Here was unequivocal, outside, objective proof that she had seen what she had seen.

"Mel," Gretchen asked later that same afternoon when he had finished paying her bills, "why did you bring me there? And why are you still following him? I don't care about Leo anymore—Mr.

Vogel. I'd rather forget about him. Please, do me a favor—no more. I don't want to hear any more about him. Understand?"

"You just asked me what he did on Tuesdays and Thursdays. And you wanted to know what he was getting his master's in. And yesterday or the day before, you wanted to know what sort of people lived there, at the trailer camp."

"I was just trying to make conversation, that's all. You're the one who brought him up—not me."

Mel performed a jump shot that made him groan. They were in the barn, where his awkwardness was much less in evidence as he dribbled and spun beneath the netless rim.

"I just want to keep an eye on him, Gretch."

She took a step away from him. His shirt was clinging to his back, and the odor, after only a few minutes of exercise, was a bit much. "What do you mean by that?"

He hitched his trousers up over his potbelly. "Nothing."

"Mel."

"Look, what do you think I spend so much time around here for?"

"I thought you'd like some extra cash, right?"

"Hey, you think my ambition in life is to be an errand boy, a gofer?" Anger gave his face an ugly look. It was the first time he had ever spoken to her like this—and it made her very uneasy. "It's eleven miles here, eleven miles back. That's a lot of gas, and it's a lot of time. I got accounts to do, you know. And studying."

"Dear, why didn't you say something before? I had no idea. You know I'll be glad to pay for the gas and the extra time, if you want."

"No, you don't get it, do you?" He had reverted to his old self, a lopsided grin restoring the charm to his ungainly, puppy-dog face. "Ah, Gretch . . ."

"What? Put down that ball. Talk to me."

He lobbed the ball into an empty hayrack. "OK, so what do you think? You're out here all alone. What am I supposed to do? Desert you? I consider us friends. And like, well, I think it's my duty to make sure you're safe."

"What do you mean, safe?"

"What did you hire me for in the first place? You were scared of the guy, right?"

"But that was before."

"Before what? You were afraid something bad was going to happen. And it did."

"Oh, Mel, don't talk foolish. There's no connection." She waved away a fly. "It was me—I was afraid something bad was going to happen to me."

"Well, something bad did happen to you. You lost your husband. What could be worse?"

"But it was a heart attack."

"Yes, and before, it was a car accident. All very natural and explainable."

"What accident? You mean Jane's? Well, yes, but . . ."

"And Leo just happened to be the last one to have seen the first Mrs. Dambar alive—to be in the same car with her. And then he's the last one to see Mr. Dambar alive. He was in the ambulance with him when he died, wasn't he?"

This was something she tried hard not to think about, that Leo, not she, had been beside him in those last moments. That he was the one who had heard his last words, who had spoken to him. She felt cheated. It was so unfair. If she could only have been with him, could have held his hand and assured him of her love, then her life might not seem so unreal to her now. There would have been a transition, a passage from the normal everyday world of married life to being a widow. Leo had stolen the end from her, the rightful end that was hers.

"Mel, I don't mean to sound harsh," she said, kicking a broken harness out of the way, "but if you ask me, it's high time you gave up playing private eye. No one has found the slightest cause for suspicion in either death. Frank's arteries were obstructed by—by fat and . . . As a matter of fact, if you didn't happen to be getting a degree in investigation or whatever it is you're studying—I'd say you were one paranoid young man."

"That's what our instructor told us last week, you know." Mel rested an arm on her shoulder. He did not seem the least offended.

"He said the best P.I.'s are totally paranoid. They've got a license to be paranoid. Otherwise, they'd be considered plain nut cases. It's the paranoid frame of mind that gives them the ability to put two and two together—to take things that seem on the outside totally unrelated and see how they're really part of a pattern. It's pretty neat, wouldn't you say? Sort of creative."

"Well fine, but I just wish you wouldn't practice your creativity on me. I can't take it. Really, I'm serious." She maneuvered herself gently so that they were no longer touching. "It hurts too much."

"I'm sorry, Gretch."

"If you're not going to want to bring me groceries anymore, I'll understand. I really didn't mean to take advantage of you." She trailed him to the hayrack, where he retrieved the smudged orange ball. "I simply can't have you playing detective when you're with me. We've got to get that straight, once and for all. If you feel it's too demeaning to be a handyman or whatever, well, Mrs. Sklar told me she can get a woman to come out and help. Mel?"

He was shooting baskets again, his loafers clattering like heels over the gray barn flooring.

"Mel, do you hear?"

"Sure thing. I just won't tell you anything from now on." The backboard shook as the ball missed the rim. "Like what I saw yesterday and the day before. I won't say a thing about that."

"What was that?"

"Lordy, Miss Dambar, I'm jes' the janitor. Can't tell you none of that."

"Stop clowning. Please."

"Can't tell you about that lady coming over to his trailer. The doctor."

"Lahey?"

"That's right. I'm not going to tell you a thing about it. And Mrs. Rendozo, she didn't see anything either. Neither did her sister."

The old dread knotted her stomach. She had thought that now, with Frank gone, it would also have been gone for good. But here it was again, as strong as ever. "I got something on the stove," she said, and as she stepped out of the unhinged barn door she reminded herself that there was nothing to be anxious about, that the worst had already happened.

The red rinse had grown out completely. She was more gray than she remembered being, though this might have only seemed so because she had gotten used to herself with no gray at all. Eating what she wanted—fresh vegetables, pasta, a little chicken every now and then—she found herself thinner than she had been in months, though without much energy. When the farmhouse came to seem as familiar as her grief, she began to wonder if Molly hadn't been right after all, if New York was not where she belonged. She would have to get a job eventually, not that she needed the money, but rather, to give some shape to her day. To have so much time on her hands, to have no one, nothing to devote it to, except herself, this was becoming as insupportable as her grief, perhaps even more so. There was nothing she could do in Tula Springs, of course. She had looked through the want ads and made a few discreet inquiries to Mr. Herbert about possible volunteer work. But nothing seemed appropriate. As far as the farm went, she could not do anything about stocking it with cows or pigs or horses, since Mrs. Sanchez had no intention of selling. The last time she had spoken to Henry, though, he had told her about a friend of his, a woman who was opening a gallery on Greene Street. She apparently needed someone to write catalogs for her. It would be part-time, but Henry was sure he could get her the job.

Sometimes she caught herself wandering aimlessly from room to room, unable to make up her mind about New York. She knew she had to start giving her life a new focus. If there were no Philippines, no Frank, then she would have to find something. Would she be happy in a Soho gallery? Probably not. But at least it would give her a reason to get out of bed in the morning.

And then, just on the verge of picking up the phone to call Delta, she would back away. The dread that Mel had revived, it had not disappeared with time as she had hoped. Day by day it seemed to encroach a little more into the space she had set aside for her sorrow and grief. And she was afraid that if she didn't do something

about it soon, it would spread like a cancer until even the grief itself
would have no room to thrive.

The dress that she used to have to wear the shawl with, because it
wouldn't close properly—now it zipped up fine. She hadn't worn
it since the funeral. But the occasion called for something dignified,
even formal. Mel had given her the address. Though she was still
uneasy about the stick shift on the Ford Escort, she made herself
drive into town alone. Once she had pulled out onto the highway,
she felt more confident, and shortly afterward, when she stalled
beside a road repair crew, she was not overly dismayed. It would
have been nice to have a license, but with Mel as a friend, it seemed
hardly necessary. Surely he would be able to smooth things out if
she were ever stopped.

The directions that Mel had drawn on a beige paper napkin
turned out to be rather ambiguous. She was supposed to make a
right on Flat Avenue, but that put her in what seemed to be the
wrong direction on North Gladiola. When she got to East Azalea,
there was no Red Spot Cafe, no Tommy Upholstery Repair. Making a U-turn she found her way back to Flat Avenue and hailed an
older woman who was coming out of the Sonny Boy Bargain Store.

"Could you tell me how to get to East Jersey?"

The woman approached the car window, an anxious look on
her homely, pinched face. "East Jersey? I believe that's off Ca-
mellia."

"Next to the upholsterer's?"

"No, you want the upholsterer, hon, you get on over to Azalea."

"I want East Jersey."

"Oh. Then I'd head for the A&P and cut through the back
parking lot. They's a pothole right before the four-way stop up
ahead, though. You keep your eye peeled." The woman fingered the
name tag on her lapel, which indicated she was a volunteer at the
hospital.

Gretchen thanked her, somewhat curtly, and headed for the
A&P by a circuitous route. She did not want to negotiate a four-way
stop with the stick shift.

In another minute or two, finding the volunteer's directions much simpler and more direct, she was at the correct address.

A plain-looking two-story house, it was nonetheless carefully tended, the trim around the windows freshly painted, the three panes on the door spotless. She took a deep breath as she pressed the bell. In a way, she was hoping he wouldn't come to the door. When she had thought about doing this, it seemed so just, so logical. Actually carrying it through, though, was quite another thing. She had to force herself to stand her ground when she heard someone approaching.

"Yes?"

He turned out to be trimmer and better-looking than she had imagined, though by no means handsome. Gretchen wished she hadn't worn her heels, for she was looking down at him, which seemed to make him uncomfortable.

"I'm very sorry to disturb you"—she hesitated a split second, wondering if she should call him "Sid" or "Mr. Lahey," neither of which seemed appropriate—"Mr. Sid, uh, Lahey. I wonder if you have a moment to talk."

He regarded her doubtfully, as if she were a Jehovah's Witness. "Well, I'm working now."

"Yes, I'm very sorry—but this is important. I'm a patient of your wife's, a former patient. And I feel—I think it's important that we discuss a certain matter."

"My wife isn't here, you know. She's at her office."

"Yes, I know."

His smile might have been a frown; it was hard to tell. "You are . . . ?"

"Pardon? Oh, Mrs. Frank Dambar."

"Well, I suppose . . ." With a stiff wave of his hand—a mock politesse, it seemed—he ushered her in.

Inside she was surprised to discover how sumptuous a nest the Laheys had made for themselves. Belying the austere exterior, the living room, though small, was paneled in a dark, gleaming wood that set off the rich, understated fabrics covering the sofa and arm-chairs. Books were everywhere, in handsome cases and open shelves

236

of burled elm adorned by Queen's Ware. Reflected in the brass Victorian coal bucket, a modest Aubusson rug added warmth to the varnished wide planks that seemed to have the original nineteenth-century square nailheads in them. All in all, it was a room that could have come right out of a magazine ad for a liqueur.

Mr. Lahey motioned her to the sofa, which, though soft, provided firm support for the back.

"As you might be aware," she said after they had exchanged a comment or two about the deplorable Oliver North, "I've recently lost my husband."

He murmured something sympathetic that she didn't quite catch.

"He died of a heart attack."

Another murmur while his eyes darted about the room.

"In any case," she went on, feeling a little more sure of herself, especially since he had agreed so readily to her views on the colonel, "before he died, I had entrusted myself to your wife's care."

"You know, Brenda doesn't really discuss her cases with me."

"No, perhaps not with you."

"She's at the mall," he said evenly, ignoring her remark. "I'm sure if you wanted to talk to her, she could make room for you today." He ran a compact boyish hand through his thinning hair, blond flecked with gray—and made another attempt at a smile.

"Mr. Lahey, Sid—if I may—I've been through a lot recently. Normally I would never dream of imposing on anyone as I am now. But I think I owe it to my marriage, to Frank, to set the record straight."

"Frank is your husband?"

She nodded, not bothering about the tense. "I loved him more than anyone else on earth. He was my whole life. To me that marriage meant more than I can possibly describe. I would have done anything to preserve it. And I did. I stuck it out. I didn't run away." Seeing the puzzled look on his face, she tried a different tack. "When I began to feel a strain in our relationship, I went to your wife for advice. I thought that maybe she could help explain what was going on. Frank, you know, had a rather unusual household."

"Indeed?" He nodded amiably, though looking somewhat anxious now, as if she might be concealing a weapon. "Would you excuse me a second?"

A teakettle had been whistling in the other room. While he went to attend to it, she tried to think of a way to make him less wary of her. After all, she was on his side. Ultimately she was here for his well-being, not just her own. Though the truth might be painful at first, in the long run it would be to his benefit to stop living a lie.

"Ah, yes," he said, rubbing his hands together as he returned to the room with a deferential grin on his wide, pleasant face.

She had hoped that he was going to offer her a cup of tea. It would make the visit seem more civilized. "As I was saying, my marriage meant everything to me. I wasn't like some of my girl-friends, who grabbed the first thing that came down the pike right after college. I had given myself a chance to mature, to know what I wanted."

"Mrs. . . . ?"

"Gretchen."

"Are you sure you want to tell me all this? I'm an architect, you know."

She regarded him steadily. "I'm leading up to something quite important. Trust me." She folded her hands over her purse in a gesture reminiscent of her great aunt Cecil, who used to terrify her as a girl. "I myself am basically a trusting person. I make it a practice to give everyone the benefit of the doubt. So I suppose that's why it took me so long to catch on. I had clear, objective evidence, but even then I was willing to doubt."

He was grasping one foot in his hand, like a teenage girl might, and stroking the loafer's soft buttery leather. "I'm sorry. I don't follow."

"What I'm leading up to is this—your wife's treatment of me was severely compromised by her personal life. It wreaked great havoc in my own mental and emotional well-being. I think I have a strong enough case to actually sue for damages. But I'm not going to do that. I think it will be sufficient to let you know the facts."

The distress in his eyes made her want to back down and reassure him. But she could not risk losing his complete attention.

"We have a lawyer you could speak to." He was squeezing the shoe hard. "Perhaps it would be better that way. Her name is Donna Lee Keely. She's with Herbert and Herbert."

"Herbert and Herbert also represents me, Sid. Let's forget about that. I'd like to keep this a private affair. Anyway, you and Brenda have been trying to have a child for some time—am I right?"

He nodded uncertainly. "She's pregnant now."

"Yes, suddenly she's pregnant—just when you're on the verge of giving up and adopting. A nice coincidence, isn't it, for Brandi?"

"Brandi?"

"Surely you know about Brandi?" She hated having to sound so cold and know-it-all. Yes, it was unfair that this decent man should have to bear the brunt of his wife's deception. But she was afraid that if she let down her guard, she would dissolve in tears of rage and pain. Mel had told her this wasn't going to be easy. And he had warned her that the worst thing she could do would be to become emotional, hysterical. It would destroy all credibility.

"Brandi's what they used to call her before we got married. I made her go back to her real name."

"Well, apparently she's been slipping. Sid, I don't like this anymore than you do, but . . ." She unlatched her purse and pulled out an envelope. "Here, read this. I want you to see this clear, objective evidence."

Since he made no move to approach the sofa, she got up and went to the armchair by the fireplace and handed it to him. Inside the envelope was a sworn notarized statement by Mel, giving the dates, times, and places of his sightings of Brenda with Leo, the most recent being only a few days ago. Mel, too, had considered it very curious that Brenda had managed to get pregnant after so many years. It was he who had urged Gretchen to confront Sid Lahey. The more she and Mel discussed it, the more everything seemed to fit together. Hadn't Brenda made Gretchen doubt herself from day one? Not once had Brenda suggested that Leo could be a real threat to her marriage. Instead she had encouraged Gretchen to believe that she was harboring paranoid feelings. Was it any wonder that she had lived with so much anxiety and dread? Who knows what Brenda and Leo had been up to? Mel even thought it possible—Gretchen did not go along with him here, of course—that there was some connection between the pregnancy and Frank's sudden death.

After glancing at the enclosed sheet for a moment, Sid Lahey looked up, puzzled. "I don't understand, Mrs. Dambar. What is this?"

"Do I have to draw you a picture? That man—your wife, suddenly pregnant . . ."

"But this is Leo, right? Leo Vogel."

"You know him?"

"A little. Brenda used to date him in college."

"Yes, she did. She was quite enamored of him, wasn't she?" Gretchen prompted.

Mr. Lahey shrugged and set the paper aside. "I suppose, but you know . . . I . . . Hey, wait, you're not trying to tell me—the baby. Leo?"

"Mr. Vogel was our handyman. I had good reason to suspect him of . . ." She broke off, for he appeared to be chuckling.

"Pardon me, Mrs. Dambar."

"I fail to see the humor."

"But Mrs. Dambar, Gretchen, surely you know about Leo."

"Know? Know what?"

"His little problem."

He had changed so completely, seemed so at ease, that she felt the same doubt again that had plagued her at the door. "I'm afraid I don't understand, Mr. Lahey."

"Well, Leo"—he was leaning forward, his voice lowered slightly—"he doesn't like women."

"What?"

"You know what I'm saying. Actually, I shouldn't be telling you this at all. He's only recently opened up to Brenda—and she really shouldn't have told me. Except that he's not really a patient. Anyway, they have been talking from time to time. It's no surprise. He's even been over to the house a couple times. Your man missed that, I see," he added, glancing over at the sheet on the end table.

"Well," Gretchen said, trying to hide her confusion, "it could be just a cover. He could be just saying that to—"

"Hey, hold on a second." His face had become suddenly hard as he rose out of his chair. "I don't know what you're up to, but let me tell you something. I love my wife, and nothing you say is going to make me doubt her. Besides, I have a chart provided by our doctor—every time we made love. You want objective evidence, I'll give you the damn chart. If not, I got work to do. The door's right over there, ma'am."

It started with the stove. She had spilled some fiber-enriched oat-meal on one of the knobs, and when she went to wipe it up, she noticed a grease spot just below it. The door to the broiler could use a once-over, and when she examined the burners and the pans beneath, she discovered a thin crust that had to be scrubbed off. Then there were the in-between places, the edges of the oven door, the raised lettering of the trademark—and the racks themselves.

After the stove it was the refrigerator. The vegetable bin had a puddle of brown water in it. The plastic lid covering the bin was speckled with margarine and low-sodium soy sauce. On the door the rubber molding needed a good scouring and the egg compartment was gritty. The chrome racks that held the food had to be taken out and scrubbed in the sink. Which gave her a good look at the sink itself. Though the bowl was clean enough, the curved edges had unseen collections of grease, and many permanent-looking stains could be lifted off with a steady application of steel wool.

The roach-repellent shelving paper in the cupboards was old and gummy. She took it up and scoured the wood beneath till it lost its shine. Then she wiped the dust from every piece of china, and with a wet rag assured herself that there would be no sticky feel to any of the cans and jars. Next was the kitchen floor. It was no good using a mop. She would have to get down on her hands and knees to make sure the job was properly done.

The bell made her look up. She was working on the strip of

linoleum next to the dishwasher, her scrubbing rhythmic, hard, and strangely pleasurable. She did not want to be interrupted. Hadn't she told Mel that from now on she would get her own groceries? She didn't need him anymore. He had caused enough trouble as it was.

The bell again. She hoped he wouldn't barge right in as he sometimes did. Perhaps she hadn't been firm enough with him. Afraid of hurting his feelings, she had tempered her remarks and so he might not realize how upset with him she really was.

"Gretchen?"

The voice startled her. It came from behind the screen door, only a few feet away from the dishwasher. She could not escape now.

"May I come in?" Brenda called out, unnecessarily loud, as if Gretchen were old and hard of hearing. "I was ringing the front bell, but I guess you . . . So I decided to come around and see. Hi."

Gretchen had gone out the kitchen door rather than let her walk over the linoleum. There by the side of the house a patch of lawn looked out onto the pond, which was fringed by weeds that sprang up as fast as they could be cut down. Gretchen had despaired of keeping a neatly trimmed bank.

"Hi," Brenda repeated, almost shyly. And when she got no response, she said, "I thought I'd return this to you."

Gretchen had not noticed how red and swollen her hands were until she reached for the envelope. The days of cleaning had taken their toll.

She did not have to look inside to know what it was—Mel's notarized statement, which, in her haste to get out of the Laheys' house, she had left behind. Stuffing it into the pocket of her khaki trousers, she looked past Brenda at the pond.

"Do you have any fish in there?"

"What?"

"In the pond?"

"Just minnows and frogs. That's all I've seen."

The sun was harsh, and both women shaded their eyes. Mrs. Sklar had been right about the weather, though Gretchen still hadn't ordered an air conditioner. With the help of a fan and her sleeping pills, she made it through the night.

"Gretchen, Sid wanted me to apologize. He said he was pretty hard on you. He felt bad that you had to leave that way."

The warmth in Brenda's voice gave her the courage to look directly at her. There didn't seem to be any anger in her face, which was now distinctly pudgy and quite pale.

"I deserved it. I still can't believe what I did. Brenda, you have every reason to be furious with me."

Brenda took the rough hand and held it a moment. "I'm too sick to get furious. You know I still have regular bouts of morning sickness. I threw up on the way to the office the other day, right in the car." She looked with dismay at her stomach. Rather than pregnant, the therapist looked plain fat.

"You mind if we get out of the sun?" she asked, releasing the hand.

Sitting on the porch a few moments later, Gretchen still felt wary. She could not quite believe that Brenda wasn't going to berate her. And in her present condition, Gretchen knew she wouldn't be able to endure it. So she tried to steer the conversation away from her, asking questions about Brenda's illness, how many pounds she had gained, and whether she would have natural childbirth.

"I'm just too scared. I'm hoping I'll be out cold."

"But I've had friends who just loved it. Once you learn to work with your body and see the contractions as—"

"Please, don't. I've heard it all, Gretchen. I've made up my mind." Brenda's knuckles were white as she gripped the arms of the low wooden chair. "Listen, I didn't come here to talk about me. Quite frankly, I'm worried about you. I don't like the idea of your being out here all alone."

Tensing, Gretchen said as breezily as she could, "Me? I'm fine. You know, I've always been petrified of being alone, but now that I am, well, it ain't so bad. And way out in the country here, it makes me feel like Karen Blixen." She laughed at herself. Brenda didn't join in.

"You actually hired someone to follow me," Brenda said after a moment's pause.

Gretchen felt the blood rush to her cheeks. "Oh, that—no, he was just an acquaintance, some kid I met when I went to get my license. You ask me, he's a little nuts. He's trying to be a private investigator or something and like a fool I let him practice on me. Anyway, I'm through with him. I've given that boy his walking papers."

"I see."

They sat quietly a moment, as if fascinated by a squirrel's incessant scolding on a nearby limb.

"You've given just about everyone their walking papers, haven't you?" Brenda said presently. "And now, here you are, just happy as can be."

Avoiding her eyes, Gretchen focused on the pines across the highway. In the distance the needles were blue and uniform as a hedge. "That's unkind, Brenda. You know I'll never recover."

"From what?"

Such a question didn't deserve a reply. Gretchen's jaw clenched.

"I'm serious, Gretchen. What is it that you'll never recover from? Frank's death? Well, eventually most people do recover. Frank himself survived his first wife and was able to go on. Let me tell you something, girl. I agree with you. You probably never will recover. Hear? Probably never will—unless you face up to the facts."

Gretchen continued to stare beyond, her face a stony mask.

"When you came to me, you were scared stiff, weren't you? And you were even afraid to admit how scared you were."

"I was scared of Leo, yes. And your husband told me, didn't he—I had good reason to be. Leo's gay," she said bitterly, looking right at her. "You never told me the truth. But he is, isn't he? And all the time he hated me because Frank loved me, not him. Leo was in love with Frank. I see it all now. No wonder I was so scared."

Brenda picked up a year-old magazine and fanned herself a moment before replying. "Leo was no more in love with Frank than . . ."

"Than what?"

"Look, don't you see what I was driving at with you? It was

244

so obvious. You weren't scared of Leo. God, no way. It was yourself, what you had done. You realized you had just made a huge mistake."

"No, I'm not going to listen to this."

"You knew that you shouldn't have married him. You were drunk when you met him. You had just broken up with someone you cared deeply about. So you launch right in with Frank, and then you wake up the next day and realize what you've done. You had absolutely nothing in common, the two of you, except an adolescent infatuation. A sexual charge. You hated his house, the way he dressed, his car, his friends, his help. It was like a prison to you—you were absolutely panic-stricken."

Gretchen had stood up, clutching in both hands the scrub brush she had inadvertently brought outside with her. She desperately wanted to go back inside, but she couldn't. She had to defend herself somehow.

"It was sex, wasn't it, Gretchen? You liked his body. But aside from that—oh, Lord. And you were so worried what your friends would say back in New York if you left him. You were determined to make the whole thing work by an effort of the will. So if anything went wrong, it was always Leo's fault. He was a convenient scapegoat, wasn't he? And you became obsessed with the thought that if you got rid of Leo, you'd get rid of all your own problems with Frank. No wonder you scared the poor guy so much. He was scared to death of you."

"Me? Scared of me?"

"Girl, you better believe it."

"But I . . ."

"You wanted to fire him from the minute you laid eyes on him. And he knew it. He's not dumb. You had him so scared he didn't know if he was coming or going. He buys you a cow to try to make friends—he takes up the carpet for you—anything to appease you, to buy time. He even starts coming to me for help, for advice. And what can I say? Not much, really. I've got to be loyal to you, you're my client. All I can do is recommend another therapist. But he's too afraid to go to someone else. You had him practically paralyzed with fear and second thoughts."

"So he's a client now?"

"No, I'd never take him on. We have too much history behind us. I have talked to him from time to time, though. But I really can't say anything very helpful, mainly because I respect our relationship, yours and mine. That means there's only one person who can help Leo now."

"What do you mean? There's plenty of therapists in Baton Rouge."

"Gretchen, don't play dumb with me, please. It's too hot."

It took a moment for Gretchen to turn around and face her. She prepared her words carefully. "I loved Frank," she said bitterly. "I don't care what you say—I loved him."

"Just like Leo did. Leo thinks he loved him, too, Gretchen. But neither one of you did, not really. You both projected your fantasies onto the poor guy. Neither one really loved him for what he actually was. To Leo, there was his father again. And you?"

"There was my husband, Brenda. My husband, understand. I loved him so much I would have done anything for him. Anything."

"Sure, I don't doubt it. You turned yourself into a maid for him, after all. Didn't you?"

Brenda glanced down at the scrub brush in Gretchen's raw hands. Feeling exposed, Gretchen abruptly set it aside. She knew she never should have discussed Frank's sex play with the therapist before. It had felt wrong, even back then, as if she were somehow betraying him.

"You're a cold, cruel woman, Brenda. To use that against me when I'm . . . Please, go away. Leave me alone."

"I'm sorry, Gretchen. I was only doing it for your own good. You've got to come to grips with what it really was. Otherwise you'll be stuck in some fantasy. You'll never be able to get on with your life."

"My God, woman, it was real. I loved him. It was no fantasy."

The sadness in the therapist's eyes was met by a fiercer sadness, one that would not relinquish hope. She had loved—and like Joan of Arc, Gretchen decided she must stake her life on this. She would not recant.

CHAPTER FOURTEEN

Though she was eighty-six, Mrs. Dagmar Hansen fully recovered from her stroke and was anxious to have her house to herself again; so Mrs. Sanchez—her daughter, many years divorced from a Cuban nationalist, who now resided in Fort Lauderdale—reported to Mr. Herbert. Hearing that Mrs. Sanchez wished to move back to her own house in the country, Gretchen was at a loss. She did not feel capable of enduring yet another uprooting so soon after the last. Pills or no pills, she slept fitfully at night while she struggled with the question of where she would go. Mr. Herbert had a number of listings in town, but nothing she saw was at all suitable. The farmhouse she had grown used to was so isolated that the apartments she viewed, the houses as well, seemed impossibly crowded by their neighbors. She might as well be back in New York.

"But you can't really expect her to move out so soon," Molly protested when Gretchen broached the idea of returning to New York. Molly's cousin, also named Molly, had sublet Gretchen's apartment shortly after Gretchen had gotten married.

"Mrs. Sanchez will be here any day," Gretchen said into the phone rather loudly. "What am I supposed to do? You told me yourself I should come back to New York."

"Of course, sweetie, but I didn't mean you could get the apartment back just like that. You have to give Molly time to look."

"Couldn't I stay with her for a while?"

"There's not an inch to spare. She's got her ex-boyfriend there and his daughter Jo. You met Jo, didn't you? She goes to Dalton and has been in two exploitation films. Molly is trying to talk her out of acting but you know how it is."

Getting nowhere with Molly, Gretchen resorted to calling Mrs. Sanchez at City Hall, where she worked as the mayor's personal secretary. Mrs. Sanchez sounded very nice and pliable and gave Gretchen reason to hope that she might get a month's extension. But then later that same day she got a phone call from one of Mrs. Sanchez's colleagues.

"Mrs. Dambar, I'm afraid you don't seem to understand what Mrs. Sanchez is going through. It's a living hell at her mother's now that she's recovered. Mary comes to work in tears every day, and you wouldn't believe the bags under her eyes. She's gained fifteen pounds, as well. I tell you, she's turning into a basket case. You got to let her have her own home back, understand? It's not fair."

"But Mrs. Mackie, I need more time." Mrs. Mackie, the Superintendent of Streets, Parks, and Garbage, had timed her call perfectly. Gretchen had just lathered her hair for a shampoo when she heard the ringing, which wouldn't let up.

"You've had three weeks to find yourself another place, Mrs. Dambar. That's one week lagniappe. According to the deal you signed, Mary has the right to repossess after two weeks' notice."

"Maybe you don't realize the special circumstances."

"Of course I'm very sorry about that. I was at the funeral myself, hon. It was a terrible blow to us all. He was very good to me in the last election—even made a speech for me at the Boosters. But life goes on. I can't sit here wondering who's going to take his place in the next election. Now I've had Mary spend a couple of nights with me, but my husband really doesn't like it. Duane says she cooks onion rings in the middle of the night. The smell wakes him up."

"Do you think Mrs. Sanchez might mind a roommate for a couple days—until I find something?"

"I wouldn't count on it. She can't sleep if there's someone else in the house. Neither can her mother. Now look, hon, I've got to run. My son Felix is due at his therapist's, and Duane and I don't want him driving his motorcycle all the way to the mall. You know how crazy that traffic can get."

So it was that not a week after this conversation Gretchen found herself installed in a rather cramped luxury apartment in Ozone. Actually, it was a condo, as Mr. Herbert explained. But she would be able to rent from the owner for as long as she liked, with no pressure to vacate unless under mutually satisfactory circumstances. What had decided her on Ozone, though, was that these were the very condominiums Frank had invested in. Furthermore, his companies had installed the shingled roofing and the plumbing. Thanks to Francine, whom Mrs. Sklar had recently promoted, foreclosure proceedings had been avoided in U.S. District Court, and with refinancing and a dynamic ad campaign aimed at the young professionals working just across the lake in New Orleans, hopes were high that The Antibes would eventually get out of the red and prove a modest success.

The lake was another reason Gretchen did not feel too uneasy about moving here, a good hour's drive south of Tula Springs. Though her unit did not look directly onto the water, only a two-minute walk from her door a quay stretched fifty yards into the brackish lake. Here she could enjoy a more expansive view than that afforded by Mrs. Sanchez's acres. Like a plain or desert duned by mild waves, the waters stretched to the horizon, marred only by the twenty-four-mile Causeway, which she could turn her back to if she wished.

The living space itself was not to her liking. Still smelling new, the condo had a sleeping loft, which she could not stand up straight in without bumping her head. Converting this into a storage area, she slept downstairs on a futon that Mr. Herbert had been kind enough to purchase for her. Next to the built-in microwave oven was a video screen that allowed all guests to be viewed in black and white as they pulled up to the gatekeeper's hut. The two-tone tub had a Jacuzzi but was too small to stretch out in. She found herself mostly using the shower, whose nozzle had four different massage settings, all of which felt pretty much alike.

The Antibes boasted three communal hot tubs overlooking the bayou that fed into the lake. With the temperature hovering in the nineties, only a few hearty souls ventured in, most residents favoring the tepid waters of the pool. Since she tended to burn and sprout even more freckles when she stayed in the sun, Gretchen avoided this area, preferring to sit beneath a modest aged oak beside the concrete levee. Though one or two older women with bleached blonde hair tried to start up a conversation when she went for her mail, the vacancy rate was still high enough for her to enjoy a modicum of privacy. She was especially thankful that the two units adjacent to hers were unoccupied.

From time to time she would find herself driving down the road, which fronted the lake, to St. Jude State College. If there was a recital or a lecture, she might drop in—or she would sit in the library, undisturbed. Once she happened to catch the second half of a program by a Colombian pianist. Music had never meant much to her before, but there was something in his playing that seemed to quiet all the whispers that haunted her—of anxiety, loneliness. She went backstage afterward and discovered he was much smaller than he seemed from a distance. For a moment she was tempted to ask him out for a drink. He seemed so awkward, so forlorn with those yellow stains on his ill-fitting dress shirt. But she was afraid, being rather young, in his late twenties, and not bad-looking, that he might think she was coming on to him. The following week she attended a lecture by a prize-winning historian from Ohio State and took a few notes on the household of Charles the Fat, emperor of the Holy Roman Empire from 881 to 887. That Friday there was a dance troupe from Guam with a question-and-answer period immediately following the performance. Though she enjoyed the native dances, she couldn't think of anything to ask.

From time to time she would go out rowing. People had warned her that if she fell in, the water might harm her. Some said it was a temporary influx of sewage, others a chemical spill from a barge, or according to the gatekeeper at The Antibes, an infestation of minute jellyfish. In any case, she had no intention of falling in. Though the water could get choppy when the wind was up, she found it generally easy to maneuver in her scull. Her favorite time was early morning, before it had gotten too hot. The long evenings would also have been nice, but there were more boats on the water then, generally speedboats, and far more mosquitoes.

After a late lunch one day at a seafood restaurant in Ozone's small, quiet business district, she happened to see a Help Wanted sign in the window of a nearby frame shop. Without pausing to think about it she went in. The owner turned out to be an unusually tall, bony fellow in Bermuda shorts and thongs with white socks. His unkempt white beard bothered her, but nevertheless she signed on when he agreed to hire her at slightly over minimum wage with two weeks paid vacation. Once, years ago, before Henry had turned to performance art, she had helped him frame a hundred and twenty-nine of his watercolors, which never sold—so she really wasn't a novice. And anyway, this was a do-it-yourself frame shop. She was mainly supposed to be there to keep an eye on the customers and steer them toward the more expensive frames. This last she refused to do, of course, as a matter of conscience. But she never mentioned this to Jerry, her boss. Jerry also managed the drive-in Daiquiri Hut down the street, a place she avoided out of vague bad memories associated with the drink. He spent most of his time at the Chamber of Commerce, where he was preparing a pamphlet on points of interest in St. Jude Parish. As a result she usually had the run of the shop and soon came to regard his visits as annoying intrusions.

Some days were slow, and she would sit for hours without a single customer. But in general she was pleased with the more regular rhythm of the work week, rising at 5:30 for an hour in her scull, followed by a leisurely breakfast and household chores, and then the shop from 9:30 to 5:30. Anxious to fill up the time when there were no customers, she began to ponder the Philippines again. It occurred to her that in all her research, there was one primary source she had slighted, the unpublished letters of her great-great-uncle, McKinley's secretary of war. Concentrating on these alone, she saw there was a possibility for an article based on the belief that he shared with his mistress, that the United States had a mission to Christianize the Catholic archipelago, at gunpoint if necessary. She had been inspired by a digression in the Ohio historian's lecture when he mentioned a colleague's recent book, based largely on the letters of a chambermaid to her aunt during the reign of George II. There was nothing like an unpublished primary source to gain attention.

The tinkle of the bell above the door made her look up. She had been writing a letter to her great-aunt Cecil's companion, asking her if she could get the old woman to record on the cassette she was enclosing any memories Cecil might have of her uncle, the secretary of war.

"Where's Jerry?"

"He's usually only in on Tuesdays now. May I help you?"

"I'll be OK. Thanks."

It was Dr. Jonsen with a cardboard tube, which he unscrewed at the workbench in the middle of the shop. She wondered if she could have changed so much that he no longer recognized her. But perhaps he was just intent on getting his picture framed and hadn't really noticed her. It was strange, she was learning, how invisible a clerk could feel. Most people never really looked right at you, always off to one side.

"This should do, Dr. Jonsen," she said a few minutes later, handing him the rasp he had asked for.

Hearing his name, he looked up from his watercolor. "Well, speak of the devil. How are you, Mrs. Dambar?"

Not knowing what to make of this remark, she smiled and said fine. He didn't seem to know what he had meant by it either, for there was confusion on his pale bureaucrat's face. With a nod of his balding head, he adjusted his glasses, which had slipped down his nose. "I've had a hell of a time with this one. Can't seem to get the right frame at home, so I thought I'd see what Jerry had on hand."

"Well, I hope you find something you like."

He went back to his frame, she to her desk. A day or two after the funeral, she had wandered down the royal-blue carpeted hall in Frank's bathrobe, meaning to feed and water the chickens, when she heard Frank, Jr.'s raised voice in the study. Pausing outside the half-open door, she saw he was on the phone. Frank, Jr., looked nothing like his father, being more angular and lean, with a sharper, sterner face. Yet he did have some of the same mannerisms, a way of cocking his head, of shrugging, that was painful for her to be around. He was throwing out technical terms in an angry manner—stenosis of the obtuse marginal, acute myocardial infarction—words that she never forgot. It was soon evident that Dr. Jonsen was on the other end of the line. Frank, Jr., was trying to find out why his father had not been warned about his cholesterol level, his blood pressure, why no preventive measures had ever been taken with him. "So you're not his regular physician—fine. But you know as well as I do that Dr. McFlug is a jerk. He wouldn't know a heart condition if it bit him on the nose. Dad never saw him, anyway, Dr. Jonsen. They just went to those Bible Study classes together—that was it . . . Well, fine, I know Dad was just being loyal to him. McFlug treated his father, you know. That's right. And of course you realize my grandfather died of a stroke, all under the capable hands of McFlug . . . Well, I'm sorry. You could have warned him about McFlug, gotten him to someone decent. It was your responsibility." Gretchen could not bear to listen any longer. She had gone on to see about the chickens, which later she had given to the banker's wife next door, knowing that Mrs. Tilly would make no mistakes with them.

"I just don't see anything that works," he commented after a half hour of silent concentration at the workbench.

"You don't like that oak?"

Staring glumly at his watercolor, he shook his head. "I'll try New Orleans someday when I have time."

"What is it? Do you have a name for it?"

"Not yet."

She was not sure what she was looking at—a partially submerged tire, the treads deep and irregular? It troubled her, for she knew it was something, yet when she looked closer, it seemed totally abstract, the apparent pattern dissolving into a maze of erratic brushstrokes. "Is that . . . ?"

"Right," he mumbled, "a gator."

Of course. The minute he said it, she saw it, the dark water lapping the hide that humped roughly above the surface. She was the one with the license, yet he was the one who had captured the beast.

"Is it for sale?"

"What?"

"I'd like it for myself."

His pale eyes regarded her for a moment. "I thought you didn't like my work, Mrs. Dambar."

"No, I like it very much."

"But when you saw my studio, you seemed so anxious to leave." A tentative smile stretched his thin bloodless lips. "You know, we artists can't be fooled. I was sort of hurt."

"Well, I fooled you then. You're good, damn good, Dr. Jonsen."

His blush was as vivid as a schoolgirl's. Somewhat embarrassed by such blatant pleasure, she looked back at the watercolor and felt again the tug, murky and primitive, so deep inside her.

The lecture had already begun when she arrived, slipping quietly into a back row. It was ill-attended, in an auditorium much too large. The subject was landscape architecture, the speaker a young woman whose voice shook as she pointed to a graph projected on a screen behind her. Gretchen looked down at the program notes. Dr. Mackenzie Reed was a native of Donaldsonville, Louisiana, Gretchen was informed, and received a B.A. from McNeese State University, in Lake Charles, and a Ph.D. from Texas A&M. She was an assistant professor on the faculty of St. Jude State College and a member of several professional organizations.

"It is recommended to keep in mind a constructive approach to detritus," Dr. Reed said, turning from the wavering graph. "Various plant fragments, usually from annual plants, are collectively known as detritus. These can provide useful nutrients to the soil if properly managed." Looking up from her notes, she seemed lost for a moment as she gazed wide-eyed at the darkened auditorium. Gretchen gripped the arm of her chair, rooting intensely for the poor girl, who was actually, with her long red hair and striking figure, quite attractive. She hoped she would soon hit her stride and overcome her stage fright.

"Pardon me," Gretchen said to the older gentleman sitting two seats over from her. "Do you by any chance happen to have a pen? I thought I had brought one with me but I can't seem to . . . Oh, sorry," she added in a whisper when he placed a finger over his lips. She had not realized how loud she sounded. For a moment she wondered if she might be drunk. But after all, she had only had one or two extra vodkas before dinner, something she allowed herself on Fridays to unwind from the shop. Yet she had opened a second bottle of wine—and what had she done with her car keys? Rummaging in her purse, she found a pencil. The keys she must have left in the car. Well, let them steal it. She hated the stick shift anyway.

Dr. Reed said something about cow oak that Gretchen started to write down. But then, pressing the pencil eraser against her nose, she began to wonder if she was really interested in landscaping. Back at The Antibes, when she had glanced through the local paper to see what was going on, the idea of landscape architecture had seemed so intriguing. She couldn't wait to get here. Now she was here and what did she see? A reed shaking in the wind?

As her eyes adjusted to the dark she caught sight of the back of a head four or five rows in front of her. The shape attracted her eye, the clean line of the skull, which was evident beneath the cropped hair. It was so much like Henry's, that shape.

An acute longing took hold of her. Was it possible that her ridiculous adolescent crush was still alive? Hadn't she buried it centuries ago—so deep that she hardly remembered where it lay herself? Oh, what a mess she had been at Foxcroft after reading *Mansfield Park*. It had taken two different therapists to convince her that the book was just a fantasy, that those cousins, Fanny and Edmund, would never have ended up happily married. So she had learned with an effort of the will to enjoy Henry as a brother. Yes, that was the word the second therapist had used—enjoy. All she had to do to enjoy him as she should was to forget about his body. Bury the body. And she did—successfully. Except for one brief unfortunate resurrection, when he had appeared on her doorstep in New York just after graduating from Yale. While he searched for his own apartment they were roommates, as well as office colleagues at Ogilvie and Mather. At home it was so much harder to forget—espe-

255

cially since he used to lounge around in his undershorts, totally unself-conscious, as if she were one of his brothers. Was it any wonder she had fled to the Philippines?

The Philippines, yes, they had cured her. After that horrible operation in Manila, when the pain was so unrelenting that she could not sleep without a handful of Percodans, she had no trouble forgetting. She was just as glad to have all the bodies buried, hers included.

The applause echoed feebly, though Gretchen clapped diligently and hard, hoping to encourage others. On her way out she avoided the gray-haired gentleman she had spoken to. He cast a sidelong glance at her going down the aisle. She wondered if he realized he had dandruff on his lapels.

In the lobby she wove through the departing crowd, hoping to find a vending machine with coffee. It would probably do her no harm to have a cup or two before driving back. She had to admit that maybe she had overdone it in the vodka department. This was the last time she would allow herself more than two.

After some wandering about she came across a machine in a corridor next to a men's room. Fumbling with her change purse, she experienced one of those meaningless coincidences that the laws of chance produce from time to time: Coffee cost sixty-five cents, and that was exactly what she had, not a penny more or less. She deposited a quarter, a nickel, a dime, another dime, one more, but then the final piece of change slipped from her fingers. Squinting, she peered down at the speckled floor. Stooping for a better look, she felt tentatively with her hands under the machine.

"Lose something?"

Someone had come out of the men's room. She had heard the door swing open. Looking over her shoulder she saw it was he.

"Some change," she said, her voice quavering like Dr. Mackenzie Reed's. "I've already put in . . ."

"I got some." One hand in his pocket, he used the other to help her stand up, for she had gotten onto her knees to reach farther under the machine.

Leo had cropped his hair—and apparently dyed it as well, a light brown. That was why the shape had seemed so apparent to her. He was clean-shaven, more so than ever, with no sideburns at all.

"You know, if I were you, I wouldn't drink this stuff," he said after depositing the final nickel for her. "Why don't you let me buy you a decent cup? There's a café in the student union."

"Oh no, I couldn't." She lifted the plastic door and reached for the Styrofoam cup. "I don't have time."

"I see."

"Well, good-bye," she said lamely and then headed for the side door, which she hoped to God was still open.

During September there were a number of lectures that she would have liked to attend, but she avoided the campus and drove instead across the Causeway for a guitar recital one Friday and on another, dinner in what seemed a dangerous neighborhood just off Magazine Street. The dinner was with Molly's aunt, Elizabeth Bellows, who was attending a software convention in New Orleans. Elizabeth laughed at Gretchen's description of Jerry, her boss, and his New Age vegetarian ways. But the older woman, who was attractive and forthright (and had never married), cautioned Gretchen about sweeping out the shop in the evenings. It should not be a part of her duties, Elizabeth advised. Gretchen spoke to Jerry about this on the following Monday. He muttered something about Gandhi and his spinning wheel, the necessity of humble chores for an enlightened spirit, but eventually caved in. A stooped, grizzled black man appeared the next evening to do the sweeping. The sight of Mr. Larkin bent over a push broom was too much for Gretchen's conscience. In a day or two she was back to sweeping up herself, Mr. Larkin having been dismissed—by Jerry, of course. She could not bear to fire him herself.

It was early October when she happened to see him in the express line at the Burger King around the corner from the frame shop. Under the artificial light his hair looked brassy, and it was really far too short for a man his age. But aside from that he was looking healthy and fit and his posture seemed much improved. After he picked up his order, she moved to another line where a hefty man would block his view of her.

"You're looking good yourself," she said somewhat stiffly after he greeted her outside the doors. Apparently he had seen her and had waited on the sidewalk until she had gotten her take-out bag.

"I'm into the Alexander Method. It's a good way to get in touch with your body, you know."

"Anyone in touch with their body should not go near a place like this, Leo." She meant to be critical, but it came out sounding like friendly banter.

With a smile, he nodded at her own bag.

"I work just over there." She cocked an elbow, pointing vaguely in the wrong direction. "My boss is a vegetarian," she added.

"I see."

"What I mean is, well, he's a very patronizing type of vegetarian. I feel it's almost my duty to have an occasional cheeseburger." She could not believe how ridiculous she sounded. Why did she feel it necessary to explain to Leo what she was doing here—as if she had been caught red-handed? "Well, anyway . . ."

"Yeah, I guess . . ." He shrugged. Then with a wry smile, he went on his way.

A week later, when she heard his voice on her answering machine, she was not altogether surprised. She was enjoying a second vodka before dinner and had the machine on to screen her calls. Leo wanted to know if she would like to hear Dr. Ruth speak in New Orleans the following week. He had an extra ticket. She returned his call later that same evening after she had fortified herself with three cups of coffee. On his machine she left this message: "Thank you, Leo, but I'm busy that night with a previous engagement."

When she hung up, she realized that he hadn't specified the night. But it didn't matter. She could not imagine how anyone in their right mind would want to go to such a thing. Surely Leo had more class.

"Oh, no, I wasn't going to see her. I meant like for you."

"Now Leo, do you really think I would want to go hear Dr. Ruth?"

"Well, you could have given it to a friend."

This unsatisfactory exchange took place later in the week on a self-service island in Tula Springs. Leo had been waiting at a traffic light and happened to look over and see her filling her tank. So, as he told her, he decided to say hello and get a little gas while he was at it.

"What are you doing in these parts?"

She watched the cents whirl by on the meter. "I stopped by Dr. Jonsen's and bought a couple paintings."

"He's good, isn't he?"

She gave a perfunctory nod. "I'm hoping to interest a few friends in New York in his work."

The chrome handle clicked. She rounded off the cents to an even number before hanging up the pump. "Well, good-bye, Leo."

He shrugged in a way that gave her pause. It was Frank's shrug, exactly. "Bye."

When she got back to The Antibes she went into the laundry room and transferred her wash into the dryer. Once inside her apartment she felt an urge to brush her teeth. With a foaming mouth she wandered from the bathroom into the living room and for a moment or two glanced at a *TV Guide:* "Where does daytime meet prime time? On NBC's *L.A. Law*. Most of the episodes this season have featured guest appearances by at least one current or former soap star. ABC's *General Hospital* alone has contributed Finola Hughes as Victor Sifuentes' girl friend; Sam Behrens as Grace Van Owen's unethical partner in private practice; and Lynn Herring as a bitter contestant in a divorce case." Returning to the bathroom she rinsed out her mouth and thought about gargling with Listerine. The bottle was empty, though. She hoped she would remember to make a note of it.

While she set up her ironing board and searched for the spray starch, she played back the messages on her answering machine.

"Gretchen, Jerry. You left the window open when you locked up last night. Just thought I'd let you know."

"Hi, sweetie, it's Moll." A brief pause. "I'm sure I called you about something but I forgot. Well, bye. Love you."

"This is Louise Stein, Lou, from 9F. We met in the broom closet last week at the gatehouse. I was wondering if you might want

259

to take in a movie with me this evening. My number is 555-2921. Thank you. I had on a yellow scarf, remember? Thank you. Hope to hear from you."

"Hello, this is Donna Murphy, your personal representative from TFI Market Research. Your name was selected by a random computer drawing as one of our lucky winners of a valuable prize. To claim your prize, Mr. Vogel, you must call this number within forty-eight hours. The number is 1-800-555-8900. Remember, to claim your valuable prize you must call this number within forty-eight hours. The number is 1-800-555-8900. Congratulations. You're a winner. And have a nice day."

"Gretch, me again, Moll. I just remembered why I called. Henry is becoming a nuisance. He's telling Molly she has to get out because you promised him the apartment for October fifteenth. You never said anything about that to me. Is he just making this all up? Please, sweetie pie, you've got to put a lid on him. He's calling her at three in the morning and she's got a new job now at Sotheby's and simply can't go to work looking like she's on acid or something. You've got to be firm with that lad, Gretch. Put your foot down. Bye-bye. I got to run."

Gretchen reset the machine. Yes, about a year ago she had told Henry he could sublet her apartment whenever Molly's cousin moved out. But that was before she thought she might want the place for herself. Surely he must realize that her circumstances had changed. And he hadn't even bothered coming down for the funeral. That was the least he could have done, especially since his loan had finally come through. Worn out by Henry's persistence, her uncle had finally settled out-of-court, giving him $35,000 of her money at prime rate instead of $50,000 at no interest. She was relieved to have the matter finally settled, but it disturbed her that she had not received a thank-you note or a call.

Planning to get in touch with him on her next sleepless night, she debated whether to phone Lou back. Lou was sixty, divorced, and worked in the bursar's office at St. Jude. She seemed nice, but desperately lonely. Gretchen decided no—and then when she went to take her clothes out of the dryer, there was Lou. The woman had a more pleasant face than she had remembered from the broom closet. And when she repeated her invitation in an offhand way, leaving Gretchen plenty of room to back out, Gretchen said yes, OK.

Lou and Gretchen had dinner first at an inexpensive restaurant on the lakeshore drive. After a couple glasses of wine Lou started talking about her husband. He had left her for a girl half his age, someone he had met in his office. She said she had had a nervous breakdown, that for a month she couldn't leave her bed. Her rage seemed overwhelming. She was afraid she might literally kill him. Lou confessed that she had even browsed in gun shops. Then she had moved away, unable to bear the thought that she might run into him at any moment. From Shreveport to Ozone, where she had lived off alimony until one day she found an opening at St. Jude. There were tears in her eyes when she told the story. Later that evening Gretchen was a little surprised when—from an unrelated comment—Lou let slip that the divorce had happened twenty years ago. In any case, the movie they saw wasn't too awful. A week later they saw another movie together. Lou talked about office politics at St. Jude this time. She said something about introducing Gretchen to a friend of hers, a professor. But for some reason, this never happened. Gretchen wasn't even sure if the professor was a man or a woman, so she wasn't too disappointed. In the meantime, she and Lou never got any closer than being casual friends. But Gretchen was still fond of her and often worried about her being alone so much of the time. Once or twice they had coffee together by the pool. And they always had a friendly conversation if they should happen to run into each other in the laundry room.

"Hello, caller."

"Hi, my name is Carol."

"Go ahead, Carol."

"Yes, what I wanted to say was that the woman on your right, Oprah—"

"In blue?"

"Yes, her—she's got it all wrong, I think. Today is the anniversary— It would have been the first anniversary of our marriage, and I'm so mad at people saying they have this rage against their husbands for dying—like they had left them. You know? It's a cop-out. I have nothing but the deepest love for my husband. He died of a heart attack. There was no time to prepare myself or mourn like the woman in back there was talking about. It just happened. I know he could have modified his diet and maybe there was job-related stress. He had been losing money and he wasn't ever good about expressing his emotions. So I'm sure his anxiety and frustration were bottled up—but we never liked to discuss money. That was one of our rules. Of course, I probably should have tried to share more of his financial worries. I could have let him talk to me more because, well . . ."

"Yes, caller, thank you so much for sharing with us. We'll have to take a break now. Don't go away. We'll be right back for more on grieving."

The full horror of what she had done did not hit home until the middle of the night when she woke up in a cold sweat. Was it possible that she had actually called "The Oprah Winfrey Show" under an assumed name? What if Kyss or Molly or Lou had recognized her voice? Oh, it was too humiliating. She never should have had so much vodka at lunch. If she hadn't, she could have returned to work instead of going home and, with yet more vodka, staring like an idiot at TV.

In the morning, feeling dreadfully crapulous, she managed to make herself presentable in time for work. Fortunately, Jerry was not due in that day. He was visiting a stepson in Baton Rouge who worked for Exxon. An older couple appeared around noon and browsed. The woman looked sternly at her balding husband and reprimanded him for touching a frame. "Hugh," she would summon him in a loud whisper, "what do you think of this?" And with a liver-spotted hand that trembled slightly, she would point to a frame that he would find something wrong with. They left without buying anything, Gretchen's gaze upon them as they stood undecided outside the shop, looking one way and then the other. The woman was well-upholstered, a roomy luxury sedan somewhat worn and faded, but not without a certain class. When she finally grabbed her husband's hand and led him away, the pout on his face made Gretchen smile and shake her head.

At her urging Dr. Jonsen had given the shop a few oils on consignment. In the afternoon she hung these and spent quite a while making tags with the names and prices. He had let her decide how much to ask and she would frequently change her mind, not wanting to undervalue the works but at the same time wanting them to sell. It was not until closing time that she got around to calling information for the number in Tula Springs. She half expected it to be unlisted, and when the operator gave it to her, she was uneasy.

"Oh, you're there."

"Evidently."

"I thought you'd still be at school. Well, anyway." Gretchen cleared her throat and looked with dismay at the black phone. "This is—"

"Yes, I know who it is."

"Anyway, I . . . I was calling for business purposes. I hope you're not eating or anything, Leo. I'd be happy to call back some other time."

"It's OK. Go ahead."

"It won't take long anyway. I just wanted to tell you that the other day—it was the strangest thing—I got a call for you on my machine. It's been bothering me, and I thought I ought to let you know."

"I wouldn't worry about it."

"It's such an odd coincidence, isn't it?"

"Who was it?"

"Some recorded message, one of those real estate gimmicks, I suppose. They said you had won something and you were supposed to call the toll-free number for your prize. I wrote the number down if you'd like it. It's here in my purse."

"No, don't bother."

She did not know what to say next. Her script had ended. She had lost her motivation.

"You still rowing?" he asked finally, breaking the awkward silence.

"Yes, as a matter of fact. How did you know?"

"I came to school early the other day and saw a scull out on the lake. Figured it must be, you know, like you."

"Oh."

"Well."

"I guess it was."

"Was what?"

"Me."

"Oh."

"Well, I got to go now. Bye."

"Thanks."

"You sure you don't want that number?"

"What number? Oh, that. No way."

"Well. OK."

Feeling slightly dazed, she hung up.

CHAPTER FIFTEEN

Molly called two more times asking Gretchen to do something about Henry. Gretchen explained that she had tried phoning him, once even at three in the morning—but he was never in. She would write him, she promised.

A week went by, then another, and still Gretchen had not written Henry. Of course, even if Molly's cousin moved out, it would never do to have Henry there in her apartment. She was thinking maybe it was time she headed back home. And if she did, she could not possibly have Henry as a roommate—could she? After all, he kept such strange hours. Yet the apartment was rather large; he could have his own room. What was the sense of having so much space in New York for just one person? And surely he could help out with the rent. It would be one way of paying her back for all she had done for him. But of course she must be mad, reasoning this way. It would never do. Henry couldn't live with her. And yet, when she thought back on his visit to Louisiana, how much fun it had been to have him around . . .

During this time Lou started asking Gretchen to go shopping at Schwegmann's, a giant supermarket almost ten miles from The Antibes. Gretchen would have preferred going to the nearby Albertson's or the Sunflower, but she let Lou have her way. It turned out that Lou was mildly interested in the man behind the bakery counter at Schwegmann's and wanted Gretchen's opinion. "I know he talks funny, with that New Orleans accent," Lou would say, "but he actually has a native intelligence, something that could be cultivated."

The man was homely, overweight, and probably only two or three years younger than Lou, though she always referred to herself as robbing the cradle. Gretchen couldn't imagine what Lou saw in him. She tried at first to dampen her enthusiasm. But this only made Lou defensive, even somewhat loyal. "Just because he hasn't had the advantages of upbringing and education," she said rather haughtily to Gretchen on the eve of her first date with Sal from Schwegmann's. After that night Sal's turquoise Chrysler New Yorker was frequently seen in The Antibes parking lot.

"Oh, yes, I know all about him," Mrs. Angie Quarles commented in the laundry room one morning when Gretchen had gone to put in a new load. Mrs. Quarles, a widow whom Gretchen had avoided in the first weeks of her move to the condos, had a boat moored beneath her apartment. Once or twice, Gretchen and Lou had gone along with her on a "martini cruise," as Mrs. Quarles called it. Actually, the boat ride had turned out to be more fun than she had expected. With a leathery tan and bleached blonde hair, Mrs. Quarles was a tough, hard-bitten woman in her late fifties who used to raise Mobilian turtles, which she had sold to Japan and France as pets. Ten thousand turtles per pond, she had had, and eleven ponds. As she piloted the girls (so she referred to Gretchen and Lou) beneath the Causeway, she would let loose with facts and figures. In 1979, just after her husband died, she bought herself a hundred gators to get her mind off the terrible end. (He had had lung cancer.) She would get forty-two dollars a foot for the gator hide. Every facet of a gator's life, Gretchen learned, is controlled by temperature. If the eggs are incubated at ninety degrees Fahrenheit, you got yourself a batch of males. Eighty-seven degrees or below and you got yourself all girls. The mama gator collects a lot of debris for her nest if the gators need more males and less if they're in need of females. They won't mate if the water temperature is too cool, and even then the damn fools only make love once in three years. "Just like my husband," Mrs. Quarles added as she swerved expertly, like a teenager, around a piling. Gretchen and Lou let out a little shriek of alarm and excitement, holding onto the gunwales for dear life.

"He's very warm, I think," Gretchen said to Mrs. Quarles as they adjusted the settings on their respective machines. "I think that's what makes Lou like him. I can see it, I think. That down-to-earth quality."

"That's not it at all, Gretchen."

"You don't think he's warm?"

"He could be ice cold, tepid, scalding hot, wouldn't make no difference, sugar. It's his looks."

"Oh." For a moment Gretchen pondered the face she had seen behind the Danish, the birthday cakes. Perhaps she had been too judgmental. Maybe he was good-looking in a way, sort of. "Well, he is very masculine."

"You ever been inside Lou's apartment?"

Gretchen shook her head.

"Well, if you had, you'd understand." The machines began to rumble. "She's got these framed photographs all over the joint. Can't miss it. Her and whatchamadig."

"Her husband?"

"Yep. Now this Sal, he's no dead ringer. But I tell you, he's close enough. In fact, the more I looked, the more I saw it."

"Oh, that's terrible. Are you sure?"

Mrs. Quarles raised her dark plucked eyebrows. "Sug, if I hadn't fallen in love with my gators, I'd have been climbing the same wall, better believe. Oh, now look at you, why did you set your rinse on warm? Always get you a good cold rinse, that's the best, you know."

On a Friday afternoon, after Dr. Jonsen's paintings had been hanging unadmired for two solid weeks, Gretchen finally succeeded in selling an oil to a high school physical education instructor. He wanted to give his wife something different for their anniversary, their thirtieth, and eventually, after Gretchen had talked herself blue in the face, pointing out all the marvelous qualities, he surrendered

267

to her sales pitch. Granted, she had given him a fifty-percent discount, but she still felt pleased with her success. For his part he looked doubtful after she had taken his VISA, and she had to reassure him over and over that he hadn't made a mistake. Buyer's remorse made his shoulders sag as he headed for the door. She just hoped to God he wouldn't show up with it in the morning.

That evening she brought a paperback with her to the water's edge, near the quay. She was afraid that if she stayed inside she would drink too much. The hardest part to get through every day was sunset. That was when she wanted the vodka the most, especially on Fridays.

She was halfway through the thermos of tea she had brought with her, trying to read in bad light, when she heard the crunch of footsteps on the brittle leaves that had fallen from a nearby oak.

"Any good?"

The lawn chair she had brought with her creaked as she shifted positions. But she did not look up. "Oh, it's nothing."

"What is it?"

"Just something I grabbed from the bookshelf."

"Austen," he said, leaning closer, for she could feel him blocking the lake's stiff breeze. "Jane Austen. Which one? Well, you shouldn't be trying to read in this light."

"It's sufficient."

He squatted down beside her chair. "I was driving home from class and I thought it might be you. You sit out here a lot, don't you?"

"No, not a lot."

"I've seen you on the quay there, standing way out on the edge."

"Well, good."

"It used to worry me when I'd see you. I was afraid you might . . ."

"What? Jump into two feet of water? It's not deep out there, you know." Her hands gripped the book as she tried out a pleasant smile on him. But it faded quickly, the smile. "Leo, let's leave each other alone—how about it?"

The pilings of the Causeway, seen from such a distance, wavered like rickety props in the wash of amber and orange. He said, "You were the one who called me last."

"That was only because of that message."

She gave him a chance to leave. When he remained there, making a little mound of acorns, she decided he was asking for it. "Did you kill Jane?"

The back of his neck turned crimson. He did not look up at her. "We were arguing—about the rug, that blue, you know." His voice was hoarse, barely audible. "She lost her head, started like screaming at me. I told her to watch out. I meant watch out for the traffic. I wasn't threatening her, but she thought I meant I was going to do something to her. We were at that corner. 'Watch out!' I said just before she pulled out. I saw it coming, the white car. But I couldn't get her to look in time. She was looking at me instead, like she thought I was going to hit her or something."

She allowed herself a moment to digest this. Then, before her courage could desert her, she said, "And me—did you want to kill me, too?"

Now he did look up at her, his eyes dark, troubled: "Yes."

It was as if a terrible weight were lifted from her shoulders. She took a deep breath, then another. For how long had she been afraid to really breathe, to do anything but take the most shallow sips of air. "Thank you, Leo. Thank you."

He had slumped down, no longer squatting, one leg cocked at an awkward, vaguely yogic position beneath him. "And you, Mrs. Dambar?"

"What?"

"You wanted to get rid of me, too, didn't you?"

"Oh no, I just wished . . . I suppose so."

They remained there a moment or two. Cars hissed over the asphalt behind them at irregular intervals, the noise breaking like waves upon a shingle beach. Before them was the vast plain stretching to the horizon. She thought she heard him say thank you before he got up and left. But it might have been her imagination.

On the walls at evenly spaced intervals, at exactly the same height, were the doe-eyed lads and lasses, the hayricks, lambs, and waterfalls, the furtive kisses, all snug within their dimestore frames. They seemed out of place, though, in the modernistic living room, which was furnished in the spare angular style that the fifties would have called futuristic. On the floor was a wall-to-wall purple carpet with an irregular zigzag culminating in a yellow starburst just beneath a glass case of porcelain figurines.

"Sit," Mrs. Howard barked when Shaerl made a move to rise from the armless black vinyl sofa. The old woman had emerged from her kitchen with a tray of hors d'oeuvres, which she presented first to Gretchen.

"Take another," she said when Gretchen grasped a toothpick that speared a baby frank wrapped in bacon.

"One will be fine. I don't want to spoil dinner."

"Nonsense, you are too thin. Look at Mrs. Dambar, will you?" she appealed to Shaerl. "Skin and bones. My darling, what have you been doing for food? You don't eat."

To appease her Gretchen put another on her plate. She was not sure it had been a good idea to accept Mrs. Howard's invitation. But the call had come out of the blue, and she had had no time to really think about it. "You will come to dinner?" said the voice over the phone. "I give you the directions to my house. You must see my house what I live in." And Gretchen had taken the directions.

"No, he's in Angola this evening," Shaerl replied after Gretchen had asked whether Leo would be joining them.

"Angola?"

"Jail," Mrs. Howard put in as she lowered her bulk into a triangular canvas chair.

"Oh." Gretchen blinked.

"It's his first field trip," Shaerl explained. "You know, he's getting a master's in counseling."

"Oh, of course."

"The state penitentiary, that's what it is—over in the next parish. I talked to him yesterday." Shaerl winced as she repositioned her legs so that her pleated miniskirt would be a little less revealing. "He's supposed to meet one of his pen pals, someone he's corresponded with for five years."

"Do you see him a lot?" Gretchen asked with a furtive glance at Mrs. Howard. The old woman had closed her eyes, so Gretchen quickly hid her second frank behind an ovoid lamp. The first had slithered down her throat with alarming ease.

"No, not really." Shaerl added a smile, excessively polite. She seemed a little wary of Gretchen, who, with her glass of grape juice, was trying her best to appear nonthreatening.

"I suppose school must be keeping you busy."

"Yes, it is." Another smile. "Do you mind?"

"What? Oh, no, no, go right ahead."

A Merit was soon lit. Shaerl inhaled deeply with a look of vast relief.

The smell of smoke seemed to revive the old woman. Bringing herself erect in the low-slung chair, she said, rubbing her swollen ankles against each other, "So what's with Mr. Leo? He still got his sweetheart?"

Both Shaerl and Gretchen looked puzzled.

Mrs. Howard adjusted her white fur collar before going on. "You mean you don't know? Oh, yes, Mr. Leo is very secret. He won't tell Mrs. Howard nothing. But she is too smart for him." Leaning closer, she began to speak in a loud whisper, a plump beringed hand shielding one side of her mouth, "Frankie tells me, no? He says I am to say this to no one. But he catches Mr. Leo in the Ozone. In a motel!" Satisfaction, moral outrage, and delight made the old woman's powdered face positively beam as she sat there nodding in agreement with herself.

"Oh, that," Shaerl said in a low voice to Gretchen after Mrs. Howard had subsided again into a semidoze. "I heard something about that too. But there's nothing to it. You know, Leo was always so ashamed of being a virgin. He was so scared Frank would find out." She regarded her cigarette a moment, half-smoked, and stubbed it out. "Leo tried to make it look like he was involved with a girl or something. I think that's why he liked me around."

"You must be mad at me, Shaerl, for what I said the last time you saw me. I'm really sorry. I just didn't understand then. Dr. Lahey told me—"

With an impatient wave of her hand, Shaerl said, "Never mind about all that. I was an idiot myself. I thought I could maybe get him to like girls. Maybe having me around, I thought he'd get more comfortable around them, less nervous. And in the meantime, I start liking him pretty bad. Can you believe it? I start getting jealous, especially when Frank told me something about this motel in Ozone. I made Leo confess later. He said he knew Frank was going to be there, and so he arranged to have this old girlfriend meet him. He just wanted her there as bait. And good old Frank took it."

"What do you mean, Frank was at a motel?"

"Relax. He was just eating at the restaurant there, one of those bargain all-you-can-stuff-inside-you places. With Francine."

"Oh." The wave of alarm had been as threatening as if he were still alive. She took a sip of the too sweet juice, which did little to calm her nerves.

Mrs. Howard did not have a separate dining room. Rather than eat in the kitchen, she had set up a card table behind the armless sofa in the living room. Loaded with covered serving dishes and a candelabrum, as well as the Peruvian lilies Gretchen had brought, the table barely had room for the dinner plates and silverware. After lighting the seven candles, Mrs. Howard had everyone join hands.

"Say something," she ordered Shaerl.

"Oh, no. Gretchen, you."

"Me?"

"Go ahead, Mrs. Dambar. Pray for heaven's sake. My poor steak is getting cold."

Gretchen felt as self-conscious as a teenager. She had not prayed aloud since Foxcroft and had always secretly made fun of Leo's predinner homilies. "We are grateful for this food—and for the company of . . . of friends."

"That's it, darling? Fabulous. We eat."

There was a spot on Gretchen's knife and her water glass had bits of orange pulp clinging to the rim. She glanced anxiously at Mrs. Howard, who would never have permitted such lapses in the other house. The old woman had a faraway look in her eye and was barely touching her food. Shaerl reached over and moved the gravy boat away from the dangling white fur.

"You think Mr. Leo will marry?"

Gretchen chewed energetically on the gristled steak before replying. "Who knows?"

"But now dat he is free, he will—won't he?" Mrs. Howard brought a spoonful of mashed potatoes to her crimson lips. "I cook dinner for him every Tuesday and Thursday—but this is no good. He is young and so smart. He needs a young woman, no? A nice blonde who stands up straight."

"Mrs. Howard, what about you?" Shaerl asked, taking a sip of wine. "Wouldn't you like to have someone come help you clean? You must get lonely here all by yourself."

"Help *me* clean? No one cleans like Mrs. Howard." Suddenly it was the old Mrs. Howard, the one who could make Shaerl flinch.

"Well, I just meant . . ."

"Never mind, young lady. You finish your steak."

Shaerl looked glumly at her plate; the mushroom gravy had congealed. "How do you like Ozone?"

"Me? Oh, it's OK." Gretchen took a bite of something drenched in cheese sauce. "I'm going back, though, in a couple days."

"To New York?"

She nodded. Molly's Molly had finally found herself another apartment. And Gretchen, just recently, had talked to Henry. She had told him that he would have to find somewhere else to live. And no, she did not think it would be a fun idea if he camped out with her for a couple weeks. She wanted the apartment for herself.

"But why, Gretchen? I thought you didn't like New York."

"I've got a chance at a job. It's a journal, socioeconomics. I sent them an article I just finished on McKinley's secretary of war. They didn't accept it, but a friend of mine there, she said they might be interested in me as a proofreader. Pays nothing, of course. Peanuts. But maybe once I'm in, I can get it published. Find out where all the bodies are buried, then blackmail the editor."

Shaerl looked doubtfully at her, then smiled.

"They are buried where I will go—in the cemetery," Mrs. Howard said, opening one eye. She had been sitting there with her eyes closed, her guests conversing in hushed voices. Now Shaerl and Gretchen suddenly became animated.

"Oh, Mrs. Howard, you're going to outlive us all."

"You will, I know," Shaerl said with a strained cheerful lilt. "Just look at her. Boy, I hope I'm that fit at forty."

"Take it easy, darlings. I bought my plot already. They don't give no refunds."

"Oh, Mrs. Howard."

"Mrs. Howard, really. You shouldn't be thinking like that."

"That's enough, girls. Quiet." Mrs. Howard wiped some potatoes from her lips. "I know where I'm headed. Mr. Leo's told me all about it."

"Don't listen to him," Shaerl said.

"What does he know?" Gretchen put in.

"He knows. Because he was there, Mrs. Dambar. And you, Shaerl, you should be ashamed. Mr. Leo was in the garden. He saw it all. And he tells me what happens. I ask him to. And he does." Mrs. Howard touched the corsage that Shaerl had given her, then bent her head as if to smell it. Outside, a dog was barking, probably the one Gretchen had seen chained outside the public library when she had driven up to Mrs. Howard's.

"The French doors," the old woman said, "they open up. And he is standing there, my Frankie. Mr. Leo say he wave, he look very excited like he want to tell Mr. Leo something. And Mr. Leo come over to the patio. Only by the time he get there, Frankie can't talk no more. Mr. Leo hold him. He is fallen to the ground. And he hold my little boy. And he say, 'What? What is it?' But Frankie just look at him. And then Mr. Leo know what it is he want to say. He is saying it with his eyes. He feel it go through his whole body when he touch him. I say to Mr. Leo, 'What? What is it?' And he say to me, 'Thank you.' That is it. Thank you."

"He was thanking Leo?" Shaerl put in timidly.

"Dummkopf, is Mr. Leo God?"

Mrs. Dambar sat quietly for a moment while the realization sunk in: So he had felt it, too, when he had touched Frank. It was a humbling thought.

"Could I have a little wine?" she said as Mrs. Howard went back to her potatoes.

Shaerl poured some from her own glass. "I can't drink all this. I've got to drive."

It wasn't sweet, she was relieved to find out. It tasted good.

"Oh, I hate you," Mrs. Howard was saying a few minutes later after she had cleared away the dishes. "I do hate you."

"Do you have any instant?" Gretchen suggested.

Mrs. Howard continued to glare at the coffeepot that sat upon a shelf of knickknacks. "Every time I have company, it stops working. Someday I will murder you, I promise."

It was the same gleaming old pot that Mrs. Howard had lectured a year ago, when Mrs. Bill Anderson and Mrs. Keely had come for the lawnmower. And Henry with his video camera trying to tape them. Gretchen tried hard not to think about this. It hurt so terribly, this memory. For she could picture Frank in it more vividly than anything she had ever thought about since—him bursting in on them so unexpectedly, his near-naked body as fresh and clean as a child's. And that look in his eyes . . .

Suddenly there was a noise in the other room, the kitchen. Mrs. Howard looked up from the coffeepot. Shaerl, in the midst of blowing out the candles, froze. And Gretchen, with the remains of the steak on a heavy platter, which she held in both hands—could not take her eyes from the door. Whether it was terror or joy that paralyzed her, she did not know.

And then the door swung open, and he stood there before them. "Hi," he said with a little wave that dispelled all the terror.

While Mrs. Howard tended to crumbs in the other room with a hand-held minivacuum Shaerl and Gretchen started on the dishes. "You creep," Shaerl said to Leo as she handed him a plate she had just dried, "you scared me to death. I thought you were a burglar. I was sure we were all going to be killed."

At the double sink, her hands plunged in water, Gretchen tried to blow a gray strand of hair from her eyes. "Why didn't you knock, Leo?"

"I always come in the back way. Howard leaves the door open for me." He had taken off his blazer and rolled up his sleeves, but his red tie sometimes dangled in the women's way as he went about putting the dishes in the cupboards.

"At night? Y'all shouldn't do that at night. By the way, how was jail?"

"A little hairy." He took a bite of strudel drenched in melted ice cream. "I was really bummed out. I don't know if I'll ever get used to it."

Shaerl loosened his tie for him, which seemed uncomfortably tight. "What about your pen pal? Did he turn out to be cute?"

Seeing the distress on Leo's face, Gretchen hastily said something to change the subject. "Oh, Leo, I was wondering if I might store a couple things with you—temporarily. I won't be able to take everything back on the plane with me right away."

"Like what?"

"Well, my scull. I thought maybe you could keep it at the trailer park."

"Why not leave it where it is?"

"At The Antibes? I can't do that."

"Why not?" Shaerl put in. She was leaning against the counter, one hand rubbing her hip. "Leo, please?"

"What?"

"Will you fix my leg. It really aches."

"Not now. Wait till the dishes are done, OK?"

Gretchen rinsed with a sprayer attachment into the second porcelain sink. "So, Leo? The scull?"

"Just leave it."

"But how can I?"

"Lord, Gretchen," Shaerl said quietly, "it's his place, after all. Why should he have to drag it out to Swamp Possum?"

"What?"

"It's his place, the condo. He can store whatever he likes there."

"You're kidding."

Shaerl reached out and grabbed her stepuncle's tie. Giving it a yank, she said, "Hey, didn't you tell her where she's been living all this time?"

He shrugged.

"I don't believe it." Gretchen paused as she took another greasy plate in hand. "How can it be yours, Leo?"

"Go on, talk," Shaerl said, giving the tie another playful tug. "You won't? OK, big boy, too bad for you." She let go. "You know he never cashed that check Frank had given him when Frank thought the whole thing was falling apart. They still kept Leo's initial investment, but the bookkeeping got messed up when Frank was writing all these checks without explaining anything to Mrs. Sklar. So Francine figured out—for tax purposes and all—that the easiest way of coming clean with Mr. Leo here was to let him have a condo, one of the cheaper ones."

"But why didn't anyone tell me?"

Leo took another bite of strudel. "It was Mr. Herbert's idea. He said there was no reason for you to know. You'd only like make a fuss. And he was tired of trying to find a place for you to live. It was taking up too much of his time. So he just took the rent checks you sent to him and then wrote me his own. It was fine for me. I got the maintenance covered, plus a little extra."

"But it's so near school for you, Leo. Why wouldn't you want to live there yourself?" She was scouring the greasy skillet Mrs. Howard had used to fry the steak.

"You got to be kidding. I wouldn't be caught dead in a duded-up place like that. All those rich old farts—forget it."

"Well, they're not *all* that old. Or that rich—just sort of."

"And the yups, they'll be next. No way. I'm going to sell that place soon as Mr. Herbert finds me someone dumb enough to buy it. In the meantime, I guess I'll just go on renting it out."

"Leo, my leg."

"In a minute."

"It hurts."

"Let's get this done first, you little baby."

The door swung open and Mrs. Howard, a Newport dangling precariously from her red lips, surveyed her domain with an im-

277

placable eye. Then after emptying the crumbs from her minivac into the trash pail, she trudged over to the sink and tested the water.

"My darling Mrs. Dambar, you must make the water hot hot. Otherwise it's no good." And reaching in with a trembling white hand, she pulled the plug and let the dishwater, which was admittedly tepid by now, go down the drain.

"So. Fabulous. Now everyone go home. I finish this myself."